G.M.HAGUE

A PLACE TO FEAR

PAN
Pan Macmillan Australia

First published in 1994 in Pan by Pan Macmillan Publishers Australia
St Martins Tower, 31 Market Street, Sydney

Reprinted 1996

Copyright © G. M. Hague 1994

This edition published 2001 by Hinkler Books Pty. Ltd.
17-23 Redwood Drive, Dingley, Victoria 3172 Australia

National Library of Australia
cataloguing-in-publication data:

Hague, G. M.
A place to fear.

ISBN 186515 6418

I. Title.
A823.3

Typeset in 10.5/12pt Plantin by Midland Typesetters
Printed in Australia

In memory of my father, A.W. Hague.

Acknowledgements

I'M ALWAYS DIGGING into the wealth of fascinating and thought-provoking material in author Colin Wilson's books, particularly *Poltergeist*, *The Occult* and *Starseekers*. Therefore I owe just as many thanks to Norm Kupke, who recommended Wilson's writing—and who is still patiently waiting for the return of the books he kindly let me borrow.

Prologue

TERRY McGANN WAS STORING a corpse in his hotel's cool room. The body lay across the top of the spare beer kegs, the only refrigerated space in town big enough to store a cadaver after the two chilled morgue drawers in the small medical centre had been taken. A couple visiting their parents had been killed the night before, their car veering off the road and smashing squarely into an old fig tree.

Using the cool room was an arrangement Connors, the funeral director, had with McGann, though it was rarely called upon. The last time the town had needed extra storage space for corpses was almost a decade before, when a young family of four died of food poisoning from fertilisers they'd used on their own vegetable garden. Connors also owned a mechanics shop specialising in farm machinery, and ran a small bus into the closest city once a week. It was always disconcerting to see him exchange his greasy overalls for a sombre, dark suit whenever anyone came to his workshop with funeral details, or if he needed to visit the bereaved in their homes. His oil-stained hands and face clashed with the clean cuffs and collar.

When Connors walked into McGann's lounge bar early that morning, pushing the doors aside the moment the publican slipped back the latches, McGann knew what the man wanted. News of the second road accident had flashed through the town's grapevine and McGann, hearing it, doubted if the dead couple from the previous day's tragedy had yet been taken away.

Soon, Jake Sanders' remains lay on two planks balanced on top of the full beer kegs, the body a shapeless bundle within the plastic wrapping. It didn't look comfortable and McGann needed to remind himself that Jake certainly wouldn't care any more. The feel of the corpse through the plastic had upset McGann as he'd helped Connors transfer the dead man from his car into the hotel through a tortuous, discreet route involving halls and doorways. More than anything the weird dead weight of the thing repulsed McGann, who until then had thought of himself as a veteran of worse experiences.

Jake Sanders was really Paul Sanders—but 'Jake' sounded better. It suited his image. He was the small town's only biker, riding a battered, chopped-up Yamaha with a roaring exhaust. He looked mean enough with his torn jeans, leather waistcoat and club badges, and a pair of cumbersome boots that always dragged their heels across the floor. He even wore a knife in a leather pouch on his belt. Everyone said it was a flick-knife, but nobody had really seen it. No-one bothered to find out how mean Jake really could be. After moving into town to be close to his ageing mother he enjoyed a sort of character status—most of the locals were secretly pleased to have a real, live biker in their midst. It was like having a celebrity living in town. Jake used this to his advantage, nurturing a form of immunity and bending a few rules. It was rumoured he cultivated a patch of marijuana behind his house, regularly harvesting and making a trip to the city every few months for cash. The two resident policemen never called on Jake's run-down property to check—and Jake was never seen toting his wares in town. Nor did they bother pulling him over when the Yamaha was heard thundering away from the hotel shortly after closing time and it was known Jake hadn't exactly been drinking lemonade all night. Jack Daniel's and coke was his taste. In the quiet country night the bike could be heard barking its way through the backroads nearly all the way to Jake's home, an old farmhand's lodgings within easy reach of his mother's house in the middle of town. People shrugged at the sound of his motor speeding through the night, saying to each other it was highly unlikely Jake would kill anyone but himself.

Now the worst had happened, although Terry McGann remembered Jake being careful with his drinks the night before. The hotel ran a darts tournament and Jake took his darts pretty seriously, pacing his drinking in favour of keeping his 'eye'. Later, McGann had been outside shuttering the windows against the overnight damp when Jake emerged from the bar, threw his leg over the Yamaha, and with a casual wave drove into the darkness, the machine's brakelights winking as it negotiated a railway crossing, then disappearing around a bend. McGann had seen Jake in much worse condition than that and the biker had lived to see the next day.

A farmer irrigating his fields adjacent to Jake's house had found the dead man and his twisted motorcycle the next morning. Jake had crashed just seconds away from home. There was no apparent reason for the spill, so it was assumed he'd swerved to avoid an animal on the road and lost control, probably while speeding in the final stretch to the house. He might have survived, too, but Jake liked to feel the wind in his hair and perched his helmet on the backrest behind him when he thought no-one was watching—which he'd done on his way home that night. Even then, the injuries to his head were only minor, but enough to stun him while he bled to death from savage cuts inflicted by the broken edges of the macadam. It was, everyone agreed, a nasty and unlucky way to die.

Throughout the day McGann was glad to be given little cause to go into the cool room. The shelves behind the small doors of the drive-in bottle shop were well stocked and the kegs didn't need changing. In fact, he noticed some of the regular drinkers switching to bottled beers, rather than ale drawn from the taps. Word had obviously got around, despite McGann refusing to discuss whether or not he was holding the corpse for Connors. A telephone call from the undertaker ruined McGann's day further. Of all things, an industrial dispute would delay transporting the dead couple already in the morgue until the next day. He needed the publican to store Jake's remains overnight. McGann could hardly refuse, though he hated the idea.

Evening came and the hotel stayed relatively quiet. Whether it was Jake's body in his cool room or just a general state of shock in the town after two fatal accidents in quick succession, McGann couldn't decide. He sent Rosemary, his only barmaid for the night, home immediately the meals were finished. She'd been more than happy to leave, throwing a distressed glance at the cool room as she walked out. At closing time, for once, he had no trouble kicking out the regulars. Then, as he went about the business of shutting down the bar for the night, McGann wished he'd invited someone to stay for a nightcap to keep him company while he finished up. His wife had long since gone to their quarters upstairs and was probably asleep. It was only him and the plastic-wrapped body now.

McGann found himself hesitating outside the cool room as he was about to go in and turn off the beer and gas to the taps. He shook away his misgivings with a grunt, pulling open the door and feeling the wash of cold air spill around him. Stepping inside he forced himself to gaze at the body-bag a moment, as if he was accepting a challenge. He noticed a mist of condensation had formed on the plastic. Then he busied himself twisting off the gas valves and closing the beer lines. He was glad to get back out.

Back in the bar he ran the draught taps dry and cleaned them, then washed down the spillage trays. Anything that might leave a stench of stale alcohol he rinsed. Usually McGann also wiped the tables and bar-top, but tonight he just wanted to leave, telling himself he'd allow an extra fifteen minutes in the morning to do it. He progressively turned off lights as he headed towards the hallway and the stairs, until he was framed in the door, his finger on the light-switch. McGann's gaze roamed the dimly lit bar in a habitual, final inspection. The last thing he looked at, before plunging the room into darkness, was the gleaming chrome of the cool room behind the counter.

The sounds of creaking wooden steps echoed through the empty bar as McGann mounted the stairs. Then came a muted splashing as he had a quick shower. Finally there was the distant click of his bedroom door closing and silence.

Downstairs a shadow detached itself from a wall. A lithe figure, moving confidently, passed between the chairs and tables to the back of the bar. The cool room had an automatic light which came on as the door opened. A square of brightness fell across the bar as the door was pulled aside, and a cloud of vapour puffed out into the room. The figure went inside, ignoring the shelves full of inviting alcohol, and went straight to the wrapped bundle lying across the extra kegs. A slim hand reached out and tugged the heavy zipper downwards, exposing Jake's white, dead face. Cuts and slashes from the accident marked the flesh. The figure stepped back and regarded the corpse intently, standing still for a long time and not even flinching when the refrigeration compressor suddenly kicked in.

A different sort of light began to fill the cool room. It slowly grew until the weaker electric globe was lost within a blinding glow. The very core of the glare was coming from the bundled corpse itself—a shifting, uneven, but brilliant radiance, like a living thing, swirling out of the body and wrapping itself around the watching figure, who remained motionless. Then the light gathered itself and drew inwards, coalescing and solidifying until, with a final, blinding flare, it dissolved into a recognisable form.

A ghostly Jake Sanders stood in the middle of the cool room, his arms held slackly at his sides. Unlike the corpse lying before him, the new Jake looked unmarked, but his face was a deathly white and blank of expression, his eyes empty, staring fixedly ahead. Then the eyes flicked down to look at the corpse for a moment. The ghost showed no outward sign of the inner rage it suffered. An anger not Jake's, but of the being now using his form. That being had never experienced anger before; didn't recognise it as part of the dementing illness building inside its mind. All it knew was that the disease had to be stopped. The sickness was a dangerous and unpredictable thing. The rage was getting out of control too, but that wasn't important.

The ghost spoke to the corpse in a soft, sibilant whisper. 'I Chose you, but you escaped. I am— *disturbed* by that. I needed you *alive*.' The spirit was suddenly, almost physically, racked by another unfamiliar emotion—a malicious spite, which made its image flicker uncertainly for a moment. The ghost allowed the feeling to grow, and began to enjoy it. Like a child born of the anger, a low, cruel laughter came from the ghost, and the being inside liked the noise it made. The spirit laughed again, and heard the sound slap eerily off the steel walls of the cool room. The corpse appeared to lie quietly, as if patiently waiting.

Upstairs, Terry McGann stirred in his bed, but didn't rise. The hotel was always full of strange noises at night.

Jake's ghostly twin hissed at the corpse, 'Still, even dead, you have a purpose in my work. Your mother is grieving, Paul. This will be my beginning. I think I should go and visit her.' He glided forward and made a smoothing gesture over the corpse. By itself, the zipper of the body-bag closed back over the dead face. The ghost became still and appeared to be gathering some inner strength. Without warning, the spirit-figure vanished.

Inside the body-bag Jake's eyes fluttered open and stared uncomprehendingly at the close blackness all around. His fingers twitched, making the plastic rustle. Then, like an exhausted man unable to fight off sleep, the corpse's eyes closed again. The room was silent once more.

1

THE GREEN READOUT of the microwave's control panel pulsed on and off, flashing an error message in awkward, angular lettering. Michael Garrett stood with his cup of cold coffee grasped in one fist and his free hand poised in front of the microwave, his fingers about to punch the switch to open the door. His mind was still clouded with sleep and he blinked in confusion.

'Damn,' he muttered, running the hand through his thick hair instead. It was a habitual gesture meant to kick his brain into gear. Putting the coffee inside the oven he fussed with the controls a moment, glancing at his wristwatch so he could key in the exact hour and minutes. Another surprise. His watch was blank. He'd been meaning to replace the battery for a while. 'Modern technology is a pain in the arse,' he said aloud to the empty house around him. Giving up resetting the microwave for the moment he simply punched in 'Reheat Beverage' and grunted with satisfaction as the oven hummed into action.

As he watched the coffee spin slowly around he considered what must have happened—another power blackout during the night. It was the third in a fortnight, causing more electronic mayhem in his household. Michael worked at home. He had a fax machine and two computers, one he used for compiling a textbook on light-aircraft safety he hoped to publish—his chosen career for the present—and another controlling the compact recording studio he'd built at the back of his house. Michael had been a part-time musician for nearly ten years without taking the final step of turning professional, playing in the evenings when he could but always keeping his day job with the Department of Aviation. The studio housed a range of electronic musical equipment, and was a way of keeping touch with music—an expensive hobby. He decided to sharpen his mind with the coffee before going to check how well the studio had survived the blackout.

He had no idea what the time might be. Sipping gingerly at his coffee, he moved into the lounge room and confronted the entertainment unit along one wall. The hi-fi, video and television system was his pride and joy, a collection of carefully chosen components with no expense spared. The video was always switched on to maintain the integrity of some regular program-recording.

10

Michael rarely watched programs as they were aired, instead videotaping them and viewing them later.

He clicked his tongue in annoyance. The display on the video recorder was also flashing, signalling that the backup battery inside the unit had somehow failed. Sighing, and thinking it was all a bit much to cope with first thing in the morning, he turned on the television and stood back, drinking his coffee as he waited for the picture to materialise.

'Now what the hell's wrong?' he said, as a snowy, flickering image filled the screen. Television reception was usually good. He'd installed a tall mast and an expensive aerial with a booster to make sure of it. He'd willingly embraced the isolation and solitude of this small country town, but he wasn't trying to escape the rest of the world—far from it. He wanted to keep well and truly in touch and the television with its up-to-date news programs in the mornings were an important part of his day. The grainy picture was showing scenes of U.S. troops disembarking from the maw of a huge aircraft. In the bottom left-hand corner the broadcasting station thoughtfully showed the correct time. It was ten past eight o'clock.

'Thank you very much,' Michael muttered. He figured a connection must have come loose on the antenna mast. He turned the television off again, finding the unsteady picture hard on his eyes, and walked back into the kitchen.

Sitting at the dining table Michael stared out one of the long windows, musing over his day. Beyond the glass, lush green farmland crowded with neat squares of sugarcane stretched as far as he could see across the slight vale, until the land turned to near-rainforest for the climb into high, darkened hills. His house was in a superb location, if you didn't mind the isolation. The nearby town of Hickory, five kilometres distant, with a population of just a thousand souls, was the only civilisation until over another hundred kilometres further on. Michael Garrett's home was a large, modern brick building, built by the previous owners of the land. An adjacent farmer had bought the house when the owners suddenly decided to retire and move to the nearest major town. Michael, in turn, snapped up the house at a bargain price when it came on the market again soon afterwards. The farmer had only bought the property to help out his old neighbours and now needed some fast cash flow himself. Michael was happy to oblige. The place suited his purposes almost perfectly. He had reasons for being very interested in Hickory.

He tapped the tabletop with his fingernail, marking each thought as it formed in his mind. The morning sunlight coming through the window felt warm on the back of his hand. First, he needed to see if the studio was in working order. Michael looked at his watch, then remembered it wasn't working. Sometime today, too, he needed to go into Hickory and pick up a parcel from the small post office. It contained a software update for his computer and Michael was hoping it would iron out some program glitches he was experiencing. He figured he might as well make up a household shopping list, since he was going into the town. And maybe the store or the small chemist's would have the watch battery. *Fat chance*, he told himself, pulling a face.

At least this morning he should be able to pass a cheque at the store without getting treated with the utmost suspicion. He'd been in Hickory three months now.

'Country folks,' he said, shaking his head as he got up to check the refrigerator. 'After another three generations they might regard me as a local—or in thirty years, whichever comes first.'

Searching through the kitchen he scribbled a shopping list on the back of an envelope. Satisfied, he decided it was time he checked the studio, but as he walked out of the kitchen he was stopped by the telephone ringing. He could have hurried through to the studio and taken the call in the comfort of his office chair, but on impulse broke his stride and plucked the extension off the wall near the microwave. The voice on the other end of the line made his heart lurch a little and by reflex his hand came up, running his fingers through his hair.

She spoke softly and a little sadly. 'Hello, Daniel Boone. How's it going out in your neck of the woods?'

Michael risked taking a quick breath to calm himself, hoping she wouldn't notice. 'I shot three Indians yesterday,' he said easily. 'Varmints were trying to steal my chickens.'

'It's the feathers that are attracting 'em. Indians like to make big funny hats out of them.'

'Hell, why didn't I think of that?' He stopped, the joke already running out. The pause was turning into an uncomfortable silence, so he asked quietly, 'So, hello Annie. How are you?'

'I'm okay. What about you?'

'Things couldn't be better. I'm making a lot of progress with my manuscript, the house is nearly straightened out—' he faltered again. 'I'm good,' he ended, lamely.

'Aren't you still missing me a bit?' She tried to sound teasing, but it didn't work. It was more like desperate. Michael found himself resenting it.

'Of course I'm missing you.' It took an effort to keep a bite out of his voice. Immediately, he could see the conversation becoming a game between them, the way it always did, one person trying to score points against the other. 'What about you? Are you going out on the town? Having some fun?'

'Am I seeing somebody else, you mean?'

'No, that's none of my business,' he said shortly. 'I meant, are you going out and seeing people, or are you staying at home for a while?' He thought, *Lying bastard. You do want to know if she's going out with somebody else already. I should hang the bloody phone up now. We're heading for one of those crazy arguments again.*

But Annie surprised him, giving him the benefit of the doubt. 'Okay, I'm sorry. Yeah—I've been going out for drinks with the girls, after work for a few hours, that's all. Nothing special. What have you been doing?'

'It's not exactly Times Square out here, you know. My idea of a night out is a six-pack on the back porch.'

'Well, what did you expect?'

14

'Nothing, nothing else,' he said, feeling defensive. *Damn it, don't start making excuses, either. It was my choice to come out here. She doesn't have to like it. She isn't living here.* He went on, 'It's very peaceful here. Relaxing, after a day's work. You should try it sometime. Why don't you come out for a visit?' This last was out of his mouth before he could stop himself. Instantly he knew it was the wrong thing to say.

'I—I don't think so,' Annie said uneasily. A burst of interference on the telephone line filled another awkward moment. 'It's a bit too soon. We'd just be at each other's throats again within the first ten minutes. Maybe later, in a month or so, huh?'

She was right, and he knew it. It was why they were struggling to stay civil over the telephone now. They obviously needed the separation and to be able to speak without looking into each other's eyes just to stop any number of stupid arguments flaring up. Their last six months together had been full of them. Michael had felt she'd begun to reject him, or he'd failed her in some way, and in the growing confusion and heartache he'd taken it upon himself to be the one who walked away. It had hurt—but he'd left her. Another crackle of static, loud enough to make him jerk the handpiece away from his ear, gave him the excuse to change the subject.

'Are you on a mobile or something?'

'No, I'm at home. What's that noise?'

'Just a bug in the system.'

'Oh.' She fell silent and he thought she was about to say something important, but she put on

15

a light-hearted manner. 'I just wanted to call and say hello—make sure you're okay.'

'Thanks, and I'm okay. You're the first person I'd ring, if I had any problems.' *Apart from the ones you cause.*

'I hope so.' She became rushed, wanting to end the call. 'Well, I guess it's time I started heading for work. It's all right for some. All you have to do is walk down the hallway, I suppose.'

'I haven't really got a hallway. All the rooms are sort of connected to each other.'

'You know what I mean.' Listening, Michael closed his eyes. He could see her shrugging. 'Take it easy, okay?' she said.

'You, too. I'll call you soon, if you don't call me before.'

'Maybe we shouldn't call each other at all.'

'No, that would be crazy. I need to talk to you—and I really do miss you.'

'And I miss you, too. I gotta go. Bye.'

'Bye.'

The line went dead, but that was one of Annie's ways. She didn't say goodbye a hundred times over the phone like many people. She just said it and hung up. It wasn't the abrupt disconnection that made an ache in Michael Garrett's chest. It was her voice—among all the other things. The memories of Anne Shannon and what they'd done together for three years still hurt him badly. Every day he wondered if they'd made the wrong decision. It was hard to remember the arguments—the spiteful comments made just to inflict wounds. He often thought that perhaps they hadn't talked enough. He realised that, once again, Annie didn't really have a reason to call him. She'd just dialled him up and said hello. Michael was guilty of doing the same to her. Maybe she was right. They were doing each other more harm than good with these pointless phone calls.

'What a great way to start the day,' he said aloud, hanging up the phone with as much force as the wall mount would allow. 'First I get another power cut, then my ex-girlfriend rings and makes me feel like shit. Wonderful.' He allowed himself a few more moments of self-pity, then tried shrugging it away. 'What the hell.'

The answer was to get busy in the studio—fool around a little, instead of working on more serious projects, like the textbook. Michael knew if he absorbed himself in some music his personal hassles would be quickly pushed back. He paused, briefly considering a second cup of coffee, but decided to get out of the kitchen while he could.

The studio was originally the family room, a large open area air-conditioned by a single, big unit. A pair of sliding glass doors opened out onto a back patio. The lack of windows made it an easy space for Michael to soundproof, especially as he didn't expect a lot of noise coming in from outside anyway. The walls were covered in special absorbent rubber, and two wooden panels coated in the same way were on standby to fit over the glass doors. Thick carpet covered the floor. The room was filled by an assortment of instruments with microphone stands stuck haphazardly around them. Several tiers of electronic keyboards stood on racks. A mess of cables connected everything to a slightly tidier section of the room—a corner where a mixing console, effects devices, a digital recorder and a computer controlled everything. Next to the console was Michael's desk and a second computer. Here, strewn paperwork and scattered reference books ruled. Behind the desk was a bookshelf which he'd hastily fixed to the wall and overloaded with more books and some bits and pieces for his computers.

This was where Michael spent most of his days. When he wasn't working on his air-safety textbook, he simply pushed his chair to the left and dabbled with recording his own music. Michael had even managed to sell a few of his tunes to aspiring young musicians back in the city, but the financial return was small—unless he was lucky enough to hit the jackpot and write a hit. Otherwise, the studio was definitely a hobby which often cut too much into the time Michael was supposed to be devoting to more serious things.

The first thing he did was go straight to one of the keyboards. He knew what he was going to find, but an irrational hope flickered until his fears were confirmed. He'd been doctoring one of the sounds built into the electric piano's program, but he hadn't bothered to save the last settings. The power blackout had effectively wiped out his changes and he was back to square one there. 'Damn it, why didn't I use my head?' he said, punching buttons to re-enter the programming facilities. When he depressed the keys in a simple major chord no noise came out of the wall-mounted speakers. He glanced over to the computer and groaned when he realised an important message dominated the screen. The hard-drive operating system had hiccuped, rather than re-instating the software with the return of power. Michael went over and impatiently re-booted the system, his fingers tapping at the typing keys until he was into the correct software. Back at the keyboard he tried a chord again, but still there was no response.

'This is going to be a bad day for music, I can feel it,' he said, looking down between his feet. On the floor an old-fashioned distortion pedal was plugged into the keyboard. The small red light denoting the pedal as 'on' was dull. If it wasn't getting enough voltage, the pedal would stop any signal getting through, even if the effect was switched off. 'Battery time,' Michael muttered, annoyed at himself for leaving the device connected all night. 'At least there can't be much *else* left to go bloody wrong.' He went to a cupboard and pulled out a cardboard box. He bought batteries in bulk, because it was much cheaper. Juggling the pedal in one hand he ripped the plastic packaging away. After fitting the battery he made to re-plug the connecting lead, absently pressing the pedal to check it. Michael stopped in mid-stride as he stepped back towards the keyboard. The small power light stayed dull. 'Bullshit,' he said, more in disbelief at how his day was going. He took the battery back out and looked around for a simple means to test it, thinking he'd somehow put in the old battery by mistake. Seeing nothing easy to hand Michael used a method he rarely employed, because he hated the taste and the mild shock. He tentatively touched the terminals of the battery to his tongue.

Nothing happened. Not even a tingle. He spied the other battery lying on the floor among the ripped packaging and scooped it up. The tongue-test revealed the same result—that battery was dead, too. Michael inspected the wrapping and saw the manufacturing date was quite recent. It was well within the shelf-life of the battery. Annoyed, he grabbed another blister-pack from the box and tore a battery free. Installing it in the pedal showed it was also no good. Licking the terminals confirmed it. 'This is crazy,' he said, exasperated, pulling a third battery from its packaging. There was no improvement. 'I must have got a bad batch.'

Suddenly, his thinking shifted and Michael realised the mystery might represent something else. More excited than frustrated now, Michael picked up an electronic tuner. It used the same type of battery and he was certain this one was okay.

But it wasn't. The battery was dead. 'This is getting very interesting,' he told the tuner in his hand. Another thought struck him and he rolled his wrist over, looking at the blank watchface. With a nervous fluttering in his stomach, he strode out of the studio and through the house to the front door, picking up a bunch of car keys on the way. His eight-seater van, stripped bare inside for carrying equipment, was parked in the driveway. Blinking in the sunlight he jammed the keys into the ignition. Twisting the starter didn't even make the dashlights glow. Michael automatically cursed, although he was mollified knowing he had a portable battery-charger in the back shed. The dead car battery was another important piece in his puzzle. He forced himself to stay calm, pushing down the flutter in his stomach. This was getting downright strange—but it was exciting, too. There was only one more thing left to test. A torch he kept in the bedroom for emergencies.

Moments later he was standing beside his bed, cupping his hand over the lens and flicking the torch on and off. The bulb stayed dead. Michael stared at the wall above his bed, thinking hard.

Sometime during the night there had been another power cut—or more specifically, something *interfering* with the local power supply grid. And whatever that interference was, it seemed, had also rendered every battery in his household lifeless. It was just the sort of thing Michael had been hoping for.

Kerry Wentworth allowed herself a snort of disgust and hit the base of the cash register with the heel of her hand. 'Stupid bloody thing! Open, damn you!' She went through the sequence for a 'no sale' again, re-reading the instructions left behind by the previous owners even though she knew the procedure by heart now. She tapped the last button with a flourish, expecting the till to slide out so she could put her cash float inside. The register answered with a long beep, signifying it wasn't going to cooperate.

'Christ, I can't believe this is happening! Is this shop bloody jinxed or something?' She was already rattled. That morning the store's burglar alarm had gone off with a raucous din when Kerry had been trying to de-activate it. The noise hadn't gone on for long, but she thought the whole town must have been woken up. She stared angrily at the cash register, willing it to behave. A voice took her by surprise.

'Are you having trouble, Miss Wentworth?'

Kerry looked up to see a vaguely familiar face peering at her between the racks of cough lozenges. She suspected the elderly woman must have tiptoed the entire length of the chemist's just to see what all the fuss was about. Kerry narrowed her eyes a moment, struggling for the name. 'Mrs North? Hello, what brings you in here so early in the morning? I've hardly unlocked the doors. Are you all right?'

'We all tend to rise early in this part of the world, Miss Wentworth,' Mrs North said primly, although a small quirk of her lips acceded approval at Kerry getting her name correct. Kerry was learning that the townsfolk of Hickory had such tiny nuances of expression down to an art form. 'I'm fine, thank you,' Mrs North went on. 'But Bill is getting a bit of a head cold and a runny nose. I thought I might get him some vapour rub to put on his chest and maybe some medication.'

Kerry shoved the till money back into a cloth bag and balanced it in an untidy heap beneath the counter before spinning around to face the shelves behind her. 'Right!' she said, trying to sound bright and efficient. 'We've got most of the popular brands here. Do you prefer any one in particular?'

Mrs North peered short-sightedly at the rows of medicines. 'Have you got anything—stronger?' she asked carefully.

'Yes, but you'll have to go to Doctor Stanford for a prescription first. I can't just give them to you.' Kerry smiled, apologising, but she got the feeling the older woman knew exactly what she was doing. She wasn't surprised to see Mrs North wrinkle her face in dismay.

'George Carter used to give them out. He didn't believe it was right that he couldn't dispense medicine which he knew perfectly well was needed— to responsible persons. Doctor Stanford turned a blind eye, too.'

'George Carter was an older and very established pharmaceutist,' Kerry explained patiently. 'I'm sure he could get away with a lot of things like that. But I'm only new on the register and might get checked out by a State inspector at any time. I can't afford to get into any trouble.'

'No, I suppose not,' Mrs North agreed grudgingly, after judging for a moment whether it was worth a second try. Finally she chose what she wanted and silently waited while Kerry dropped the items in a paper bag. When Kerry fumbled with change from the bag of money below the counter Mrs North raised an enquiring eyebrow.

'It's out of order,' Kerry said, nodding at the till. 'It needs fixing. We had another power cut last night and it seems to have upset the electronics in this silly thing.' *If you tell me George Carter could always get it to work, I'll scream*, she added to herself.

Mrs North nodded knowingly. 'The new clock radio my son bought me isn't working properly, either. It took me hours to read all the instructions to get it right, and now it's gone all funny again.

23

There must be something wrong with the power.' Her face fell into a sulk at the memory.

'Well, the power's either on or it's off, really—' Kerry began, then stopped, realising the older woman wouldn't appreciate being lectured by a young newcomer to town. 'Yes, you're most likely right,' she said, quickly changing tack.

'I must be off. I told Bill not to go out until I had something on his chest, but he won't wait forever.' Clutching the bag to her, she shuffled towards the door. Kerry pulled a face, listening to Mrs North's shoes scuff loudly on the threadbare carpet.

'You did creep up on me, you old bag,' she muttered good-naturedly, then plastered a cheerful smile on her face and waved, calling, 'Have a nice day. I hope Bill gets better.' Mrs North lifted a hand above her shoulder in reply without turning around, and disappeared out onto the footpath.

The next hour passed uneventfully. Kerry abandoned trying to get the till to work, instead taking change out of her money bag and making a note of every sale on a slip of paper. One of the conditions of Kerry's taking over the chemist's was that she adhere to a long-standing agreement with the grocery store next door. It ensured they didn't double-up on some of the faster-moving goods. The agreement almost guaranteed a certain cash turnover for both businesses, keeping them alive. She was learning quickly about small-town politics and, most importantly, recognised the value of building personal relationships with the local population. Kerry made an attempt to note the name of everyone who came into the chemist—if a name was offered—and remember them when they came again. She tried to make it easy, associating some names with particular traits. For example, Mrs Dunbridge was easy. She was another elderly lady who needed a cane to walk, dragging one foot almost absently behind her. Jeff Butler was simple to remember too, but for more unfortunate reasons. A man about Kerry's age, he was the mechanic at the garage. His bumbling, inexperienced attempts at conversation whenever Kerry drove in for petrol were both touching and a little alarming—the latter due to the sense of desperation that was creeping into his manner. It soon became common knowledge in town Kerry was 'available' and, no matter how many times she told herself she was imagining things and being vain, some of the younger males in Hickory seemed to regard her in a more lustful, rather than merely friendly, way. Lately, Jeff Butler had taken to buying pointless little things from the chemist's and using the excuse to stand around and talk. These exchanges were always awkward. Kerry struggled to find mutual interests, yet didn't want to sound too encouraging, either. Often she found herself glancing hopefully at the door, because someone else coming into the pharmacy was usually enough to drive Jeff away. The mechanic's infatuation sparked a paranoia in the pharmacist, too. Whenever any of the younger men of Hickory came in Kerry felt a mixture of emotions—her need to establish herself with the townsfolk clashed with a panic that any friendliness might be interpreted as a sexual invitation. It wasn't the sort

25

of problem she'd envisaged when deciding to buy the business.

Thinking about it now, Kerry suddenly resolved to get a 'not interested' message across to Jeff Butler. Maybe it would help her to see everyone else in a kinder light.

She was fiddling with a sunglasses display, discounting the older stock, when two men walked into the pharmacy, one behind the other. Kerry left the sunglasses so she could get behind the counter before they reached it. Seeing her, the second man flashed a cheerful smile and backed off, deferring to the other. The first was tall and pale with a bony frame and lank, black hair hanging over his forehead. He strode straight up to one of the glass cabinets and waited.

'Hello, can I help you?' She was immediately puzzled, because she needed to actually place herself in front of the man to capture his gaze. His eyes slid away from the shelves of medicines and looked uncertainly into hers.

'My name is John Powers,' he said in a flat voice. 'Mr Carter should have arranged for some insulin for me. It's due by now.'

A diabetic, Kerry thought. *That's why he looks a little unhealthy, that's all.* But there was something else in Powers' demeanour she found unsettling. 'Sure. It came in two days ago. George said not to bother calling you, because you knew it was coming.' Kerry waited for a response, but Powers simply kept looking at her. A sudden thought surprised her—if she dodged to one side would his eyes follow her, or would he still stare at the same spot? His blank gaze was giving her the creeps. 'I'll

26

go and get it. It's in the refrigerator out the back,' she said, glad to move away from the man. Then she hesitated, concerned about turning her back and leaving the place unattended, but there was no choice. Unless she was willing to pay for an assistant there were going to be plenty of times she'd need to let her guard down. She just had to trust a little in the small-town attitude and hope petty shoplifting wasn't an issue with the adults, at least.

Returning with the insulin Kerry saw she needn't have worried about any stealing. In fact, Powers looked as if he hadn't moved a muscle since she left him. His hands were still placed neatly side-by-side on the glass display case. His eyes were staring implacably at the shelves of goods in front of him. Glancing at the other customer Kerry noticed he'd moved a discreet distance away. 'Here's your insulin, Mr Powers. Is there anything else?' Again his attention fell in a peculiar and unnerving way on her.

After a pause, during which Kerry had time to wonder if he was going to say anything at all, he said, 'Some hypodermics. Two packets.'

This meant she had to get the store keys from under the till and open a glass case mounted on the wall. She fumbled getting the key into the lock. *Take it easy. This guy's okay. You'd be a little weird too, if you were a bad diabetic.* Kerry knew from the type and amount of insulin Powers needed that his condition was quite severe. She got the two packs of needles and slipped them into a paper bag, putting the insulin in after them. Making some calculations on the notepad she told him how much it cost. He seemed to become confused.

'The till's broken—that's why I added it up on paper. You can check it, if you like. I don't mind.'

'No,' he said slowly, reaching for a wallet from his pocket. Now he appeared reluctant to pay and Kerry wondered if he usually got some sort of discount. Before she could think of a way to ask politely he took some bills out and offered them. 'That's fine.'

'That's too much,' she said, managing a smile. 'I don't want to start out by charging too much!' She handed him one of the notes back, expecting a smile in return, but Powers calmly placed the bill back in his wallet. Kerry counted out the rest of his change into his palm and he did the same, his face not altering as he tucked the money away. 'Thank you,' she said, feeling her cheerful facade begin to crumble. Without another word Powers picked up the paper bag and walked out of the shop. Kerry watched him go, letting out her breath between her teeth in a slow whistle.

'A strange guy, huh?' the other customer called, moving closer to the counter.

'He's just a bit under the weather, I guess,' Kerry said, unprepared for the question. The man surprised her by thrusting his hand towards her.

'Michael Garrett. I haven't been in here since you took over.'

Kerry shook his hand. 'Kerry Wentworth. No, I didn't think I'd seen you before.'

'I'm new in town, too. Been here about three months. Hey, we should stick together—' Michael stopped, seeing an alarmed expression flit across

28

her face. 'It's just a figure of speech, you know. I was only kidding.'

'No, I'm sorry,' Kerry recovered. Knowing he wasn't a true local she felt safe saying, 'I've—ah, been getting a few subtle offers from some of the lads, I think.' She laughed self-consciously. 'I'm not sure, actually.'

'The new girl in town. It's understandable,' Michael said, smiling widely and hoping she'd take it innocently. He saw she was pretty beneath the severe hairstyle and unflattering white uniform, which nevertheless failed to hide her trim figure. She had dark, almost black, hair pulled back into a ponytail, and an attractive face that needed little make-up.

'I guess so. Anyway, what can I do for you, Mr Garrett?'

'Call me Michael—or Mike, if you like.' He looked genuinely appalled that she wanted to address him so formally. He glanced around the pharmacy. 'Ah, batteries. The alkaline type. They've only got the normal ones next door, and they're not very good for the sort of stuff I use them for.'

'I've got some over here in the film section,' she gestured for him to follow. 'Not many, though. How many do you want?'

'Just one or two will get me out of trouble, but can you get me some more?'

Kerry handed him two batteries and looked in dismay at the empty rack left behind. She had no idea how to order more stock. Michael mistook her hesitation for a reluctance to buy more purely on his behalf.

'I'll buy a whole box, actually. That way you won't get landed with any extras. I'll pay for them now, too.'

'No, really that won't be necessary—'

He cut her off with a wave. 'I buy them by the box all the time, honestly. Look, do you mind if I test these?' He held up the two packages in his hand.

Kerry was surprised, but shook her head. She watched as Michael peeled the plastic wrapping off one of the batteries and tentatively stuck the terminals against his tongue. He let out a funny sound and jerked the battery away from his face. Kerry couldn't stop herself bursting into laughter.

'What did you do that for?'

'I didn't think it would work,' he said, embarrassed.

'But they're new!'

'Yeah, I know.' He was frowning now. 'Hey, did you have a power cut in here last night?'

Kerry jerked a thumb at her cash register. 'Sure did. It seems to have killed my till.'

'Really?' Michael looked strangely interested, but didn't explain further. He looked down at the battery in his hand and muttered, 'They must have been closer to my—' He caught himself, suddenly smiling at Kerry again. 'Sorry, I'm trying to figure out something and I've got into the habit of talking to myself. It must be from living alone,' he added, making a joke of it. He held up the batteries. 'Well, these will obviously do fine, thanks.'

Kerry looked a little perplexed as he paid for them, then they stood and chatted about the funny ways some of the locals treated newcomers.

They also agreed that Kerry would call him when the batteries arrived—hopefully on the next delivery from the city. Satisfied, he went to leave the shop, but paused a moment halfway to the door. 'Can I pay you with a cheque?' he asked.

'Will it bounce?' she said, joking.

'Hey, you're turning into a Hickory local faster than I am,' he said, grinning and waving a goodbye as he walked out. She watched him go, noting he was of average height, but had broader shoulders than most. Kerry decided he looked like a man who tried to keep himself in good condition.

Nice guy, too, she thought, then found herself comparing Michael Garrett's style to the unsettling behaviour of John Powers. *Well, one out of two's better than nothing,* she shrugged, trying to dismiss the episode. But before she could put her mind to other things, Kerry had to admit Powers' weird manner had upset her. Only then could she dismiss him and get her concentration back.

2

THE BEST PLACE they could have met was Terry
McGann's hotel. But the last thing these men
wanted was somebody outside their select group
to witness the meeting, and besides, it was long
past McGann's closing time. Instead they waited
until after midnight and gathered in the small
town's library, which was attached to the school.
It was common for John Powers to have lights on
there until the early hours of the morning. Nobody
passing by would give it a second thought. Powers
had established a reputation for sleeping little and
working late.

There were only four men, plus Powers himself
watching over them with his stony gaze. They sat
around a study table, though nobody used it to

keep notes or any documents. It was simply habit that these men needed to sit around a desk or table to provide the environment for discussion of serious matters. Greetings were exchanged, then a short, bespectacled man stood up and announced the meeting was beginning. He had thinning grey hair that made him appear older than his forty years. It was actually an advantage for him, considering his profession, but that didn't ease his frustration when he looked in the mirror each morning.

'They're coming—and they're coming soon,' he said, his voice heavy. 'There's no turning back now.'

'There was never any turning back,' someone said quickly, harshly. 'I'm no longer sure we even had a choice in the beginning.'

'We had a choice. At least we'll all benefit from this, rather than be ignorant of something fantastic happening under our very noses.'

'Some *choice*. We wouldn't have stayed ignorant, and you know it. And what would have happened when we did notice something going on? The same thing that happened to Jake Sanders?'

'I'm convinced Jake was an accident. Besides, the rewards should ease your conscience,' the first speaker reminded him dryly.

'Conscience?' another man spoke. 'He said some people might be removed if they looked like being a problem. Was Jake Sanders an accident, or was he *removed*? What about that couple the other night? If our population is *removed* at this rate, there'll be no-one left inside a month—and that's certainly not the sort of project I agreed to be a part of. It's more like something straight out of Nazi Germany.'

'Don't overreact. We all understood some people might need to be—ah, inconvenienced. Not that I agree with it,' he added hastily. 'But there's too much at stake now for us to worry about the likes of Jake Sanders. Besides, it might well have *been* an accident. The couple who died in the car crash most likely were.' He turned to Powers, hoping for confirmation. There was no change in Powers' expression, and he continued to stand absolutely still at the window, where any movement outside would attract his attention, and he could also keep watching and listening to the men at the table. 'Anyway,' the man went on, 'let's not get excited. We're committed—and we've been committed for a long time now. There's no changing our minds.' He looked around, waiting for someone to comment. Instead, it was Powers who spoke, his voice flat yet somehow authoritative.

'You have one week.'

There was stunned silence. The man standing stared at Powers, appalled. 'What? There's supposed to be at least a month!'

'A week. Then it will be over. It's a matter of—timing,' he ended vaguely.

'Timing! Changing from a month to seven days is something a little more drastic than damned *timing*!' He thought for a moment, then suddenly pointed an accusing finger at Powers. 'Nothing's changed, I'll bet—damn you! It was always going to be like this. This is just your way of keeping us off-balance and under control,' he said bitterly,

34

then he became slightly smug. 'Well, we're not sure everything's ready. What do you say to that?'

'You are expected to be sure. We have you gentlemen to attend to any problems. That is why you are here. As you agreed, you will take care of the containment and make certain we aren't disturbed in our program. So, you have a lot to discuss tonight.'

'For Christ's sake, what are we supposed to do? Build a wall around the whole town?'

'You people *are* the wall. That is your work.'

The four men looked at each other, exchanging expressions of disbelief and helplessness. There was another silence, until someone asked hoarsely, 'Why do you need us at all?'

'Indeed, things should be different in the future,' Powers conceded with a nod, then added with a chilling lack of emotion, 'Your type of input into the program may become unnecessary.'

3

GAVIN PACKER STEPPED out into the backyard and took a deep breath of the fresh morning air. It was promising to be another beautiful day. It was a shame, he realised, that it would probably be marred by a funeral. He meant to go into town and check first, but it seemed logical Jake Sanders would be buried today. Gavin and his small family wanted to attend the service.

A clutch of chickens noticed him standing near the back door and came scurrying closer, hoping for scraps. 'What are you bastards doing out again?' he asked. At the sound of his voice the fowls began strutting, competing for position. 'All right, all right,' he sighed, his moment of revelling in the new day ruined. 'I might as well get it out the way.' Gavin ducked quickly back into the house and grabbed a bag of feed from a high shelf. Some of the birds had instantly gathered around the back door and Gavin's sudden re-emergence made them scatter in a flurry of feathers. He ignored them, striding towards the chicken coop. Recognising the moment, the fowls scrambled to follow.

At the wire-mesh enclosure the birds that hadn't escaped saw him coming and got excited, too. Gavin pushed the makeshift gate open wide and walked to the furthest corner of the pen. The fowls all followed, those from outside being lured back through the gate. He spread a generous amount of feed over the ground and stepped back, watching them greedily peck at the dirt. Then he quickly checked the nests and found only half the usual number of eggs. Gavin swore, because this meant the escaped birds had laid the rest in any one of a dozen places around the yard and he'd have to go searching—which was why he didn't particularly like them running free. Gavin's nine-year-old daughter, Beth, usually found it a delightful game looking for the stray eggs, but she wasn't always available.

Thinking of his daughter made him look at his watch. It must be nearly time she got out of bed and ready for school. He raised his eyebrows in surprise, seeing his watch had stopped, then he shrugged. Judging by the early-morning sunlight it certainly wasn't late yet. If he shook Beth now, she'd have time to find the rest of the eggs. His thoughts turned back to the escaped chickens and how they had got free. Gavin left the coop, pulling the gate firmly closed behind him. He went to one corner of the enclosure where earlier he had noticed that the mesh was pushed apart. Carefully putting the eggs down on the damp grass, he knelt and twisted some loose strands of wire together, closing the gap. It would need to be done properly, later.

Cradling the eggs again Gavin went back into the house. His wife Linda sat at the kitchen table and nibbled a piece of toast, stirring a mug of tea with a spoon in her other hand. She was a small woman with brown hair she had cut boyishly—and sensibly—short after getting annoyed with constantly brushing it out the way as she bent over her vegetable garden. Despite spending so much time outdoors, her fair skin refused to darken. Only the freckles became more pronounced. She was already dressed in baggy overalls, ready for the garden. The family dog, a labrador called Mandy, was watching with despairing eyes as Linda's toast got smaller. Linda ignored the dog, giving her husband a look as she saw how few eggs he carried.

'They got out again,' he explained, opening the refrigerator and putting the eggs inside. 'The rest'll be scattered all over the damn yard again. I'll get Beth to search around before she gets ready for school.'

'Did they get in the vegetables?'

'I didn't look. Most likely, I suppose. Have we seen Sleeping Beauty yet?'

'Not a peep. She hasn't even opened her bedroom door.'

Beth had developed a sudden desire for privacy,

closing her bedroom door whenever she was in there. Her parents were shrugging it off as another 'stage', which wasn't doing any harm. Gavin walked down the hallway and knocked gently on his daughter's door. There was no answer, so he quietly turned the handle.

The first thing Gavin noticed in the gloom cast by the drawn curtains was an unusual, yet oddly familiar, smell. Then he realised the gloom itself was peculiar, because Beth had never bothered closing the curtains before. He stood uncertainly in the doorway, waiting for his eyes to adjust, and finally saw his daughter crouched on the end of her bed.

'Beth? Are you okay?' He was answered by a sniffle. Gavin stepped across the room and pulled the drapes apart, filling the bedroom with sunshine. Now he blinked in the bright light as he looked down at her. She was huddled, her knees drawn up to her chest, near the foot of the bed. Beth's pale face looked back at him, her eyes wide and damp. 'Honey, what's wrong?' Gavin said, concerned. He went to sit on the bed next to her, but stopped himself. He saw what the smell was now—she'd wet the bed in the night.

Immediately he felt sorry for her. She hadn't done this for years and Gavin figured she was worried about what her parents would think. 'Oh, Beth,' he said, carefully lowering himself down onto the bed, avoiding the damp patch. He put an arm around her shoulder, drawing her close. 'Did you have a problem in the night? A nightmare? Hey, it happens to everyone now and again.'

But she was silently shaking her head, her dark hair brushing his chest. 'Are you sick?' he tried, automatically putting a hand to her forehead. She felt hot and clammy, but that could have been a result of her crying. When Beth spoke her voice was small and frightened.

'I saw Jake standing outside in our yard last night. He was just staring at my window. It *scared* me. It scared me so much I wet the bed.'

Gavin felt a sinking feeling in his stomach. Jake Sanders had become a good friend of theirs after he called in one day to buy some fresh eggs and got interested in the Packers' attempts at self-sufficiency. He had visited often after that—the Packers lived on one of the backroads to Jake's home. Jake would squat somewhere in the backyard, chatting and surveying the small collection of livestock the family kept, or wandering among their vegetable gardens and the young citrus fruit trees bordering the property. He especially had a soft spot in his heart for Beth, displaying a kindness and affection he probably wouldn't have liked known about in the front bar of the hotel. Sometimes he stayed late into the night, sharing a meal and bringing out a joint or two of marijuana once Beth had gone to bed.

When news of Jake's death reached the Packers the day before, the first thing the parents did was discuss long and hard how Beth would take it. She was at a most impressionable age, being old enough to understand, yet too young to cope properly. Beth came home from school very distraught, but holding herself together with the childish hope that her parents would dispel the awful story she heard from some of the other kids. But her mother could do nothing except shatter that hope, crying too, and confirming the stories were true—Jake had been killed in an accident. Together, Beth and Linda spent hours in tears and rocking in each other's arms. After Beth finally calmed down Gavin and Linda waited and watched, hoping she had come through the worst.

Now Gavin believed he was dealing with some sort of emotional relapse, brought on by Beth's dreaming of Jake Sanders. He hugged his daughter tighter and tried to think of gentler words, but sadly understood the circumstances didn't allow it.

'Beth, you must have dreamt it. You know you can't have seen Jake.'

'But I *did*. He was standing there, like he was thinking of coming inside, the way he always did.'

Gavin glanced towards the window. He remembered, too, the way Jake had always seemed oddly reluctant to come into their home, as if becoming a part of the Packers' domesticity and family ways would have been in conflict with the tough biker figure that he liked to keep up. Unexpectedly, it disturbed Gavin that Beth claimed to have seen such a *particular* image of Jake, then he mentally shook his head. Gavin tried to sound both understanding and firm.

'Beth, we talked about this a lot yesterday. And we all shed more than a few tears, remember? But Jake's dead—it's just one of those terrible things that happen in the world and we have to learn to accept it. It's not easy, I know, especially when you're your age. We'll probably all dream about him for a little while, because we'll be thinking about him so much.'

'I didn't dream about it,' Beth whispered, her lips moving against the fabric of his shirt. 'He was there. I saw him.'

Gavin wasn't sure what to say next, so in a reflex action he tried to humour her. 'Hey Beth, you couldn't possibly have seen Jake here without your mother and I knowing about it, too. You know what he was like. He *always* rode his bike, and we would've been woken up.'

'His bike's wrecked,' she replied simply.

'Yeah, but if you're talking about a *ghost*, then that doesn't mean—' Gavin stopped, realising he was getting onto dangerous ground. He'd had no intention of mentioning ghosts or any such thing. 'Look, this is getting a bit silly. I think you've just had a bad dream, don't you? You'll feel a lot better if you have a shower and get dressed. What do you think?' Beth looked up at him with wet eyes and Gavin could see her making up her mind that it was pointless trying to convince her father. At Beth's dumb nod he released her and she ambled slowly towards the bedroom door, picking up items of clothing as she went. 'Beth?' he called after her. 'Do you still want to go to the funeral?'

'Yes, I want to say goodbye.'

'Well, I guess that's what funerals are for,' Gavin conceded heavily. He'd been against the idea of Beth going, saying the service would be too intense a scene for a nine year old. But Beth insisted she wanted to be there and Linda didn't believe it was good to shield their daughter from such things. Gavin had reluctantly agreed. 'Okay,' he sighed. 'I think maybe you shouldn't go to school today, then. I don't know what time the funeral will be—I'm not even sure it'll be today yet. It seems pointless to send you to school if it is, though.' Quietly, Gavin was glad of the excuse to keep Beth close.

'Okay,' she said, uncaring. A day away from school held no consolation. As she disappeared down the hall Gavin had an inspiration and called her back.

'I'll tell you what,' he said. 'Let's make a deal. Have today off school and come to the funeral, but if the funeral's not until *tomorrow*, I want you to go to school tomorrow and stay *there*. Then we can all go and visit the grave later, together. We'll take some fresh flowers.' Gavin knew he was giving himself the slim chance of still keeping Beth away from the funeral.

'Okay,' she said again. She was too drained to argue.

While Beth headed for the shower Gavin gathered up the soiled sheets from the bed and took them straight to the laundry, dumping them in the washing machine and dialling up a long wash cycle. Then he went back to Beth's bedroom and tried hauling the mattress out to put it in the sunshine to dry and air, but he had to call for Linda's help. As they struggled with it through the house Gavin explained what had happened. When he came to what Beth claimed she saw, Linda stopped suddenly and let the mattress drop to the floor.

'She said that?'

'I tried to tell her it must have been a dream,

but she's not going to buy that yet.' Gavin saw Linda had something else in mind. 'Why?'

'Oh, nothing, I suppose,' she shook her head, changing her mind. 'It's just my own imagination getting carried away, too. Last night Mandy went right off, growling and carrying on like crazy. All the hackles went up on her back, like I've never seen her before. I was going to wake you, but it wasn't like somebody was prowling around outside. It was funny, really. I didn't know what to do, then she started to calm down again anyway.'

'I didn't hear a thing,' Gavin admitted guiltily.

'You never do.'

'No, I know.' He was a very sound sleeper.

They got the mattress outside and returned to the kitchen for a cup of tea. Beth was happier now, out of the shower and scouring the yard for eggs. Gavin watched her through a window.

'You know, it's still pretty early,' he said. 'I'm thinking about taking some eggs into town for Elaine Sanders—just as an excuse to see how she's going.'

'I'd expect a lot of other people will be checking on her,' Linda said, looking at him over the rim of her cup. 'I'm not sure too many of them will appreciate the "hippy from the commune" calling in.'

'Fuck them,' Gavin said, making sure Beth wasn't within hearing range. 'Elaine and I get on really well. I'm genuinely concerned about her welfare. Besides,' he shrugged, 'I've met a lot of locals by now, while I've been working, anyway. They know we're not like that.' Gavin earned money during the cane harvesting season, stock-piling the cash to pay the utility bills during the rest of the year when he concentrated on making their property more self-supportive.

'Well, I agree you should go now, early, before the crowds gather. You know there's nothing like a good death in the family to bring your friends out of the woodwork,' Linda added dryly.

'I'll find out when the funeral's being held, too,' Gavin said, rising from the table.

He could have taken the battered Ford trayback they owned, but Gavin opted for his ten-speed bicycle and a satchel. Petrol was another com-modity they used sparingly and it was only a ten-minute bike ride into Hickory. By the time Gavin was pedalling out of his driveway and along the road, the sunshine was starting to dry the dew from the grass. In the distance he heard the grum-bling of a tractor, but the height of the sugarcane growing around him prevented him seeing where it was working. The morning air was only stirred occasionally by a fitful breeze and he made good time into town.

Coasting along the main street Gavin waved to Mr Bartell, the grocery store owner, who was putting out magazine posters and collecting the piles of newspapers that had been delivered before dawn. Bartell had only just unlocked his doors. The pharmacy next door wouldn't open for another hour. Gavin had already met the new chemist, an attractive young woman called Kerry, when he'd needed some cough mixture for Beth.

He wasn't so self-sufficient or independent as to reject the benefits of modern medicine—especially when it came to his daughter.

A minute later he was pulling to a stop outside Elaine Sanders' small house. His brakes squealed, attracting the attention of an older woman who was walking through the garden towards the rear of the house.

'Good morning,' he said easily. 'Is Elaine awake?'

The woman stopped and regarded him warily. Gavin was a big man with a rather wild appearance, with his shaggy red hair and full beard. 'No,' she said. 'I can't seem to rouse her, but I expect Doctor Stanford gave her something to help her sleep. I was going to make her a cup of tea.' She now seemed undecided what she should do.

Gavin jerked a thumb at his satchel. 'I've brought her some fresh eggs.'

The woman nodded wisely. 'Yes, but I expect she won't need so many of those things now— groceries, I mean. Not without young Jake to share them with.'

I'll bet you would have cheered her up no end, Gavin thought, but said instead, 'Yes, she'll miss him very much.' He looked around, checking the angle of the sun. 'I might put these eggs around the back somewhere out of the sun.' Without getting off his bike he leaned forward and opened the gate, backing away to let her through. It was a little obvious, but he felt sure he would be doing Elaine Sanders a favour by encouraging this woman to leave. 'Can I tell Elaine who called, if I see her first?' he asked, urging her on further.

46

'Mrs North,' she announced primly, reluctantly stepping through onto the footpath. 'Have we met?'

'I've worked with your husband, Bill. I'm Gavin Packer.' *As if you don't know,* he added silently.

'Ah,' she said, narrowing her eyes and instilling all her understanding into the single sound. Gavin stayed quiet and she was obliged to move on. 'If you do see Elaine, tell her I'll be back later.'

'I'll do that,' he nodded, giving a small wave. He watched as she shuffled away. Only when Mrs North crossed the road did he feel safe to dismount and go through the gate.

The garden was meticulously kept, with sharp-edged lawns and beds of flowers weeded to perfection. A wrought-iron bench was perfectly placed for sitting and enjoying the sun, surrounded by all the colourful plants. Gavin knew Elaine Sanders was responsible for it all, except for Jake actually mowing the grass, and he suddenly decided to offer doing it for nothing—perhaps he could trade it off with some babysitting, if he and Linda wanted to spend a night in the city. It was unlikely they ever would, but he thought it might be good enough to coerce Elaine into accepting his charity. He made a perfunctory knock on the front door, then moved around the back. He knocked again on the laundry door, but there was still no answer. Gavin glanced around for somewhere to put the eggs. Then he heard the buzz of an electronic alarm clock going off. 'Wake up, Elaine,' he muttered. 'Let me in.'

He waited for the noise to stop before knocking again, but the raucous sound kept on. 'She must have taken a damn packet of sleeping pills,' he said aloud. He tried knocking louder, hoping to be heard over the top of the alarm, and called out, 'Elaine? Are you awake? It's Gavin.' He looked around, worried about attracting too much attention from the neighbours. The alarm didn't stop. 'Bugger this,' he grunted. Gavin moved to one side of the house and stood underneath some open casement windows where the alarm seemed loudest. After checking again that no-one was watching, he gripped the bottom sill and pulled himself up, popping his head between the casements and looking quickly through. It was the bedroom, but he was surprised to see the bed neatly made.

'Maybe she didn't stay here last night,' he told himself. It didn't sound right, though. As he'd ridden into town Gavin realised there was a possibility that someone had stayed with Elaine Sanders overnight and he shouldn't have been so concerned—but he couldn't see her leaving the comfort and familiarity of her own home. He went back to the front of the house, stepping onto the small porch. The street was empty, Mrs North's figure had disappeared. Someone could have been watching him through the drapes of any of the nearby houses, but he risked cupping his hands around his face and peering into a French window.

The room beyond the glass was shadowy and at first he saw nothing. Gavin was about to give up, pulling away from the window, when he noticed something bad—a pair of stockinged feet projecting out from behind a sofa.

'Oh shit,' he said, feeling his stomach lurch. He quickly tried the front door, but it was locked. For a moment he thought about breaking it down, but on a hunch hurried back to the rear of the house. The laundry door was unlocked, giving him access to the whole home. Gavin told himself wryly he'd probably saved Mrs North from a nasty shock. He was pretty sure what he'd find.

Stepping inside he trod carefully, his eyes unaccustomed to the darkness. There was an unnatural stillness in the air being shattered by the alarm. He moved through the kitchen, noticing a half-prepared cup of drinking chocolate on the bench with two white tablets beside it. Entering the lounge room he found himself on the opposite side of the sofa. Now Elaine Sanders was in plain view and Gavin let out a groan of pity.

Whatever killed her had happened fast—some sort of shock or massive heart attack. She must have dropped instantly, sprawling on the floor. A glass of port she'd been carrying lay next to her outflung hand, the liquor a dark stain spread across the carpet. Gavin knew immediately there was nothing he could do for her. He also knew he shouldn't touch anything and leave it all for the police to deal with properly.

But Gavin didn't hesitate to sidestep into the bedroom and hastily pull the counterpane off the bed. At the same time he yanked the power cord for the alarm from the wall. Back in the lounge he balanced himself carefully, placing his feet in the clear spaces within the confined area between the wall and sofa where Elaine Sanders' body lay. He gently dropped the bedspread over her. It wasn't just an act of decency or respect.

Gavin couldn't bear the expression of pain and terror locked on the woman's face.

4

AN AIR OF anxiety and grief closed down on Hickory. Normally when unexpected, even tragic, events occurred, gossip would flare up like a struck match. People would have something *important* to talk about, seeking each other out in the street, the words ready on their lips, each eager to voice an opinion first.

But four deaths within days of each other was different. It was as if the town's sensibilities were overloaded. The events were unsettling in a strange and frightening way. Some began treating them with an almost fearful reverence, as if to discuss things too much might cause them to be the next stiffening occupant of Arnold Connors' makeshift hearse. Usually people would enthusiastically claim to be the last person to speak to, or see, the victim of an accident. Now they shied away from the privilege, muttering only vague recollections and guarded references to other people having been closer, or spoken later, than themselves.

A solid sheet of leaden cloud slid across the sky, enhancing the effect of a town in mourning. It didn't rain. A fitful breeze kept scooping litter from the few rubbish bins in the main street, the wind rattling the paper cups and balled wrappers along the gutters. Standing in the doorway of her pharmacy Kerry watched them roll past and considered how undignified it might look if she chased after them and put them back in the bin. She prudently took too long to decide, seeing the scraps get blown too far away for her to catch. A chill caught her unexpectedly and she stepped hurriedly backwards, shielding herself behind the plate glass windows. She thought about closing up and going home.

Everyone else was—well, almost everyone. It was as if the town itself had died, too. Only Terry McGann was actually preparing for a big one, with a whole town full of thirsty funeral-goers soon to descend upon his establishment. And the betting agency down the road was still operating. Behind the agency's sign-covered frontage Kerry could just make out a few figures scrutinising the glowing television repeaters. Dark clothing suggested a few avid punters were placing their bets before heading off to the graveside service. If Kerry had been closer, she would have noticed the gamblers needed to peer harder at the video monitors today—some unusual interference was making the satellite link jumpy and unreliable. The agency was staying open mainly because it was government-owned and boasted a satellite link to the major racecourses in the country and a computerised betting terminal. With such a system in place, the authorities held little sympathy for small-town funerals—even when it was a double-attraction at the cemetery. The betting shop wouldn't be closing.

Arnold Connors had made an exemplary effort to quickly process and prepare Elaine Sanders' body. By postponing Jake's funeral for a day and convincing Sergeant Riley, the more senior of the two local policemen, that there was nothing particularly unusual about Elaine's death, Connors avoided the awkwardness and delay of an autopsy and arranged the funerals so that mother and son could be buried at the same time. Her husband Gordon, already in the ground some ten years now, would be reunited with both members of his family. A second grave was quickly dug beside Jake's. Someone suggested it was somehow a beautiful and touching thing that a mother and her son would be interred at the same service. Connors was simply glad to get rid of the backlog in his funeral business so he could concentrate again on replacing the diesel injectors in Harvey McGow's Massey Ferguson tractor. The two car crash victims were on their way to the city, the stricken parents acceding to the solicitor's insistence that friends wishing to attend a funeral in the city far outnumbered the family considering a service in the country. Connors figured that, by the law of averages, things should settle down again. Besides, he could ill-afford any more funerals like the Sanders', where he'd now have to squeeze the costs out of a deceased estate, there being no remaining family.

Kerry turned away from her doorway, thinking about making herself a fresh cup of coffee and using that as a time-gauge. If no-one came into the pharmacy by the time she'd drunk it, she might as well shut up shop. There was an emergency telephone number on the door, anyway. A sound from the footpath outside stopped her and she peeked through her window displays to see what had caused it. Next door, Mr Bartell was gathering together the wire-framed posters advertising his magazines and newspapers and propping them inside his doorway. Kerry braced herself against the breeze and went out, waiting for Bartell to reappear.

'Closing, Mal?' she called, when he came back out to retrieve an ancient bubblegum machine. Bartell looked up at her and gave her a sad smile. She noticed he was wearing a dress shirt and tie under his customary white grocer's coat.

'I wasn't going to go to Jake's funeral. I liked him and everything, but the store's pretty important—' he gestured helplessly at the doorway. 'But his mother Elaine's a different matter. We've known each other for many years. She helped look after my mother, when her illness turned bad.' He stopped for a moment, gazing into the distance, lost in the memory. 'I have to pay my last respects. Silly, isn't it?' He smiled wistfully again. 'I should have said my thankyous while she was still alive to hear them.'

'I'm sure you did,' Kerry said sympathetically, startled to find herself thrown into a personal conversation.

'Oh, I did,' Bartell said. 'But you always feel, in these times, you could have done more—when it's too late. Are you going to the funeral?'

Kerry realised it was really only a polite question. 'I don't think I knew either of them well enough to attend the service. I know I *could*, because of being here—' She meant her slightly prominent position as Hickory's pharmacist and being part of the business community. And she had spoken to both the Sanders several times. Bartell was nodding, understanding. 'But funerals are a family and friends thing. I think I should stay away.'

'Then perhaps you could do me a favour?'

'Sure.' Kerry was surprised again.

'If I left you the keys to my store, could you look after anyone who wants anything urgently? There'd be no need to take any money—just make a note of who called and what they got. I'll get the money from them later.' He saw a flicker of indecision on Kerry's face and didn't realise it came from her disappointment. She'd already half-accepted she could have the rest of the afternoon off, but now she didn't want to refuse Bartell any help. She wasn't going to get home early after all. He went on, 'Oh, I don't expect you to stay open the extra hour I do, of course. I should come back after the funeral I know, but I've decided if I'm going to give myself the afternoon off, I might as well do a job of it. I expect there'll be a decent turn-out at McGann's afterwards.'

'What about your keys?' she asked, forcing herself to sound unconcerned and obliging.

'I have a spare set. I could get them back off you in the morning.'

'I can't see any problems then,' she said, groaning inwardly.

Kerry followed him into his store and he showed her the door-locks and where the things most likely to be needed were kept. 'Don't bother, unless it's really urgent,' he said. On her suggestion they carried several litres of milk back to the pharmacy and left a note on the grocery store window saying limited stocks were available next door. 'Thanks for this,' he said, suddenly looking awkward. 'I really appreciate it. I hope I can return the favour sometime.'

Kerry had it on the tip of her tongue to quip, *Okay, next funeral it'll be my turn to go out.* She decided Mal Bartell's sense of humour wouldn't cope with it at the moment. Instead she repeated, 'Really, no problems, Mal. Any time.'

'I'm not leaving just yet. I'll bring you the keys when I do.'

Kerry went back to her pharmacy and grimly surveyed her domain. Right now it looked more like a prison. The depressing weather wasn't helping her frame of mind. She put on a compact disc, a little louder than usual, but she only had relaxing, ethereal music, suitable only as background noise. The way Kerry felt now, it sounded morbid. She needed something lively to kick-start her into a better mood. She turned the music off after a few minutes and tried the radio, hoping to catch something—perhaps a controversial talk-back topic—to make her think.

The radio answered her with a weak signal interspersed with vicious bursts of static. No amount of knob-twiddling could make it go away.

'Damn it,' Kerry muttered. 'Nothing works in this bloody place.'

There were a lot of things that needed attending to in the pharmacy since she'd taken over. The previous owner, George Carter, had been there a long time and collected a lot of rubbish in the process. Old stock, old paperwork which could have been thrown out years ago, old equipment too out-of-date or antiquated to use, filled every nook and cranny. It was a mess and Kerry would be spending long hours sorting it all out. She tried devoting time to it now but, although she persevered, her heart wasn't in it. Mal Bartell called in half an hour later, dropping in his keys and staying a moment to offer more thanks and extend an invitation to Kerry that she might like to walk over to McGann's hotel for a drink after work. She didn't decline, but stayed non-committal, saying she might be tired by then.

After he left Kerry tried once more to get enthusiastic about some stock-control ledgers she wanted to revise. Her mind kept drifting to aimless subjects and she often found herself sitting motionless, staring into space. She was like this when somebody walked quietly into the shop.

'Hi, Kerry. How's it goin'?'

Kerry jumped, yanked back into the real world. Jeff Butler, the infatuated garage mechanic, was standing at a nearby display rack. He looked nervous and fidgety, his hands thrust into the hip pockets of his jeans. The jeans, she saw, were clean, and he was wearing a respectable, if slightly rumpled, collared shirt and polished boots. Her next thoughts were a silent curse at herself for being caught. Obviously she wasn't bustling around and busy, her usual barrier to Butler's awkward advances. She was sitting around doing nothing—ripe for a deep and meaningful conversation about petrol or engines.

'Hello, Jeff!' she said brightly, pasting a smile across her face.

'How's business?'

'Oh, pretty slow today. Must be the funeral, I guess.'

He began fingering a row of shoe inserts, studying the instructions on the plastic wrapping intently to avoid meeting her eyes. 'Yeah, I'm going. Jake was on my darts team. Good bloke. Bloody shame he's gone.'

'What time's the service?' Kerry asked, hoping it would be soon.

'Three-thirty. Then everyone's going back to McGann's for a few drinks.'

Kerry stopped herself from turning and looking at the clock. 'So I've been told.'

'Actually, a few of the guys are having a barbecue this Saturday afternoon for Jake, too, like a memorial service—just some beers and steak. We get together a lot anyway. It's good for a few laughs,' Butler said, shrugging. Kerry tensed herself, sensing an invitation was coming. 'You should come along,' he added casually, but she

58

could tell by the way the words were forced out that they hadn't been easy for him to say. In fact, he was nervous as hell.

'I'm—ah, not really a barbecue person,' she said, feeling trapped. 'And a whole bunch of people I don't know would sort of make me very shy,' she added, grasping at a half-formed inspiration. It back-fired.

'Hey, that's okay. I could pick you up. If you're with me, it wouldn't be so bad.'

Christ, how do you say you've got something else to do in this town? Kerry thought desperately. Then she remembered her earlier resolve to send a 'not interested' message to Jeff Butler. Kerry took a deep breath and firmed her voice. 'Look, Jeff. I don't think I want to get involved in anything like that right now. I like being on my own, okay?'

A range of emotions quickly jumped across his face, making him look ugly. Kerry felt a flutter of alarm at how suddenly he changed. When he spoke next, there was an angry edge to his voice. 'Hey, I'm not trying to lay anything on you, all right? I'm just trying to be friendly, okay? It's not a big deal.'

'I know, Jeff.' Kerry held her hands up in surrender, frightened by his short temper, but trying to hide it. 'Don't get me wrong either, right? I only meant that I'm the sort of person who likes being alone. I'm not a big fan of barbecues or social gatherings.' The lies were stacking up, but Kerry was prepared to lie through her teeth, given Butler's sudden twisted expression and flashing, irate eyes. *This guy's as stable as a bloody rocking horse. It's a great day we're having today, Kerry*

Wentworth. Welcome to Hickory—home of double-banger funerals and loonèy mechanics.

He was abruptly, openly angry now. 'You know what? I know your problem. I think you've got a pretty fucking high opinion of yourself, don't you? Is that it?' Butler was snapping, jabbing a finger at her. 'Don't you think—'

Kerry cut him off. 'Jeff, you're blowing this out of proportion. Don't get so upset—'

In turn he interrupted, mimicking her words. 'I'm blowing this out of proportion. Fancy words, right? Too fancy for a dumb-as-dogshit mechanic?'

Kerry tried getting mad herself, though it took an effort to drag some anger through her fear. 'Jeff, take it easy! You're getting carried away.'

The harsh tone only encouraged him and Butler took a step backwards, pretending horror. Before he could figure out his next jibe a voice called through the open doorway.

'Hello? Are you open?'

Kerry could have cheered. A fierce look, a mixture of fury and frustration, came over Butler's face and he stared at her, daring her not to answer so they could finish the argument. She held his gaze, but said loudly, 'Come on in. I'm open.'

A tense moment followed, then Butler let out a hiss of disgust and spun about, striding down the length of the shop towards the door. Halfway, he met someone coming in, but kept a determined set to his shoulders so the other person had to dodge into a gap between the displays to avoid being knocked aside. The move was so blatantly aggressive the new customer twisted around and stood a moment, watching Butler's retreating figure with surprise. Kerry recognised it was Michael Garrett, as he recovered and moved towards her.

'I'm beginning to worry about the standard of customer you're attracting here,' he said, coming to the counter.

'He's a bit upset,' Kerry explained, hearing a tremor in her voice. She cleared her throat and tried acting casual by brushing a non-existent strand of hair away from her face. Too late, she realised her hand was shaking and she quickly put it back down behind the counter.

'Are you okay?' Michael frowned, then threw a quick glance towards the front door. Butler had disappeared.

Again, Kerry felt she could be honest with Michael—probably because he was a newcomer to town, too, and therefore a kind of kindred spirit. 'Well, he—ah, frightened me a little,' she admitted. 'Maybe I took things the wrong way and I shouldn't have said—' She stopped and shrugged. 'Who knows?'

'I see.' Michael smiled and he raised an eyebrow. 'One of your amorous friends?'

It took Kerry a second to remember what she'd told him before. 'Oh! Yes, actually he's the main one. I think he wants to take me home, feed me up and have babies before the end of the week.'

'Typical country courtship,' Michael agreed easily, then added teasingly, 'They get that way with all these animals around.'

'Animals?' Kerry suddenly found herself suppressing a laugh. 'I thought it was sugarcane they farmed out here?'

'You've noticed?' he asked, looking innocent.

'Just a bit—I'm waiting for someone to plough up my front lawn and plant some more damn sugarcane. It's everywhere.'

'I know what you mean. I'm told the place looks naked when they've cut it all down.' He sighed theatrically and changed the subject. 'Anyway, I had to come into town to get some milk—which it looks like I can't get—so I thought I'd check on those batteries, even if it's a bit soon. Any luck?'

'I called a supplier today and they claim they'll be on the next truck out. At least, I think that's what he said. The line was bad and I kept losing the connection. But I *can* sell you some milk. Didn't you see the sign on Mr Bartell's window?'

'No, I didn't. Have you got some here? I didn't really look beyond the fact Mal was closed.' He reached into a pocket for his wallet, mumbling, 'I'll have to make another trip in tomorrow for the batteries.'

'Where are you living?' Kerry asked, getting the milk.

'I bought the new brick place on Jonas Road.' At her uncomprehending look he added, 'Turn right at the bridge, then again at that overgrown tennis court.'

'Oh, I know it,' Kerry nodded. 'George took me there for a look. He didn't know you'd already put an offer on it. Look, I can bring those things out to you after I close tomorrow, if you like.' She

62

surprised herself, not quite sure why the offer came out.

Michael glanced up from his wallet. 'That's a bit out of your way, isn't it?'

'It'd save you a trip in. Call it customer service.'

'Okay,' he said, a little nonplussed. 'So that's about six o'clock, right? Well, I'm usually having a beer on the back porch about then. Watching the sun go down. Care to join me?'

It wasn't what Kerry had been intending—to invite herself to his house. But suddenly she found the thought of having a normal conversation with somebody, where she didn't need to be polite or on her guard, appealing. Michael seemed a nice enough guy. 'I don't suppose you might have a cold wine instead?'

'Certainly, but it's Chateau Cardboard moselle. Is that okay?'

'My favourite,' she smiled back, feeling better. The bad taste left by Jeff Butler's nastiness was almost gone. 'Sure, I'll have a drink. About six o'clock, then?'

He walked out of the store carrying his milk and waving goodbye with his free hand.

The rest of the afternoon dragged on. Around four o'clock Kerry noticed cars beginning to line the street. People returning from the cemetery were heading for McGann's. They were dressed in their Sunday best, many of the toughened cane farmers looking awkward and uncomfortable in their good clothes. The overcast sky was bringing an early sunset and she suddenly determined to close half an hour early, at five o'clock. If Mal Bartell could have half the day off, then Kerry figured she sure as hell could treat herself to thirty minutes of extra freedom. She hung around the front door and watched the mourners filing through the lounge entrance of the hotel. Kerry ducked back when Jeff Butler pulled up nearby, his hard-worked farm utility ridden carelessly over the kerbing so he could park in a small space. She saw him glare at the pharmacy, but didn't think he could see her among the displays. A flutter of unease passed through her.

By the time five o'clock came the hotel was the brightest place in the street. It was too early for the streetlamps to automatically switch on. Everything else was gloomy, but it seemed the patrons of McGann's had managed to shrug off their depression. A growl of noise and laughter floated across the street as Kerry fumbled her key into the front door. She turned and looked at the hotel. Framed in the brightly lit windows people were lifting glasses and smoking. A game of darts had started. The place beckoned to her with warmth and friendliness—she felt certain many people would genuinely welcome her. But one of those people would be Jeff Butler. Either that, or he would make her feel bad, and Kerry didn't want to see him at all anyway.

'Looks like the whole town's in there,' she said aloud. 'Well, it's going to be a warm drink and an early night for me.' She hurried around the side of the building to where she parked her blue station wagon. A minute later, pulling out onto the road, she threw one last glance towards the hotel. Someone was silhouetted in one of the windows, looking out onto the street. Kerry felt certain that person was looking directly at her, and not in a casual way. Something told her it was Jeff Butler, and that he'd been waiting to see her leave, but there was no way of telling for sure.

'I'm developing a very healthy problem about that guy,' Kerry told herself. 'I *must* be imagining half of it. He's just a silly country yokel.' But in her heart, she knew it wasn't so simple. She was scared Jeff Butler might start causing her a lot of trouble.

Kerry's house was an older, timber structure set on two-metre-high stumps to guard against the mild flooding that often came with the wet season. It was a rickety-looking place with fading paint and a slightly lopsided appearance thanks to several of the stumps starting to settle. Inside, the previous owners had put in a greater effort, and that was why Kerry had decided to buy it. All the floor coverings had been taken away, revealing the wood beneath. This was stripped and polished to a warm lustre. The interior walls were painted to complement the floors. Much of the furniture was old too, so it fitted in. Adding a few personal touches of her own, Kerry had made it home. The outside, she figured, would have to wait for another day and a few more dollars.

She stood on the small patch of lawn at the base of the steps and let out a whistle. Nothing happened. Somewhere around the place there should have been a dog, a mongrel she'd called Monty. After three years in the city Monty was enjoying his new-found space and freedom, so Kerry wasn't surprised when he didn't answer her call. Shrugging, she let herself in the front door and quickly turned on a few lights to push back the gloom. In the bedroom she carefully hung her uniform so she could wear it again the next day. Kerry wasn't particularly fussed about wearing the matronly white every day, but for the moment it saved her having to worry about what to wear to work each day. She changed into jeans and a T-shirt and immediately felt more human. As an afterthought she pulled a light windcheater over her head. Then she went into the kitchen and made a cup of milk coffee in a saucepan on the stove, even though she knew the caffeine might spoil her plans of an early night. A small debate formed in her mind whether to bother cooking a major meal. Giving in, she plucked an instant Chinese meal from the larder and put on the kettle, gently chiding herself for being lazy with the quick just-add-water meal. While she waited for the kettle to boil she put on some music.

Sitting at the table alone, eating the meal straight from the plastic packaging, Kerry was content and comfortable. She liked her own company. The few serious relationships she'd had had suffered from this—the men involved unable to understand that there were times when she just wanted to be by herself. She didn't feel lonely at all, but simply enjoyed being by herself.

After picking through the makeshift meal, forcing herself to eat it all, Kerry washed the food down with the dregs of her coffee. She looked into the empty container and grimaced. 'Cooking for one is a bummer,' she said. 'It's not worth the effort to do anything decent. If I'm not careful, I'll have to start taking a handful of my own bloody vitamin pills.' Considering how she might cook properly more often—and coming up with the answer of a guest or two—her thoughts suddenly turned to Michael Garrett. She glanced out the window. The lower sky was turning red with its first touch of the sun, which had finally dropped below the cloud level. Michael, she remembered, should be having a cold beer about now and watching the sun go down. 'Now, why is a guy like that all on his own?' she wondered aloud. She amused herself with several outrageous possibilities, then tried to imagine what the next day was going to be like, joining him for that drink on his back porch. 'Actually, it sounds like a good idea right now.'

She got up and went to the refrigerator. There was an open bottle of white wine that she'd been slowly drinking with the occasional cooked, night-time meal. Now Kerry poured out a glass and took it to the back door, which she unlocked, swinging it wide. A draught of cool evening air made her glad she was wearing the windcheater. The back entrance to the house was like the front—a long set of wooden stairs. Kerry settled on the top step and, nursing the wine in both hands, looked out over the canefields and the darkening sky. Her house was on the rim of the town, so the view from her back door was nothing but farmland set out in orderly squares. The symmetry of the cane-fields was spoiled by the Hickory River cutting a jagged, tree-lined path across the landscape like a mad giant's untended hedge. Kerry was glad the river was there. If there had been only neat, regimented crops of sugar, then the complete corralling of the land might have upset her—as if the 'country' wasn't the countryside any more, but a greener suburbia, designed and given a shape like anything else man-made. Instead, however, the winding river was like a statement of defiance by nature that the farmers were forced to work their way around, and that made Kerry glad. It was a funny sentiment, she knew, but it gave her a nice feeling.

Some movement at the edge of the nearest cane attracted her eye. The area was in such deep shadow Kerry couldn't decide what it was, and she felt her nerves jumping until Monty wandered out, sniffing the ground. The dog looked up to the house and, seeing his owner, broke into an excited scamper across the grass and up the steps.

'There you are, you rotten thing,' Kerry said, strangely relieved. Living out here on the edge of the canefields didn't bother her normally and she briefly wondered why she felt so uptight. 'Why aren't you here protecting me? What am I feeding you for?' Monty was busy trying to lick her face and she struggled to fend him off without spilling her drink. The dog was mostly German Shepherd, with a dash of another breed that took some of the size off him. 'Settle down and let me finish my drink,' she told him. Monty awkwardly sat his rump on the step between Kerry's feet and was happy to be scratched behind the ear in exchange for staying still.

Kerry sipped her drink and played a game with herself, watching the sky turn darker and the slashes of late sunlight on the cloud growing shorter and deeper in colour. She was trying to pick the exact moment when there was no sunlight left in her part of the world. The sun changed to a vivid crescent on the horizon and Kerry gazed at it intently as it slipped away. Now there was only a fading glow and she watched it die. Finally, she couldn't decide if there still was a gentle radiance left, or if she'd been looking so hard at the sun its image had been left on her retinas.

Besides, a light was shining among the trees on the river.

Kerry frowned. It was a strange light, with a disturbing quality she couldn't quite put her finger on. It looked *unnatural*—but of course it did, she told herself immediately. Nothing *natural* gave out that much light at night. Even a big fire wouldn't glow like that, with an intensity that would have discouraged looking directly at it, if it hadn't been diffused by the trees. There was something else, too. Despite its brilliance, the light didn't seem to radiate much beyond its own hot core.

'What's that, Monty?' The dog appeared to understand—his ears pricked up and he stared at the distant light. A growl rattled his chest. 'Someone fishing? A gas lantern?'

Kerry took her eyes off the light a moment to gaze to either side of the house. There were only four homes spread along her road, each one nearly two hundred metres from the next, with sugar growing in the gaps. Hers was the oldest home and the only one built well off the ground on stumps. Normally she could at least see the lights of the other houses sparkling through the tops of the cane, but tonight there was nothing. The streetlamps finished at the beginning of her road. 'Everyone's at the funeral—well, the pub,' she told the dog. 'Except for whoever that is.' She nodded at the light. Monty growled again.

Instinct or intuition—she didn't know what it was—but suddenly Kerry knew there was something wrong about that light. She stared at it, mesmerised for a moment, and it seemed to shimmer back, as if to mock her. 'Hey, what the hell *is* that?' she asked the dog again. Monty was agitated now, growling softly all the time, but trembling, too. The rest of the night suddenly looked unnaturally black and menacing. Kerry realised there were no night sounds either. No calling birds or squealing fruit-bats. Even the frogs were silent.

'I think we'd better go back inside.' She rose quickly and stepped inside the house, beckoning the dog to follow. Kerry wasn't happy until she'd closed the door and turned the key. 'I must be going crazy,' she told Monty, who was now staring and growling at the closed door. The dog looked up at her and gave a single wag of his tail before resuming his worried posture. 'Take it easy, Mont,' Kerry said. 'The door's locked. We're safe.' But the animal wasn't easily appeased. Kerry fed him, hoping it would settle him down, but Monty only took time out to eat then went back to occasionally growling at the back door.

Kerry decided to read a book rather than watch television. With a fresh glass of wine she snuggled into one of the lounge chairs and started to read. It was hard to concentrate on the pages and her mind kept slipping back to the light next to the river. Twice she got up and went to the kitchen to peek through one of the windows. The glow was still there. Monty was driving her nuts, too. The dog wouldn't settle down and kept pacing the room, then stopping and cocking his head to listen, or staring nervously at the wall, all the time whining and growling softly. It started to get on Kerry's nerves and she finally snapped at the dog.

'For goodness' sake! Will you lie down or something?'

Monty reluctantly dropped where he was and put his head on his paws. Still, he continued to grumble to himself and risked the odd gentle whine.

At nine o'clock, as Kerry was thinking of calling it quits, the lights in the house flickered for several seconds. 'Damn, not another power cut,' she cried, half-rising from the chair and thinking about dashing to the kitchen for candles. But the lights only faltered a moment longer, then managed to hold on. At the same time Kerry thought she saw a similar glimmering reflected through the curtains. 'Now what? Lightning?' she asked out loud. She went to the window, twitched the drapes aside and waited to see if another flash occurred. There was nothing, and no thunder. 'Okay, have it your way,' she told the black sky. While she was up she decided to satisfy her curiosity again and went into the kitchen. Now there was no sign of the odd light in the trees and she felt better about that, though she still couldn't understand what had scared her before. 'Well, the fish can't be biting tonight,' she told Monty, who

71

was following her around. Heading back to her chair Kerry walked past her bedroom door. She could see the power fluctuation had lasted long enough to wipe out the settings on her clock radio and she groaned. She detoured into the bedroom and sat on the bed, peering down at the clock's controls. When she'd remembered how to reset it Kerry glanced at her wristwatch for the correct time.

The sweeping minute hand was still. Her watch was stopped.

'It was like a bright light—but it was a really weird-looking light. I can't describe it. You had to be there.'

'It'd be someone fishing. Maybe they were using the light to attract the fish, draw them into a net.'

Kerry looked at Michael Garrett, wondering if there would be any point in telling him about the bad feeling that seeing the light had given her. She decided it was too hard to explain. He didn't seem so keen on convincing her with his fishing theory, but Kerry couldn't tell if it was because he simply didn't care, or he had something else in mind that he didn't want to mention.

'Maybe,' she shrugged, encouraging him to try again if he wanted.

They were sitting on Michael's back verandah on two old canvas deck chairs. The sun was setting and, like the day before, it was now visible for the first time, dropping below the blanket of cloud hovering over the Hickory area like a pall of pollution. Michael had given Kerry a quick tour of the house, showing her the home-studio last and briefly describing what he did there. Then they went outside and Michael got the drinks. The conversation came easily as they shared their experiences of moving into Hickory, but soon Kerry couldn't stop herself telling him about the night before.

'You don't like the fishing theory?' he asked.

'No, you're probably right. It's the first thing I thought of, too.'

'Why didn't you go and have a look?' He sounded teasing.

'Oh sure!' she shot back. 'I'll wander down there in the middle of the night and probably stumble into the local lads brewing their own moonshine, or practising witchcraft. Good idea, Michael.'

He laughed. 'Okay, maybe it would be a bit rash. You could've gone down there this morning, I suppose,' he added, not seriously.

'I wouldn't have a clue where I was going. I could only point out roughly where it seemed to be from my house.'

'Actually, there's a good track all along that riverbank and every so often they've built barbecue areas. It's very nice. I took a drive down there one day, just for the hell of it.'

'But this was much further on than those barbecues, I think. I haven't actually seen them. But this was quite a way up the river—or are you telling me the good people of Hickory were having a night-time sausage sizzle after their heavy day at the cemetery and McGann's afterwards?'

Kerry was keeping her tone light and funny, but Michael began to guess she'd been more than a little spooked. 'I'm sure the track keeps going for a while, a lot further than those barbecue areas,' he said absently, thinking over a few possibilities. 'I've got an idea. Maybe one of the farmers has some broken machinery down there and he was trying to fix it. Like, he had an arc light and a small generator. Those things can be pretty bright.'

'I didn't hear any generator.'

'You'd be surprised how quiet they can be, these days.'

'Look, don't worry, Michael.' Kerry was touched by what she decided was his genuine concern. 'Whatever it was, it went away. So it's not such a big deal, really.' He was looking at her strangely, so she added, 'Okay, if it comes back I'll give you a call. You can dash over and have a look for yourself then, if you like.'

'All right, I'd like that,' he said, obviously satisfied and puzzling her even more. 'Make that a promise and I'll be happy.'

'It's a promise,' Kerry nodded, laughing suddenly. At least, it felt good to know someone was willing to come over if she got into any trouble, or got too scared. A mental image of an angry Jeff Butler hammering at her door crossed Kerry's mind and she pushed it away again, annoyed at herself. She'd be imagining monsters under her bed next.

'Another drink?' Michael asked, rising and pointing at her glass.

'Just one, then I'd better get home. I've got a child to feed.' At his surprised look she added, 'A four-legged one.'

He hesitated at the doorway. 'I was thinking about asking if you wanted to stay here for dinner. I haven't got much to offer, but I'm sure I can rustle up something decent.'

'No, I don't think so, thanks.'

'No problem. It was just a thought.'

She caught a glimpse of disappointment on his face as he turned back into the door. Kerry had refused feeling slightly uncomfortable in her white uniform, and tired too, worn out from a day on her feet. She hadn't meant to discourage him as such, so she called into the house, 'Hey, why don't we do it properly? If you want to cook me dinner one night, I'll make something for dessert and bring it with me.'

'Hang on a second.' His voice sounded muffled, his head inside the refrigerator. When he walked back outside, handing Kerry her glass, he looked pleased. 'That's a good idea. Any night in particular?'

She surprised him by breaking into a chuckle. 'When that guy Jeff was hassling me in the pharmacy yesterday, he invited me to some barbecue, or a wake, or something—I'm not sure what it was now. Anyway, I said no, which is why he got upset, but I remember thinking at the time—how do you say you've something else to go to? In this town?' Michael laughed with her. 'So anyway, any night's okay—except maybe Thursdays,' Kerry added quickly. 'I stay open a few extra hours and I'd have to rush around.'

'Well, how about the day after tomorrow? That'll give me time to buy a few groceries and things.'

'And when you do, drop into the chemist and tell me what you're going to cook, so I can do a dessert to match.'

'That's a deal.'

They talked some more while they finished the drinks, then Kerry left. In her car, driving through the quiet streets, she felt good. She liked Michael Garrett. He didn't seem to regard her as anything except a newly-forming friendship. After the sideways glances from most of the younger men in town and the difficult, and now alarming, advances by Jeff Butler, Michael's more mature behaviour was very welcome.

The headlights picked out her front steps, revealing Monty sitting waiting for her. 'Yes Monty, I'm late,' she said aloud. After locking the car and petting the dog enough to calm him down Kerry let herself into the house and went through her usual routine of getting changed. In the kitchen she propped herself on the open door of the refrigerator and looked for something to eat. The shelves were looking decidedly bare.

'I should have stayed for dinner after all,' she said to Monty, who was watching from the middle of the floor. Determined to have a proper meal Kerry pulled some frozen chicken pieces from the freezer and put them into the microwave, dialling up a defrost setting. The readout told her it would take fifteen minutes to thaw, giving her enough time to prepare some vegetables. Taking some greens and a few carrots from the crisper-drawer she pulled a face. They'd been in there a bit too long and were rather limp and sad-looking. Kerry decided to chop them all up and throw them into a stir-fry mix with some rice, then lay the chicken pieces on top. It would make quite a lot, but she could keep the leftovers for her lunch the next day. So the cooking smells wouldn't tease Monty too much, she fed him.

With perfect timing Kerry had the vegetables nicely sizzling in a pan when the microwave announced it had done its task. She rearranged the chicken and seasoned it, then programmed the oven to cook it right through. Now all she had to do was wrap the scraps and the empty dog-food tin and put them in the bin, in order to eat in a clean kitchen.

The council-provided rubbish bin stayed wedged under the back steps to stop any stray dogs from tipping it over. Kerry opened the back door one-handed, more intent on making sure the newspaper wrapped around the scraps didn't unravel and spill the contents.

When she looked up and out into the night, Kerry stopped dead at the top of the stairs. 'Damn,' she whispered, letting her breath out slowly between her teeth.

The strange and brilliant light was burning again, nestled among the trees.

Monty started growling and it made Kerry jump nervously. 'Don't start, Monty!' she snapped, then instantly regretted it, bending down to pat the dog. 'Sorry, I know you're only doing your job. You scared the hell out of me, that's all.' Monty gave her a reproachful look. Again Kerry stared to either side of the house, but as before the other homes were dark. Apparently no-one else was worried or outside checking the distant glow—not that she would see anybody standing in their yards anyway, she realised. It suddenly occurred to her that the tall sugarcane, combined with the low-set homes, probably meant her neighbours wouldn't be able to see the river, or the hot glare either. She grabbed Monty's collar and dragged him back into the kitchen, pushing the door closed hard with her free hand. It slammed against the jamb, rattling the house.

'Jesus, I hate that thing,' she told the dog. 'I don't even know what it is—I mean, it's only a *light*, for Christ's sake, but I still hate it. There's something weird about it.' She stood in the kitchen and wondered what she should do. A popping sound came from the chicken in the microwave, reminding her what she'd been doing. The frying pan still sizzled and Kerry went over and turned the heat down, giving the vegetables a quick stir at the same time. She didn't feel hungry at all now. Just flustered and a little scared. 'He's going to think I'm a bloody idiot,' she said, thinking of Michael. 'Still, a promise is a promise,' she decided, glad of the excuse.

Kerry went into the bedroom and took a scribbled note from the pocket of her uniform—the piece of paper Michael had written his telephone number on. Her finger shook slightly as she punched at the numbers on the telephone. 'This is crazy,' she muttered, listening to the clicking of the signal being processed. 'I'm going mad. It's only some bastard fishing, and they're miles away too.' The instant she resolved to hang up before he could answer, the other receiver clattered and Michael's voice came through.

'Hello?' He sounded cautious.

'Michael? It's Kerry. I thought I'd ring to say your light's back again, if you really want to have a look.'

It took him a moment to understand what she was talking about, then he sounded excited. 'Is it? Are you okay?'

'Sure I'm okay. I thought you might want to have a look, that's all.' Kerry tried to sound casual, but a tremor had crept into her voice. She wondered if he could hear it.

'I would. You've got me intrigued about the thing now. Do you mind if I drop over for a minute?' His voice was neutral, as if he didn't want Kerry to think he thought her silly or overreacting.

'That's why I'm calling, remember?'

'I'll be there in a few minutes.'

Kerry couldn't bring herself to leave the front door open, so she watched out one of the windows facing the road until she saw a pair of car head-lights moving slowly up the street. Then she opened the door and the van put on a brief burst of speed until it pulled up next to her station wagon. Michael got out.

'Still there?' he called.

'It was a minute ago. Come in, have a look.'

Michael bounded up the stairs, but before he could follow Kerry through the house he had to take a moment to acquaint himself with Monty, who made it clear he wasn't happy with this sudden intrusion. In the kitchen Kerry gestured at the back door and watched him open it. Instead of looking out into the night with him, Kerry stayed back and watched his face for a reaction. Immediately, a frown creased his forehead and she worried the light was gone, so she squeezed in next to him to look, their shoulders and hips touching. If he noticed this small intimacy, he didn't show it. He was too intent on staring out into the night.

'You're right,' he said, after a long and thoughtful silence. 'There is something different about it. I can understand now why you're not so comfortable about it.'

'Good. Then I'm not going crazy,' she sighed. 'So, tell me what the hell is it?' Looking into his face Kerry caught a whiff of the beer he'd been drinking before—then realised he'd probably had another one or two since, as well. She didn't mention it, though she wondered if he were completely sober.

'I don't know. I'm tempted to go and have a look.'

'What? Now?'

'Why not? It's the best time to find out.'

'Why don't I ask Mal Bartell tomorrow, instead? I'm sure he knows about everything that happens around this place.' Kerry was more concerned Michael was suffering from bravado—too many beers and maybe some silly urge to impress her. Going down to the river tonight, even though it was still early, didn't sound like a good idea. Michael hadn't taken his eyes off the distant glow.

'Ah—but what if Mr Bartell doesn't want to tell you?' he asked carefully.

'Oh, come on! I'm sure it's not that big a deal. You're worse than me, imagining things and making it sound like some weird small-town conspiracy.'

'Then we *can* go down and have a look, right?' There was a sparkle in his eye now, and Kerry figured that perhaps he was only teasing.

'No way. I might have been right before—it might be the local lads brewing their own moonshine, or growing their own drugs. It *could* be something like that, and I don't think they'd like us barging in to say hello.'

'Chicken,' he said, smiling.

'You've got that right. Just convince me that thing isn't going to come through my window tonight and murder me, and I'll be happy.'

Michael sighed and looked back out into the night. 'Well, I really don't know what it is, and I can see why you think it's a little weird. There's something about it which I find a bit strange, too. But it's definitely a long way away and I doubt that whoever it is and whatever they're doing, they'll be worried about the likes of us. I'm sure Mal Bartell will give you a perfectly straightforward explanation for it, anyway.'

'Okay, you say I'm safe. I guess I can sleep on that. So, have you got time for a quick bite to eat? I was in the middle of cooking some dinner when I called you.'

'I've got something bubbling away myself at home, so thanks anyway.' Michael looked sorry.

'Then how about a quick coffee?'

'Sure—but a quick one.' This made him happy again. 'I wouldn't mind getting in a few hours in the studio tonight, before the urge to work goes away.'

81

'What a life,' she said, rolling her eyes, then asked him seriously. 'Why are you working tonight? Haven't you got all day?'

'I wasn't kidding. Sometimes I get the urge to get stuck into a project and I'll work for hours without a break.'

'So I disturbed you, calling up and telling you about this?'

'No, not at all. I told you I wanted to have a look at your ghostly light. I'm glad you called.'

She felt a curl of worry in her stomach. 'Hey, who said anything about *ghostly*?'

'Sorry. A bad choice of word, but you know what I mean.'

'Yes, unfortunately I do,' she said, glancing out the door.

They sat at the kitchen table and drank their coffee. As they talked Michael's gaze kept straying to the back door, but he was more intent on Kerry's attempts to explain something with her hands when the night sky flickered. He only saw it from the corner of his eye.

'This weather is amazing,' he said lightly, getting up to have a look. 'All this cloud, but not a drop of rain, and now we're getting lightning. I don't hear any thunder though—' he stopped, reaching the back step. After a moment he said quietly, 'Well, the light's gone.'

'Was that your lightning? The light going out?'

'Could have been. Maybe it *is* an arc light, and they just threw the switch on the generator. That'd make it sort of flicker for a moment.'

'Forget it, Michael. I'll ask Mal in the morning.'

'I've got a better idea. Why don't we go and

82

have a look in the morning? If it's people fishing or a broken-down tractor, there's bound to be something there that'll tell us.'

'But I have to work in the morning.'

'I know. We could make it really early, just after daybreak. Hey, it could be the only excitement we get all year.'

Kerry looked at him, wondering what his motives might be. Was he really interested? He seemed to be, which itself was a little weird. So interested that he was willing to get up at the crack of dawn for a drive down to the river? The next thought startled Kerry. Was he looking for an excuse to stay the night? *Getting paranoid again, are we?* She realised he was waiting for an answer and she shrugged, giving in, half because she wanted to know what the light was, and because she liked Michael's company.

'Okay, I'm game. I'll go for a look in the morning. You can pick me up and we'll solve this mystery once and for all.' She said this quickly, in case Michael did have thoughts of inviting himself to stay the night. 'If you want to make it around six o'clock, we can walk part of the way along the river. I wouldn't mind the exercise.'

'We can go in my van, then you can chuck Monty in the back and bring him along.'

'A bit of extra protection, right?' It was Kerry's turn to tease.

Michael gave her a wry look and gestured at the dog, who was sitting on the floor, trying to scratch away a flea from behind his ear—and looking decidedly unaggressive. 'Yeah, right. Whatever you say.'

Michael left soon afterwards, promising not to be late in the morning. Kerry waved from the top of her steps and waited until the tail-lights were disappearing down the road. The next thing she did was make sure all the doors and windows were securely locked.

'We need to get back in time for me to change into my uniform,' Kerry told Michael as they pulled out of her driveway the next morning.

'Why do you bother?' he asked, glancing across at her. 'You won't poison anyone just because you're wearing jeans and a T-shirt, will you?'

'Jeans and a T-shirt! I wish!' Kerry wound down her window and lifted her face to the chill morning air rushing past. Behind them Monty tried to get a footing on the back of her seat so he could sniff the open air, too. 'I'm a respected member of Hickory's business community, don't forget.' At Michael's snort of disgust at her assumed manner she grinned at him. 'At least I'm not the drug-addict musician living in the Hordens' old place.'

'Drug addict? Is that what they call me?'

'Not yet, but don't push your luck or I'll start the rumour myself.'

He laughed. 'Okay, you're a respected member of the Hickory business community. You have my most humble apologies.'

As they drove into the edge of town Kerry could see it was early enough to beat even the country folk of Hickory. The streets were empty and the stretches of dew-laden grass were undisturbed except for the wandering tracks of a dog, the pawprints dark smudges in the silvery frost. The clouds above the town were breaking up now and the sun managed to provide occasional watery patches of warming yellow light. Michael swung the van right, avoiding the main street altogether and heading for a street which eventually petered out into a dirt road leading to the river. With the bitumen running out and the vehicle rattling along the gravel track they also lost the little sunlight they'd seen, plunging into the shadow beneath the thick canopy of trees hugging the river. Michael slowed down considerably and Monty got excited, sensing he was going to get out soon.

'Hang on a minute,' Michael told the dog. 'We've a bit to go yet.'

'Cheerful place,' Kerry said, pulling a face.

'A bit of sunshine would brighten it up, I suppose. In the middle of the day it's quite pleasant.'

The trees opened into a natural clearing and in the middle of it a concrete barbecue had been built. The track kept going and Michael drove on. 'There's another two of these yet. We'll park in the last one and walk from there. That's as good a place to start as any, and I'm not sure there's somewhere I can turn the van around safely further on.'

'How do we know where we're going, by the way?'

'I thought we'd time ourselves. If we know we've got half an hour to fool around, we'll walk down the track for fifteen minutes, then turn around. We'll either find something, or we don't.'

The last clearing was smaller than the others.

Michael parked the van close to the barbecue and turned off the motor. The following silence was almost complete, broken only by the ticking of the van's cooling engine. Kerry said, 'Even the birds aren't out of bed yet.'

Michael frowned and listened. 'It is very quiet, isn't it?'

Monty started whining anxiously, eager to get out. 'Okay, okay,' Michael said, opening his door. He went around the back and opened the tailgate. Monty rushed out and immediately put his nose to the ground, running around in mad circles, uncertain which new scent to follow first. Michael sauntered towards the river's edge and looked at the sluggish green water flowing past. A scum was rimming the bank, trapping floating leaves.

'Is it deep?' Kerry asked, coming up behind him.

'I think so. It looks like it.'

She looked doubtfully at the water for a moment. 'So, what do we do now?'

'Start walking, I suppose.' He suddenly grinned at her. 'This was a good idea last night. Now I have the feeling I'd be happier in bed.'

'Don't start complaining,' she said, reaching out and grabbing a handful of his jacket. 'Come on. Let's get going.' Kerry began walking away, but turned around and stepped backwards a few paces. 'What time is it?'

'Six-thirty.' He started after her.

'Okay. Let's walk for fifteen minutes and turn around. That'll get us back here at seven o'clock. That's plenty of time for me.'

Kerry detoured back to the van to wind up her window, just in case. As she went past the barbecue she stopped and frowned. 'Hey, Mike. How long has this place been here?' she called.

Michael had been passing down the other side of the van and had to circle around. 'What? Hickory, you mean?'

'No, dummy. The barbecue areas.'

'There's a plaque at the first one commemorating some founding father of the town. I read it the last time I was here.' He thought a moment. 'I can't remember exactly, but it's a couple of years at least. Maybe more.'

'But look.' She pointed at the barbecue. The concrete cradle for burning wood was completely clean and unmarked. It wasn't even blackened. The mesh grill for cooking on was similarly unmarked, except for a coating of rust.

'Maybe it's a new one. An addition,' he said after a while.

Kerry looked around the clearing. There were still no sounds of wildlife. Only Monty, scampering near the edge of the sugarcane, made any noise. Without warning a shiver went through her. She shook it off. 'Maybe,' she said, feeling her imagination was getting the better of her. 'Let's go.'

They set off down the track, Kerry whistling and calling Monty to stay close. Walking side by side, each staying in their own wheelrut, Kerry and Michael were quiet for a while in a companionable silence. Both had their hands thrust deep into the pockets of their coats. Michael kept looking towards the river, waiting for the first sign of what might be causing their mysterious light. At times it was difficult, because the track swung out from the water's edge and followed the sugarcane instead, but he was expecting another clearing or at least some evidence of vehicles. Kerry suddenly laughed.

'This is a wild goose chase, isn't it?'

'Probably,' he agreed, almost too easily and shrugging. 'But let's do the fifteen-minute bit. It won't kill us.'

She raised an eyebrow at him. 'Hey, there's nothing you know that I don't, is there? Something you're not telling me?'

Michael put on an innocent face. 'Did I tell you about the cannibal natives they say live in the canefields? They've been getting a regular feed off Hickory for decades.'

'Very funny. You know, nobody knows we're out here. We could get run over by a cane harvester and nobody would know. Turned into little cubes of sugar and finally dissolved in someone's cup of tea. What a way to go.'

'What an imagination, you mean,' Michael said. 'You should be writing books, not handing out pills.'

'Have you seen those harvesters?'

He nodded. 'They're like something out of a Star Wars movie. All screws and cutting blades and everything. Crazy-looking bits of machinery—' he stopped and looked ahead. They were cresting a small rise in the track, revealing a clearing in front of them. There was no barbecue, just a natural open area within a stand of trees. 'Hello, this looks interesting.' Michael strode purposefully down the opposite incline. Kerry was suddenly filled with an urge to stay where she was and observe from a

88

distance. She didn't want to go on. In fact, a feeling of dread was making her want to turn around right then and return to the van. However, Michael was already well ahead with Monty zig-zagging along with him.

'Faithful bloody dog,' Kerry muttered, and unhappily set off to follow.

As they got closer to the clearing it was obvious there was something unusual about it. Michael stopped at the edge of the trees and waited for Kerry to catch up.

'See that?' he asked.

The grass inside the clearing was bent and broken into a large, circular swathe, as if a whirlpool had formed in the ground.

'What could cause that?' Kerry stood still, but Michael was already moving slowly into the circle. He bent down and examined the grass.

'I don't know. It looks like they had a big vehicle down here and needed to drag it around in a circle. Maybe it was broken down and they had to turn it around so they could tow it out properly.'

'You'd think they'd have made more of a mess of the surrounding area,' Kerry said, looking around. The rest of the clearing seemed undisturbed.

'That's right.' He crumbled some dirt between his fingers. 'Perhaps it was only a plough or something.'

Kerry felt very uncomfortable. Something about the place upset her—the same way seeing the light from her back door did. 'You know what it reminds me of?' she said suddenly, then bit her lip, sure Michael would think her silly.

'No, what?'

'Don't laugh, will you?'

'No, of course not.'

She hesitated a moment more, before saying, 'A crop circle. Do you know what I mean?'

Michael nodded slowly. 'Like they get on those farms in England. The strange patterns crushed into the barley crops and such. I'd forgotten all about those,' he said absently, then looked up at her. 'I thought somebody owned up to doing them?'

'Someone admitted to carving out the more elaborate ones, but they've actually been around for centuries.'

'A crop circle,' Michael murmured. He stood up and came back to her, looking at the entire area. 'Do you think we should tell someone?'

'Who? And why? Someone must know what this is all about. Besides, you're probably right, it was only a bit of bogged machinery.'

'I guess so, though I've got a hunch now it wasn't.' Thinking hard he stared at the patterned ground.

'Do you feel okay?' Kerry suddenly asked him.

He looked at her knowingly. 'You mean, do I feel a bit nervous? A bit on edge?' He nodded quickly. 'It's strange, but I do. I don't know why, but this place is a bit creepy.'

A noise from the direction of the cane made them both jump and look up. Monty was worrying something on the edge of the field.

'Monty, leave it!' Kerry called, walking quickly towards the dog. Michael hurried to keep up.

Monty saw them coming and reluctantly backed away. He was skittish and the hackles on his back were partly raised. On the ground was a small bundle of ragged fur. At first it wasn't clear what it was, until they saw the long, rodent tail laid out behind the dead creature.

'It's a bandicoot,' Michael said. 'Poor thing. They live in the cane and get killed when the farmers burn the crop for harvesting—along with everything else, of course. Snakes, birds, mice— it's like a mass panic when the flames start.' He tentatively reached out with his foot and nudged the body with his shoe. They heard a crispy, crackling sound.

'But they haven't burned the cane,' Kerry said, confused.

'No, that's right. I don't know what happened to this little fella.' Michael bent down for a closer look. 'He's been well and truly cooked, that's for sure.'

'How?'

Michael threw a glance back at the crushed circle of grass, but Kerry didn't notice. She was busy giving Monty a warning look as he edged back towards the carcass. Michael decided to keep his thoughts to himself, saying instead, 'You're the chemist. You tell me.'

'No thanks,' Kerry shuddered. 'I can do without poking at dead animals this morning.' She noticed that the shaking feeling hadn't entirely gone away and she felt slightly sick. 'Mike, I'd like to head back now. Do you mind?'

'Of course not. Are you okay?'

'Yeah, just a bit sick all of a sudden. Probably

because I haven't had a decent breakfast and I'm looking at a bandicoot burger right now. I'll be all right in a minute, but I'd like to get going.'

They headed back the way they'd come. Kerry had to stop and get angry with Monty before he would leave the dead animal. She felt better as soon as they'd gone back over the rise and the clearing was hidden from view. On the walk back they kept to small talk and didn't discuss the swirling pattern on the ground. Just before they reached the van their movement frightened a pheasant which had been foraging in the cane. Screeching in protest it burst out of the greenery in front of them in a flurry of feathers. Kerry let out a squeal and Michael yelled 'Whoa!' The bird was gone before they could register what had happened.

Kerry had to stop and get her breath back, holding her fluttering stomach with one hand. 'Shit, that scared the hell out of me,' she said, uncaring of her language in front of Michael.

'You and me both,' he agreed shakily.

'Do you realise that's the first bit of wildlife we've seen this morning? And it had to scare me half to death.'

'There's the bandicoot,' he reminded her.

'Wild*life*, I said. That thing was deader'n a doornail.'

'Yes,' he said, suddenly thoughtful again. 'Though I suppose this place is full of tame animals and birds when there's people around eating and cooking stuff.'

Kerry didn't answer. They got back into the van and drove back towards the town. As they passed close to the first two barbecues Kerry tried to see if the stonework in those was blackened by fires. She didn't ask Michael to stop so she could check for sure, and it might have been a trick of the early-morning sunlight—but even getting only a quick glimpse as they passed, she could have sworn the concrete was clean. There had never been anything cooked on these, either. The *bandicoots* around here were somehow getting fried to a crisp, but nobody was using the barbecues. And this was for—how long did Michael say since they were built?

A couple of years, at least.

5

ARNOLD CONNORS WAS starting work earlier every morning to beat the backlog of jobs filling his workshop floor. The new diesel injectors for Harvey McGow's tractor still hadn't been done. The suppliers in the city had sent Arnold the wrong parts, so the tractor lay in what looked like a million pieces all over the concrete floor. Harvey was screaming he needed it back and why the hell did he let Arnold talk him into driving the damn thing all the way into town? It was supposed to save him time, rather than Arnold doing the work out at the farm, and now he'd had the tractor twice as long as he should.

Harvey McGow, Connors was beginning to realise, could be a pain-in-the-arse son of a bitch.

Connors took on any smaller jobs he could while he waited for the new injectors to arrive. There was a tune-up, an oil change and an automatic transmission service—easy stuff to keep the cash flowing. Unfortunately, none of these were proving to be as easy as expected. Almost nobody in Hickory owned a *new* car. They drove their vehicles into the ground and walked away from them when they wouldn't run any more, or when Connors couldn't perform one last mechanical miracle. He continually battled with rusted bolts, stripped screwheads and engine parts buried under years of grime and old grease, turning simple jobs into frustrating tests of his patience. That morning he'd even cross-threaded a spark-plug on Mal Bartell's Ford—he hadn't done that since his apprenticeship days a long time ago.

It didn't help his temper when the telephone started ringing.

Connors was underneath a car, attempting to service the transmission without putting the vehicle on the hoist because he couldn't be bothered shuffling cars around the workshop to give him clear access to the lift. Doing the job this way was awkward and Connors was getting angry, mostly because he knew he was being lazy and that in the end it was likely to cost a heap of extra time—more than he would've spent moving the cars around so he could use the hoist. The shrilling of the phone made him curse and he slid out from under the car, the metal wheels of the Lazy-tray grating on the dirty concrete. Before he got to his feet Connors reached for a piece of rag and wiped the oil from his hands.

As he walked towards his office he looked rue-fully at the early morning sunshine flooding through the wide door of his workshop. It was going to be a beautiful day for a change and he was going to be stuck in this dump probably until after nightfall, if the right injectors turned up. He reckoned he should have called an off-day for himself and done the bus run to the city instead. His wife June was doing it today, and that always worried him, even though she'd been driving the buses for years. She just seemed so nervous driving the sixty-seater.

It was only eight o'clock. Connors had been there since five-thirty. He considered not answer-ing the telephone at all, on the grounds that he theoretically wasn't open yet—and that he felt tired and fed-up. But they'd only call back again, and most people knew to let the phone ring on forever in case he was under a car or something. Entering the office he pulled a face at the mess of paperwork scattered across his desk. It was another thing he needed to do something about and he didn't ever seem to have the time any more. He picked up the receiver.

'Conners' Workshop,' he said gruffly. The name hardly catered for his differing talents, but he nor-mally didn't care and right now he didn't give a damn at all. The voice at the other end belonged to a woman—an older and respected member of Hickory's community. Her name was Heather Meares. What she had to say turned Connors' stomach cold. It was the last thing he wanted to hear.

'Okay, Heather,' he said quickly, interrupting

an enthusiastic fresh repetition of the same story. 'I'll go over and take a look. And don't worry Doug Riley with this just yet. It's probably just a dog or something. If I think it's something worse, like kids maybe, I'll call into the police station on my way back and speak to Doug about it myself.'

He said goodbye and hung up, the telephone still squawking as he put the handpiece down. The woman, he knew, was sometimes incapable of shutting up. Connors looked through his office door at the cars and the tractor awaiting his attention. This matter was going to waste another half an hour of his day, but it had to be checked out. The feeling of tiredness suddenly grew, making his bones ache. 'Another ten years, Arnold-me-boy,' he said aloud, but softly. 'Retire at sixty. Maybe keep the bus route a couple of days a week, but the rest of this can go to hell. I'm getting too old to be crawling over motor cars and carrying damn corpses.'

At least, he realised, he now had an excuse to go out into the sunshine.

Something or someone had been seriously fooling around with Jake Sanders' grave. The freshly dug square of earth already had a border of whitened bricks mortared around it and a mixture of gravel spread across the top. Once the soil settled into place, pressed down by the gravel, a neat layer of white pebbles would make the site identical to Gordon Sanders' grave beside it. There was no headstone yet. It would be some time before the ground hardened again enough to allow a marker to stay properly upright.

But inside the neat oblong of bricks it looked like a small eruption had occurred, the earth spewing up to push aside the packed gravel and leave a small, untidy crater. In fact, it looked as if something had pushed up from *below*, digging its way out. Gravel and clods of damp earth were scattered for some distance around, as if something had impatiently burst upwards from the dirt. This notion made Arnold Connors frown, a curl of unease teasing his gut. He looked around the cemetery, seeing the surrounding stonework wet with frost and gleaming in the early morning sunshine. Nothing else seemed disturbed. Heather Meares had spotted the problem first thing that morning, when she put fresh flowers on her husband's grave. She was probably right to give Arnold a call, though it really couldn't be too big a deal, could it?

Maybe the council boys accidentally buried a live snake or a bandicoot when they filled in the grave. Weird, but it could happen. And there was a lot of damage for an animal. Connors tilted his head to one side and regarded the mess again. It *could* have been done by something digging downwards, he supposed. Maybe a dog, or a bandicoot trying to take advantage of the loose earth to make a new burrow. But the thing niggling at his mind, ruining the theory, was that he couldn't remember anything like this ever happening before since he'd begun undertaking for Hickory—and that was a very long time.

He knelt down beside the grave and used his

hands to scoop the soil and gravel back inside the borders of the grave, finally using the flat of his palm to smooth it all down. The first time he touched the dirt a shiver of unease ran through him, and Connors muttered a curse at his own foolishness. He'd been around corpses and graves almost all his life, taking over the business from his father. He knew there was nothing to fear. He finished repairing the damage and stood, slapping his hands together and stepping back to admire his handiwork. It didn't really matter, he figured. If it had happened when the white pebbling was in place it'd be a different matter, the dark soil would have spoilt the effect. A noise from somewhere behind him made Connors spin around nervously.

Two young boys, each about ten years old, were pushing their bicycles happily through the graveyard, balancing along the edges of some of the graves and chattering to each other loudly. Both were carrying satchels of school books. Connors recognised them. One was Kevin Stanford, the town doctor's son. The other was Ainslie McGregor—a flash-sounding name, Connors thought, for a tearaway kid who was always getting into trouble. He wondered what the good doctor would say if he knew his son was hanging around with the likes of Ainslie. At least it seemed the kids could show enough respect not to ride their bikes through the cemetery. The two boys instantly modified their behaviour when they saw Connors watching them. As they drew close they called out polite good-mornings to him.

'Good morning, boys,' Connors nodded, then a

thought came to him. 'Hey, you kids, come over here a minute.' A doubtful look passed between them, but the boys walked over. 'Do you two walk through here every morning? On the way to school?'

Predictably, it was Ainslie who replied. 'It's a short-cut,' he said, tilting his nose up defiantly. A lock of thick, unkempt hair fell across his face and he tossed it back with a shake of his head. 'We're not doing any harm.'

'I'm not saying you're doing anything wrong,' Connors said, holding up a placating hand, but already tempted to take a swipe at the boy, too. This kid could put across a sly insolence without even trying. 'Tell me, do you ever see any dogs or anything, rooting around the place? Digging up things?' As he watched the boys' eyes widen dramatically, Connors started shaking his head. 'Now, don't start getting any silly ideas. We're just talking about a dog or something, knocking over the flowers or maybe scratching a hole to lie in, all right?'

Kevin and Ainslie exchanged another look, this one the tacit decision whether or not to treat this grown-up with complete honesty, or with the guarded mistrust most adults deserved in the minds of ten-year-old boys. Finally Kevin answered meekly, 'I don't remember seeing any dogs.' He was a thin boy with pale, freckled skin and red hair. A direct contrast to his friend, who was heavy-set with a dark complexion.

Ainslie was looking at Jake's grave. 'Has somebody been digging up the bodies?' he asked, suddenly excited.

Connors sighed and admitted to himself he'd probably made a mistake asking the two youngsters. 'No, nothing like that! Something's been making a bit of a mess, that's all. Don't go telling any silly stories at school now, hear me? You'll only frighten the younger ones.'

'No, Mr Connors,' they chorused back at him, but the undertaker figured it was too late.

He shooed them away, sending them off towards school and calling more instructions after them not to make anything dramatic of it all. But once they were out of his hearing, he could see the boys avidly discussing something and regarding the gravesites around them with a new, awed reverence.

'Damn it,' he said, annoyed with himself, then he tried shrugging it away. There was nothing he could do now. He looked at the grave once more and decided to take a drive to the council's depot, find out who had filled the grave and just casually ask if anything out of the ordinary had happened. Then he'd have to get back to his mechanical business and get some work done.

The next morning Heather Meares called again. Apparently she was now a self-appointed guardian of the cemetery, because she'd diverted her normal morning walk to go past there so she could check that everything was all right. Mainly, she explained, because she didn't want anyone tampering with her husband's resting place.

And she wanted to know why Connors hadn't done anything about the damage to Jake Sanders' grave. Nobody had even filled in the hole. As

Connors listened to her, his uneasiness returning more strongly, he prudently didn't tell Heather he *had* repaired the damage.

This time the hole was a little bigger. It had the same appearance as before, as if something had dug its way up from below, rather than something burrowing downwards. And Heather Meares was mistaken—it was Elaine Sanders' grave this time. Connors was expecting to find that the same animal had returned to mess up Jake's resting place again. It would have made more sense. This was more than upsetting—it was downright spooky. Connors took the time to do a quick tour of the cemetery, looking for similar holes in other graves. He didn't find any. On his way he found a garden rake carelessly left behind by one of the council workers. Connors picked it up and used it to repair the damage to the grave. He didn't like the idea of using his bare hands this time. When he'd finished he stared thoughtfully at the rake as if the tool might give him the answer. The day before, Connors had spoken to the two men who'd filled in the Sanders' grave after the service. They'd both given him dumb looks.

He looked down at the grave again. It sure as hell looked like something was trying to dig its way out. *What would you find if we brought up the coffins again? The lids loose? Black dirt under Jake's fingernails? Those nails would still be growing, right? They did, for a while. Maybe they'd all be broken from clawing at the gravel.*

Connors snapped out of it, physically shaking

himself. 'You'd better stop thinking shit like that right now,' he said, his voice flat and lost in the open air. 'You never have before and there's no reason to start now. When a man's dead, he's dead—you know that better than most.'

Connors heard chattering voices approaching and turned to see the two schoolboys, Kevin and Ainslie, making their way through the cemetery again. They stopped short when they saw him and Connors could see the amazed looks on their faces as they realised he was standing next to the same grave. The garden rake in his hand told them what he'd been doing.

'Keep going, you two!' Connors called, suddenly angry. 'You've no business in this place—and hey! Hey!' He didn't notice he was brandishing the rake aloft. The boys were hurrying on without answering. Connors took a few steps after them. 'Hey, you kids! You can start walking around the cemetery from now on. This isn't a bloody public footpath, all right?' He stopped, out of breath. The boys were running now, awkwardly pushing their bikes and dodging between the graves. They disappeared through the far gate.

Connors stood still, trying to calm himself down. He ran a hand across his face. 'Jesus Christ,' he whispered. 'I must be going crazy.'

Kevin and Ainslie were already late for school, so they had little chance to discuss seeing Arnold Connors again in the cemetery. Then Ainslie got into trouble for trying to pass a note to Kevin about it in class, so he had to spend his morning recess picking up litter under the stern supervision of the Assistant Headmaster. It wasn't until the lunch break when, clutching their packs, they were able to hurry to the furthest corner of the school-yard and sit together in a patch of shade too small to allow anyone else to join them.

'So, what do you reckon?' Ainslie asked, prising the lid off his lunch.

'About what?' Kevin was trying to sneak a look at Ainslie's sandwiches. Kevin's mother was in the habit of providing him with healthy, boring lunches, while Ainslie always brought simple but tasty meals.

'About Connors being back in the cemetery this morning, stupid.'

'Oh.' Kevin feigned interest in his lunch. He'd been thinking about the graveyard in class and decided it worried him—and he'd already seen a look in Ainslie's eye which normally spelled trouble.

'Well?' Ainslie asked impatiently.

'Well, Connors yelled at us not to say anything or do anything. And he said we couldn't short-cut through the cemetery any more.'

His friend dismissed his words with a wave. 'I heard that. Don't worry. He'll never be there to see us.' Ainslie leaned closer. 'But what do you think he was doing there this morning?'

Kevin mumbled into his sandwich, 'Fixing the grave, I suppose.'

Ainslie was relishing watching Kevin getting more uncomfortable. Then he made the mistake that Arnold Connors so wished was correct: 'The *same* grave, right? Where Jake Sanders is buried.

That's two nights in a row somebody's tried to dig him up—*or he's tried to dig his way out.*'

Kevin went pale, the freckles on his face standing out even more. 'Don't say things like that,' he said hoarsely. 'That sort of stuff only happens in movies and things.'

'Yeah?' Ainslie looked smug. 'Beth Packer told Julie Gainsborough she saw Jake standing in their backyard the night *after* he died.'

Kevin sat still and stared at him, then tried to pretend the news didn't worry him. 'I heard that,' he lied, shrugging it away. 'They're girls,' he added, as if that explained everything.

'Maybe, but Beth Packer's not normal, like the rest of them. Her mum and dad are hippies. I reckon if she says she saw a ghost, then she must've seen something.'

Kevin blinked, needing a moment to digest this. 'All right, so why don't you go and tell Connors about it?'

'What? Are you kidding? A couple of kids like us, telling Connors that it's Jake Sanders messing his own grave when he goes for a walk in the middle of the night?'

Kevin took another bite of his sandwich and considered reminding Ainslie that he hadn't actually included *himself* in the plan to approach the undertaker. While he was trying to chew and swallow the wad of bread and meat in his mouth, Ainslie dropped his punchline—which Kevin had known full well was coming.

'Besides, we haven't got any proof, have we? Like, we haven't seen Jake's ghost *ourselves*, right?'

In his haste to speak and stall anything further

from Ainslie, Kevin swallowed hard, the unchewed food hurting as it pressed down his gullet. 'And I don't *want* to see one,' he finally gasped, his chest burning.

'Of course you do!' Ainslie spread his hands. 'Seeing a real, live ghost! It'd be like seeing God, or Batman, or somebody like that.'

'Batman'd be okay,' Kevin agreed reluctantly. 'Not a ghost, though.'

'We should spend a night at the cemetery. Wait and see if he comes out—it'd be fun.' Ainslie pointed an excited finger. 'I bet he comes out at midnight! They always do.'

Kevin was appalled, even though he could have guessed this was what Ainslie was building up to. 'You want to go to the cemetery at midnight? To see a ghost? You're *crazy*.'

'But it's only Jake. He was good to us kids when he was alive. Why would he be any different now?'

'Because he's *dead*, for Christ's sake.' The blasphemy didn't come naturally from Kevin. He struggled with any bad language, after countless warnings from his father. He looked around guiltily, afraid somebody heard him.

'Don't panic, nobody heard you say it,' Ainslie said, wryly amused at the panicked expression on Kevin's face.

Kevin wasn't convinced. His voice trembling, he said, 'Yeah? Why don't you look behind you— *slowly*.'

'What—?' Ainslie frowned, then casually gazed about.

Leaning against the next tree, almost hidden in

the deep shadow, was John Powers, the school's—
and the town's—librarian. His eyes were two hot
points of anger glaring out from the dimness of
the shade, and fixed on the boys.

'Oh-oh,' Ainslie muttered. 'I hope he didn't hear
us. I hate Powers. He's *weird*.'

'He's sick, that's why.'

'No, that's not why he's weird.'

'What are we going to do?'

'Get out of here. Just pick up our stuff and head
along the fenceline so we don't have to walk past
him.'

They gathered their lunchboxes and satchels,
being careful not to appear hurried or concerned.
Neither dared to cast another glance towards John
Powers as they stood and made their way down
the edge of the schoolyard. Kevin thought he
could feel Powers' eyes boring into his back. The
two boys made it to a concrete play area where
they sat close together, whispering secretively so
the other kids nearby couldn't hear.

'I hate him,' Kevin admitted.

'Everyone hates him, dummy.'

'Do you think he heard us?'

'No way.' Ainslie shook his head, but didn't look
so convinced. 'He was probably just suspicious
because we were staying away from the other kids.
He wouldn't have heard any of the stuff about the
cemetery, that's for sure.'

'Well, it wasn't such a hot idea, anyway.'

'Come on, Kev.' Ainslie was suddenly enthusiastic again. 'It'd be great fun. We could take
torches, and some food and everything. There's
really nothing to worry about. It's just a bunch of

dead people—and they're buried deep in the ground.'

'But I thought you *wanted* to try and see a ghost? That was the whole idea.'

Ainslie realised he'd made a mistake. 'Yeah, I know—' He paused, screwing up his face. 'Look, it's just a fun thing, right? If we see a ghost, okay we see a ghost. But we probably won't and we'll just have a laugh. Maybe we'll see Connors' dog, or whatever it is digging up the graves. Besides, we don't have to be there for long. Just around midnight, for half an hour or so.'

As Ainslie started to press his argument harder, Kevin backed off just as fast. Shaking his head, he said, 'It's all right for you. You can sneak away from your house almost any time you want. Your mum and dad wouldn't know if you were away for a week—' Kevin stopped and looked unhappily at his friend. 'Well, you know what I mean,' he added lamely.

'It's okay,' Ainslie shrugged.

After an awkward pause Kevin said, 'If my dad checked my room and saw I wasn't there he'd go crazy.'

'Yeah, I know.'

'Maybe we could go and have a look this afternoon? After school?'

Ainslie gave him a dry look. 'It's really not the same. You're supposed to look for ghosts at night—and at midnight, if you can.'

Kevin felt stung and a little embarrassed about his comfortable, protective home life, and that he couldn't find the courage or the opportunity to sneak out at night. He felt weak and cowardly, yet

108

it wasn't his fault his parents loved him and looked after him, was it? It wasn't his fault Ainslie *could* creep away—and even stay out all night—because his mum and dad were too busy drinking and arguing to worry about him.

'I'm sorry, Ainslie. I really don't think I can do it. I'd get found out and I'd be in trouble for weeks.'

'Don't worry about it. It's no big deal.' Ainslie shrugged and tried to sound unconcerned, but Kevin could see he was disappointed. Ainslie suddenly hissed, 'Hey, don't look now, but you-know-who is back.'

John Powers was walking through the crowd of schoolchildren. Most of them saw him coming and gave him a wide berth, the games and tomfoolery breaking and flowing away from him as if Powers was a predator shark moving through a school of fish. His eyes searched the students' faces as they passed. When he saw Kevin and Ainslie, he stopped his hunting gaze and stared at them across the top of the squealing, playing children filling the concrete area.

'I think we're in trouble,' Kevin said.

'We don't have to go near him,' Ainslie said, sounding more confident than he felt. 'We don't have Library class until next week now. He'll have forgotten us by then.'

'But why does he have to be so *weird*?'

At eight o'clock that night Ainslie lay on his side in front of the television, his head propped on one elbow. His older brother Grant was out playing basketball. He wouldn't be back until late. Hickory could only field four basketball teams out of the entire town and the age-limit of the players was a very flexible matter. Grant got to play a lot because he was tall for his fifteen years and an effective player even though there were several adults among the teams. After the games everyone went down to McGann's for drinks and the publican turned a blind eye to Ainslie's older brother having a few light beers. Later, Ainslie knew Grant would take a six-pack over to a friend's house and (unknown to their parents—and it was doubtful they'd care anyway) watch R-rated videos until late into the night. Ainslie had heard that his brother usually struggled to drink more than two of the beers before he began feeling sick, and the ten-year-old only had a vague notion of what R-rated videos had to offer.

In Ainslie's house Mr and Mrs McGregor were preparing to go over to a friend's place to play cards. They thought nothing of leaving their ten-year-old son by himself. This was Hickory, after all, and nothing bad happened here. And he had the television to keep him occupied, even though the reception wavered between snowy and unwatchable.

The telephone rang as Ainslie's father walked past it. He answered it expectantly, thinking it would be their friends with a last-minute request to pick up some more liquor or something to eat on the trip over. Instead, the voice made him frown and he held the receiver towards Ainslie.

'It's for you. One of your friends.' Ron McGregor's puzzled expression asked why one of

110

his son's friends should be calling at this time of night—late, for a ten-year-old. But he didn't say anything. It was time for them to leave and he didn't want to get held up by something that probably didn't matter anyway.

Ainslie was surprised too, but he slowly went over and made a show of clearing his throat noisily, gaining seconds while his father walked out of earshot, before he put his lips to the mouth-piece. 'Hello?' he asked quietly.

'It's me.'

'Kevin?'

'Who else?'

'What's wrong?'

'Nothing. Let's do it.'

'Do it? Do what?'

'Go to the cemetery. Tonight, at midnight.'

Ainslie felt himself go cold at the thought—he didn't know if it was through fear or excitement. But there was something different about Kevin's voice that made him hesitate. 'Are you okay? Hey—are you at *home*? You haven't run away or anything?'

'Sure, I'm at home.' Kevin sounded flat and emotionless.

'How are you going to get away? Won't your parents find out?'

There was the smallest hesitation. 'No. Dad's got his rural clinic tomorrow. He'll want to be on the road by five o'clock in the morning, so he'll go to bed early. Mum always goes to sleep with him. I can sneak out later, no problem.'

'They won't get up in the middle of the night to check on you?'

'They never do.'

This didn't sound like the caring, concerned parents Kevin had been worried about earlier in the day. 'Are you *sure* you want to do this?' Ainslie asked, hoping for some clue which might explain his friend's strange manner.

'Of course I'm sure. What about you? Are you turning chicken?'

'No!' Ainslie denied, hotly. 'It was my idea, remember?' When Kevin didn't answer he went on, 'Okay, I'll come around and pick you up. Just after eleven o'clock. I'll be waiting under the mango tree next to the swings.'

'No, I'll meet you at the cemetery. Later, too—'

'Why at the cemetery?' Ainslie cut him off, scared at the thought of going into the graveyard on his own. 'Why can't we meet outside somewhere?'

'We'll meet at the cemetery gates, then. If my mum and dad start stirring, I might have to leave as late as I can. At least you'll be there to see anything, if something happens and I'm running late.'

'Yeah? So now who's getting chicken?'

'Not me. Don't worry, I'll be there.'

Ainslie sighed, frustrated. He wasn't used to not being the one in control. 'Okay, I'll see you at the gates, just before midnight. Bring some food and something to drink. Maybe we can stay out a while. We have to make an *adventure* out of it, right?'

'If you like.' Kevin was non-committal, annoying Ainslie further.

'I've got a torch and I'll grab some snacks from

the refrigerator. Don't forget to wear something black, okay?' Ainslie looked up to see his parents waiting impatiently for him to finish so they could tell him they were leaving. He lowered his voice more and put his mouth closer to the handpiece. 'Look, I've got to go. I'll be there—so don't let me down, okay?' He hung up quickly without listening for Kevin's response.

After his parents walked out the front door and Ainslie had locked it after them, he turned around and his eye fell on the telephone. He thought about Kevin Stanford's sudden bravado about going to the cemetery. It seemed so out of character Ainslie wondered if his friend was trying to trick him.

'Well, now I've got to go,' he said aloud. 'Just to make sure Kevin goes.' He thought about the cemetery and what it would be like to be there alone at midnight. 'He'd *better* go,' he muttered.

Ainslie had ridden his bike through darkened streets many times before. The shadowed alleys and shuttered shopfronts of Hickory held no fears for him. Terry McGann's hotel was still ablaze with lights, a few dedicated drinkers propped against the bar while the publican started closing down. Ainslie gave the place a wide berth in case Grant was still in there somewhere. As he rode a knapsack bounced against his back. He could feel the hard edge of a torch and the round lumps of some apples. It was all he could find for food, but it was okay. It was the thought that counted. These were the supplies for their adventure.

Ainslie resisted the urge to detour past Kevin's house. It was tempting to wait outside until Kevin actually left home, which meant Ainslie could avoid the cemetery if he *didn't*. But then again, Kevin might already have left and be hiding near the graves, leaving Ainslie to hang around outside his house until it was too late. That would give Kevin an advantage in their friendship—Kevin could say *he'd* gone that night, while Ainslie didn't make it. Because of Kevin's strange manner on the telephone, Ainslie was becoming more and more convinced that his friend had devised some sort of trick: maybe to conceal himself somewhere in or—more likely—near the cemetery and wait to see if Ainslie had the guts to see it through. Kevin might even jump out of the darkness and try scaring the life out of him. Ainslie resolved to be prepared for that.

It was cold, and his breath puffed out in clouds of vapour that whipped over his shoulder as Ainslie turned his bicycle into the street approaching the cemetery. The graveyard was at the end, and that part of the street was looking unusually dark. He realised it was because the last two streetlamps were out—an unexpected bit of bad luck. Ainslie gritted his teeth and rode on. He had the torch, and he knew the darkness wouldn't be so bad once his eyes adjusted to it.

The night seemed to get even more chill as he left the last streetlight behind. The gates to the cemetery were wide open, two long, low wrought-iron sections the same height as the concrete wall surrounding the entire plot. Ainslie parked his bike against the wall, then decided that if he needed to hide himself quickly the bicycle would give him away. So he pushed the machine to rest against the inside of the wall. Just those few moments alone inside the cemetery's perimeter were enough to make a creeping feeling run down his spine, and Ainslie hurried back out to sit on the roadside kerbing. He shrugged the backpack off and, as he lowered himself down, another thought came to him.

'Kevin?' he said in a loud whisper. 'Are you here? Don't muck around, if you are.' He waited a short while and added, 'I'll punch the shit out of you, if you're trying to scare me.' There was still no response. Unhappy, but satisfied he was alone, Ainslie sat down to wait. He looked at his watch, tilting the face to catch the light. It was ten minutes to midnight.

He sat watching the street, waiting for the familiar sight of his friend pedalling his own bicycle towards him. The minutes passed with no sign of Kevin. It wasn't long before Ainslie felt too fidgety to simply sit and wait, so to waste time he slowly walked back to the nearest working streetlamp. Dawdling in its glow, he had to contend with moths and mosquitos buzzing around his face, so he returned just as slowly to the cemetery entrance. He sat down again, then immediately got up and started cautiously checking the nearby shadows for another bike. Soon he decided that if Kevin did want to scare him, he wouldn't leave his bicycle anywhere Ainslie might find it. It was probably inside the perimeter wall.

This brought him back to the cemetery gates and he stood staring anxiously into the dark, but with no success. He was hoping for the giveaway gleam of chrome from the handlebars. The grave-yard was surrounded on the other three sides by canefields. The blackness of the night within the cemetery was complete and unbroken. There were no distant lights to silhouette the tombstones. Only the white stoneworks showed, glowing slightly with a faint reflection of the distant streetlights.

'What the hell am I going to do?' he asked himself softly. 'Kevin couldn't be in there, could he? Not Kevin *Stanford*. He'd be wetting himself, just because it's dark.'

As if to answer him the faintest pin-point of light suddenly appeared, hovering above the ground some distance into the graveyard. Ainslie sucked in his breath with a hiss. 'Kevin? Is that you?' he called. No-one answered. It was impossible to tell what the light could be. With a sinking heart Ainslie knew he would have to go closer to find out. He told himself he didn't want to go any-where near any damn ghosts, that's for sure—even if, in theory, they might be friendly—but the alter-native was that it was Kevin playing a trick out to its fullest, taunting Ainslie and trying to scare him away, so that the next day in school Kevin could have the last laugh.

'Fuck it, fuck it, fuck it,' Ainslie murmured des-perately. He used the word often, but mainly to impress his friends who still considered such lan-guage too much of a risk. Now he really meant it. His gut was roiling with tension and fear at the idea of walking through the graveyard. Then he remembered the torch. Relieved, like a boy reprieved from punishment, he pounced on his backpack and wrestled out the flashlight. Flicking on the button Ainslie was rewarded by a weak yellow beam. It was better than nothing. Taking a deep breath to give himself courage, he cautiously took a few steps through the gates.

Immediately he discovered that, low though the torch's batteries were, the wash of light was enough to ruin his eyesight outside the beam. Thus, he found himself trying to shine the torch in all directions at once—and seeing nothing in his haste. The circle of orange light flickered over the headstones, reflecting back from the white marble or the deeper, gold-flecked black grave markers, and casting odd-shaped shadows, too. Ainslie found himself wishing he hadn't used the torch after all, but at the same time he couldn't bring himself to turn it off.

'Kevin?' he called out again. 'Come on, is that you?' There was no reply. The pin-point of light still appeared to hang in mid-air. Ainslie felt he hadn't gotten any closer and he dared a quick glance over his shoulder towards the gate. He saw that in fact his nervous shuffling had only taken him a few metres from the perimeter. 'Kevin! You'd better answer me! I'm getting mad.' But he knew he didn't sound mad. His voice was quavering.

Ainslie was staring so intently into the night that he strayed off the gravel path slightly, his ankle bending as his foot landed on the uneven grass edging. He stumbled and fell sideways, reaching out quickly to steady himself and placing a hand on the slick, wet marble of a headstone. As he regained his footing he kicked out a spray of loose stones and he let out a yelp of surprise.

Somewhere among his own noise Ainslie thought he heard a moment of soft laughter.

He froze and listened hard. Nothing. His heart was beating painfully in his chest and his breath was roaring in his ears. The torch suddenly faded out and Ainslie desperately bashed it against his leg. The light returned, weaker and flickering. 'This is crazy. What am I doing here? I don't need this shit.' Ainslie tried to muster up enough anger to convince himself to turn around and leave. He recognised he could use the same excuse—anger at Kevin for not doing things properly—the next day at school if Kevin started teasing him. The argument firmed in his mind and he spun around, turning his back on the strange light, but before he could begin retracing his steps towards the now-inviting cemetery gates another sound stopped him. He heard a quick burst of boyish giggling somewhere behind him, from the same direction as the pin-point of light. Ainslie turned back, relief flooding through him.

'Stanford, you pig! I *knew* it was you. I'm going to kill you!' Ainslie hurried a few paces back towards the light, not caring as his torch again faltered to a feebly glowing bulb. He was confident he could pick his way through the graves from there onwards. Then his resolve wavered slightly as he realised where he was heading— straight towards Jake Sanders' grave. Ainslie had envisaged that he and Kevin would observe the grave from a distance, not stand right *next* to it. As he moved closer Ainslie expected Kevin to

118

reveal himself at any moment and step out from a nearby tombstone. The weird light was puzzling him, too. Small and intense, it had no shape, yet it didn't seem to throw any light on the area surrounding it.

Ainslie suddenly decided to swallow his pride completely. 'Hey, Kevin. I don't like this stuff any more. Come on out, okay?' Ainslie kept walking towards the light. Now he could at least pick out the black squares of dirt and gravel that were the Sanders' graves. 'You win, all right? You're braver than me—I admit it. You can tell anyone about it too, if you like.' He was now less than five metres from the gravesite.

The bright light shimmered and moved. Ainslie stopped, startled. Something stretched and seemed to grow within the glare, hidden by it. The dirt beneath was disturbed as if by an invisible hand. Then, like a curtain falling aside, the light subsided to reveal a tall figure. It took a moment for Ainslie's eyes to adjust and he urgently pointed the torch, its faint light hardly making any impression on the darkness. But Ainslie could see enough.

Jake Sanders stood on top of his own grave looking down at the young boy.

Terrified, Ainslie screamed once, twice, then through his fear an instinctive loyalty to his friend came uppermost in his mind. 'Jesus! *Run, Kevin!*' He couldn't take his eyes off the spectre to search for Kevin. Ainslie started stepping backwards, stumbling. 'Jake's here! It's *true*! He's come *back*!' He tried to wait to see if Kevin had appeared from hiding and was hurrying to escape too. That

119

instant of time seemed like a whole year to Ainslie. He couldn't wait any longer. Spinning around he began to run down the path towards the gates. A crawling feeling on his back anticipated the touch of the ghost's hands, grasping for him. Ahead, he suddenly saw something blocking the path. A small shape, silhouetted against the faraway streetlights.

As Ainslie automatically ducked to one side, hoping to dodge around whatever—or whoever— it was, he realised too late it was Kevin Stanford standing in the centre of the path. Ainslie tried to call out again to his friend to run for his life, but he tripped a second time on the rough edging of the walkway and cannoned painfully into a headstone, the fall punching the wind out of him and cutting off his words. The torch was flung from his grip and he heard it smash against something nearby. Whooping for breath and trying to ignore the pain Ainslie pushed himself to his feet. His terror was like a physical weight bearing down on his shoulders. 'Kevin,' he croaked, tears in his eyes. 'Can't you see him? Get going! Run!'

Through his blurred vision Ainslie tried to see his friend, but Kevin had vanished. Movement close by caught his attention and he twisted around to look. His hope turned to roiling fear when he saw a figure too tall and grown-up to be Kevin push itself off the ground from where it had been lying, hiding in the shadows of a tomb. Something about the size and shape of the figure rang alarm bells in his mind too, but these were swamped by his overwhelming fear.

'Kevin? Where are you?' he cried, denying the

almost certain knowledge in his heart that his friend wouldn't answer. Instead, soft laughter came from the dark figure rising from behind the grave. Helpless with terror, Ainslie watched it move closer, reaching forward and grabbing his arm above the elbow.

Then Ainslie recognised who was holding him—but it made everything worse and he began screaming. A hot, clammy hand twisted itself into his hair and hauled his head backwards until it hurt so much it stopped his screams. Ainslie had a second to see the panorama of sparkling stars in the sky above before darkness closed over his mind.

Brief images came to him, like a sleeper being regularly awakened from a deep sleep, then allowed to rest again. There was movement, but in a way that was somehow different. There were smells, too. Smells he didn't recognise, except for one—the damp, reedy stench of the riverbank where he'd searched for freshwater mussels and built dams with his friends. Then there was a light, and it reminded him of a light he'd seen before only recently. He was taken towards it. Things weren't happening so smoothly now and he realised it was because he was struggling. It was no good. The light came closer.

It swallowed him.

6

A DIFFERENT MEETING. Another place. Five figures glowing slightly, like the walls of the strange room around them.

'Who called this meeting?'

'It was my request.'

'You must have good reason. There is too little time available to us to be wasted indulging in politics. We will be Arriving soon.'

'This is nothing so simple as mere politics. Kann appears to be turning corrupt.'

A thrill of emotion filled the air. A physical shuddering as the figures reacted to the words.

'Are you sure? He is one of our oldest Watchers. Why would it take so long to begin?' Others made noises of agreement.

'Kann has also been sleeping for a long time. It is only our Arrival which wakens him. He may have been corrupt for some time. Still, we can't be certain.'

'He expects to be taken with us. What if he is? Can we do this? It has never been done before.'

'It's probable he is already trying to reverse the corrupting cycle. If it was ever to be achieved, Kann would be the one to do it.'

Another voice, this one angry. 'Why must we take the risk? Our course of action is clear—move on to an alternative. Kann is no longer an option.'

'His corruption isn't confirmed.'

'How can we find out?'

There was a sound which could be interpreted as dry laughter. 'Soon we will be in a position to ask him ourselves. And I'm sure he has taken that possibility into account. He will not want to be left behind—and I don't expect he will be, unless it's necessary.'

'What do we do?'

'Continue as we are,' replied the one who had called the meeting. The words caused a worried silence.

'Can he make an error? Ruin us?'

'Kann may do anything, but he will never ruin us. We are his passage back to a normal existence and he won't risk that. We must wait for him to reveal clearly his condition before we can decide how to act. Until then the program will continue as planned. We have no time to spare, even for Kann, even if he is corrupt. In the end, we can always leave him to his Changing.'

This time the vibration in the room was an

123

expression of sadness—and disapproval.

'Well?'

'Wouldn't that be—irresponsible?'

'Explain yourself.' The reply was sharp.

'He will still be powerful for some time—but very unstable.'

The angry voice spoke again. 'It has happened before, and we shouldn't associate ourselves.'

'Be calm! Remember, this Arrival has been planned for a long time. To change direction now could bring more risks than controlling Kann, if need be. We are committed to an action—to this Arrival.' There was a pause. 'We do not get a second chance.'

No-one questioned this. Such emotions and conflicts of opinion were unfamiliar to them. Reluctantly, one by one they left.

7

'I'LL BET YOU'VE called to tell me again what a brilliant cook I was last night,' Michael said. He tucked the receiver into his chin and idly tapped a few keys on the computer in front of him. He'd been thinking about Kerry Wentworth all day, and their relaxed meal together the evening before. Michael had already rejected a few lame excuses to call her up, but now Kerry was calling him instead, solving the problem.

'Nothing so nice, I'm afraid,' she replied, then he heard her ask a customer to wait one minute while she finished the phone call. It gave Michael a moment to worry about Kerry's tone and wonder if he might have upset her.

'Why? What's up?'

'I've just been told one of the kids is missing from the school.'

'I haven't got it, honest,' he said, smiling.

'No, they're organising a search party. Apparently his parents thought he was staying over at a friend's place, and now they know he *isn't*, it means he's been gone two days.'

'Oh, I see. It's that serious,' Michael said, regretting his flippancy.

'Doug Riley's asked if anyone who isn't tied up in essential services can give them a hand. I thought you might come in. It's a bit—well, presumptuous of me, I know, but—'

'No, you're right,' Michael interrupted her. 'Of course I'll come in. Where's everyone meeting?'

'At McGann's, of course. At four o'clock. I expect they'll be worried about running out of sunlight early this time of year.'

'Are you coming?'

'I've got to stay here in case one of the parties finds him and they need anything from my dispensary.'

'I guess it won't be a stroll in the park, anyway,' he muttered, running a hand through his hair and thinking hard. 'I'd better rug up, I suppose. This could go late into the night. I'll drop in to see you before I go to the hotel. I need some batteries for my torch, anyway.'

He said goodbye and hung up, then hurried into the bedroom to find some warmer clothes.

Michael felt self-conscious as he walked into the circle of men gathered around the police sergeant

126

standing on the hotel's step. Doug Riley, Hickory's senior policeman, was making a list of who was banding together, then assigning them search areas. Riley's only assistant, a constable called Griffith, had apparently already left to search a section of the town. Everyone's attention was on Riley and only a few curious glances went Michael's way. Michael decided to speak with someone—anyone—just to establish contact, and noticed a man close to his own age who also seemed uncertain of his surroundings. The man was large and strong-looking, his long red hair and bushy beard giving him a rather wild appearance. Like Michael, he had a large torch hanging from a loop on his belt.

Michael moved closer and said quietly, 'Obviously this is the place for the searchers to meet?'

The other man replied, nodding. 'I only just got here myself. I don't really know anybody here.'

'That makes two of us. I'm Michael Garrett.' He held out his hand.

'Gavin Packer.' Gavin shook his hand. He noticed Riley direct a look towards the two of them.

'This town seems to be having a run of bad luck,' Michael said, lowering his voice to a whisper.

'Maybe we'll get a happy ending this time.'

'He's been missing nearly two days?'

A frown crossed Gavin's face. 'I can't understand how any parent can fail to realise their ten-year-old child is missing until two days have gone by.'

'It's a bit strange,' Michael agreed. 'I can't really

judge. I'm not a parent,' he said, hoping to lighten things a little. Gavin's frown didn't go away, so Michael felt obliged to add, 'I guess now the important thing is to find him.'

Before Gavin could answer Doug Riley called out to them. 'You gentlemen have come to help?' He didn't sound either friendly or grateful.

'Yes,' Gavin replied for the both of them.

'Mr Packer and Mr Garrett, is that right?' Both men nodded. Michael was startled, as he hadn't actually met the policeman yet and didn't expect to be recognised. He reminded himself it was a small town.

'You two can come with me and three others.' Riley mentioned three more names, then looked directly at Gavin and Michael again. 'We'll be searching the riverbank. As you two are new to the area, try and avoid getting lost yourselves.' The policeman was barely managing to stay civil, and Michael couldn't understand why their help didn't seem particularly welcome.

Gavin spoke up. 'You think the boy is only lost? You're not concerned something worse might have happened?'

Riley looked at him stonily. 'This is Hickory, Mr Packer. We don't have problems like that. This lad is an ill-behaved juvenile who has gone too far this time and got himself lost—that's all.' Dismissing Gavin he raised his voice. 'Let's get going. Don't forget, his name is Ainslie McGregor.'

But Gavin stopped everyone by calling, 'Is anyone else coming to town to help? Any other police, or the civil emergency services?'

Riley looked annoyed and pointed his finger at him. 'Don't start, Mr Packer. I'll decide when things require assistance from outside. If you only want to be obstructive and upsetting to everyone here, I'd prefer you went home and left us to it.'

Instantly a tension grew among the gathered men. They all turned and watched Gavin, waiting to see what he'd do. Gavin hesitated, then backed off, waving a hand. 'Okay, I was just asking.' Riley glared at him a moment longer, then turned on his heel and stalked towards his vehicle. The three other men assigned to their search party followed and climbed into the wire cage on the back of the police Ford pick-up for a ride to the riverbank. Michael called out that he would take his own van, then turned to Gavin.

'Want a lift with me?'

'It might be better.'

They walked quickly over to the van. Michael waited until they were inside before saying lightly, 'Wow, that turned into quite a heavy scene. I don't think our friendly local policeman likes us— he certainly doesn't like you. Is it something we've done?'

'I haven't had much to do with him. I'm surprised myself. I had to speak with his deputy, Griffith, the other day and I expected Riley might pay me a visit, but it didn't happen.' Michael waited for Gavin to explain why he'd had dealings with the local police, but instead he went on, 'It's probably because we're the new kids on the block. Anyway, now I don't like *him* either—or his methods,' Gavin added, looking annoyed.

'What do you mean?'

'Well, he's not giving this search much thought. I heard two women talking in Bartell's when I was in there grabbing a pocketful of chocolate bars— to keep me going and for young Ainslie, if we find him.' As if to prove it Gavin pushed his hand into his pocket and produced a wrapped candy. He offered it to Michael, who shook his head. 'These women were saying Ainslie's taken nothing. Only his bicycle and the clothes he was dressed in—and maybe a knapsack, but that's not unusual, apparently.' Michael looked puzzled, so Gavin explained: 'It means this is not some kid who's run away from home to prove a point to his parents. We're not going to find him camped out in a drainpipe somewhere. He didn't take any extra clothes, or his favourite toy, or book, or anything. Wherever he went, he intended to come home again—and Riley must know all that himself.'

'I see what you mean,' Michael said, concentrating now on keeping pace with the police vehicle in front. It would take them a minute to reach the river. 'You seem to know a bit about these things.'

'I was involved in the army reserve for a few years and we did a lot of emergency services support. Most of it's commonsense, though. That's why I can't understand why Riley's got us doing this search on our own. This is a big area to cover and the boy's been out there two days already. In this weather he'll be freezing at night and suffering from exposure. The first thing Riley should have done is call in some extra manpower—like the army reservists,' Gavin said with

130

a shrug. 'There must be a unit nearby.'

'Maybe he thinks local knowledge will be more valuable than a bunch of strangers trampling all over the place,' Michael said. Gavin didn't answer immediately. They were approaching the edge of the town where trees and bush ran into a curving bend of the river itself, beginning what the locals called the riverbank area. There, they would stop and begin searching on foot, pushing through to the barbecue areas. As the the van braked to a halt Gavin leaned across the cab and spoke quietly, surprising Michael with his sudden closeness and the intensity of his expression.

'If the situation weren't so serious and the suggestion so ridiculous, I'd be wondering if Mr Riley *already* doesn't expect to find young Ainslie alive. That's why he's not trying too hard. He *knows* it doesn't matter.'

In front of them the other men were jumping from Riley's vehicle and listening to instructions from the police sergeant, who threw several impatient looks towards Michael's van. Michael was shocked by Gavin's statement and stalled for a moment, holding his door half-open. He stared at him. 'What are you saying? How can he know? Why would we be searching at all? It doesn't make sense.'

'That's what I just said. It's a ridiculous suggestion, right?' Gavin pushed his door open and dropped to the ground.

Riley made them spread out along the treeline between the water's edge and the wall of sugarcane with its adjoining track. This put the men nearly twenty metres apart, but having driven this way with Kerry a few days before, Michael knew that as they progressed they would be alternatively squeezed together, then stretched even further apart by the winding course of the river.

'Keep your eyes sharp,' Riley called. 'We could be looking for something as small as one of his socks, or a handkerchief half-buried in the dirt. Then again, we might stumble over his bloody bicycle, plain as day.' He looked towards a tall, thin man standing closest to the river. 'John Powers, you concentrate on the water. Look for anything metallic under the surface, or tyre tracks in the mud—and point out anything floating. If he's been in the water for two days, he's going to look more like a fucking log than a ten-year-old boy,' Riley finished brutally. But Powers, Michael noticed, wasn't upset by the policeman's blunt words. He recognised him from when Powers had been in Kerry's pharmacy several days before, but if Powers recognised him he didn't show it. He made no attempt to nod a greeting or acknowledge Michael.

They all started off together, working their way parallel to the river. At first it was easy going, but as they left the cleared space of the picnic area and moved into the trees Michael soon found himself slipping into a bad habit. It was something bush searchers were prone to do, he knew, and he'd been warned about it several years before, the first time he had to search dense bushland for clues to a plane crash. Simply, he was worrying more about where he was putting his feet—and his own safety—rather than looking for signs of a lost child. Long grass, thick tufts of rogue sugarcane and stands of trees, their branches low to the ground, made it a struggle to walk in a straight line. After only a few minutes Michael was frustrated with fighting through the undergrowth. He found himself close to Gavin Packer.

'Are we doing this right?' he puffed, clawing under a branch.

'More or less,' Gavin replied, sounding a lot fitter and not quite so out-of-breath. 'I'd be having someone quickly checking all the cleared areas first, but—' he stopped and shook his head quickly. Then he startled Michael by suddenly yelling, 'Ainslie? Ainslie! Can you hear us?' There was no answer. Nobody else followed Gavin's example and called out.

They broke out of the bush into the first barbecue area. Already it was getting darker. Michael looked to either side along the line of searching men and realised that with John Powers on the waterline and the others more or less on the dirt track or close to the cleared space next to the cane, he and Gavin were getting the worst of it, battling their way through the stands of bush. He wondered if it had been a deliberate placement by Riley, to put the two of them in the centre of the line.

'Anything, John?' Riley shouted to Powers.

'Nothing,' Powers replied, his voice flat and emotionless.

'Has everyone got a torch?' Michael asked loudly, holding his up.

'Don't worry yourself about that, Mr Garrett,' Riley called. 'I doubt we'll be searching after dark.'

Michael was surprised, but a look from Gavin stopped him saying anything. Then they were back into thick bush and he needed to concentrate again on where he was walking.

The rapidly failing light made things worse. Michael felt the surrounding bushes and trees were deliberately reaching out towards him, clutching at his clothes. Off to one side he heard Gavin shout out Ainslie's name regularly and he found comfort in the man's calling himself, like a beacon on a dark night. There was still enough daylight for him to catch glimpses of Gavin's clothing as he moved among the trees. Again, Michael discovered he'd unconsciously returned to worrying more about actually making his way through the bush safely, than hunting for a lost boy. He tried harder, looking around him and searching the undergrowth for any tell-tale signs, perhaps a scrap of torn clothing. It occurred to him how futile their attempts could be. How damn *big* the world was, and how easily a small boy might disappear forever. What were the chances that he, Michael, could pick just one section of the surrounding land and miraculously stumble across Ainslie McGregor? Maybe Sergeant Doug Riley was right to be angry and cynical about the whole effort—especially if Ainslie *was* a juvenile who'd run away from home and didn't want to be found.

But that's probably not true, Michael's mind went on. He stopped, wiping aside a thick spider's web and forcing himself not to think about whatever eight-legged monster lived in it. He remembered Gavin's story of the two women in Bartell's store

134

discussing Ainslie's disappearance. *Wherever he went, he intended to come home again.* Michael knew Gavin Packer no better than he did the policeman, but Gavin's words and quiet authority had a ring of truth about them, whereas Riley's behaviour seemed almost irresponsible in a man of his position. Another silken strand pressed against Michael's face and he tried to duck beneath it. He felt it break, and at the same time thought he felt something fall down the back of his jacket. Squirming around he tried to brush the fabric with his hand, then changed his mind and quickly pulled his coat off and inspected it. He couldn't see anything, and the ground at his feet looked devoid of creatures, too. Michael shrugged his jacket back on, expecting the tickling sensation of a spider trapped in his clothing at any moment.

When he pushed his way out of the bush into the next barbecue clearing Gavin was waiting for him. The others were gathered in a tight group talking quietly to themselves. Cigarette lighters flared in the gloom.

'You okay?' Gavin asked. 'You fell behind.'

'I thought a bloody spider dropped down my back. I stopped and took my jacket off to shake it out. I didn't find it, though.'

'There were a lot of spiders in there,' Gavin nodded. 'I think it's because there's not much birdlife around to prey on them. None, as a matter of fact.' He tilted his face to the sky and listened intently. Michael did the same. Gavin was right. There wasn't a bird in sight, or to be heard.

'That's pretty strange, isn't it?'

'It's got me beat.'

Michael saw the other man was genuinely puzzled by the lack of birds. He was about to question him further when Riley broke away from the other group and called out.

'We'll do one more section, through to the last barbecue area, then we'll call it a night.' Without waiting for a response he turned away again and headed off, the rest of his companions spreading out to their allotted positions. Michael glanced towards Gavin and got another look warning him not to protest about calling off the search at nightfall. He walked across the clearing, giving the open areas a searching gaze, then before he plunged into the bush once more on the opposite side he pulled the torch from his belt and flicked the switch. A bright glow dazzled him momentarily. The new batteries he'd bought from Kerry were in good condition, but he decided to turn the torch off again in the interests of getting the maximum use from it. It was getting very dull within the trees, but he could still see for a while yet.

The first thing Michael did this time was pick up a fallen branch and use it to pull down any spider webs he needed to negotiate. It slowed his progress even further, but he couldn't bring himself to just crash through the webs and hope the spiders made good their escape. Somewhere nearby Gavin was still regularly calling out Ainslie's name, but his shouts were getting fainter as he pulled ahead of Michael's more cautious pace. Michael began cursing at his own timidity and tried to move faster. He realised that once again he was forsaking actually *searching* for the lost boy in favour of making his way safely through the scrub—which defeated the purpose of the exercise. He impatiently poked at the next web barring his way. The daylight was so dull now he'd been lucky to see the silhouette of the spider against the lighter upper branches. The web didn't break, so before he tried again Michael switched on his torch. The silk net gleamed in the light and a dark-brown spider the size of Michael's palm began to vibrate, make the web shiver. The creature spun around, revealing two rows of black eyes glaring balefully into the beam.

'Sorry, pal, but I win,' Michael muttered, taking another swipe with his branch. He suddenly cried out in alarm and stepped away as the spider deftly launched itself onto the branch and ran rapidly towards Michael's hand. Hurriedly dropping the branch, Michael took another step away and shone the torch on the ground. The spider crawled off the branch and kept advancing across the leafy dirt towards him. In a reflex action Michael stamped his foot down hard. Revulsion rose in his throat as he felt the soft body squash under his boot, but he kept his weight down to make sure. Lifting his foot away Michael bent down and put the torch close to the ground. With a strange compassion he wanted to make certain the spider was dead, and not in agony. The brown body was a curled-up mess of broken legs and wetness. Michael felt even sicker at the sight and quickly straightened again.

He realised he hadn't heard Gavin call out for some time.

'Damn, he must've got well ahead of me.'

Unhappy, Michael began moving forward again. It was a cardinal sin to lose contact with the rest of the search line and Michael was annoyed with himself—he knew better. He kept the torch on the ground in front of him for unexpected holes or branches that could trip him. With a guilty conscience he gave up searching for any signs of Ainslie McGregor and concentrated on getting through the bush and into the next clearing. He still couldn't hear Gavin calling and wondered, with a pang of anxiety, if he was heading in the right direction. Michael turned around and shone the torch back the way he'd come. It was hard to tell, but he judged by the trail of broken twigs and trampled undergrowth that he'd been drifting slightly to his right. 'That's okay,' he said aloud, taking comfort from the sound of his own voice. 'The worst I can do is find the track along the sugarcane.' He thought about it some more and convinced himself he couldn't get lost. He was boxed in on all sides by recognisable features—the river, the track, and the two barbecue areas. All he had to do was head in any direction and he'd reach familiar territory eventually.

He saw a light flickering through the trees some distance away. Michael called, 'Gavin! Is that you? Hold on a second, will you?' No-one shouted an answer, but Michael began pushing his way towards the light, which was already becoming lost in the scrub. 'Hey Gavin, wait a minute!' Going as fast as he could Michael tried to close the gap, but the light stayed tantalisingly out of reach and behind the trees. He called out several more times, but didn't hear any answering shout.

It didn't mean much, he told himself—he'd only met Gavin that evening and the man could be half-deaf for all Michael knew. He was relying on the fact that Gavin had been the only other member of the search team carrying a torch, so the jumping light in front had to be him.

In his haste Michael kept running straight into more spiders' webs. Groaning in disgust he tried to pick the sticky stuff off his face and clothing as he moved. He hated the way darkness was closing in fast around him. What he could see of the sky above, through the trees, was now a deep orange speckled with the brightest stars. His torch didn't seem to make much impression on the bush around him, reflecting instead off the closest leaves and not penetrating far. Michael soon didn't care who was carrying the light in front of him—even Riley would have been a welcome sight.

He was beginning to feel lost.

A large dead tree lay across his path and Michael lightly vaulted across it, the soles of his shoes barely touching the wood. His eyes were fixed on the glow ahead and he only flicked the torch down to the ground on the other side of the tree for a moment, to make sure of his landing. Too late, his senses warned him that the area on the far side was a little *too* flat and clear. He plunged thigh-deep into icy black water, scattering the solid layer of dead leaves and scum floating on the top which had tricked him. It was a tiny inlet on the bank of the river, a backwater where the trees continued into the stream itself. Michael yelled in surprise and shock at the cold, and instinctively held the

torch high so it wouldn't get wet. He felt his feet
sucked into thick, clinging mud—and sink deeper
with every move. He swore loudly and grabbed
hold of the fallen tree, draping one arm over the
trunk and twisting around to face it. He kept still
a moment, calming himself, then used the torch
to look around him. The water lapped noisily.

He allowed himself the luxury of a string of
curses. The line of mud on the water's edge, now
shining blackly in the torchlight, had been hidden
by the tree. Now it was easy to see. At the extreme
edge of the torch-beam, beyond the backwater
where the river's current had little effect, the
ground ended in a sheet of black water. Michael
realised it was a combination of bad luck and bad
management that had brought him to the exact
spot on the river where he could be fooled, the
still water camouflaged by floating debris. If he
hadn't been so busy trying to catch up with Gavin
he would have—

The thoughts froze in his mind. *If I'm in the
water, where the hell did Gavin go?* Ignoring the cold
water slopping at his crotch Michael changed his
grip on the tree-trunk so he could turn and look
at what he'd been running towards. The flickering
light which he'd assumed to be Gavin's torch
seemed to be stationary now, keeping at a teasing
distance that stopped him from seeing any details.
But it appeared to be waiting for Michael to
resume the chase.

I don't get it, he thought, and pointed his torch
at the light, but the beam failed to penetrate far
enough. *That damn thing's got to be hanging out over
the middle of the river, doesn't it? So what the hell is*

it? Someone in a boat? That didn't make sense. Michael had just been chasing it across solid ground. In fact, nothing immediately made sense and a curl of unease hit his stomach as he was reminded of the strange light shining in the trees behind Kerry Wentworth's house, and how it had made them both feel oddly uncomfortable. This light wasn't so bright or big, but now that he looked hard at it Michael thought it had the same qualities—intense, yet not apparently casting any glow on the area around it. A small voice in his head suggested he should get more excited—he might be closer to finding some answers to a few questions he'd been asking lately. But in the darkness, just having had a lucky escape from possibly a worse accident, he felt more scared than excited.

'Hello? Is anyone there? Out on the river?' he called, feeling slightly foolish. He couldn't think of anything else to say. He was answered instead by a shout from behind him. He turned to see a bobbing light coming towards him along the riverbank.

'Michael, is that you? Are you okay?' It was Gavin.

He took a moment to answer. 'Yeah, I'm okay. I fell in the bloody river. I wasn't watching where I was going—' The torch dazzled him as it swept across the ground, then finally settled on his face. Michael put up a hand to protect his eyes. Gavin made his way across to the fallen log, balanced on top of it and reached down to help him up.

Seconds later Michael was standing on firm ground, squelching in his wet jeans. He swore for a while longer, before saying, 'Thanks. I feel like a bloody idiot. Where're the others?'

'Waiting in the next clearing. It's not far up the bank. That's why I heard you yell out.'

'Were they very concerned about me?' Michael muttered, stamping his feet and trying to shake some of the water out.

'I told them to wait, because I'm the only one with a torch. What happened?'

'I fell behind. I didn't realise it was happening. I was so worried about dodging the damn spiders I lost contact with the rest of the search line.' Michael's face became embarrassed as he went on to admit, 'Then I got confused and started heading in the wrong direction, I think. Anyway, I saw your torch through the trees and tried to catch up. Next thing I know, I'm in the bloody drink.' Remembering, Michael turned and looked out into the blackness of the river. The strange light had disappeared.

'It wasn't me,' Gavin said, puzzled. 'You must have been tricked by something. The moon, perhaps—' He paused. 'Though the moon's not up yet, I think.'

'I know I was tricked *now*,' Michael grunted, returning to rubbing and squeezing his wet clothing. 'And it wasn't the moon or anything like that. It was a light, like a torch. And it was moving. It definitely, *deliberately* kept its distance from me as I chased it.'

'A cloud of fireflies?' Gavin asked, doubtfully.

'No, it was a *light*. Besides, I've seen something like it before—' Michael stopped, again thinking of what he'd seen from Kerry Wentworth's back door. Suddenly, he didn't want to talk about it. It made him nervous. 'Look, I'll tell you about it later.'

Gavin was taken by surprise, and finally said uncertainly, 'Okay, if that's the way you feel about it. We'd better get back to the group anyway. Riley will be spitting blood, waiting for us.'

Sergeant Riley was indeed mad, barely keeping himself under control by replacing his anger with a heavy sarcasm. As Gavin and Michael came into the clearing he called, 'Mr Garrett, we're having enough trouble searching for the lost boy, without having to retrace our steps all the time to pull you out of the mud.'

Everyone was now just a dark figure in the gloom. Michael found himself biting back several harsh retorts, telling himself they wouldn't help the situation.

'I was too busy looking for signs of the boy to watch where I was going,' he said lamely, hating his weak response.

Riley let out a grunt of disapproval, turning it into clearing his throat with a hacking cough, then spitting a lump of phlegm to the ground. 'Well, you don't have to worry yourself any more. We'll stop searching and postpone it until morning. It's getting too dark—' He stopped, momentarily surprised to see John Powers emerging from the bush nearby. Michael expected Riley to say something acerbic to him too, but the sergeant quickly recovered to say, as if Powers' arrival hadn't interrupted him, 'The sun's nearly gone. It's time to quit.'

It seemed John Powers, Michael told himself wryly, was beyond reproach.

Of the six men Michael would have guessed they were neatly divided about whether this was the right thing to do. Riley didn't seem concerned at all over cancelling the search. John Powers had only heard Riley's final announcement, but he didn't protest. One man nervously shuffled his boots in the dirt, but Michael could tell he wasn't going to speak up.

Gavin said softly but clearly, 'It's a pity Ainslie McGregor can't postpone being lost until the morning, too.'

Riley immediately rounded on him, dropping any pretence of being professionally courteous. 'Mr Packer, I see no point in having people wandering around in the dark and getting lost themselves just like your friend here. I've got four-wheel drives checking the backroads and tracks, but I *don't* want anyone stumbling through the bush or the canefields. It's stupid, and I'll be the one held responsible if we have any more fuck-ups.'

'We've got two torches,' Gavin replied stubbornly. 'We could split into two groups of three and at least check all the open areas along the river, like the track and some of the clearings further on.'

'Well, I'm *sorry* I didn't make arrangements to suit *your* planning, Mr Packer,' Riley said heavily. 'I'm supposed to be back at the police station to check with the other searchers—and that's exactly where I'm going. Anyone who wants a lift back into town with me had better come along now.'

Gavin turned to Michael. 'Can I borrow your van, if I stay out here a while longer? You should go back and get changed.'

Michael heard himself say, 'No, I'll hang around out here with you. I've got a torch, so it's stupid

144

to waste the opportunity.' Silently, he called himself all sorts of a heroic fool. In fact the last thing he really wanted was to stay out. 'It's only the legs of my jeans that are wet, and I'll keep warm as long as we're moving.'

'You have no objection to us searching a while longer?' Gavin asked Riley, formally. 'Of course, no-one will hold you responsible if we have any problems. These other men can witness that.'

There was a tight silence, then Riley snapped, 'If you two want to fool around in the dark and play heroes, then I can't really stop you.' He raised an arm, jabbing his finger at them in the growing darkness. 'But God help you if we have to come out looking for you, too. Stick to the clearings or the tracks. *Don't* go searching in the cane. You newcomers don't know how much that stuff can be a fucking maze, especially at night. Leave it alone.' Riley spun around and started walking away, calling over his shoulder, 'Anyone who doesn't want to stay, come with me now if you want a ride back to the station.'

The others broke away. Only the one man who had seemed unhappy before hesitated slightly, then followed too. Gavin and Michael watched them disappear into the darkness down the track. Neither moved nor spoke until it was certain Riley and his group were well out of earshot.

'Well,' Gavin said with a sigh. 'Not exactly your friendly local policeman, is he? I can't *believe* he's stopping the search now.'

'I've got no idea what he's doing—or what he's got against us. I've never even spoken to the man before.'

145

'Nodding a good morning to him is about as far as I've got, too. No doubt we'll find out what his problem is one day.' Gavin peered at Michael. 'Are you sure you want to stay out here? You're wet, and it's getting pretty cold.'

'Really, I'm only wet from the crotch down, which is no big deal. As long as we keep moving I should be fine.'

Gavin flicked on his torch and used it to glance at his watch. 'It's just past six o'clock. Much as I hate to give in so easily, we'll only have an hour or so's life in these torch batteries. After that, Riley's right. I've just remembered the moon won't be rising until late. We won't achieve much stumbling around in the pitch blackness—not on our own, anyway. A larger group of us, working together, might have made the odds worthwhile,' he added, sounding slightly bitter.

'Why do you think Riley quit so easily?' Michael asked, flicking his own torch on and off to make sure it was still working.

'I have no idea. It's certainly beyond any of the search-and-rescue guidelines I've been trained in. Now is not the time to be calling off your search parties. In theory, after two days out on his own, Ainslie McGregor would be well and truly suffering from some sort of exposure—and we have to consider what must be keeping him out here, too.'

'You mean he must be injured, right? I was thinking about that myself. Otherwise he could have made his own way home—unless he is just lost.'

'I doubt whether he's lost. There's not a lot of people around this part of the country, but the

146

place is crisscrossed with farm tracks and minor roads. In two days somebody would run into him sooner or later. There's the possibilty he's stuck up a tree, or trapped by a rockfall, but you're right. The odds are he's hurt. That's what must be stopping him coming home.' Gavin paused, then added, 'Of course, he could already be dead. Snakebite, a bad accident—who knows?'

'Wrong time of year for snakebite,' Michael said soberly, his mind filling with a vision of them finding a dead child in the darkness. A shiver ran through him.

'Unlikely,' Gavin nodded, 'but he might have disturbed something.' He took a last look up the track. Nothing could be seen or heard of Riley and the others. 'Well, let's get started.'

'How are we going to do this?'

'Let's just head down the track and each try and search one side. It's not much, but better than nothing.'

Michael thought of the circular pattern crushed into the grass further on. 'There's something down there you might like to see, too,' he said. At Gavin's questioning glance, which he felt more than saw in the dark, he added, 'See what your first impressions tell you.'

They set off to the track, then, taking a wheel-rut each, swung their torches in an arc to either side. They moved in silence for a while, then Michael asked, 'How long have you been in town, Gavin?'

'Not much longer than you. I got into Hickory in time for my daughter Beth to start the school year here.'

147

'They say you're a hippy,' Michael said, laughing to take away any offence.

'No, we're only trying to be a little self-sufficient. We grow our own vegetables, run a few chickens—that sort of thing. We've got some livestock too, but mainly to keep the grass down. It's hardly worth the effort to slaughter anything for meat when you can buy the same quantity of, say, lamb, so cheaply. Besides,' he admitted wryly, 'we've fallen into the trap of getting too damn attached to the animals.'

'I don't blame you. I think I'd have the same—' Michael stopped abruptly, cocking his head to one side and listening. He turned on his heel, swung his torch towards the cane and peered intently where the beam splashed over the thick green stalks in their orderly rows—the 'drills' of sugarcane. Between each drill was a gap originally wide enough for a tractor tyre. Now the plants were nearly fully grown there was enough room for a man to squeeze along the rows. Down these gaps his torch barely penetrated more than a few metres.

'Did you hear something?' Michael asked. Gavin joined him, shining his own light into the cane.

'No, but you obviously did. What was it?'

'I'm not sure. It sounded like—' Michael hesitated. 'Well, this is going to sound stupid, but it was like someone laughing, actually. Quietly, to themselves.'

'It'll be some sort of a bird, or an animal,' Gavin said, not very confident.

Michael lowered his voice to a whisper. 'My first thought was that some of the guys who just left

148

have doubled back and are playing stupid games, trying to scare us.'

'I doubt it. I'll be bloody wild, if they are.' Gavin concentrated for a moment, searching the cane. 'Well, I can't see or hear anything now. What do you think?'

Michael checked the nearest drills one more time and sighed. 'Okay, it can't have been anything worth worrying about. You're right—it must have been some sort of animal. Let's keep going. Maybe we shouldn't talk to each other,' he suggested reluctantly. 'We probably need to keep our ears open, as well as our eyes.'

'Good idea.'

They moved off again. Michael was feeling uncomfortable, walking so close to the sugarcane, despite having the powerful torch. He felt jittery, imagining something would launch itself out of the wall of greenery and attack them. It was difficult to keep remembering they were searching for a lost and probably very frightened young boy. Michael found himself more concerned with his own survival.

Soon the two men were walking up the slight rise which, in daylight, would have revealed the crop circle, as Kerry had called it. 'It's down here,' Michael said, breaking their silence and pointing with his torch. Again, the eerie feeling he and Kerry had experienced came back. The darkness made it worse. Gavin didn't hurry, maintaining his patient search of the bush on his side of the track. In the light of the torches the men's breath came out in thin clouds of steam now. The temperature had dropped rapidly with the setting sun.

Michael reached the crushed circle first and waited for Gavin to catch up. The other man was still looking, probing with his torch among a cluster of rocks, then he shone it on the ground at his feet and walked over. He stopped in surprise as the light revealed the clear arc of crushed grass. He cast about with the beam, tracing the edge of the circle completely around until it came back to them.

'Interesting,' he murmured after a while, disappointing Michael. He bent down and picked at the grass.

'Any ideas what caused it?'

'Some farmer storing his machinery here for a long time, I suppose.' Gavin stood again and walked towards the centre of the circle. Michael called after him.

'It's something a bit weirder than that—I know you're thinking that yourself. That's why you're saying it's "interesting",' Michael challenged him. Gavin didn't answer him and Michael watched as he dropped to his haunches and examined the centre of the circle, his crouched form silhouetted by the torch held close to the dirt. 'I found it the other morning, when I was walking down here with Kerry Wentworth—the pharmacist.'

'I know her. Nice lady,' Gavin replied without looking up.

'Kerry said it reminded her of those crop circles they get in England. You know the ones?'

'I know what you mean, but I haven't seen or read much about them.'

'They've been happening for centuries, but nobody's ever been able to explain them properly.'

Michael was slightly taunting, hoping to goad Gavin into moving his thinking away from the obvious—or safe—answers. Neither did he want to mention the bad feeling the place gave him. He wanted to see if Gavin would mention it.

Gavin stayed silent, scratching at the ground. Finally he rose and slowly stepped back. 'Hey, Michael, let's not get carried away. We came out here to look for a lost kid, and instead we're getting spooked by unfriendly policemen, night-time noises and, well—' he gestured at the circle and shrugged. 'There's probably a perfectly ordinary explanation for this. Interesting maybe, but still ordinary. When you really look at it, I don't think there's anything to get spooked about. If this was daytime we wouldn't be giving it a second thought.'

'Don't you—feel something?'

Gavin looked about him and shrugged. 'It's night-time, we're in a canefield—or next to one anyway—and we've just had a bad scene with Riley. Of course I feel a bit rattled, but I won't say it's because of this place. Though I must admit it *does* seem to have a bad vibe.'

Michael opened his mouth to reply. He was going to say the circle looked even stranger in the clear light of day, and that Gavin's 'bad vibe' didn't go away in the daytime either, but a noise coming from the cane nearby stilled the words in his throat. It was the same noise as before, clearer this time. Both men heard it.

A low chuckle of laughter.

Gavin reacted angrily, shining his torch towards the sugarcane and calling, 'Who's there? Who is it? We're not out here to play games and I don't think you're being very funny!'

There was no answer and he was too far from the canefield for his torch to do anything other than wash over the outer stalks. Michael added his beam, reaching a little further and discovering a black square in the wall of cane, a track leading straight into the field. Michael vaguely remembered it from his earlier trip.

'Let's take a look,' Gavin snapped, striding towards the cane, his torch-beam dancing wildly across the ground in his haste. Michael hurried to catch up.

'Let's be careful, Gavin. Remember, Riley told us not to go into the cane,' he said.

Without faltering Gavin said, 'You don't have to come, if you don't want to.'

'Of course I'm coming!' Michael was immediately angry. 'I'm just saying we have to be careful. Let's not rush in. We just heard someone *laughing* at us, don't forget. Not a lost child crying.'

'We won't go far.'

They went quickly to the edge of the sugarcane and worked their way towards the track, flicking torch-beams into the drills, but really more interested in investigating the path leading into the canefield. When they reached the gap in the sugar the men shone their torches together. The track extended only thirty metres or so into the canefield, then became a T-junction, branching off to either side.

Gavin sucked in his breath with surprise. Michael simply stared. Standing at the apex of the intersection was a small boy. He wore torn clothing and his feet were bare. A mad grin was spread across his white face. He let the torches settle on him for a few seconds, then let out a childish peal of laughter and dodged away further into the cane.

'Ain—Ainslie! Ainslie! Wait!' Gavin yelled, running forward.

Michael followed, calling, 'Hey, Gavin! Take it easy! How do you know it's Ainslie?'

'Who the hell else could it be, for Christ's sake?' Gavin answered sharply over his shoulder.

'Well, he's not acting like a lost kid, for a start!'

They reached the intersection, both of them puffing from the short run. Gavin pointed his torch in the direction the child had gone. The track, which went straight for only a short distance before bending away again, was empty.

'Damn!' Gavin swore, moving off once more.

'Gavin, look! Don't just go rushing in. There's something I don't like about this. Something strange.' Michael tried to sound like the voice of reason, but already he could feel the high walls of cane closing in around them and it made him twice as nervous. Something about the child's fleeting appearance and the mad expression on his face had Michael thinking things weren't right. His instincts were screaming at him to be very careful. 'He's not *acting* like a kid who's been lost for two days,' he repeated.

'He didn't look like a kid who just left home, either,' Gavin said. 'We can't ignore him. I just want to talk to him—see if he will tell us his name.' He raised his voice and called, 'Hey! Don't run away! We're not going to hurt you.' Gavin stopped suddenly to listen properly and Michael nearly bumped into him. The thick vegetation all around seemed to soak up every sound except for the rustling of the upper leaves, as if the cane stalks were whispering to each other about these strangers trespassing among them. Just as unexpectedly Gavin strode off again, leaving Michael behind. The next bend in the track was a right-angle turn with a small, cleared space just beyond it where an irrigation pump was mounted in a wire cage. The track continued into the darkness. Gavin kept going with Michael keeping close.

'Shit, Gavin. This stuff *is* like a bloody maze,' Michael said, adding reluctantly, 'Maybe we should quit right now and get some help. Riley's right. *We* might get lost too.'

'We might never get this close again, either. Stress and exposure can do crazy things to a person—especially a child. Most likely this is Ainslie and he's temporarily lost his mind. God knows I would, wandering around in this cane for two nights. We have to try, Michael. Believe me, it could be a matter of survival for this kid.' Gavin halted suddenly again, but this time he switched off his torch and turned towards Michael. 'Switch off yours, too,' he said.

'But why—?' Michael began, then obeyed.

Gavin stayed quiet for a few long seconds, then said, 'Look up.'

'What?'

'Look up. At the sky.' He stretched his arm upwards and Michael realised he could, at least dimly, *see* Gavin in the light of the star-filled sky. He tipped his head back and stared at the heavens.

Gavin said, 'See that long, curved tail with the red star near its head?'

'Not really,' Michael admitted, feeling stupid.

'Well never mind, because I can. It's Scorpio, and it's a big constellation which will be hanging above us for some time yet. As long as I can see it—or a few others for that matter—then I know all we have to do is head in that direction and we'll get back to the river.' Gavin waved at the sugarcane on one side. 'Even if we don't find the right track and have to force our way through the cane, as long as we go in that direction we'll get there, okay? We can't really get lost. So, come on.'

'Okay,' Michael nodded, convinced that Gavin would be able to lead them out of the cane, but still feeling they were taking on too much on their own.

Another low cackle of laughter came from somewhere nearby and Gavin quickly switched his torch back on. He called, 'Ainslie, is that you? Stay where you are a moment. We only want to talk to you.' The beam flickered too hastily over a small, running form. When Gavin snapped it back to the same place the child was gone. 'Ainslie! Wait!' They stood, vainly shining the torches about them, not sure which direction to look. A squeal of high, excited laughter came again, this time from further up the trail. Both men swung their lights that way in time to catch another flitting image of the boy running into a side-track.

'He moves bloody fast for a sick, lost kid, too!' Michael grated, his nervousness turning to frustration and anger. This time Gavin didn't answer.

They ran towards the end of the trail.

This track ended in a T-junction, too. Gavin and Michael stood undecided at the corner, shining the torches each way and seeing nothing. 'Perhaps we'll have to split up,' Gavin said grimly.

'Like hell!' Michael was quick to respond. 'You might be able to find your way out of this shit, but I won't have a hope.'

'All right, so which way?'

Michael heard the resentment in Gavin's voice, but ignored it. He knew they were both getting rattled by what was happening. This was no time to start arguing between themselves. He looked in each direction, hoping for a clue. As he turned his head, something caught his eye to make him turn back. 'Look,' he said, not sure he was seeing right.

A light was glowing from within the cane. It came from yet another side-track, throwing a white square out onto the opposite wall of plants.

'Now what?' Gavin muttered and began moving cautiously towards the light. Michael followed, and now the whispering of the upper leaves of the cane seemed to be hissing a warning at them, telling them not to go nearer. Michael tried to close his mind to the sound. He started thinking again of the strange light behind Kerry Wentworth's home, and the similar thing which had led him blindly into the river. He felt that same strange mix of emotions—fear, but also of being on the verge of discovering something important.

The side-track revealed itself more as they moved closer. It was filled with light and Gavin switched off his torch. They paused at the corner, instinctively holding themselves back from stepping into the glow, like escapees trying to avoid being caught in a spotlight. Gavin looked at Michael quickly.

'Okay?' he whispered.

'Okay? Sure, but what the hell do you think it is?' Michael was startled by Gavin's suddenly wary, almost frightened, manner. The man had tackled everything else so matter-of-factly before now.

'God knows, that's why I'm not rushing in—like you keep telling me.'

Gavin took a deep breath to steady himself and stepped around the corner into the light. What he saw made him rock backwards onto his heels and fall against Michael, who was close behind him. Recovering from the knock, Michael looked up the side-track for himself. He felt his stomach go cold.

Two figures stood bathed in the glowing light. One was small—the boy they'd been chasing. The other was a grown man, standing almost protectively behind the boy. It was impossible to see any other details. The brilliant luminescence shone from a point just behind the two figures, silhouetting them and creating a halo-like effect.

'My God,' Michael muttered, 'what *is* this?' Then fear burst inside him, taking over. Gavin's answer made it worse. He recognised one of the silhouettes.

'It's *Jake*,' he croaked. 'It's Jake Sanders!'

Jake's corpse stood silently and absolutely still. The blinding light behind him flickered and moved skittishly, sometimes reflecting off the broad leaves of the sugarcane and allowing Michael and Gavin to see the corpses' faces. The boy had a deathly pallor, and his expression was one of immense sorrow and regret beyond his years. Suddenly he jerked, as if someone had painfully prodded him, and he stretched one of his hands forward, curling his fingers in a beckoning gesture. The boy called out in a broken voice.

'Come and meet Jake. He's going to come and visit you all anyway, so you might as well meet him now. Get it over and done with.'

With a terrible, calm deliberation Jake's corpse raised an arm high. The light glittered off the steel blade of the flick-knife he held.

Every nerve in Michael's body was screaming at him to run. Without consciously understanding, he knew that to go closer to the glowing figure— to let it come within reach—would be the worst thing they could do. But incredibly, he realised Gavin was actually taking a step towards the corpses and their accompanying, blinding light.

'No, Gavin!' Michael snatched a handful of Gavin's collar and hauled at him hard. Gavin stumbled and fell backwards, and Michael literally dragged him by his jacket back around the corner of the tall sugarcane. He heard mocking laughter and was terrified the two figures would follow. Michael fell to his knees and put his face close to Gavin's.

'Get up!' he shouted. 'We've got to get out of here. We've been tricked into some sort of a trap and you're the only one who can take us back out!'

Gavin nodded, confused and disorientated, but he heaved himself to his feet. For a moment it looked as though he was going to dash back around the corner into the side-track and Michael prepared himself for a flying tackle to bring the man back down again—not that he was feeling any strong desire to save anyone but himself. Only it was true—Gavin *was* the only one of them who could lead them out of the cane. He was relieved to see Gavin shake himself instead, like a man coming out of a daze. He growled, 'Let's go,' and trotted quickly back in the direction they'd come, switching his torch on to light the way.

It was too easy at first—and Michael knew it. He waited for something to go wrong. Gavin was confident of his heading and it seemed they would simply leave the canefield the way they'd entered. They didn't speak, the only sounds the tramping of their feet and their panting breaths. Michael's fear heightened everything—the sounds, the sharp, sugary smells of the plantation, and the sight of every threatening shadow. Then the laughter started again, regularly now and echoing out from the cane all around them. It alternated from the throaty chuckle they first heard, to loud, shocking screeches of boyish delight which made the men flinch and duck their heads.

'Ignore it! Keep going!' Michael yelled, his voice cracking. Gavin waved a hand.

Coming into a straight stretch Gavin pulled up suddenly. Blocking the path ahead of them, the boy was waiting. His white face glowed at them, the grin an evil expression of malice. They heard a coy voice which, rather than coming directly from the boy, seemed to echo inside their minds.

'Wait for Jake. He's trying to catch up.'

'Jesus!' Michael spun around. Behind them the darkness was complete—the light had disappeared. But the blackness was even more threatening and Michael could easily picture Jake's corpse moving along the track after them. How the boy had got ahead of them Michael didn't know. 'What the fuck do we do?'

'We have to get out of the cane—back to the van. This way,' Gavin said, and plunged straight into the cane. After a moment's hesitation Michael followed.

They were moving with the run of the cane drills, but many plants had fallen or were pushed to one side, barring the way. Some of the leaves reaching out were sharp-edged like razors and the two men quickly learnt to hold their arms up protectively in front of their faces. Pointing the torches forward was useless. The laughter kept drifting around them, but more distant and indistinct.

'Keep going with the cane!' Gavin yelled, the words punctuated by his grunts of effort. 'Follow the furrows. If you find yourself running against the plants, you're going in the wrong direction.'

Michael shouted back something unintelligible, saving his concentration to fight against the plants. In the darkness every fallen sugarcane plant was an unseen slap against his face and body as he crashed against it. He tried to keep Gavin's torch in sight as it danced crazily in all directions. He quickly became exhausted and feared they were headed the wrong way—pushing deeper and deeper into the cane. Then unexpectedly Michael was stumbling over open ground. Somebody grabbed his coat by the sleeve and he heard Gavin snap at him.

'This way—towards the water. Let's get away from the cane for a while.'

Michael found a moment to marvel at Gavin's presence of mind. They fell, gasping for breath, into the soft sand next to the river. They both lay trying to gather their senses. At first Michael was too exhausted and shocked to care if he needed to run any further, then he croaked, 'Will they follow us out?'

Gavin took a long time to answer, then he surprised Michael by laughing and saying harshly, 'How the fuck would I know?'

It started Michael laughing too, though it was more of a maddened giggling. Reaction started to set in and he could feel the muscles all over his body begin to loosen and quiver.

It was short-lived. Gavin urgently hissed something at him and the panic and fear in his tone made Michael's nerves snap steel-tight again until it hurt, making it hard to breathe.

'Michael! Be quiet! Listen!'

Michael clamped down his feelings and forced himself to listen.

There was a soft, whining sound building in the air. It was mechanical, like a machine building up to speed. It grew steadily louder.

'What the hell is it?' Michael asked.

'I don't *know*, for Christ's sake!' Both of them still had their torches switched on, but in the same instant the beams flickered and died. Michael bashed his torch into his open palm, but there was no response. Gavin propped himself up and stared back towards the canefields. Michael did the same, tensing himself and ready to run.

A white round object, glowing with an intense light, appeared in the air above the canefield. The whining noise was louder now, but too quiet to be in proportion with the fantastic spectacle in front of them. Michael held his hand in front of his face and squinted against the light through his fingers. He tried to judge the object's size, but could only determine it would be nearly fifteen metres wide.

Then it vanished—and the noise with it. It disappeared so suddenly the men were blinking for several moments at the image left on their retinas, not the real thing. It all happened so quickly Michael was left wondering if he'd seen it at all. The night had reverted to darkness and silence. Only the sugarcane could be heard, the upper leaves whispering their secrets. Michael waited to hear the laughter again, his heart pounding, but it didn't come.

'Goddamn, I sure can pick 'em,' he said, softly to himself.

Beside him Gavin flopped back onto the dirt and groaned with exhaustion. Neither of them said anything for a long time. Michael was lost in his own thoughts for a while, then when he snapped back to the present he began to think Gavin may have fallen asleep through fatigue.

Gavin spoke as Michael was about to give him a shake. 'Now I think we should go home,' he said dryly.

8

ANNE SHANNON DIDN'T lie to Garrett when she told him 'a few drinks with the girls' was about the sum total of her social life since he'd moved away. Anne didn't feel like going through all the usual rigmarole involved in those boy-meets-girl, girl-meets-boy situations. She even felt beyond that sort of thing now—too *old*, as a matter of fact, she told herself wryly. The three years spent with Michael Garrett had taken her away from late-night bars and partying hard until the sun came up—her previous lifestyle. Anne wasn't a vain person, but in the past, before she had made a commitment to Garrett, she'd recognised herself as attractive and smart enough to play the mating game any time she wanted, and she'd played it well. A succession of broken-hearted men littered her life and Anne hadn't particularly cared. If they had been so foolish as to take her too seriously, or read too much into the way she simply enjoyed their company, then that was their own fault, right?

This time Anne knew she was on the receiving end—it was *her* heart breaking. Michael had found the strength to walk out of their affair. Her relationship with him had been stormy and exhausting. He'd been so withdrawn at times it drove her crazy, as if she was living with a completely different person—but part of that was because of his job, she'd grudgingly conceded. Back then, Garrett was a safety officer for the Department of Aviation, sometimes going away for days while he investigated some light-aircraft accident in the middle of nowhere. He used to say Anne wouldn't understand enough of his work to make it worthwhile talking about it, and judging by the news coverage on the television, he must have seen a few things you wouldn't want to remember either. Twisted, mangled bodies among the debris of a crashed aircraft strewn through bushland. Other times, he'd be as warm and loving as a girl could wish. Anne never could tell if he did these things deliberately, switching his moods at will, maybe just to test her. At the same time Anne often tried a few of her own tricks that she'd always used to keep her men in line—and that was mostly when the couple clashed. Vicious arguments that left a sour taste in the air for days, until one or the other backed down enough to apologise for their behaviour, without necessarily conceding the point they were divided over. That could be left to brew for weeks, causing another round of heated words later.

Their arguments became frequent and often pointless—arguing for argument's sake. All the facts added up to the conclusion that their separation was a good move, although the idea had come out of the blue for Anne, with Michael dropping it on her in the middle of yet another quarrel. It wasn't until later that she realised he must have been thinking about it for a while, because his solution of moving out of the city and using his accrued long-service leave to take a year off work must have needed a lot of figuring out. And to gamble everything on some half-arsed project about writing a government textbook on his work, selling the townhouse and buying a new home in the backwoods of absolutely nowhere—well, you didn't come to that sort of decision in the heat of the moment. Anne had felt cheated—deceived and angry enough to not back down this time. She kept her bitterness boiling and refused to ask him to explain himself properly.

Then he was gone, and instead of feeling relieved, Anne hurt even more. That was why she couldn't stop herself calling him up for no reason, but when the conversations seemed to be turning to some sort of reconciliation—something they'd both agreed couldn't, no, *shouldn't* happen—her stupid pride dug its heels in and stopped her saying the things she wanted to say.

It wasn't long before a girlfriend planted the notion in Anne's mind that a new man in her life was all she needed. It was an illogical and not even vaguely attractive thought at first, but Anne slowly began to agree it was something she would probably have to try if she ever wanted to exorcise the demon of Michael Garrett from her heart. It seemed silly, too, that she was having so much trouble shaking off the bonds of a man she'd fought cat-and-dog with for most of the time they'd spent together.

Finally, Anne accepted an invitation to a night out on the town—just to see what might happen. One evening, against her own rebellious thoughts, she found herself spending a long time in front of the mirror before she left to go out. Maybe the tight skirt was a little *too* tight these days around her rump, but the waist was still okay. At least being tall helped. The blonde streaks through her brunette hair, teased into curls around her face, had seemed like a good idea a month ago. Now Anne decided she looked like someone trying to trim too many years off her age. She sighed, hearing the door bell ring. It was too late for any more damage control now.

She found herself squirming in a crowded, smoky bar. The band was too loud and everyone had to shout at each other to be heard. The faces all around her were lit up with alcohol and excitement, their eyes bright and their mouths wide open with laughter or yelling conversation. The two girls with Anne, Julie and Leanne, seemed to fit right in with the crowd. Obviously it was a place they came to regularly, as several people called out greetings. Anne was introduced to a rapid succession of complete strangers, but the formalities didn't go further than trading names at a shout. The loud music meant you needed to put your lips close to the other person's ear if you wanted to say anything at length, and Anne felt ill at ease with that. Leanne disappeared, then returned carefully nursing three drinks. She used her elbows to clear a way through the crowd. Anne was glad when her two friends turned their backs on everyone else so the three of them could talk. At the same time the band took a break, replaced with taped music at a slightly lower volume.

'How the hell do you guys do this every weekend?' Anne asked, throwing a pained look at the bodies pressed in around them. She took a sip of her drink. It was a scotch and coke, but the cola was flat and watery from too much ice.

'Come on, lighten up, Annie,' Julie said, looking amused. 'This is a great place. You've just been out of the scene too long.'

Her words had the opposite effect. 'Annie' was a name rarely used by anyone except Michael, and hearing it brought back a painful reminder of the reason why Anne was here.

'It's a bloody meat-market,' she replied sharply, but her tone was lost in the noise.

'Of course it is. You're the one who wanted to meet someone new, remember?'

'No, I didn't. I only agreed it might be a good idea for me to get out a little more. I didn't say anything about meeting anyone.'

Leanne and Julie exchanged a sly glance, tacitly agreeing to drop the subject for the moment. The look wasn't lost on Anne, but she ignored it.

Leanne stood on tiptoes and tried to look over

the crowd. 'I can't see him,' she complained.

'He'll be here,' Julie said. 'He's always here. I'm surprised you haven't noticed him before.'

'Who's this?' Anne asked, half-guessing already.

'The latest love in Lee's life.'

'Yeah? What's his name?'

'Oh, she doesn't know yet,' Julie said dryly. 'Lee saw him here last week, but he got away before she could make a move. She's determined to do better this time.'

'How does she know he's available?' Anne felt childish and certainly immature, talking like this. It had been too long.

'He's *always* available—early in the night. You just have to get in quick.' Something in the way Julie said this made Anne think she was expressing more than just an opinion, but Julie stopped any further questions by gesturing with her empty glass at Anne's half-full drink. 'Come on, it's my buy. Get that in you.' Ignoring a warning voice inside her, Anne bolted the rest of her scotch down and watched her friend push her way through the crowd towards the bar. Leanne started a conversation about the band and their music. Anne was glad to talk about something comparatively neutral.

The next hour passed quickly. The drinks were going down fast—too fast, Anne noticed, but she couldn't seem to do anything about it. She got a genuine shock the first time it was her turn to buy the drinks, discovering the steep prices late-licence bars charged these days. She felt odd flashes of guilt, figuring Leanne and Julie were sacrificing their normal style of night out in order to keep

Anne company. She couldn't make up her mind whether or not she was enjoying herself. Worrying about this was tipping her indecision towards making excuses and catching a taxi home, letting the two girls do their own thing.

Anne was on the brink of catching the right moment to announce her departure when Leanne suddenly stiffened with excitement. 'There he is,' she hissed loudly, jerking her head over her shoulder. 'He's wearing the red American college sweater.' Anne tried to discreetly have a look, but Julie blatantly and coolly eyed him across the crowd.

'Yep, that's him all right.'

Leanne hurriedly leaned forward and pulled a cigarette from a packet sticking out of Julie's purse. 'It's the quick or the dead,' she announced, slipping away. The other two watched her sidle close to the man and coyly ask him for a light. Puffing a stream of smoke into the air Leanne struck up a conversation and didn't leave his side.

'I didn't even know she smoked!' Anne laughed, amazed.

'Only when she has to,' Julie said, shrugging. 'Our Leanne's not backwards in coming forwards, that's for sure.'

'You don't approve?' Anne raised her eyebrows, surprised.

'I've been there—done that,' Julie said shortly. She avoided Anne's eyes.

'What, with him? Does Leanne know?'

'No, and I wouldn't want to spoil her fun by bad-mouthing the guy, just because we didn't hit it off so well. It doesn't matter,' Julie said softly, dropping her own cigarette to the floor and grinding it with her shoe. Despite the thick atmosphere Anne smelled the acrid stink of burning carpet. 'Well, it's only you and me now, pal. Unless she gets the big knock-back, which I doubt.'

'Hey, at least it's cheaper for us to buy drinks,' Anne said brightly, trying to cheer Julie up. 'He can buy 'em for her.'

Julie laughed and tipped her glass towards Anne in a salute. The rims tinkled against each other and they drank together, but Anne was feeling a little unhappy, too. Now she felt obliged to stay around and keep Julie company, just when she'd been psyching herself into making a move home.

Anne was quite drunk. A passing parade of men had tried their luck with the two girls, but all were rejected as too tall, too short, too silly or any one of a dozen other different excuses, mainly by Anne. Julie was starting to look a little frustrated, but managed to stay understanding. Anne's biggest problem was she no longer knew how to do this. In her younger days she could have survived the entire night without spending more than ten dollars, accepting offers of drinks from the hopeful males who gladly bought them in exchange for a chance to try their best line. She couldn't even feel attractive. It was a long time since she'd dressed herself with the express purpose of luring a man—and that was what she'd done tonight, Anne had to admit, if only to herself. So despite the fact that she and Julie were attracting a lot of attention, Anne convinced herself their admirers were all the wrong sort of person, and it was most likely her fault.

The band was playing even louder and it seemed an impossible number of people were crammed into the bar when Leanne suddenly reappeared next to them, her prized catch in tow.

'Hey girls! I want you to meet Clay.'

'Who?' Anne asked, confused by the noise and the alcohol swirling around her head. Clay leaned close and put a familiar hand on her shoulder to steady himself.

'It's Clay,' he explained. 'Short for Clayton.' He shrugged, as if apologising for having a difficult name.

Anne immediately decided the man had a definite *cuteness* which probably seldom failed him when it came to girls. Although Julie's comments earlier put a seed of dislike in her mind, Anne couldn't help smiling back at him. 'Oh. Well, hello—' she said, then felt stupid. She wished she hadn't drunk so much. Julie was offering her hand and name, obviously disclaiming ever having met Clay before for Leanne's sake. The four of them tried to have a meaningful conversation, but it was hopeless with the loud music. Anne quickly started to get a strange feeling—that Clay was paying her a lot more attention than he should have. More than he was devoting to Leanne, anyway. At first she told herself it was the alcohol making her imagine things. A chance came for her to find out.

'My buy,' Leanne announced merrily. She was too drunk to care whose turn it was supposed to be. Anne noticed an alarmed look pass over Julie's face and figured it was because she didn't want any time with Clay without Leanne, which might become awkward.

Julie escaped this by quickly saying, 'I'll come and give you a hand.'

Startled, Anne found herself alone with Clay. He didn't waste any time.

'I'm glad Leanne brought me over to meet you. I was sort of hoping she would.' He leaned close to speak, but didn't pull away again, giving Anne the full effect of his thick, dark hair and soft brown eyes. She knew exactly what he was doing, but still couldn't bring herself to draw back.

'Really? Why?'

'I wanted to meet you. I was just about to come over and introduce myself when Leanne came over. I saw you over here with Julie—but I, ah, actually know Julie from before—'

'I know,' she interrupted, adding the lie, 'She told me all about you.'

'I gather Julie doesn't have a great opinion of me.' He managed to look humble.

'Something like that.'

Clay glanced over his shoulder towards the bar. 'Look, I know this is a bit quick, but what's the chances of you and me slipping away together? Get away from this place, for a start. I can hardly hear myself talking.'

'God, I couldn't do that to Leanne. She'd never speak to me again.' *That's good, Anne,* she told herself savagely. *You didn't actually say you didn't want to—you only said you wouldn't want to hurt Leanne.*

172

'Leanne's nice, but—you know. She's not exactly my type.'

'How do you know I'm your type? You just met me.'

'I don't know,' he laughed, and took another look towards the bar. 'But I'd like to find out.'

'Well, thanks for the compliment, but I still don't think Leanne will see it that way and I don't want to upset her. Besides, I was thinking of going home. I'm tired.'

'Then she doesn't have to know. Look, there's a quiet bar on the other side of the street. It's just a little piano bar. Instead of going home, go in there and I'll meet you in fifteen minutes or so. I'll make my own excuses and duck away.'

Despite being intrigued and excited by his brazenness, Anne was also a little amazed by his gall. 'You expect me to wait alone in a bar for you at this time of night?'

'It's a nice place. No-one will hassle you.'

'Clay, forget it. It's not going to happen, anyway.'

'If you change your mind and leave, I'm going to check out that bar fifteen minutes later, okay?'

'Forget it, all right? I'm going to go home—by myself. Take Leanne home with you instead. She's crazy about you.'

'I'll still check the bar out, just in case—' Clay was cut short by Leanne and Julie returning with the drinks.

Events appeared to conspire against Anne—or go her way, depending how she looked at it. Julie suddenly met an old boyfriend and the flame of passion was briefly rekindled by several more scotch and cokes. Now Anne felt a burden to Leanne, who was coming on stronger to Clay but wasn't noticing his guarded responses. Anne knew he was keeping his options open.

The alcohol and smoky atmosphere peaked for Anne soon afterwards. A feeling of tiredness, of being too drunk, and a mild headache telling her the band's next set was going to be too loud, all combined to make her feel drained. She told Leanne and Clay she was leaving and asked them to pass her goodbyes on to Julie, who was too buried among the crowd for Anne to bother getting to her. Leanne flashed grateful eyes at Anne and missed Clay trying to send messages of his own. Anne winked back at Leanne and ignored Clay.

The chill, clear air outside hit her like a slap in the face, making her head spin. There was a taxi rank just up the street, but there was a queue of drunken people and no taxis. Anne took her place at the end of the line. To avoid conversation with any of the drunks waiting with her, she immersed herself in her own thoughts and found herself mulling over Clay. He was all right, she decided, as long as you took him for what he was—a sleazebag. In a way, he didn't pretend to be anything else. In fact, he was probably exactly what Anne wanted right now. Someone *she* could use, and kick out the door in the morning. It was a shame Leanne was in the way.

What would Michael say, if he knew you were looking for a one-night stand? Who cares? It's none of his damned business any more!

Anne snapped at herself for letting her thoughts

go in all the wrong directions. Then one of the other people in the queue chose that moment to vomit their night's drinking onto the footpath and Anne had to quickly back away. The stench revolted her and made her own stomach turn. Her eye caught the lights of the piano bar on the other side of the street and she suddenly decided that at least it would be better to wait in there for the queue to disappear and the taxis to become more plentiful.

And if he comes over—he comes over, she told herself, stepping off the curb. A drunk at the taxi rank begged her not to leave but she didn't hear him. *He can keep me company until I get a taxi, that's all. Leanne can't complain about me waiting in a bar instead of being spewed on by drunks. If he comes in, it's not my fault. I told him to forget it.*

9

CLAY'S SECOND-STOREY flat was nestled on the river foreshore. It was impressive and expensive—like his car, his clothes and, Anne noticed, just about everything else.

'Very nice,' she said, looking through long, plate glass windows at the lights of the city reflected in the river. 'Did you win the lotteries or something?' Anne allowed herself a small grimace, hearing herself slur the last few words.

'Yeah, the genetic lottery,' he said from the refrigerator, where he was dropping ice cubes into two glasses. At Anne's puzzled silence he explained, 'My parents are disgustingly successful and rich, and I unashamedly take advantage of the fact.'

She watched him slop a large measure of scotch into each glass and top them up with coke. Just the thought of another drink made her head swim, but it was too late to change her mind. She'd already accepted his offer. 'Well, at least you're honest about it. Do you actually *do* anything as well?'

'I work in Dad's company and I like to think I contribute something.'

'You sound guilty.'

He put a drink in her hand. 'A bit of paranoia, I'll admit. Take a seat.' She sat down on the two-seater lounge facing the windows. Clay dimmed the lighting in the flat and sat down too. He used a remote control to turn on some soft music. The couch was just big enough for both of them, their thighs and shoulders touching. Anne briefly wondered how many other women had found themselves here like this. *Don't start that sort of rubbish. You're a big girl. You know what you're doing.*

'Do you smoke?' he asked.

'No, thanks. I never got the habit.'

'No, I mean *smoke*.'

'Oh—yes, sometimes. I don't get the opportunity that often. I can take it or leave it.'

'I've got some stuff here. It's not very strong. Do you want to try it?'

No sense in doing things by halves, Anne told herself. She realised the alcohol was making her careless, but that was as far as her commonsense got. 'Okay, but just a little bit. I'm not used to it.'

Clay produced a half-smoked joint from some-where beside the seat. Anne thought it must have been waiting there, ready. He lit it and the sweet-acrid smell of marijuana filled the room. He drew on the joint twice, using dramatic movements and sucking his cheeks in hard. Then he made a show of holding the smoke in his lungs a long time before tipping his head back and expelling a blue cloud up towards the ceiling. He gave the joint to Anne, holding the end between the tips of his fingers.

'Does your Dad know you're spending the family fortune on drugs?' she asked dryly.

Clay either didn't hear her tone, or decided to ignore it. 'Probably,' he nodded. 'I wouldn't be surprised if my father knew everything I do. I represent a sizeable investment on his behalf. I'm sure he's keeping an eye on me.'

'Great,' Anne said, gingerly taking a drag on the joint. The smoke made her eyes sting and her throat tickle, but she determinedly kept a lungful down as long as she could. 'Where's the hidden cameras?'

'No, nothing like that,' he laughed, taking the joint back.

They finished the joint, Clay smoking most of it. The scotches were drunk too, while Clay tried to make light conversation. Anne answered in monosyllables. The smoke had gone straight to her head and combined with the alcohol to make her feel strange. Clay's voice echoed in her ears and she couldn't move. She closed her eyes and felt frozen in her seat. Anne realised she was waiting for him to make a move—the first touch of his fingers, or his breath on her face as he leaned close to kiss. With a spark of panic Anne suddenly wasn't certain she wanted either.

It was a kiss. There was an instant when Anne smelled the spirits and marijuana on his breath, then Clay's lips pressed against hers, not hard at first, but with increasing pressure as she didn't object or turn her head away. Unbidden, excitement flushed through her in a warm flood and she opened her mouth. Clay's tongue ran against hers and Anne pushed against him as his hand ran quickly, impatiently, from her knee to beneath her skirt high between her legs, one finger rubbing against her panties.

Too fast, too quick. Michael was never this fast.

Again she pushed the stray thought away, angry that it had managed to intrude at all. Clay's lips moved from her mouth to nuzzle her neck while he hastily changed hands. His left hand moved under her skirt and kept touching her. His right fumbled with the buttons of her shirt, twisting the top two open and sliding inside to cup a breast. He let out a moan when he discovered she was naked under the shirt and he could tease the nipple with his fingers.

Feelings and emotions were whirling through Anne's mind with dizzying speed. The drugs in her system were making it ten times worse and stopped her from grasping just one thought for longer than a moment. She wanted some sex—wanted it more and more as Clay's hands and lips touched her and lust built up inside her. But at the same time she wanted Michael Garrett's sort of sex—caring, loving sex, not this rushing conquest that needed to be done before the drugs wore off. Anne couldn't make up her mind. Clay's left hand, awkward because of the way they were sitting, worked its way under her panties, caressing her, and Anne automatically opened her legs a little wider to give him room.

Jesus Christ, Anne. Make up your mind. Do you really want this or not?

Clay had forced more buttons of her shirt open and was kissing her breasts now, running his tongue around and across her nipples. Anne felt them go hard. Involuntarily, she raked her fingers through his hair and across his back. Suddenly he stopped and pulled away. Anne didn't know if she was glad or disappointed, but she was breathing hard and she felt hot, both physically and sexually. Clay slid off the seat and knelt between her legs.

'Let's loosen up a little,' he whispered. He reached forward and found the zipper on the side of her skirt, drawing it down.

Now, Anne. If you don't want this, you have to tell him now.

The words didn't want to come and the room spun slightly for a few seconds. She didn't say anything.

He pulled her skirt off, taking her shoes with it as he took the garment over her feet. He hooked his fingers into her panties and pulled them off, too. Prising the rest of her shirt buttons apart he opened the tails wide and kissed her breasts again, moving down to her stomach and the tops of her thighs. Then he stopped, leaning back and holding his hands out to her.

'Come down here,' he said, pulling her onto a thick rug in front of the seat. Anne moved beside him and lay on her back, feeling the soft fibres against her bare buttocks. Clay started to take his

180

own clothes off, awkwardly tugging at them as he sat on the floor next to her. It looked ungainly and unromantic, so Anne closed her eyes. He took a while, and the next thing she heard was the crackling of cellophane.

'Help me,' he asked softly.

She opened her eyes. He'd unwrapped a condom and was holding it out towards her. Anne felt resentful. Obviously he'd had this ready too, along with the drinks, the soft music and the joint—and it was too soon to worry about contraception just yet, anyway. But at the same time she was glad Clay had thought of it. After three years of monogamous sex and being on the pill, Anne wasn't used to acting so cautiously. She helped him put the condom on, smiling reassuringly at him when Clay looked momentarily embarrassed about the difficulty it caused them both. Lying back again Anne waited, expecting the foreplay to continue. The room around her did another lurching spin, so she closed her eyes once more.

Instead, he surprised her by rolling on top of her and jerking between her legs, probing with himself. Almost absently, he kissed her face and neck. 'Come on, Anne,' he whispered against her ear.

After a moment, a now confused and disappointed Anne reached down and guided him inside. She wasn't quite ready and it hurt a little, but Clay didn't seem to notice her resistance. He was thrusting quickly, breathing in sharp hisses. Anne let him move against her without responding herself. He soon orgasmed, his whole body tensing, then turning limp as he let his weight

181

collapse onto her. He groaned quietly and went still.

Suddenly angry, Anne wriggled against his weight until he came out of her. She put a hand down to her crotch and made sure the condom hadn't come off. Clay took the hint and rolled off her.

'Are you okay?'

'Yes. You were getting heavy.'

'Sorry.'

There was a silence, then Anne asked bitterly, 'So, what happens now?'

She hadn't meant to say anything like it. Amongst her anger and disappointment the last thing Anne wanted was to start a confrontation. She realised her disappointment wasn't so much at Clay's lack of sexual finesse, but that *overall* he hadn't been what she was looking for—a replacement for Michael Garrett, even if only for a single night. Anne was angry at herself too—more than at Clay, really. That was where the bitterness was coming from.

'Hey, give me a chance. Next one I'll take my time. I'm sorry,' he added defensively. 'You know what's it's like.'

Anne sat up and leaned back against the lounge suite. She was torn between telling Clay what it was *supposed* to be like, or keeping quiet and just getting out of there as fast as she could. Instead, like a barrier breaking down inside, she startled herself by suddenly bursting into tears and crying hard. Anne covered her face, trying to hold the wetness back with her hands. A small voice in her mind suggested the drugs and alcohol were really getting on top of her now. Anne was usually a lot stronger than this. Clay put a hand on her arm and murmured something, but she ignored him. He stayed for a while, then she felt him get up and move away.

At the clicking of a door Anne jumped up and gathered her clothes. In the dim light, her eyes blurred by tears, she needed to search for her panties, but she was determined to find them. They were hidden under the rug and she wondered if it was deliberate. Pulling her clothes back on, she heard a toilet flush as she buttoned up her shirt. Anne expected Clay to return at any moment, but he still hadn't appeared by the time she was fully dressed and had found the telephone. She dialled a taxi company, and ordered a cab. The operator asked for the address and Anne groaned, feeling the tears come back into her eyes as she realised she didn't know where she was. Clay came back into the room. He was wearing a loose tracksuit.

'What are you doing?' he asked, though he guessed.

'What's the address here?'

'Don't go. Stay the night. I've got a spare bed, if you want.'

'Just tell me the fucking *address*!'

After she repeated it to the taxi operator Anne hung up and started crying again.

The idea to go and visit Michael Garrett came to her during the taxi ride home. Anne knew she was still stoned and more than a little drunk, but she convinced herself the drugs were a good way of breaking down the barriers towards acting the way she *wanted*, instead of how her stupid pride and pig-headedness dictated. The last time she'd spoken to Michael it'd been his suggestion she come up. Well, she was going to take him up on it. There were still some things that needed to be said between them. She couldn't be happy or feel free—if that was to be the result—until she'd spoken to him again.

Back in her flat, Anne's mind began to work with a clarity and purpose which she gladly welcomed—even though she thought it may have been another stage of the marijuana coming to the fore. She needed to pack—that was easy. She also had to straighten out some paperwork at the office where she worked, so that whoever tackled it in her absence wouldn't have too many problems. Anne was conscientious about her job, a secretarial position with a firm of solicitors. She was also sure enough of her ranking and respect at the office that she could take a few days off unannounced. It didn't matter that it was now the early hours of the morning, she had her own key to get in. It would also allow her to leave notes and organise things while nobody else was around. To get away from the place while her employers were actually there might not be so easy.

And there was one more bonus.

Anne had picked up the telephone to call Michael and tell him she was coming, then realised what time it was. She decided to send him a fax instead. It would be waiting for him on his machine when he got up in the morning and besides, it was an effective way of avoiding him changing his mind and saying she couldn't come. By the time he read the fax Anne would be well on her way and out of contact.

It was just after three o'clock in the morning when Anne pulled out of her driveway. The city streets looked deserted. It was a good time to start her trip, she decided, as it was around an eight-hour drive to Hickory. Anne hoped no police patrols pulled her over out of sheer boredom. She was still completely calm and under control, but in reality her blood alcohol level was likely to be over the legal limit. The effects of the joint seemed to have disappeared, at least.

In the office she dithered over what to put in the fax, having second thoughts about what she was doing.

'Listen to your heart instead of your damn head for a change,' she told herself aloud, and scribbled a simple note. After feeding it into the fax machine Anne waited for the slip of paper confirming the message had been sent. It took another ten minutes to deal with her workload and write a more explanatory letter to her boss, saying she had a family crisis (Anne knew the truth might be more palatable, but decided to leave *that* until she returned). Then she was out the door and back into her car. It still wasn't four o'clock. She could be in Hickory in time for lunch.

Anne's planning went awry because she'd forgotten about spending most of the night in a loud, crowded bar and how much she had had to drink. Not to mention the sex and drugs later in the night.

185

'Sex and drugs and rock 'n' roll,' she smiled to herself at the cliché. It was now eight o'clock in the morning. The sense of adventure she'd felt as the sun dawned was gone now, leaving behind a tiredness which made her eyes feel gritty and her shoulders ache. She was heading north, still on the main highway, so small towns and truckstops were frequent. Filling the tank two hours before also gave her a coffee—plus a second which she nursed on her lap—but everything was starting to catch up. Twice she felt herself drifting towards sleep, only to wake up with a jerk and thank God she was still on the road. 'Maybe some breakfast will get me going again,' she decided, seeing a billboard advertising bed and breakfast another ten kilometres down the road.

It was a big roadhouse with a modern restaurant. Anne didn't realise how hungry she was until she smelled the cooking odours drifting from the kitchen. She sat at one of the tables. A few truckers gave her interested looks, but she feigned not to notice them. She ordered a big meal of bacon, eggs, fried tomatoes and mushrooms, and sipped her coffee while she waited for the food.

Am I doing the right thing? I'm sober now—and straight. Is it still such a good idea? I could turn around now and call Michael when I got home. Tell him I changed my mind. He'll understand.

But Anne didn't want to back out now. That was why, she realised, she'd left town on the spur of the moment. When it felt like the right thing to do. Now she was having second thoughts, there were already four hours of driving behind her which would be wasted if she turned around.

Besides, the fax was sent and within the next thirty minutes or so somebody at her office would find the notes and the rearranged work. She had to go through with this thing, even if Michael turned her away at his front door.

The breakfast arrived and Anne hungrily ate it all, then finished the rest of the pot of coffee. As she rose to leave she felt bloated and heavy—not refreshed and awake as she'd hoped. In fact, it felt like a grade-A hangover headache was building, too. After paying the bill she stood outside next to her car, the early-morning sunshine making her eyes water. Beside the restaurant, invitingly bracketed by lush green lawns and shady trees, the motel section of the roadhouse beckoned to her. She wondered if the management would rent her a room at a discount if she promised to leave by five o'clock that afternoon. Not that Anne wanted to stay that long—just long enough to grab two or three hours sleep and be back on the road after lunch. That would still put her in Hickory before nightfall.

The motel owner was a friendly woman more than happy to give Anne the room at half-price as long as she vacated by six o'clock in the evening. Giving Anne the key and telling her how the attached tag made the air-conditioning and power work, the owner thoughtfully showed her to a unit furthest from the bustle of the petrol pumps and the restaurant. Opening the door she bade Anne a good sleep and left.

Anne drew all the curtains and immediately went into the bathroom for a warm shower. A few minutes later, dried off and walking naked around the unit she switched the air-conditioner to a low setting, so the room wouldn't get too hot as the day got older, then slid between the cool, clean sheets of the double bed. She let out a moan of pleasure—the linen felt so good against her skin, and the mattress was firm, supporting her aching bones. Anne put her head on the pillow and closed her eyes.

The buzzing of a telephone woke her. Anne opened her eyes and struggled for a moment to remember where she was. The room was much darker, the drapes silhouetted by a grey light. She located the telephone next to the bed and fumbled the receiver to her ear. 'Hello?'

It was the motel owner. 'I see your car's still there. It's four o'clock and I thought you might like a wake-up call.'

Anne was stunned. 'Four o'clock! In the afternoon?'

'You've had a good sleep,' the owner laughed kindly. 'You looked like you needed it.'

'Yes, I know—but four o'clock—' Anne swung her legs off the bed and sat up. She felt dizzy for a moment. 'Look, thank you. I must get a move on.' She hung up, stood, and tried to gather her thoughts. She felt disorientated and time-lagged, needing another shower just to wake up properly.

Ten minutes later, in a change of clothing and feeling wide awake—if still a bit muddled by the time of day—Anne decided she was now running so late she had to call Michael and tell him what had happened. She called reception and learned the telephone system would automatically record the cost of her call—all she had to do was stop in at the office and pay for it. Next, Anne dialled Michael's number. After a series of connecting clicks and buzzes she heard a tone indicating the number she was trying to reach was out of order.

Anne glanced at the receiver in her hand with a puzzled frown. 'Don't tell me the idiot hasn't paid his bill.' She broke the connection and dialled again with the same result. 'Damn,' she said, hanging up. There was the option of ringing the exchange operators and asking them to test the number, but Anne suspected they would only confirm what she already knew—that there was a problem. The best thing she could do now was get on the road and maybe try again later. It was possible too, that the problem was at this end. If she drove for an hour or so she might move into a different exchange area and have better luck.

She was hungry again, but decided not to waste any time on a sit-down meal. After filling the car she bought a steakburger, a large cup of chips and two drinks—one for later—and drove out of the roadhouse with the food opened and ready on the seat next to her. It was going to be messy, but Anne was starting to get anxious about the amount of time she'd lost. Already she was going to arrive in Hickory well after dark.

An hour's driving brought her to the last major city before turning off the main highway onto sec-ondary roads. Anne stopped at a long-distance pay phone and tried Michael's number again. It still answered as unobtainable or out of order. Cursing under her breath Anne stepped out of the booth and took a moment to stare up at the sky. It was past five o'clock. There was little more than an hour of sunlight remaining and she still had three more hours of driving to do.

'This is not turning out the way it was supposed to,' she grumbled, getting back into the car.

Stopping at another roadhouse, she used their toilets, then went into the store to buy the latest road map. The assistant, a young mechanic covered in oil, was surprised at where Anne was headed. He gave her precise instructions about the turn-off onto the minor highway which, he explained, wasn't well marked.

He wasn't kidding. Anne drove straight past the intersection, catching sight of a faded, leaning signpost as she did so. Doing a U-turn she went left into the road, but stopped the car suddenly, surprised at what she saw. The bitumen ahead was narrow and broken-edged, with no line-markings in the centre.

'Shit, they call this a highway?' Anne said, wondering if she was going the right way. She backed the car up and squinted in the failing, late afternoon light at the signpost. It confirmed she was definitely on the correct road. 'Hickory! More like Hicksville. Who the hell wants to live all the way out here?'

But Anne wasn't even close yet. There was still nearly three hundred kilometres to travel with only two towns spaced evenly between—each smaller than the last, with Hickory the third and smallest.

'Talk about living out beyond the black stump,' she sighed, and pressed her foot back down on the accelerator.

*

At the first town Anne filled the car up again, just in case any petrol stations further down the road were closed for the evening. Despite the big sleep at the motel, Anne was beginning to feel exhausted. The last fifty kilometres had been plagued by kangaroos leaping across the road in front of her, and it was a strain to see them first and take action to avoid them in the deepening twilight. It was that time of day when there wasn't much sunlight, but the car's headlights made little impression on the gloom ahead of her.

There was a long-distance pay phone at the garage and Anne again tried to call Michael while the attendant filled her car and cleaned the wind-screen. She got the same disconnected signal. On a whim she dialled her own number back in the city and heard the telephone ringing. The problem, it appeared, must be at the Hickory end of the line.

The next town was in darkness except for lights glowing from the local hotel. Anne was thirsty, but couldn't find the courage to stop and buy some-thing over the bar. It was stupid, she knew, because the people out here were probably a damn sight more friendly than city folks and there would be nothing to worry about. But there were only another hundred kilometres to go and she would survive. Something else occurred to her as the hotel lights slid past—she would have to make Hickory in time to ask at the pub for directions to Michael's house if she couldn't get through to him on a local telephone. Glancing at the clock in the car Anne calculated she had nearly ninety minutes to complete this last stage of the journey—

assuming the hotel closed at ten o'clock like most did.

As she left the last houses of the town behind, the road narrowed even further. Enhancing the effect—something Anne hadn't experienced before—she was well into sugarcane country now, and the tall fields of cane plants hemmed in closely on both sides of the road. Anne figured if a kangaroo or any other animal fled out onto the road from the cane, she wouldn't have a hope of seeing it in time. Reluctantly, she shaved another five kilometres per hour off her speed. The cassette she was listening to finished and ejected out of the player, bringing a burst of static as the radio automatically came on. Anne twiddled with the tuning knob and found the local ABC repeater, but it was already sinking below a sea of hiss and static. Instead, she rummaged blindly in the console and dug out another cassette.

Anne was calculating she only had fifty kilometres to go when a bright light began to fill her rearview mirror. Something was coming up behind her—and quite fast. It had to be a local driver, she decided, though for some reason a worm of tension grew in her stomach. The lights had to be someone who knew the road well and had large spotlights on the front of their car, to be travelling so quickly. The road had been empty of any other traffic until now, and Anne hadn't seen any farmhouses—because of the tall sugarcane, she figured—but *somebody* had to live out here, she told herself. Every now and then there were side-tracks running into the cane with a makeshift postbox and a name roughly painted or chalked onto a sign. So the sugarcane didn't grow itself, and besides, there was a whole town full of people somewhere ahead. It shouldn't be so surprising to see other traffic on the road.

Still, she found herself flicking nervous glances at the mirror, watching the light getting brighter and nearer. Anne waited to see the distinctive pinpoints of headlights, but couldn't pick them out of the glow. It was just a white glare filling her mirror.

The light vanished.

'Oh well,' Anne said aloud, feeling relieved. 'That solves that problem. They must have turned off into one of the properties.'

She drove on for another few minutes, then a similar glow began to build on the skyline in front of her. 'Ah, the bustling metropolis of Hickory, no doubt,' she said. But a puzzled glance at the odometer told Anne there was still well over forty kilometres to go. The town couldn't be big enough to cast a luminescence into the sky like that—it had to be something else. She thought about local drivers and farm trucks with spotlights again, but somehow she knew it wasn't going to be that simple.

This time the light seemed stationary. She slowed down even more, hoping it might go away again before she reached it, but the hot white glare stayed where it was, as if waiting for her. In contrast everything else looked even darker. From her side windows the passing fields of cane were a black, impenetrable wall. Anne started looking for another side-track, so it would be easier to turn around if she wanted to.

Turn around? What the hell do you think might be up ahead, that you'll want to turn around and run from?

She didn't know—couldn't even begin to guess. Only an unexplained fear, beginning to whisper louder and louder in her mind, was insisting things weren't going right. Still, Anne told herself it was impossible to know what to do until she knew for sure what lay ahead. Looking quickly around the car Anne stretched over into the back seat to lock one of the rear doors. She reminded herself there was every chance there was nothing to worry about at all.

As she negotiated a long, sweeping bend Anne knew that whatever was causing the light would be revealed beyond it. The glare was so bright it had to be close. Then she saw it. Something was sitting squarely in the middle of the road, blocking it. Anne hit the brakes hard, locking the front wheels and bringing the car to a squealing, crooked halt. The engine stalled.

'What the *fuck* is that?' she yelled, staring through the windscreen. The light coming from the object bleached her face white, but she'd gone deathly pale anyway.

It was a wide, glowing craft in the classic saucer-shape of a UFO, with a smaller extra dome on the top. It filled the entire road, the edges of the craft missing the sugarcane on either side by scant centimetres. It was hovering just above the surface of the bitumen.

Jesus Christ, Anne! Don't—don't just sit *here!*

As her panic started to swell, dangerously close to being out of control, Anne's only coherent thought was that she must keep the car moving. Sitting there with the doors locked could invite all sorts of terrors, but if she was travelling at speed in any direction she *must* be safer—though she couldn't have explained why she felt threatened, other than being confronted by something unknown. Her instincts were telling her to run—get away. It meant turning the car around within the narrow road. The motor started again immediately and Anne, her hands trembling badly as they gripped the wheel, hauled the steering in a hard lock before edging the car as close as she dared to the narrow, but deep, drainage ditch between the road and the canefield. She did the same in reverse, craning her head over her shoulder to look out the back window and try and judge how close the rear tyres were to the opposite ditch. The saucer continued to float motionlessly above the road, as if dispassionately watching Anne's frantic efforts.

It needed another forward-and-reverse before Anne was satisfied she could straighten onto the bitumen. As it was she gunned the motor too hard and the back wheels spun, breaking away on the slippery, grassed shoulder of the ditch and threatening to slide sideways into the drain. For a heart-stopping moment Anne accelerated even harder, then the tyres gripped and the car sprang forward down the road. The glowing craft quickly disappeared from her rear-view mirrow, hidden by the bend, but the white glare still filled the skyline.

Then, once again, it simply disappeared.

'Now where have you gone, you freaky bastard?' Anne muttered through her teeth. Tears were running down her cheeks. She realised she was driving too fast. Her theory that safety lay in staying on the move didn't require her to go at break-neck speeds, especially on such a bad road, but it made her feel better. It was only fifty kilometres or so back to the next town. She might even make it before the pub closed, but that didn't matter anyway. Anne was going to hammer on the door, or the door of the police station—*any* damn door—and scream the place down until somebody let her in.

In the distance ahead of her a white glare began to grow behind the horizon.

'Oh *God*, no—fuck you, I'm not stopping this time,' she said, trying to fight back the tears and replace them with a cold anger. She had to struggle with the steering as the car nearly failed to take the next bend. The left-hand tyres spat grass and dirt into a ditch as they slid off the bitumen, but Anne managed to keep the car under control. She slowed down a little.

It was as if the saucer was taunting her. This time it blocked the road at the end of a long straight, giving Anne plenty of time to stop, if she wished. She put her foot down and the car surged forward. The saucer didn't move—and suddenly, shockingly, Anne felt frozen in the seat, the accelerator flat to the floor, her hands like stiffened claws on the steering wheel. The white, glowing craft seemed to rush towards her and when impact seemed inevitable she closed her eyes and couldn't help a scream of horror.

Nothing happened.

There was only an open road in front of her. For an instant Anne thought she heard a whisper of laughter inside her head, but told herself it had to be the hiss of the tyres on the road. Gasping with shock Anne hurriedly corrected the car's drift towards the edge of the road. There was nothing she could do but keep trying to reach the last town. Anne prayed that with every minute passing bringing her closer to a community, the UFO might be less interested in her.

Now the light was slowly growing all around the car. Anne looked desperately in the rear-view mirror, the side mirrors, and turned to check through the rear quarter glass, but she couldn't see anything. She noticed the shadow of her car racing along bitumen beside her.

The saucer was directly above her.

She wound her window down and stuck her head out, her hair whipping about her face. Something large, round and white hovered above the car, keeping pace.

'*Leave me alone!*' Anne screamed at it, before ducking back inside the car, bashing her head painfully on the window edge.

Then the car died. Everything—the motor, the headlights, even the cassette player which had still blithely played soothing music—all stopped dead. Anne found herself coasting along in silence and absolute darkness. In the same instant the saucer vanished again.

'Oh God, oh God—' Anne moaned, fumbling with the ignition key. In her haste she turned it back too far and locked the steering. She was too panicked to have the presence of mind to use both hands and press the disengage button to unlock the wheel again. The car began to drift towards the edge of the road and Anne cried out in horror. She stamped her foot on the brake, but without the motor running to supply a brake booster the pedal felt squashy and ineffective. Teasing her, dragging out the inevitable, the car gently coasted off the road. The ditch wasn't so deep here, serving only to snare the front wheel and guide the car like a tramtrack until it hit a concrete culvert and threw the vehicle to the left, into the cane. Anne screamed again, expecting a terrific crash, but the thick cane cushioned the impact. The seatbelt cut painfully into her collarbone, but that was all.

Now there was absolute silence, apart from the soft ticking of the motor. Anne sat in the driver's seat and tried to regain her senses. She felt trapped, hunted—and terrified. She opened her door, unclasped her seatbelt and fell to her knees beside the car. Dampness soaked through her jeans, but she didn't care. The stink of rich mud was all around her. She stayed like that for a while, her head bowed, half-expecting to be sick. Slowly Anne pulled herself to her feet, using the open door for support. Her eyes had adjusted to the darkness and she saw a carpet of stars in the black sky above.

'Where have you gone now?' she asked the sky.

On the opposite side of the road a white glow appeared above the cane.

'No!' Sobbing for help, Anne shoved herself away from the car and began running along the

edge of the cane. She wanted to hide inside the tall stalks, but she was hoping for a gap, just a niche, which would let her push deeper into the field first. Her prayers were answered with a narrow side-track. Dodging into it Anne screamed when something loomed threateningly over her. It was a tall irrigation gun, the water nozzle pointed like a weapon into the air.

With a gentle hissing noise the saucer swept over the cane, moving out of sight beyond the high plants. Anne fought her way past the huge sprinkler, tripping on the hose and then the tractor wire. After that the track seemed clear. She tried to decide how deep to go before burrowing into the cane.

The sound of soft laughter floated around her.

'Who's that? Who's there?'

There was movement on the other side of the sprinkler, closer to the road. A small figure, like a child, fleetingly appeared in the track. And more laughter.

'Hey! For God's sake *help* me. Please don't do this to me. Oh God, what's happening?' Through her terror she knew it wasn't a child she'd seen.

Anne didn't wait any longer. Getting down on her hands and knees she pushed into the drills of cane. Roughly ten metres into the plants Anne sat and hugged her knees to her chest. Her heart was pounding and her head hurt. Every nerve in her body was jangling, making the muscles jump and twitch. She determined to stay exactly where she was—unless something found her—until daylight. Anne didn't dare look at her watch to calculate how long that meant she had to stay there.

She only lasted an hour. By then the cramps in her legs and arms were unbearable and she badly needed to urinate. She decided to move and carefully see if the car was salvageable. From the moment she hid in the cane there had been no lights, no saucers—nothing.

She pushed herself to her feet, allowing herself a whispered groan at the pain it caused. Then she dropped her jeans and squatted again, urinating on the spot she'd occupied. After dressing again, she cautiously made her way back out of the plants to the side-track. Her nightsight was excellent now and the tall irrigation gun stood out plainly against the starry sky. Further into the field the track appeared to end in a solid wall of sugarcane. Anne decided to creep out onto the track and check her car from a distance—just watch it awhile and make sure it was safe to approach.

At that moment the saucer silently floated out above the canefield. A brilliant white beam, like a searchlight, stabbed down from underneath it and made a circle of light on the ground. The circle raced across the cane plants and onto the track, heading straight for Anne. She knew it was coming for *her*.

Letting out a cry of horror she desperately tried to dive back between the stalks of cane, but something that felt like human fingers gripped her arm and used her own momentum to swing her further out into the open. She fell on her back, her knees raised defensively. There was only a moment, when she glimpsed a small, lithe figure moving towards her. Then the circle of intense light blinded her, trapping her in its glare.

10

'I THINK IT'S all about ley lines,' Michael admitted wearily.

'*What* lines?' Kerry asked, sipping her wine to keep her hands busy. Her face was pale, having heard Michael and Gavin's story of their experiences during and after the search through the sugarcane. Gavin had just suggested the shining object rising out of the canefield was typical of just about every UFO story he'd ever read, when Michael responded he wasn't so surprised—in turn startling his two companions.

'Ley lines,' he repeated, 'spelt l-e-y.' He took a long drink himself from a beercan. The three of them were in Michael's kitchen—the back verandah didn't feel so safe at the moment. The two mén were struggling with a shared, mild shock after their escape from the canefields and the story had affected Kerry the same way. The first thing Michael had insisted on when they reached his van was to have several drinks at his house and get Kerry over to hear what had happened. Gavin worried about Linda and Beth, but a quick telephone call to check on them and give Linda Michael's number made him feel better—although he came back grumbling about how bad the connection had been.

'Ley lines? I've never heard of them,' Gavin said doubtfully.

'You wouldn't have, unless you indulge in the sort of research I've been digging into for a while.'

'And that is?'

'Well, it's hard to explain.' He paused, choosing his words. 'You know, a lot of strange things happen in this world,' Michael began cryptically.

'Yeah? I wish you'd told me that before we went wandering around in the canefields.'

'That was your idea, don't forget.'

'But you didn't exactly object. Besides, I was looking for a lost child. You obviously expected something more.'

'No, I didn't expect anything—but I wasn't completely surprised when things started getting weird, either.'

Kerry saw Gavin was becoming irritated. 'Mike, you're not making much sense.'

'Okay, but it *is* hard to know where to start—explaining, I mean.' Michael paused again and frowned, frustrated because he knew that whatever he said, his words wouldn't be taken easily.

'Look, all the strange things that *do* happen—anywhere, right? Did you know they often happen in straight lines?'

'Straight lines,' Gavin echoed flatly. He raised his eyebrows at Kerry and she gave him a hurried, hopeless shrug.

'All right,' Michael sighed. 'Here's something a bit easier to imagine, instead. It's got a connection.' He sat forward in his chair, propped the beer between his knees and chopped one hand into the palm of the other to emphasise his points. 'Take some of the oldest religious places of worship, for example, and some of the new ones, too. You've heard of Salisbury Cathedral in England—well, Salisbury, at least? It's a very old town and, of course, it has an equally old cathedral. And Stonehenge?' Kerry and Gavin both nodded readily. 'Okay, so if you also take into account several other places of ancient worship in the same area, like Old Sarum and a couple of recognised Druid meeting areas, you can actually draw a straight line through them all on a map. It's called "the Old Sarum ley", in fact.'

'So, it's some sort of coincidence,' Gavin said. 'If you think about it, there's got to be enough churches and places like that to be able to draw a straight line almost anywhere. They're all over the place.'

'No, believe me. This is a documented phenomenon. Most people involved in this sort of work—whether they're trying to support it or shoot it down in flames—accept that ley lines exist. There's different arguments about how they came about. And if they're deliberate or not, of course—

including your theory that it's only a coincidence. But many researchers are satisfied enough to regard them as fact.'

Kerry sighed. 'I hope this is all going to make sense. You're telling us all the old churches were built sort of in a straight line? Okay, but what's that got to do with anything happening here?'

'I'm getting there,' Michael said patiently. 'It's not just churches. Lots of things—strange things, paranormal events—seem to happen along these lines. The ley lines are like lines of—of *power* running across the face of the world.' He waited a moment, expecting a protest that he was going too far. Kerry and Gavin stayed silent, but looked more doubtful. 'Look, here's another example. Some of the most famous hauntings, or the really big poltergeist stories, are often found to be situated smack on top of recognised ley lines. It's as if the paranormal phenomena gain the power to occur from the ley line they're on.'

'Wow, that's getting confusing already, but all right—how many of these ley lines are there?' Kerry asked carefully.

'Hundreds—possibly thousands.' Michael gestured at Gavin. 'There is the problem of establishing exactly what could be an actual ley line, and what might be just a coincidence. Like Gavin says, there's so many churches and things all over the country it's not hard to draw a straight line almost anywhere.'

'Given that point,' Gavin nodded, 'I'll buy the ley line story for the moment. Now tell us what it's got to do with the situation here—although I've got a hunch what you're going to say.'

Michael shrugged, but refused to be drawn into cutting his explanation short. He counted off points with his fingers. 'UFO encounters, flying saucer stories, unexplained lights in the sky—those sort of reports. They also seem to be related to ley lines. Instances of UFO sightings almost always seem to occur in areas where ley lines are suspected to exist.'

Kerry got up and went to the refrigerator, returning with some fresh drinks. Taking one of the beers from her, Michael pulled a face. 'Sorry. I'm not being a very good host. Thanks.'

'I'll have to say you've got some pretty weird hobbies, too, from the sounds of it,' she said, sitting down again.

'It's not one hundred per cent a hobby. I worked for years in the Department of Aviation. Unexplained aircraft, or more importantly *unauthorised* aircraft flying in airspace which we considered clear and safe for commercial flights, was a serious subject. Every instance was supposed to be checked out, if we could. Mostly, they turned out to be light aircraft piloted by irresponsible people goofing around, or lost, not realising the danger they presented by being in airspace that traffic controllers were using to route passenger flights. Sometimes these idiots got away with it, and sometimes we managed to track them down and give them a rap over the knuckles. But *sometimes* nobody could come up with a decent explanation about exactly who was flying what, and where. Now, that's only the "lights-in-the-sky" stuff which we're supposed to investigate. It doesn't include the blatant UFO reports from pilots who claim to see little green men in flying saucers off their starboard wing. We got a few of those, too.'

'That was your job?' Gavin asked, fascinated.

'For a while. I got so interested in it, I kept up my own records even after I got promoted to another section.'

'And that's where you heard about these ley lines?'

'Basically. I started digging around in some UFO books, mainly to learn more about what *wouldn't* be UFOs. Like cloud formations, or the sun reflecting off another aircraft much further away than it looked—things like that. The ley lines tickled my curiosity, which is why I read a bit deeper and found out about the churches and the poltergeist stuff.'

'Now I get it,' Kerry said, looking at Gavin for confirmation. 'You think Hickory is on one of these lines.'

'I can show you,' Michael replied. 'Hang on a second.' He stood and disappeared in the direction of the back room.

Kerry and Gavin gave each other a look, but didn't say anything. He smiled helplessly and shrugged, and Kerry returned the comment with a shake of her head. Michael came back into the room carrying a rolled-up map in one hand and a piece of paper in the other. He looked troubled.

'Michael, what's up?' Kerry asked.

'It's a fax,' he said, sitting down without watching what he was doing, keeping his eyes on the paper. 'I didn't notice my machine had run out of paper until now and this was in the memory, waiting to print out. I should have seen it before.

I must walk around in a daze, most of the time,' he added, annoyed with himself. 'It's from Anne.'

'Anne?' Kerry suspected she might be prying, keeping her voice neutral.

'She's my—well, my ex-girlfriend, for want of a better description. She says she's coming out for a visit.'

There was a silence, then Gavin said carefully, 'It's possibly not the best time for her to come visiting. Not that I want to interfere with your personal affairs, Michael—'

'No, I agree,' Michael said quickly. 'But it looks like it's too late to stop her.'

'When does she arrive?'

'I don't know.' Michael held up the fax for them to see. The note was handwritten, but the bottom half of the page was missing, just a garbled, electronic nonsense.

'The fax machine broke down,' Kerry said.

'Maybe. I sent a fax to a colleague of mine yesterday—it was about the strange lights out the back of your house, actually. He's interested in that sort of thing too and looks after anything I need back home. I figured the fax would give him something to think about. I guess the next one will make his eyes fall out. Anyway, the machine seemed to work perfectly well then.' He read the coding at the top of the paper. 'She sent it early this morning.' He gazed out the window. 'She should be here by now, maybe.'

'Are you worried?'

Michael thought about it. 'No, not yet. It's a big drive for Anne. I wouldn't be surprised if she doesn't do it all in one go. If she's not here by

207

tomorrow evening I can start to panic. God knows what I can do, though.'

'Tell Doug Riley,' Gavin said, wryly.

'He's the last person I'd tell at the moment. Judging by the way he searches for lost children, I can't see him getting too excited about my ex-girlfriend not showing up for a re-match of our last argument.' Michael went quiet, lost in his own thoughts.

After a moment Gavin said gently, 'Don't worry too much just yet. You're probably right. She's doing the drive easy and most likely holed up in a motel somewhere for the night. So come on, what were you going to show us on the map?'

'Oh—oh, right. Yes, look at this.' Michael pulled himself together and became business-like again, unrolling the map and spreading it on the floor between them. He grabbed an ashtray to weigh down one corner that wanted to curl inwards. The map showed the Hickory region, with small coloured marks inked in by Michael dotting its surface. 'Okay, so here we go. I started mapping out known UFO reports as they came into our department. At first, I had this vague idea about predicting where the next report might come from and maybe doing something about it. Getting some photographs—something like that. I stuck to reports only within our State borders, because it would be unrealistic for me to travel any further and it would be beyond our jurisdiction, anyway, if I wanted to try conning some financial support from the department. It became obvious this area here was the busiest around, so to speak, and I took a bit more notice. Next, I began taking notes and keeping this map. When I got some spare time I went back over the old records, too, marking in any promising reports from the past.' He looked up at them. 'Of course, there was more than a fair share of crank callers. People mistaking comets, falling stars, satellites—you can use your imagination. That was the hardest part, really, trying to sort the rubbish out from the real thing.' He stopped for a quick swig of beer. Gavin and Kerry were leaning forward in their chairs, staring at the map. 'Then I tried to chase up any other weird or unusual events—not necessarily UFO things. That was even harder and I didn't find much. Two happened right here in Hickory—a family of four all died of food poisoning about ten years ago, though it's stretching a point to call that weird or unusual. It's more of a tragic mistake, really. But I'll explain the other in a moment.'

Michael stopped again, straightened up from the map and reached across to grab a pencil from a nearby table. Then he leaned over and plucked a book from a shelf to use as a straight-edge. 'So, the day came when I couldn't pretend any more. I had to make up my mind if I was achieving any-thing or not. Now, look at this.' Michael lay the book on the map and used the edge of the cover to draw a light pencil line between several of the ink markings. Then he turned the book around and drew a second line. 'See? That's what I came up with. What do you two make of it?'

'It's amazing,' Kerry whispered, after a moment of stunned silence. 'The lines cross at a perfect ninety degrees.'

'Yes, but look *where* they cross.'

'I know,' she said, quickly. 'My brain's trying to cope with one thing at a time.'

Gavin was shaking his head, unwilling to accept what Michael was telling them. 'According to this, Michael, what you're saying is we're living in the Grand Central Station of flying saucer traffic, right? Hickory is the exact centre of all this UFO activity.'

'That just might be the case,' Michael said, adding ruefully, 'In fact, the other night every battery I had in the house went dead somehow, which is definite evidence of electro-magnetic interference—the sort of thing usually associated with UFOs. But the batteries at your store, Kerry, were okay. Maybe a saucer landed in my backyard—it might have been that close.'

Kerry could see Michael was half-joking and decided she preferred it that way. She turned back to his map. 'But you haven't got anything marked for Hickory except this one blue dot.' She jabbed at the map with her finger. 'Is that a UFO sighting—or is that the family who were poisoned?'

'The red dots are UFO sightings—that's been my problem for so long. Where those two lines cross—*right on top of Hickory*—there have never been any reports of UFOs. And no, I decided the poisoning was too inconclusive to include,' Michael said. 'But that blue dot is what convinced me I was onto something.' He touched the map in several places with his finger. 'Here, here and here are all UFO sightings within the last ten years. This blue mark here is one of the oldest churches in the area, this one's an Aboriginal sacred site, this one *here* is the last camp site of a party of our early explorers. These guys simply disappeared. When a follow-up party found the camp they discovered everything as if the two explorers were still there. Their bedding was laid out, the camp fire had burned out—it hadn't been extinguished. In fact, a meal was still suspended over the ashes. The animals had disappeared, too.'

'Natives,' Gavin said. 'Nothing so strange about that. They killed quite a few of our early explorers.'

'But there were no signs of a struggle—and that raises another question. Even if it *wasn't* natives, the camp site wasn't plundered by anyone later on, either. It was as if the place had attained some sort of sacred status and couldn't be touched.'

Gavin blew out his cheeks in a long sigh. 'This is pretty wild stuff, Michael. If we hadn't seen what we saw tonight, I'd be calling you crazy and getting the hell out of here.' He looked at Kerry and saw her shiver uncomfortably.

Now Michael tapped the map where the two lines crossed. The word 'Hickory' was partially obscured by the blue ink mark next to it. 'I know, but this is the wildest of them all. This is Hickory's sole claim to fame.'

'I have a feeling it's going to be a good one,' Gavin said, grimly.

'I think it is,' Michael answered with a wry smile. 'Try this. A few years ago, as all this was starting to come together, I had the chance to come out here and have a quick look around. A light aircraft went down about three hundred kilometres west of here and my department had to send someone out to check it over. I leapt at the chance and volunteered to drive out, because I saw I could investigate the crash then detour this way to the coast on the return journey, through Hickory, then continuing on to the main highway and heading straight back up to the capital. It was a pretty large detour, but I was keen to have a look around. One thing I wanted to see for myself was if the town had any really old churches, so I was disappointed to see our only church was comparatively recent, and, I discovered from old Father Johnson, not built on the original site. That's significant, see? Because most of our churches are built on the same sites as the old ones, especially in places like Europe, even if the previous building belonged to a rival denomination and was destroyed because of it. There's some churches over there they claim were erected on the same sites where pagan rituals had been held centuries before.' Michael paused to get his breath. 'I spoke to Father Johnson again just after I moved to town. The poor old bugger's starting to lose his marbles and didn't remember me, which I'm glad about, really. I probably struck him as a bit strange myself, at the time. Anyway, he'd also told me there used to be another church, a Mormon building, that was built over a hundred years before. A group of settlers came out here to start their own community long before anyone thought of farming sugarcane here. It was when they were just beginning to establish themselves that a priest appeared—this is in the middle of *nowhere*, right?—and offered them his spiritual guidance.

212

They accepted, eventually, and it turned out he was Mormon, which was lucky in a way, because the Mormons keep accurate old records. Still, let me tell you, it took some real digging this time to get their story, because they *definitely* don't like anyone to know about this one. They want to keep it well and truly buried.'

'You're going to say something terrible happened,' Kerry said unhappily.

'You got it. Typically, the first building they put up was a church, while they lived in tents around the area. It turned out a good thing, because apparently a strain of influenza started to wipe out the group and the church got its first customers into the cemetery. They must have brought the bug with them. By the time the epidemic had run its course there were only twenty Mormons left— less than half the original community. By the way, anthropologists suspect it was the same influenza which accounted for a large portion of the Aboriginal population out here. In comparison to other parts of the country, real *local* natives are scarce. The tribes never really recovered.'

'And the rest of the Mormon group?' Gavin asked expectantly.

'The story gets worse. They started seeing the ghosts of those who died from the influenza. At first it was put down to hallucinations and indications of the sickness taking hold of someone new, but then it became so prevalent and frightening the survivors took to locking themselves into the church at night. Only the priest, a man calling himself Isaiah, used to roam the area alone. Then one night, without warning, he simply barricaded everyone inside the church and set fire to it. It was like his mind just snapped and he went homicidally insane. But he didn't know two people were still outside and watched the whole thing. They claimed Isaiah exhibited an incredible, evil power and danced around the church while it burnt, frightening the watchers so much they didn't dare try and save anyone inside. All they could do was listen to the people trapped inside, screaming in pain for Isaiah to let them out. When it was clear nobody was going to escape the inferno, they claim Isaiah stepped into a white, shining door which appeared near the church, and he vanished into the air.' Michael let that sink in before he went on. 'Those two people survived the journey back to tell the story. Incredibly, they kept their faith with the church, and the Mormon religion being what it is, they made a good record of the whole event. However, they don't like to make it a well-known episode. Despite *that*, when the next settlers tried this area apparently they were aware of the story and made a point of keeping clear of the Mormon church site. They began building the Hickory of today where it still stands as we know it. But you can try guessing what they *did* erect on the old church site. Any takers?'

Kerry had been mesmerised by the tale. Suddenly there was a noise at the window and everyone jumped. Kerry's dog, Monty, snuffled his nose against the lower glass and reminded them he was still waiting outside. Snapped out of her reverie Kerry tried a relieved laugh, but it ended up a nervous shudder. She said, 'I suppose you're going to tell us we're sitting on the damn thing right now.'

'Close—because we've been there,' Michael replied. 'Actually, it's barbecues.'

11

MAL BARTELL KEPT his general store open an extra hour. While he admitted it wasn't particularly nice to prey on the misfortune of others, facts were facts. And tonight's fact was that a lot of searchers would be returning from tramping around in the bush looking for a lost boy. Most of them, he knew, would head straight to McGann's for a beer and a meal, but some were teenage boys and Mal could whip up a decent burger and a can of coke, if need be. It would be cheaper and quicker than eating at the hotel anyway, and Mal knew most of the locals were open to saving their money for drinking liquor, rather than paying extra for a plate of food over the bar when anything to fill an empty stomach would do.

It turned out he wasn't exactly inundated with business—he wasn't aware Doug Riley had instructed most of the searchers to go home once it was too dark to see. But Mal Bartell wasn't a man who'd accept his own judgement may be in error, so he stuck to his original plan and kept the doors open. He decided to pass some of the time by checking his stock. The small black-and-white television wasn't working anyway and even the radio was just a scratchy noise. Mal was surprised no-one had done anything about *that*, yet. It was unusual for the radio signal to be bad for so long. He wondered if it was one of those strange occasions when everybody expected someone else to complain, so in the end nobody did.

He put a clean piece of foolscap on his clipboard and went to the first shelf. After doing the same thing for so many years Mal knew exactly where everything was supposed to be and he could see at a glance if stocks were missing or down. He took his time, noting what he needed to order. It could be a funny old business, he reminded himself. Some items came and went in waves. Normally he sold about two cans of black shoe polish a year, but now he'd got rid of all his stock, four cans, in the last week. A few funerals in town weren't necessarily the worst thing for everyone, he told himself. He automatically looked about the shop, a guilty expression on his face, as if somebody might have heard his thoughts.

A noise came from the far end of the store.

'Hello?' Mal took a few steps backwards, trying to see beyond the end of the last shelf. He was puzzled, because nobody had walked into the store for some time—and he would have seen them if they did. 'Is anyone there?' It was possible, he realised, that somebody had been browsing down there for a long time, but not very likely. Not in this town, anyway. Not without saying hello by now.

When no answer came Mal frowned. It meant he had mice, or—God forbid—even a rat or two helping themselves to the merchandise and disturbing the shelves. It was to be expected, really, in a shop this old, and Mal hadn't seen a Health Department official ever, so it wasn't as if he had great cause to spend a lot of money fumigating the store against pests. What annoyed him most was when customers confronted him with tins of food with chewed labels, or packaging with holes neatly gnawed through. Usually he had to give the stuff away then. People could be righteous and disgusted at the idea of consuming smallgoods from a shop with an obvious rodent problem— until they were told they didn't have to pay for it. Then it was usually a case of, 'Well, it's only the label, isn't it?' or 'The little bugger hasn't eaten much,' and the 'spoiled' goods went straight into the shopping bag—for free.

Another noise came, this time from the other side of the shelf Mal was working on. The goods on the top level were too high for him to see over, but he stood on tiptoe and tried anyway. Clicking his tongue with annoyance he went quickly down the short aisle and looked down the other side. No-one was there. He checked the other two aisles as well, thinking his hearing was playing tricks. Now he was sure the shop was empty.

'I'll set a few traps overnight,' he said aloud, threatening the small furry creatures he imagined were now listening in trepidation. 'That'll fix the problem.'

The tinkling of glass came from a nearby shelf. Mal quickly went over, pulled a few jars of preserves aside and peered into the darkness at the back of the shelving. Nothing moved. 'That's it,' he declared, stepping back. 'I can't have pests running all over the shop at night.' Tucking the clipboard under his arm Mal went back to the front counter, stopping on his way at the tiny hardware section and picking out a couple of mouse-traps. In the refrigerator where he kept supplies for making sandwiches Mal took out a slab of cheese and carefully cut off the hardened yellow face, then chopped two small squares off it.

He hated setting mouse-traps. After baiting them his hands trembled as he gingerly tried to catch the thin metal arm into the trigger and hold down the tension of the trap at the same time. He imagined it was going to snap closed the instant he took his fingers away and catch him. Mal concentrated, not daring to breathe as he very slowly released the spring, waiting to see if the trap was set or if it was going to crack closed. From the edge of his vision he suddenly sensed someone walk into the store and stand waiting for him to serve them, but Mal kept his eyes on the mouse-trap. There was only a few millimetres to go before he could be sure it was safe.

'Is my grocery order ready, Mr Bartell?'

For a moment Mal didn't look up, his task not

yet completed, though his curiosity beckoned. The customer's voice was somehow familiar—but not quite recognisable, either. And the use of 'Mr Bartell' was unusual, unless it was a young child, and Mal could tell this person was an adult. The mouse-trap appeared set. He wasn't actually touching it now, and the spring-loaded arm stayed where it was. Wearing an apologetic smile, Mal raised his face to the customer.

Elaine Sanders stood a metre back from the counter, her dead eyes staring steadfastly at him.

She was wearing her best dress. In his terror this small, almost insignificant fact etched itself into his memory as if it was carved there with a knife. Elaine would have been buried in that dress only days before, he knew, but it was already ruined. So was Elaine Sanders. She looked like she'd clawed her way out through the dirt of her grave. Black soil was smeared all over her and caked in the creases of her clothing. The fingernails of her hands, crossed characteristically in front of her stomach, were torn and filled with dirt. Behind the filth Elaine's skin was a sickly white, almost grey.

Mal tried to scream, but the sound came out a hoarse squeak. Backing away from the counter he came hard up against the shelves behind him. He stood frozen with horror, staring at the figure in front of him.

'Do you have the latest *Women's Weekly* yet?' she asked, taking a tottering step forward, leaning her weight onto one hand on the counter. It was a familiar habit, but Mal only registered that the wretched thing was coming closer to him. He couldn't decide if what he was seeing was *real*.

Was it a ghost? A figment of his own mind? Or was it the terrifying alternative—a solid, walking corpse? Fear was locking his thought processes. He wanted to scream again, but couldn't.

There was a small, snapping sound. Mal's eyes flickered down. He saw the mouse-trap had sprung, snaring Elaine Sanders' fingers and cutting deeply into the softened, rotting flesh. She didn't seem to notice.

An instant of hope flared in Mal's heart as he registered a shadow moving along the windows, announcing somebody was walking along the footpath towards his door. The hope died when he also noticed something *wrong* with the way the shadow was moving—a slow, laboured approach. A figure filled the entrance, silhouetted by the glare of McGann's from across the street and staying just outside the square of light cast through the open shop doorway. Mal knew who it was. With the last few steps he'd recognised the scuffling, scraping shuffle of the worn riding boots.

His head spinning, Mal felt his legs weaken and he began to slide to the floor, his back rubbing painfully against the shelves behind him and sending a shower of goods clattering down. He briefly, madly, wondered if he might wedge himself under the counter and wait for everything to just go away. Without any emotion, Elaine Sanders' blank eyes watched him sink to the floor.

'Any fresh milk, Mr Bartell?' she asked, over the sound of the dragging footsteps on the store's lino-leum floor behind her. 'You needn't worry your-self. Jake will help me carry it.'

12

THEY'D BEEN TALKING for an hour now, the conversation going around in circles. All they'd managed to do was frighten themselves.

'Come on, guys. Let's make a damned statement here! What do you think you actually *saw* tonight?' Kerry could tell neither Michael nor Gavin wanted to answer first, but she didn't give them a chance to slip the question. She looked challengingly at them in turn. Michael finally spoke up.

'I guess I came here specifically to look for these things, so I should be happy to say we found one. We saw a flying saucer, a UFO, whatever you want to call them—'

Gavin cut in, 'You came *looking* for them?

That's why you moved to Hickory?' He was astonished.

Michael explained, 'Well, to find them would have been the icing on the cake, and I figured Hickory was the best place to look if you use all the ley line information I'd gathered—'

'But it's all only a theory! You sold up everything and moved here, where it will probably be impossible to unload this piece of real estate again, right?' Gavin gestured at the house around them, 'In the hope your ley line theory would bring you a real, live UFO?'

'Sort of,' Michael shrugged, ignoring Kerry's attempt to break in. 'I've already got enough material to write a small textbook on light-aircraft safety anyway. I wasn't going to be financially ruined by it all, if that's what you mean. I might have found myself stuck in a real quiet neighbourhood, that's all.' He smiled ruefully. 'As it is, you and I nearly got run over tonight by part of my theory—and it's not *my* theory, don't forget. It's been around a long time. Now, if I can gather some more information, maybe get some good photographs, I might have a monster bestseller about UFOs in Australia on my hands.'

'Still, I have to say I admire your commitment,' Gavin said, shaking his head.

'I don't believe you two!' Kerry cried, finally getting a word in. 'Forget about the UFOs. If something round and shaped like a tea-cup zooms overhead *I'll* tell you it's a flying saucer, okay? No argument! But what about the *ghosts* you say chased you out of the canefield? Where the hell did *they* come from, for Christ's sake?'

223

'Take it easy, Kerry,' Michael said gently. 'I was coming to them. It was pretty scary stuff, that's for sure, but now I look back, I'm not so certain we didn't overreact.' Gavin gave him a doubtful look, but Michael ignored him. 'I've remembered something vague from my ley line research which might explain it for us.'

'*Might* explain it? Well, okay. If it tells me Jake Sanders isn't going to walk through my front door, I'll listen all night.'

'It won't take long, but here goes.' Michael took a deep breath. 'Okay, try this. It's a pretty popular theory that UFOs use a driving force that either utilises a strong magnetic field, or it at least greatly affects any magnetic field around it—in this case, the Earth's. This isn't science-fiction guessing. This is the sort of thing the experts are suggesting is the next logical step in propulsion systems, next to nuclear energy, if only they could figure out how to make it work. Now, the Earth's magnetic field is such a hugely influential thing—to put it mildly—governing all sorts of natural laws and physics. So, who knows what sort of damage, or what sort of effect, a thing like a UFO could cause by travelling near Earth and disturbing our magnetic field?'

There was a puzzled silence, then Gavin tentatively asked, 'Do you mean the UFO might have caused the ghosts to appear?'

Michael nodded. 'It's possible it disturbed the natural fabric of our—' he paused, looking for the right word. 'All right—our *dimension*—enough to cause a paranormal event. In fact, there is a term, "paranormal anomaly", which is like a ghostly occurrence that is accidental or unexpected.' He smiled apologetically. 'If the concept of ghosts isn't enough on its own.'

'But that child spoke to us—threatened us, in a way. I certainly felt threatened, that's for sure. We didn't just observe some sort of unnatural anomaly, as you call it. We were made a part of it.'

'I agree. It wasn't a direct threat, but it scared the hell out of me. And it does spoil the theory, too.' Michael ran a hand through his hair. He suddenly looked tired and drawn. 'It is all pretty fantastic stuff—hard to take seriously, in many ways, but I can imagine how a fluctuation in the magnetic field could cause a ghostly appearance—a glimpse of another dimension, perhaps. I *can't* explain how those two figures that appeared could relate directly to us. The child spoke to you and me—and that's weird.'

'Hey, whoa, guys!' Kerry said, holding her hands up. 'You're supposed to be making me feel better, not frightening me half to death.'

'Sorry, but I'm speaking my mind as the ideas come up. I don't like the sound of it any more than you do.'

'Then let's discuss something a bit closer to home and leave the ghost stories until daylight,' Gavin sighed. 'I want to head home myself. You're getting me worried, too. But what about Doug Riley? We might bump into him tomorrow, or he may even come looking for us to check how we went with the searching. How are we going to treat him? I mean, why didn't he want us to go into the cane? Did he know something?'

'He certainly seemed concerned we might go in there. In hindsight, I think it's possible he may have known about the UFO. If he did, then so did that guy John Powers, the school librarian. Those two were as thick as thieves.' Michael shook his head slowly as he understood his own words. 'This is getting crazy.'

'That man is definitely weird,' Kerry said, pulling a face. 'I know he's a chronic diabetic and everything, so he doesn't look very healthy sometimes—you know what I mean? But still, he gives me the creeps.'

'I agree he had the same attitude as Riley, too,' Gavin said thoughtfully. 'Like he knew we were wasting our time looking. Now we know for sure, because I reckon that child we saw tonight wasn't alive. No way.' He shivered a moment at the memory and his face darkened. 'You wouldn't think the ghost of a child could be frightening— more likely tragic. But that thing tonight was evil in the true sense of the word.' He looked up at Michael and said quietly, 'We did the right thing, getting the hell out of there. I don't think anybody was overreacting.'

Michael rubbed his eyes and seemed about to argue, then he gave in. 'Yes, you're right,' he said tiredly. 'All the scientific theories about other dimensions and magnetic fields aside, I feared for my life the moment we saw those two figures. But—God, were they ghosts, Gavin? Did we really see *ghosts*?'

Gavin took a deep breath before he answered. 'Actually, my theories get even more confusing. We know for a fact Jake Sanders is dead. To be correct, we can't be so certain of Ainslie McGregor—in fact, we can't even be sure it was Ainslie we saw. But if you asked me to make a choice, I'd swear on a stack of Bibles those two things were too solid to be ghosts, if you know what I mean—not that we can claim to be experts. It's like they were walking bloody corpses. But when that kid suddenly popped up on the track in front of us, I think that was something different. And that weird laughter coming from all around us. That was something different, too. And what about that crazy light? It seemed to have a life of its own. I'd say we were confronted by two totally separate entities tonight. The corpses—and maybe somehow their ghosts, too. That kid suddenly appearing nearly scared me to death—there was something terrible, really evil, about him. Didn't you feel it, too? See it?'

'I know what you mean, though it's hard to describe. If he wasn't some sort of evil spirit, then he got around mighty quick for a damned walking corpse.' Michael rubbed at his face and looked very tired.

' "Damned" would be right,' Kerry said softly. 'God, this conversation is incredible. Are we all going mad? And hey, I thought we weren't going to talk about ghosts tonight?'

'It's a bit hard not to,' Gavin said wryly.

Michael sighed. 'The point I was getting to is this—we can hardly go to Doug Riley with all this if we think he may be involved in some way.'

Kerry groaned. 'That in itself is fantastic, too.'

'The whole *thing* is fantastic. Can you imagine trying to call somebody outside this town and explaining it? That we're being invaded by ghosts and UFOs that kidnap and kill schoolchildren, but the local authorities seem to think it's okay?' Michael's short laugh sounded shaky. 'I wouldn't know where to start! Apart from maybe the sensationalist magazines, anyone else would hang up on you in the first two seconds.'

'You don't think the UFO killed that boy, do you?' Kerry looked even more worried. 'You haven't said *that* before. I thought he must have been killed in some sort of accident, and all that stuff you were saying about magnetic fields, he was just—' she stopped, unsure now exactly what she'd been thinking.

Michael was frowning, having only made the connection himself as he'd spoken. 'It's a possibility we have to consider,' he said slowly. 'Judging by how Riley was searching for the boy, you'd think he already knew there was no point. And by the way he didn't want us to go looking in the canefields, it suggests he also knew we'd get a big surprise if we did. There's a slim relationship there.'

'This is getting very complicated, Michael,' Gavin warned. 'Perhaps too complicated. Let's not read too much into things. Maybe Riley did know Ainslie was dead, but for other reasons. Perhaps there was a criminal investigation going on already and he couldn't let on the boy was killed—maybe he was waiting for someone to make a mistake and give themselves away. And we saw for ourselves those canefields are a maze for the unwary—especially at night. It was good advice not to go searching in there on our own, really.'

'Okay,' Michael held a hand up in surrender. 'So maybe we should make sure of a few things before we start screaming UFO invasion at the top of our lungs to the world. But I still don't think we should approach anyone in this town, at least.'

'The whole town? Surely there must be somebody we can talk to?'

'Who knows? What if all this conjecture is true? Riley is our head policeman—supposedly one of the most trusted figures in town. So who the hell else is involved with him? John Powers, the librarian, for one, right? I can imagine a few others in the chain of importance between the policeman and the town librarian.'

'Now you're imagining a conspiracy including the whole town, Michael.'

'I'm only trying to think of every possibility. It could be a bloody big mistake to go talking to somebody we figure can be trusted, only to end up like Ainslie McGregor—or Jake Sanders, for that matter.'

Kerry was frightened. 'Christ, Michael! What are you saying now? Surely that's taking things too far!' She paused, biting her lip as she thought. 'I think we should try and talk to somebody outside of Hickory, at least. There must be someone.'

'Well, there is,' Michael nodded. 'There's the colleague of mine I told you about. The one I sent the fax to the other day. I'm sure he'd listen, even if it's all a bit much to swallow in one lump. He won't hang up on me, I can be sure of that.' He sighed again and glanced at his watch. 'It's too late to call him now. He's been a very ill man for some years—he's in a wheelchair most of the time, unless he's going through a good patch. I don't want to disturb him now and besides, he'll be in a better condition to absorb all this in the morning.' Michael stared out the window for a moment. Monty was still sitting hopefully on the other side of the glass, and at Michael's look he woofed and snuffled at the window. Absently Michael got up and went to the door, calling the dog inside. Whining and wagging his tail happily Monty sniffed each of them, then settled on the floor next to Kerry. Sitting down again Michael said, 'I just wish we knew a bit more. It's hard to know where to look, though.'

Gavin was looking at his watch, impatient to get home to his family. 'I wouldn't like to be found eavesdropping under Doug Riley's kitchen window. God knows how he'd react if he caught us.'

'No, it's too risky.'

'But what about John Powers?' Kerry asked, tapping a finger against her front teeth as she thought. 'You know, tomorrow night's late-night opening for the library. We can be certain he's not home if you want to look through *his* kitchen window.'

There was a silence and they all looked at each other.

'Damn,' Michael said softly. 'It's taking things into our own hands, I know. But I wouldn't mind just a quick look. It couldn't do any harm and there's not much chance of getting caught, like Kerry says.'

Gavin stood, preparing to leave. 'It's still a risk. And what do you expect to see?'

'Who knows? Anything—maybe nothing. Papers, or perhaps just something that will tell us he knows more about what's going on than he's been telling.'

Shrugging on his coat, Gavin said, 'Well, whatever we decide to do, I'm sure broad daylight tomorrow will give us a different perspective. We'll have to do something, though. Nothing takes away what we saw tonight. *That* still happened, right?' He walked to the front door and opened it, but stopped and gave Michael and Kerry a strange look. 'What a way for three people to meet, hey? Still, it's been nice to meet you both properly,' he added with a rueful laugh, then he did a small mock-bow. 'Why don't you come out and see me tomorrow? Meet Linda and Beth,' he asked Michael. Then he said to Kerry, 'You couldn't get away from the pharmacy, could you?'

She shook her head, but Michael said, 'Okay, around lunchtime. I'll need until then to write all this down while it's fresh in my memory, and I'll try that telephone call and see what sort of reaction I get. He might send out an ambulance with a straitjacket.'

'You'd better tell them to send three, then.' Gavin waved goodbye and pulled the door closed behind him.

Kerry and Michael didn't speak for a while. She scratched Monty behind the ears, then she looked up when she felt Michael's eyes on her, his expression firm.

'Don't take this the wrong way, Kerry, but do

you want to stay here tonight? Things are a bit weird and scary, but we should get a few answers tomorrow. I don't like the idea of you being alone at home. Maybe just tonight, at least.'

Kerry was nodding. 'No, you're right. I was thinking of asking you anyway. I'm feeling jittery enough as it is. If I was at home alone I'd go crazy.' She patted the couch next to her. 'I can sleep on this, if you've got a few spare blankets.'

'I'll sleep there. You can have my bed—'

'Really, Michael. If you don't mind Monty staying here next to me, this'll be fine. I won't take him into your bedroom and he'll drive us both nuts if he can't sleep beside me. This is the best way, and I'll fit on the couch no problem. It's too small for you, anyway.'

'All right, you've convinced me,' he smiled. 'I'll get some blankets.'

They were both surprised to notice it wasn't that late, though Michael was tired. He turned on the television, but none of the channels was watchable due to heavy interference. It occurred to Michael there might be a connection between this and the night's events, but felt his mind was already overloaded and he couldn't find the energy to try discussing it with Kerry. Instead, he invited her to choose a movie from the collection of videos he had.

They watched it for nearly an hour, before Michael jerked awake to see Kerry's face close to his. 'Michael, you're falling asleep again. Why don't you go to bed?'

Michael suddenly felt a strong urge to reach up, pull her face down to his and kiss her. And if she didn't complain he would draw her to him and hold her tight. Looking into her eyes he was almost sure Kerry wanted him to. Was there a yearning there? An invitation to take this chance, while they could? Then his commonsense told him this surely wasn't the moment. And if he was wrong and Kerry objected—well, they had enough problems already. To hide his thoughts and the moment of hesitation they caused he yawned, stretched and nodded. He realised he was exhausted. 'You're right. Will you be okay?'

'I'll watch this for another ten minutes or so, but I'm nodding off myself.' Kerry gestured at the television. 'I'll be all right. I can turn everything off.'

Michael stood and stumbled off towards his bedroom. He paused in the hallway and turned back, inviting Kerry to help herself to anything in the refrigerator and the bathroom, including his toothbrush. Then he wished her a goodnight and left.

In his room he undressed and crawled into bed. Strangely, despite how tired he felt, Michael found himself staring at the ceiling. After a while he rolled over, leaned out and pulled the curtain away from the window, then settled back to look out at the night. Once his eyesight adjusted he could see a large portion of the sky filled with stars. He wondered if he would ever look at the night sky again in the same way he had before this night—so naively. Right now, he wouldn't have been shocked to witness echelons of UFOs cruising like advancing waves of bombers over the canefields.

Michael's mind turned to Anne Shannon.

Where was she? Was she all right? He told himself again there was nothing to worry about, that all his logical thoughts were most likely correct. Anne wouldn't be doing the trip in one drive and she was probably sleeping in a motel somewhere. Tomorrow she'd arrive—it would be bad timing and Michael wasn't sure what he was going to say to her, but at least he'd know she was okay. He realised he wasn't so uptight about Anne's imminent arrival as he'd expected he might be. It didn't seem to be so important any more.

All their theories and fears about ghosts and UFOs weren't preying on his mind, either.

In fact, the biggest image to fill his imagination was a picture of Kerry Wentworth snuggled under a blanket, asleep on his couch.

Gavin needed to drive back through Hickory on his way home. Nothing looked particularly different as the headlights of his utility swept across the fences and parked cars, but now he couldn't help imagining something sinister in everything he saw. Even the lights of McGann's blazing out into the road didn't look welcoming. Gavin suddenly saw the hotel as a trap—the shining lights a lure to the unwary, drawing them unsuspectingly closer, to some terrible thing inside the building which would pounce like a trapdoor spider from its lair. *The unwary.* He let the term roll through his mind again. *Like any newcomers—like the three of us. Michael, Kerry and myself. We're all new to the town. Did that mean something?* He shook the idea away. It didn't make sense. Who, in an old country town like this, was considered a newcomer? Someone who'd only lived here less than a year? Ten years? Where did they draw the line? It was too vague a notion to consider seriously.

At least the lights of his own home looked inviting. He parked close to the house, seeing Linda and Beth through the window, sitting together in the kitchen. He guessed they were doing Beth's homework.

He stepped into the house and tried to return their greetings cheerfully. They looked at him anxiously and for a moment Gavin was at a loss as to what they expected. Then he remembered.

'Ah, no luck,' he said grimly, hoping his manner wouldn't betray the many other things that had happened. 'At least, our group didn't find him. Maybe one of the other search parties that haven't returned yet . found him. Doug Riley's pretty certain the boy's run away from home and doesn't want to be found, which makes it twice as hard.' He turned around, closing the back door and slipping the lock. This wasn't lost on Linda, who frowned at him. Beth was again engrossed in the schoolwork in front of her, so she missed the look her parents exchanged. Gavin took the chance and very quickly put his finger to his lips. This made Linda frown even more, but she didn't say anything.

After giving them a condensed, watered-down version of the evening's searching he realised he was very hungry and started to cook a meal. Linda left Beth to complete her homework on her own and began helping Gavin. As they stood together in front of the stove, tending the contents of a simmering frying pan, Gavin could feel the tension in his wife's body. She wanted to know what was really going on. A few times she glanced at him, as if expecting their closeness would give him the opportunity to whisper a clue, but he ignored her looks.

Not surprisingly, Beth was bundled off to bed with almost undue haste. Gavin was still eating, so he gave her a kiss goodnight and let Linda make sure their daughter actually got into bed. Beth tried to protest, saying she was too old to be packed off and tucked in like a baby, but Linda gave her the look reserved for occasions requiring 'no nonsense whatsoever' and Beth subsided, grumbling, under the bedclothes.

When she came back into the kitchen Linda didn't waste any time. 'Gavin, what's going on? Why did you lock the door?'

His mouth full, he motioned her to sit at the table with him. He swallowed and said, 'Linda, I want us to be a bit more careful for a while, okay? Lock the doors at night, that sort of thing.'

'Why? Is it something to do with this missing boy? What's happened to him?'

'In a way. Something happened tonight which makes me want to be more careful—' He stopped, looking frustrated. 'Look, can I ask you to trust me on this one, Linda? At least until I know more. I can't really explain it to myself yet.'

He knew it was a mistake the moment the words were out. Linda's expression hardened and she pressed her lips together. 'What? You're saying there's something you can't tell me? Since when? I'm your wife, Gavin. And I want to know why you suddenly think it's best to lock the doors—'

'Okay, okay,' he said, holding his hands up. He paused, trying to think of the best way to explain, before he went on. 'Well, tonight while we we searching, we saw a UFO.'

Linda looked at him blankly, confused for a moment. 'A UFO? A flying saucer? Is that it? Flashing lights in the sky—that sort of thing? That's why you're locking the doors?'

'No, it wasn't just flashing lights in the sky,' he said, trying to keep his voice patient. He took a leaf out of Michael's book. 'In fact, Michael and I nearly got run over by the damned thing.'

'Michael? Who's Michael?'

Gavin realised that no matter what he said, Linda was going to answer him with another question, so he decided to start from the beginning again. He explained that he and Michael had continued searching because they had torches, they had gone into the canefield, and been chased out by the UFO. Gavin still deliberately kept some details of the story from Linda. It was the first time in their relationship he'd felt a need to hide anything from her, but he felt that the very idea of a UFO and a possible threat from it was enough for one night. Right now, he didn't want to mention any ghosts or corpses—especially as one of them was their friend Jake Sanders. Glancing through the window out at the night Gavin convinced himself this wasn't the time for ghost stories. He knew it wouldn't be long before he told Linda the rest of it—probably in the morning, in fact, when daylight wouldn't let things seem so frightening. And besides, he reminded himself,

Michael was supposed to be coming over to see him. It would be too difficult to discuss everything in front of Linda without her knowing the whole tale.

When he'd finished, Linda stared down at the tabletop, thinking. There was a trace of sarcasm in her voice as she asked, 'And what did Doug Riley say about it all? Is he calling in the air force? The army, or the navy?'

'Are you taking me seriously?'

'All right, I'll take you seriously. You got chased out of a canefield by weird noises—nothing else—and when you reached the river again something *like* a flying saucer flew away over your heads.'

'It's not as simple as that. I know what happened, and I know what we saw.'

Linda suddenly gave in, visibly slumping in her chair and putting her head on one hand. 'Okay, I'll go along with you, but I fail to see why it's necessary to lock the doors at night. I just got out of that habit. That's one of the reasons we came here, remember? Now I've got to do the opposite.'

'Maybe not for long. Michael and I will be checking a few things out. This was probably a once-in-a-lifetime thing and we'll never have to worry about it again.' Gavin had a flash of inspiration. 'Michael used to work in the Department of Aviation. He's going to make some discreet inquiries. He might even get some answers tomorrow morning.' It sounded hollow to Gavin, because he knew so much more and had been face to face with the dead Jake Sanders. 'While I think of it, let's leave Mandy outside, too. She can be a guard dog for a change, like she's supposed to be. I'll put some old bedding down under the rainwater tank—she sleeps under there most of the day, anyway. A barking dog's worth a hundred locked doors, any day.'

Linda nodded tiredly. 'Okay. And I get to meet this guy? Michael?'

'Tomorrow, around lunchtime.'

Gavin was glad Linda had forgotten her question about Doug Riley. He wasn't sure how he would have answered that, either.

Linda didn't meet Michael the next day. Beth's school called early in the morning and asked if Linda could fill a vacancy in the canteen. In fact, there were several vacancies, and the tuckshop was going to be hard-pressed to cater for all the kids. Under those circumstances Linda could hardly refuse.

She was still determined to get to the bottom of Gavin's wild stories of UFOs in the canefields. Linda had a deep-seated scepticism about such things and had only reluctantly treated it all with the same seriousness as her husband. She suspected the whole thing would soon be revealed as an elaborate prank, or a simple case of Gavin and Michael getting confused by a piece of cane-farming machinery. She'd seen the harvesters many times and even though they obviously couldn't *fly*, they were large, quite out-of-this-world looking contraptions that, on a dark night in the middle of strange surroundings—complete with weird noises—well, she figured even her practical and sensible Gavin might get a fright and come home with a crazy story.

Linda believed the entire episode would soon be forgotten, due to lack of evidence.

Gavin didn't speak to her of the night's events again, mainly because Beth kept close all morning before school and he didn't get a chance. And he certainly wasn't going to pull Linda aside and quickly explain he'd neglected to mention a couple of corpses in his recounting of the story. Besides, with the warm, friendly morning sunshine pouring through the kitchen windows, he, too, couldn't help thinking it all seemed a little too bizarre to be real. It needed a rethink.

For that reason, when Michael arrived, Gavin made them coffee and purposely suggested they sit outside in the shade of a wide mango tree. They sat sipping from the mugs and watching the Packers' small collection of domestic animals and farmstock going about its business foraging for food. The two men briefly discussed what Gavin and Linda hoped to achieve in the way of self-sufficiency. It brought a stab of memory for Gavin about Jake Sanders—they used to do the same thing, in the same spot, too, except it was usually with a beer or a joint. A sudden mental picture of Jake standing on the canefield track framed by the glowing, ghostly light turned Gavin's stomach cold. Unaware, Michael seemed to be interested in learning about their lifestyle, only interrupting with pertinent questions. In such an unthreatening setting, Gavin hoped the two of them wouldn't be inspired to act hastily or stupidly when they came to discuss what had happened the evening before.

And he had a fresh theory to try on Michael.

'I had an idea about last night,' he admitted, finally broaching the real reason for their meeting.

'I've done a couple of things too, but you go first.'

'What about chemicals? Is it possible they spray the cane with some sort of insecticide which affected our behaviour? We might have absorbed something through our skin. Remember all the fuss about Agent Orange in Vietnam? I'm thinking we might both have been hallucinating.'

'It's a good thought,' Michael nodded, taking another sip of his coffee. 'But that means we both had the same hallucination. That's almost impossible.'

' "Almost" is right. But if we were both affected, I could have suggested to you what I was seeing— Jake Sanders' corpse—and that was enough to plant the image in your mind, too.'

'Can you remember what he looked like? Last night, I mean.'

'Pretty much, though Jake never changed anyway. He was always wearing jeans, T-shirt and that leather jacket. It usually needed a heatwave before he took that jacket off. That's how I recognised him, despite that blinding glare.'

'Still, I think if we carefully compared what we saw, including that child, we'd find too many similarities to support the idea of a shared hallucination. You might be able to put the thought of Jake in my head, but I wouldn't necessarily see him the same way as you. The way he dresses makes it easy, but what about the way he was standing? Looking? And what about the light? We both saw that, too.' Michael shook his head. 'The more I think of it, the less likely it seems.'

'It was just an idea,' Gavin said, disappointed. 'Anyway, what did you manage to do?'

'Nothing—that's the thing. Have you tried to make a long-distance call out of this town lately? It's like the lines are cut. Now that I think of it, it's been bad and getting worse for a while now. Even local calls are full of static and rubbish.'

Gavin agreed, thinking of the night before when he'd telephoned Linda from Michael's home. 'What about that fax? The one you received, I mean?'

'It might have been there for over twenty-four hours. Faxes use a digital signal, they don't need such a high-quality connection. Maybe the lines failed completely in the middle of the fax, which is why I only half-received it. I couldn't fax out to my friend today—I tried to call him first. Now my fax machine says it can't connect with his at the other end. It's possible my unit's broken down, but I doubt it.'

'This sort of stuff's beyond me. I'll take your word for it.'

Michael leaned closer, his face grave. 'Then I'll tell you something else you *will* understand. All this got me thinking, so I did some checking out. Have you noticed how bad the television reception is? It's unwatchable. The radio's just as bad, and that's almost unheard of these days. At first I told myself it's what I should expect if I'm going to live in the middle of nowhere. But then I figured the *radio* reception was a different thing altogether. You can get crystal-clear radio in

242

some of the most isolated places in the world. We're not in the same league at all in this country. So I went for a drive and stuck my head inside the betting shop. The manager in there is tearing his hair out.' Michael began counting things off on his fingers, 'He's lost the satellite link for the race broadcasts. He can't call anywhere long-distance to find out what's going on, and his computer-betting system is down too, so he can't even let the punters bet on the radio broadcasts, if they could get *them* anyway.' Michael sat back again, spreading his hands now to make his point. 'The computers are a land-line system, related to telephone cables. The television satellite link is broken. So it means, short of a damned carrier pigeon, there's no long-distance communication out of this town.'

Gavin thought it over, his expression troubled. 'That's crazy, Michael. And it doesn't make sense, either. It's not as if we're really isolated. We can always simply jump in the car and drive away. The nearest town is only an hour or so distant.'

'That's right,' Michael said quietly. 'And it makes me wonder what would happen if you tried to do exactly that.'

'Oh, come on! Now you're saying—'

'Gavin! There's only one road out of town, right? And if you wanted to stop anybody using it and leaving town, who would you use?'

Gavin didn't reply for a moment, knowing there was only one answer. Reluctantly, he said, 'Doug Riley.'

'Right again.'

'But what about your friend—Anne, isn't it? Maybe she can tell us if there's anything unusual on the highway when she gets here.'

It was Michael's turn to look concerned. 'That's something else I'm worried about. She hasn't got here yet, and I would've expected her to have arrived by now. It's possible she's changed her mind.' He paused and added wryly, 'We have a— well, a difficult relationship. Maybe she turned around and went home, and now she can't get through on the phone to tell me.'

'I'm sure she'll be okay,' Gavin said, though it sounded inadequate. He took a deep breath, then let it out in a long sigh. 'So, what the hell are we going to do, Michael?'

'I figure Plan A is the only thing we *can* do. Let's take a peek through John Powers' windows. It's a start.'

'I feel like we're getting out of our depth. It shouldn't be up to us to be poking our noses where they don't belong.'

'I know what you mean—but I'm damned if I can ignore it, either.'

They met in the car park next to Kerry's pharmacy at 7.30 p.m. It was properly dark by then and the extra cars wouldn't be noticed—a lot of people parked there after hours if they were in McGann's hotel. Despite that, Gavin alarmed Michael and Kerry when he suddenly loomed out of the darkness on his bicycle.

'You scared the hell out of me,' Kerry said, watching him lean the bike against the wall.

'Sorry, but I wanted to leave the utility with Linda.'

'What does she think about all this?' Michael asked.

'She's convinced we're going crazy, but didn't mind my coming tonight to check a few things out. I didn't tell her exactly what we're doing. I think she's hoping this is all some sort of phase I'm going through and eventually I'll lose interest.'

'I'm sorry I didn't meet her today—but then again, having her husband raving on about flying saucers was probably enough. A total stranger doing the same wouldn't have helped.'

Gavin was thoughtful. 'She worked at the primary school today, in the canteen. She said a lot of kids were away and no-one knew why. There isn't a flu going around the town or anything. A couple of reliable parents didn't show, either. That's why they called Linda in.'

They looked at each other in silence. The news had an oddly ominous ring to it.

Gavin asked, 'So, anyway, do we know where we're going?'

Michael gave a dry laugh. 'By a brilliant piece of detective work, I looked up Powers in the telephone book. He lives just down the road and around the corner. We can walk there in five minutes. We've got an hour before he closes the library, and maybe a few minutes more while he locks up.'

'*Everybody* lives just around the corner in this place,' Gavin said, moving off. 'By the way, I took a detour past the library. It looked like he's in there on his own.'

They walked past the front of Kerry's pharmacy and under the verandah of Mal Bartell's store, keeping close to the windows and hugging the shadows out of the streetlights in case any curious souls over the road in McGann's might want to call attention to them. The hotel was quiet anyway, no-one was leaning in the windows or doors as they did when it was busy. Kerry glanced in through the dark glass of Mal Bartell's store as they passed.

'And there's another strange thing—' she began.

Suddenly she stopped and let out a small squeal, backing away from the windows. Michael and Gavin quickly moved to her side.

'What's wrong?' Michael asked urgently.

Kerry put a hand to her chest to quieten her thumping heart and catch her breath. 'Christ, I just scared the hell out of myself! I thought I saw someone else pressing their face against the other side of the glass, but it must have been my reflection. No-one's been in there all day.'

Michael cupped his hands around his face and peered into the window. He didn't see anything. 'It was closed early this morning when I went past, but I didn't give it a thought. Where is he?'

'That's what I was about to say. There's a note saying, "Closed. Gone to the city for business", for goodness' sake! Apparently it's unheard-of. Somebody commented today that there are three things certain in life—death, taxes and Mal Bartell's store being open, with Mal behind the counter. He's never done anything like this before.'

'Look at the note,' Gavin said, frowning in the bad light at the doorway. 'It looks like it was written by a child.' It was true—the letters were large and ill-formed, and scrawled untidily across the paper. Gavin looked down at the footpath. 'He must have left after he brought in the newspapers. Otherwise they'd be still out here.'

After giving it some thought Kerry replied, 'I don't know. I didn't see any delivered myself. Maybe they didn't get through for some reason? Perhaps Mal can't get back to town either?' In the gloom she didn't see the look passing between the two men.

'It'll be something like that,' Gavin agreed flatly. 'Come on, let's not waste any more time.'

Michael thought most of their caution was being wasted now. The town was so quiet it looked like there was a good chance they would get away with their plan easily.

'God, the place is so dead, it's creepy—or am I letting my imagination get the better of me?' Kerry kept her voice low.

'I know what you mean,' Gavin replied. 'There's a bad vibe in the air, no doubt about it.'

'Normally you'd hear televisions and radios coming out of the houses, too,' Michael said. 'And people trying to talk above them. I think that's contributing to the quietness.'

Kerry shuddered as she walked, hunching her shoulders deeper into her jacket. 'If it wasn't for the lights, you'd think it was a ghost town. There's no *people* around.'

Michael tried to ease her mind by chuckling and saying, 'We don't *want* any people around. We're going to break into someone's house, remember?' Gavin, walking slightly ahead of them, gave him a sharp glance over his shoulder. Nobody had suggested breaking in before, only looking through a window if they could.

Michael led them around a corner and everyone breathed a sigh of relief. The side-road was darker, its streetlamps spread well apart. Kerry and Michael felt better, because there was less chance of their being seen, then Gavin put a dampener on their spirits by pointing out one of the houses they were passing.

'That's Elaine Sanders' house—Jake's mother.'

'Poor woman,' Kerry said. 'The shock of his death must've killed her.'

'Shock? I'll say it was a shock. I was the one who found her body. I knew her quite well and I went around there that morning to see if she was all right. I found her collapsed in the lounge room. I had to cover her face—it looked like she'd seen a ghost—' Gavin's voice slowed as he spoke, listening to his own words. He stopped in mid-step and, turning to face Kerry and Michael, whispered, 'You don't think it's possible—?'

They all stared at the house. It was in total blackness.

'Is it worth taking a look?' Michael said.

'What for, now? Anyway, we'd have to turn on some lights to see anything, and that might really bring somebody running. I didn't think to bring my torch—Christ! I suppose we're going to have the same problem at Powers' place.'

'Lots of people leave lights on, if they know they're coming home after dark,' Kerry reminded him. 'But you're right—lights in a dead person's home might attract some attention.'

248

'It may be worth coming back later with a torch,' Gavin mused aloud. 'Later in the night, too. We'll see how we go at Mr Powers' house first.'

Powers' home was a sagging, weatherboard structure that had seen better days. For years it had been the unofficial residence of Hickory's schoolteachers, since the times when one teacher sufficed for the entire town. In later years, there had only ever been four teachers at most, two of them teaching the primary children, a librarian who doubled as the town's curator of books as well, and the last concentrating on the small group of high school students. The latter was barely surviving the slash of the Education Department's financial razor. Most of Hickory's youth went to boarding schools for their high school education.

By default Powers was living in the house by himself. Two of Hickory's teachers were a husband and wife, who preferred to find their own accommodation. A third teacher lived with his girlfriend. Gavin had found all this out by the most obvious means—asking Beth, who had launched into a seemingly endless discourse on the more private details of her teachers. Eventually, Gavin had gently put a finger to her lips. He'd walked away amused, wondering if Hickory's schoolteachers were aware their private lives were under such close observation all the time.

Kerry was right. Powers had left a light on. But the drapes were tightly drawn behind the closed windows, allowing only cracks of light to escape. After making sure as best they could that no-one was watching, the three vaulted the low, sagging fence and moved quickly into the deeper shadows of a side wall. There they waited again, expecting to hear someone call out a challenge.

'Has he got a dog?' Kerry whispered fiercely.

'It's a bit late to worry about that!' Michael hissed back, annoyed they hadn't considered it before.

But no ferocious animals leapt out to attack them. Michael waited a few moments more, then led them around the back. As they went he tried peering through the tiny gaps between the curtains, but each time he dropped away from the window shaking his head with frustration. They did a complete circuit of the house, ending at the back door. He put his hand on the knob, but didn't turn it.

'I say if it's unlocked we go in and have a quick look around.'

'What if he comes home early?' Kerry said, glancing around.

'He won't.'

'What about a burglar alarm?'

'It'd be the only one for a thousand kilometres around. Besides, if the door isn't locked, he's hardly going to have an alarm set, is he?'

'For Christ's sake, Michael,' Gavin said impatiently, pushing him aside and grabbing the doorknob himself. The door swung inwards with a faint creaking. Immediately, a strong smell drifted out to greet them. Kerry wrinkled her nose.

'Well, there's fact number one about Powers,' she said. 'The man lives like a pig.'

'Pigs are quite clean,' Gavin muttered absently, moving cautiously inside. Like most of the old houses in that area, it had an enclosed back porch

250

which doubled as a laundry and had the toilet at the opposite end. An inner flyscreen door led into the kitchen and it was there Powers had left the light on. A square of illumination fell into the porch, but did little to push back the gloom. Michael and Kerry crowded in after Gavin, who went straight to the flyscreen and let himself in.

'Anybody home?' he called softly. No-one answered and he turned to Michael with a shrug. 'Well, here's your big chance.' Without replying, the others followed him into the kitchen.

'Let's not take too long,' Kerry said. 'I can't believe the stink in this place. Powers must have no sense of smell.'

'He's not the best of housekeepers,' Michael agreed, running a finger along a benchtop. It was covered with a layer of dust and grime. He looked around the room. Everything seemed to be in its place, stacked on shelves or hanging off hooks. The sink was clear. Yet the whole kitchen appeared unclean. 'There's something wrong here, but I can't quite pick it.'

Gavin's voice came from the lounge room. 'It's the same here. The place is filthy. Still, that's not exactly a crime.'

Michael left Kerry in the kitchen to see the lounge for himself. The rooms were separated by an arch and enough light from the kitchen spilled through for them to be able to see. There, dust coated everything except for one lounge chair, the cushions shiny in patches from use.

'It must be his favourite chair,' Michael said. 'Obviously it's the only one he uses.'

Gavin was pushing open a connecting door that

led into a bedroom. Inside, a single bed was roughly made. Beside it a small table held a wind-up alarm clock and nothing else. He bent down to examine the clock more closely and saw it was stopped. Clicking his tongue in annoyance Gavin checked the drapes were drawn closed, then flicked on the light. Michael came to the doorway, a worried look on his face, and watched him.

'Might as well,' Gavin said, shrugging and gesturing towards the lightswitch. 'No-one can see us. How can anyone tell it's not Powers in here?'

'You know what these country towns are like by now. A nosy neighbour might remember he's supposed to be at the library at this time.'

'I get the impression Mr Powers is the sort of fellow the neighbours might watch, but they couldn't give a damn if an army of burglars went through his house. He's not a very likeable man. Beth tells me everybody at the school hates him—even the other teachers don't seem that well disposed towards him. Anyway, I just got suspicious about something and I wanted to see it properly. Now I'm glad I did. Look at this.' Michael moved closer as Gavin grasped one corner of the bed-clothes and gently pulled them back a way. 'See? Look at the line of dust across the pillow.'

'I don't get it,' Michael frowned. 'These covers haven't been moved for ages. The bed hasn't been slept in for a long time. He must use another bed somewhere.'

Gavin shook his head. 'This is the only bedroom. Either he sleeps on the floor, or maybe on that chair.'

Just then Kerry called them from the kitchen,

stopping them discussing it further. They hurried back and found her standing in front of an open pantry. The stench of refuse and spoiled food was even stronger.

'Check this out,' she said, moving back to give them room.

There were assorted tins of food and preserves, but also several packets of biscuits, flours and grains, and bottles of sauces. The tins were still okay, but in all the perishable food the rotting process was well advanced. Thick clumps of green mould had taken hold wherever they could.

'God,' Michael choked, pulling a face. 'Why doesn't he throw it out?'

'That's not the question.' Kerry looked at him seriously. 'Why doesn't he *eat* it? And the refrigerator's locked, too. I don't understand that.'

'How do you lock a refrigerator?' Gavin asked, moving over to it. He quickly checked the outside of the door and found nothing, then he tested it, pulling gently at first, then with increasing strength with each attempt. When it still didn't open he gave Kerry and Michael a look, then heaved on the door. It opened suddenly, the door-seal separating with a sticky, ripping noise. A new, putrid stink of decomposing food filled the air and Gavin, gagging on the smell, backed away from the refrigerator.

'Christ!' he said, putting a hand to his nose. 'It smells like something's dead in there.'

It was worse than the pantry. All the food kept in the refrigerator was perishable and everything was well and truly rotted and decayed. It was a sickly, sour combination of curdled milk, shrivelled vegetables and tainted meats.

'This guy doesn't know how to put the garbage out,' Michael said, indicating with a pained expression for Gavin to reseal the door.

'No, I just *told* you,' Kerry said wonderingly. 'I reckon he doesn't know how to *eat*. At some stage in the past, even though he had all this food, he stopped eating—and he doesn't care about the mess.'

Michael nodded slowly, accepting her idea. 'Then he doesn't know how to sleep, either. Gavin had a hunch and checked the bedroom. The bed hasn't been slept in for a long time.'

Kerry went still as another thought came to her. 'Now *I've* got a hunch,' she said, and began opening the drawers, searching.

'What are you looking for?' Michael asked.

'I'm looking for—' Kerry stopped, staring down into the drawer she just opened. 'No, I'm not. I found them.' She reached in and pulled something out, holding it up for them to see.

'What is it?'

'Insulin,' she said simply.

'His insulin?' Michael looked at Gavin. 'That's right, I forgot to tell you. Powers is a diabetic.' He turned back to Kerry. 'Shouldn't that stuff be in the fridge, too?'

'Yes, this batch will be ruined, but that's not the point. He's not *taking* it.' Kerry rummaged through the drawer some more. 'Hell, there must be two or three years worth of the stuff here. It's amazing.' She pulled out another vial and held it up. 'I can tell you, because of the type and grade of this insulin, that Powers' condition is pretty

severe. If he wasn't to take his regular dosage—
and I know he injects it, because he buys needles
from me—I'd expect him to become very ill and
maybe even die within a short period of time.'
Kerry gestured down at the open drawer. 'But
judging by this, he hasn't injected himself for
years. He *should* be dead!'

'That's crazy.' Gavin went over and looked in the
drawer. It was filled with unused insulin and packets
of needles. 'How the hell does he keep going?'

'I can see something in this, you know,' Michael
said quietly. 'He doesn't need to eat—he may not
even know he's *supposed* to eat. I doubt that, but
it would explain why he seems to be ignoring the
food already in here. I wouldn't mind betting he
doesn't need to drink, either. And when he comes
home in the evening he doesn't do anything
except sit in that chair and wait for the sun to rise
again—because he doesn't need to sleep. I'll take
another guess, too. That his personal hygiene
sucks—'

'I remember Beth saying something like that
once,' Gavin broke in. 'I was going to snap at her,
but Beth's a good kid. If she says the guy smells,
then he probably stinks pretty bad. How do you
know that, Michael? What are you getting at?'

'Look, Powers doesn't pass a close inspection
like we're doing now. That's why the windows are
shut and the curtains are drawn, but he's either
getting lax about the back door or maybe he
doesn't even understand the concept of locking it.'
Michael paused and looked around, as if
confirming his theory again for himself before
daring to tell the others.

'I think Powers is doing a very bad job of being *a human being*.'

Kerry and Gavin stared at him. A dreadful understanding came over both of them, reluctantly at first, but Michael already looked convinced and they were surrounded by some incredible clues. It needed an incredible answer.

The moment was broken by the unmistakable sound of a car pulling up in front of the house. Michael swore and rushed quickly to the lounge. He forced himself to keep calm, and moved one of the curtains aside a fraction so he could see out.

'Oh-oh, we're in a shitload of trouble. It's a police car. There's only one person in it, as far as I can see. I'll bet it's Riley.'

'How the hell does he know we're here?' Kerry said desperately.

'Maybe he doesn't—*Wait*, Gavin!' Michael had seen Gavin reaching to turn off the bedroom light. 'He might not know we're in here, but if he sees that light go off he'll know somebody is. He hasn't moved yet. Let's just sit tight a second and see what he does.'

They waited tensely, expecting Michael to tell them to run at any moment. He stayed with his eye to the gap in the curtain. It wasn't long before he announced with a relieved sigh, 'He's lighting a cigarette. He must be waiting for Powers to come back. He's certainly not acting as though he knows we're in here, thank God.'

'Do you think he's the same as Powers?' Kerry asked in a small voice.

'No, he's not weird like Powers. Not from what

we've seen, anyway. But if he comes visiting here, then he must know what Powers *is*.'

'Christ, and what's that, Michael?' Gavin asked, sounding despairing.

'I don't know, Gavin. All I *do* know is he's not like us. He's not the same as you or me.'

Gavin was nodding tiredly, pinching the bridge of his nose between his thumb and finger. Then he seemed to recover. 'Okay, okay—look, we've got to get out of here. We'll have to go straight out the back door, over the fence at the back and into the house behind. That'll get us into the next street and Riley shouldn't see us.'

'Powers will know somebody's been here,' Kerry said, thinking of the bedroom light.

'Maybe he'll think it was kids. They seem to hate him enough. I'm surprised it hasn't happened before now.'

'Let's get going,' Michael said, coming away from the window. 'The library doesn't close for another thirty minutes yet, but Riley's here waiting. Maybe he knows something we don't— like Powers is closing early.'

Moving carefully to avoid any loudly creaking floorboards in the old house, the three went back outside and stood behind the house. Michael winced as the back door squeaked again as he closed it.

'Why'd you bother with the door?' Gavin whispered.

'No sense in giving us away too easily. He might just think he left his own bedroom light on—you never know.'

'We couldn't be so lucky,' Gavin muttered.

257

'Come on. As long as we walk in a straight line to the rear, the house will hide us from Riley.' He set off, leading the way, then paused at the back fence.

'What now?' Michael asked impatiently.

'This time I *am* checking for dogs.'

'I'll tackle a dog any time, before I take on Riley.' Michael jumped the fence then turned to help Kerry over. They hurried down the side of the house. Just metres from the road, and comparative safety, Michael kicked something in the darkness. It rattled over the ground with a metallic clanging and they all broke into a run. Michael waited for someone to yell out to them, but instead he heard the sound of a window being slammed closed, and a few moments later a front door hastily crashing shut. In the stillness of the night, above his own panting breaths, came the clicking of a lock.

Out on the road they slowed to a walk.

'They're more scared of us,' Michael said, catching his breath even though they'd only sprinted a short way.

'It seems like everybody's locking their doors now,' Gavin said. 'Maybe we're the only dumb bastards who don't know what the hell is going on around here.'

They stayed close together, walking along the street and half-expecting to see the lights of Riley's police car swing into the intersection at the end. Michael didn't know what they should do if that happened. The further they got from Powers' house the better he felt, so he wanted to keep moving. He nearly groaned aloud when Gavin suddenly stopped and went tense.

258

'Look,' he said tightly.

Kerry and Michael followed his gaze, but couldn't see anything unusual. There was just the same, silent row of houses.

'See that light?' Gavin pointed. 'Not on this street, but the next—through the trees at the back of this house? That's got to be Elaine's place. There's a light on inside Elaine Sanders' house.'

Kerry felt a chill of fear. 'Maybe it's been on all the time and we didn't see it before because it's at the back.'

'Maybe.' Gavin moved closer to the fence and tried to see past the home in between. 'I think we should have a look. We can cut through this yard and hop their back fence.'

Kerry felt someone squeeze her arm. It was Michael. 'Don't worry,' he said. 'We'll just take a peek, this time. It's probably someone looking after the house, or a relative who came here for the funeral.'

They couldn't be so lucky a third time with dogs. As they crept down the driveway towards the rear fence Kerry looked at the front porch of the house they were passing. She noted the closed front door and thought that as it was a chilly night it wasn't so unusual that people would be shutting up their homes against the cold. But at the same time Gavin was right. Hickory was supposed to be a safe place, and front doors were normally left open until the owners went to bed. Tonight every home looked closed up tight. It was as if the town was instinctively aware something bad was going on, an unspoken cognisance that it was time to lock the doors and windows—and not to go outside if something strange was happening in the street. Kerry hadn't heard anything said in her pharmacy, but then again, being regarded as a newcomer she probably wasn't entitled to be privy to such things. Kerry liked to believe it was more the intuitive closing of ranks unique to a small community like Hickory. Everyone knew what to do without saying anything.

Then she saw the dog sitting on the front step, watching them.

Kerry nearly let out a cry, expecting, as her eyes met the animal's, that it would raise the alarm. 'There's a dog on the porch,' she hissed at Michael, clutching at the sleeve of his jacket. Gavin heard and the three of them froze. The dog's black eyes watched them stonily, two glaring points reflecting the distant streetlight. Then came a noise—a slow, rhythmic thumping—and Kerry couldn't help a giggle of relief. The animal was wagging its tail.

'Some guard dog,' she whispered.

'Don't complain,' Michael said. 'I didn't see—'

At the sound of their voices the dog began to growl and laboriously hauled itself to its feet. It was obvious now it was an older animal, unsure of what it was seeing until the unknown voices told it the three people were intruders. It began to bark, a husky, deliberate challenge.

'Keep going,' Gavin urged, running to the back fence. This was a low wire mesh, only a token gesture marking the boundary. All three of them hurdled it easily. Michael hoped the dog wouldn't be bothered to do the same. They heard someone yelling at it to be quiet.

260

'I don't think we're very good at this,' Michael said, looking back at the fence and waiting to see if the dog was pursuing them. No-one answered him. Gavin was staring at the lit window in Elaine Sanders' home. He could see now there was no way they would have missed it passing by before. In the minutes since they'd last gone past, somebody had come visiting. The thought inexplicably made his stomach tighten with fear. Something was wrong.

He recognised the window as the kitchen's, and the curtains were pulled aside. But because the house was mounted on short stumps the sill was too high for them to see inside. He motioned for Michael to give him a hand, leading him over to an ornate wrought-iron bench. Between them they carried it beneath the window and the two men climbed up to stand side by side and look cautiously over the sill.

'My God,' Gavin whispered. Kerry heard his voice tremor with awe.

'What is it?' she hissed, and began to push her way up onto the bench. Michael turned and looked at her, the shocked expression on his face made plain by the light spilling out of the house. Kerry could tell he was going to stop her and say she shouldn't look, but she determinedly stepped between them and stood on her toes to see. The scene inside the kitchen was enough to make her legs go weak, and she had to grip the wooden sill hard to prevent herself from falling back.

Elaine Sanders' corpse sat at the kitchen table, holding a hand of playing cards. On the other side of the table sat Mrs North. Her face was set into such a grimace of madness and terror that drool was escaping from her slack mouth and tears ran freely down her cheeks. Mrs North held cards too, but she was locked in staring horror at the figure in front of her. The corpse's head was tilted down, as if studying her own cards, but the face was expressionless and blank—the look of the dead.

Time seemed to stand still, then Kerry jumped violently and stifled a scream when she felt hands grasp her around the waist. It was Michael, helping her down off the bench. Gavin stood behind him, his white face clear in the darkness. She hadn't even noticed them leaving the window.

'We've got to help her!' Kerry hissed desperately.

'There's no point,' Gavin said calmly, though he felt anything but calm. 'Did you see the look on her face? She's snapped—lost her mind, I'm sure of it. She wouldn't know it if we *did* help her. We've got to be strong and walk away. We have to think of ourselves, now.'

Kerry turned to Michael for support, but he nodded gravely. 'I think we'll just say we've seen enough for one night, and go home,' he said quietly. He looked pale, too—and as frightened as Kerry and Gavin.

Kerry seemed about to protest, then she whispered sadly, 'God, I think we're *all* going mad.'

13

GOING INTO THE library was a spur-of-the-moment decision for Gavin, something he certainly hadn't set out to do. When the three of them returned to the pharmacy car park Michael suggested going back to his house again to discuss what they'd seen. Gavin turned down the offer. He didn't want another late night filled with so many frustrating questions, and no real answers. He was also feeling shaken and more than a little scared. Somehow he had a gut feeling—despite not having any proof—that Elaine Sanders' corpse wasn't one of Michael's 'paranormal anomalies' or the result of any disturbed magnetic fields. Gavin thought it was something more deliberate than that, something which wasn't a random act of nature or God. Something—or *somebody*—had brought her from the grave. As to *why*, he couldn't begin to guess.

Gavin wanted to get back home to Linda and Beth. He wanted to be protective, although he had no idea how—or really *what* they needed protecting from. His uneasiness grew when he heard Kerry ask Michael if she could sleep on his lounge again, and Michael readily agree. Gavin couldn't blame Kerry for not feeling safe alone in her own home.

So he pedalled off, waving goodbye. Then the idea came to him to detour past the library again. Gavin wanted to see if Powers was still there, or if he knew Riley was waiting for him at his home. It wasn't quite 8.30 p.m. and Gavin could reach the library before then.

The library was a small extension of the town's municipal building. It had rows of casement windows opening out at forty-five degree angles and Gavin needed to position himself exactly to see if Powers sat at the reception desk without blatantly looking through the front door— although the windows still being open was indication enough that the library hadn't closed for the night. Bright fluorescent light, starkly white against the darkness of the rest of the building, showed orderly lines of bookshelves and, near the front door, Powers' bowed head. Gavin figured the librarian must be reading something on the desk in front of him.

'So, you don't know you have a visitor waiting at your house, unless Riley's early,' Gavin mused, undecided what to do next. He'd intended riding straight home, but another idea was coming to him.

Gavin told himself he was casual and unafraid, but he also couldn't deny the nervous fluttering in his stomach. He rode his bicycle onto the footpath at the library's front door, dismounted and put the bike on its stand. Out of the corner of his eye, he noticed Powers look up at the sound of the metal stand scraping on the concrete. Trying to stay nonchalant Gavin walked to the double glass doors and pushed. The door rattled, but didn't budge. It was locked. It was enough to make Gavin panic a little—what was he supposed to do now? Just walk away? Or ask Powers to open up on the strength that it wasn't quite 8.30 p.m. yet? He tried the other door tentatively and was relieved to see it swing aside.

Inside the library the air was as chilly as the night outside. Powers wasn't bothering with any heating for his patrons' comfort and, Gavin realised, it would have been pointless with all the open windows. Immediately he noticed a faint smell of decay, a foulness lingering about the room. That would be Powers himself, the stench of his home ingrained into his clothing and even his skin. Gavin wondered if he would have noticed it normally, without knowing what he did now about the man. There was something else to think about, too: perhaps Powers was aware of the problem, which would explain the open windows on such a cool night. But surely the answer would be to keep himself and his surroundings cleaner? Not attempting inadequate solutions such as opening the windows instead? Gavin remembered

Michael's comment, *'I think Powers is doing a very bad job of being a human being.'* This might be another example of Powers behaving strangely—even illogically—as if he didn't understand a basic, simple concept, or was incapable of figuring out an easy answer to a simple problem.

Startled, Gavin realised Powers was looking at him, waiting for him to speak. He saw the librarian's expression was almost blank, with only a trace of annoyance, perhaps, in the dark eyes.

'Ah, good evening. I would like to join the library. It's one of those things I've been meaning to get around to and never have. I was just going past and I thought—'

'I'm just about to close,' Powers cut him off. His voice was as devoid of expression as his face. A flat, inflectionless sound.

'Well, I haven't read anything for ages—much as I'd like to—so it'll only take me a moment to choose something. I could probably do that while you're closing up.'

Powers' gaze didn't falter. It was so unnerving the way those eyes stared at him. Gavin found himself waiting for the other man to blink. A silence stretched out, then Powers turned away and opened a drawer.

'You'll have to fill out this card.' He put it flat on the desk and slid it towards Gavin. Leaning forward to take it Gavin suffered a stronger whiff of Powers' stench. It took an effort not to pull back involuntarily. Without being asked, Powers placed a pen within reach. Gavin quickly scribbled his name and address and gave the card back.

'Thank you. I appreciate this. It's good to have

a library, even in a small town like this, don't you think?'

'Books are a source of power,' Powers said cryptically. 'You may have two fiction and two non-fiction titles for two weeks.'

'Ah—right. Thank you.' Gavin was momentarily nonplussed by Powers' reference to 'sources of power'.

The empty stare came back and another silence threatened, so Gavin moved towards the shelves. There weren't many and they were all placed so Powers could turn and keep watch over them, if need be. Gavin wasn't trying to hide behind them, anyway. He wanted a chance to study his quarry without the other man knowing. Pulling down a few books at random Gavin made a show of riffling through the pages, but he stood with his body angled so he could look over the tops of the covers at Powers.

The librarian sat unmoving at the desk, staring at the spot Gavin had occupied. As Gavin watched, Powers' head slowly drooped downwards, like a man falling asleep.

How the hell does this guy get away with it? Gavin thought, feeling pressured and unsure of himself. *Surely somebody in this damned town got concerned sometime that their local librarian—and teacher, for that matter—isn't anywhere fucking near normal! What's wrong with these people?* Gavin wasn't sure what he'd been hoping to achieve by coming into the library. Michael was trying to tell them Powers may not even be human. *Not human, for Christ's sake! What is he, then? Did he step out of a UFO? Maybe we should have checked the carport for a flying saucer.* Realising his mind was filling with wild ideas, Gavin told himself maybe he wasn't acting so normal either. The trouble was, Michael Garrett's crazy theories were looking better and better, while Gavin's tendency to find more common-sense answers was losing ground. He took down another book and stared at the cover without taking in any of the words. *It's the insulin. That's what's bugging the hell out of me. Powers could be as nutty as a fruitcake about his food and the refrigerator. He could eat a burger at Mal Bartell's store three times a day and survive. He'd probably get mighty unhealthy—and he sure as hell looks unhealthy—but he'd survive. And the hygiene thing could be the product of a totally unbalanced mind. The man's going insane and no-one's got the courage to do anything about it. But the damned insulin's a different thing altogether. Kerry says he shouldn't be alive without it—and I believe her. And he can't get it anywhere else. So how come he's alive?*

The answer is—he shouldn't be.

Michael says Powers is doing a very bad job of being a human being. Well, add to that he's doing a very bad job of being a diabetic, too.

A small, beeping alarm sounded and Powers stirred, thumbing his wristwatch to stop the alarm. He stood and turned around, looking for Gavin.

'You have to go.'

'Okay. I've found these already.' Gavin held up two books and hoped they weren't anything inane or inappropriate, he'd taken so little notice of what he'd been looking at. It was a relief to see they were both military history books. 'Do you want a hand closing the windows?'

'No.' Powers worked his way along the line of windows, pulling each one shut. Gavin went to the reception desk and waited for him.

When Powers came back he sat and flipped open the book jackets, removing the identity cards in each. Then he stamped the return date on the flap. Gavin saw that each time the stamp was upside-down. Powers didn't seem to notice.

'Actually, we were on the same search team looking for Ainslie McGregor, do you remember?'

Powers appeared to consider the question for a long time, then answered simply, 'Yes.'

'I was surprised Doug Riley didn't continue the search the next morning either—not that I know of, anyway. Did he—ah, say anything to you?'

'The child's parents found a note. He ran away. They are looking in the city.'

'Really? That's news to me—good news though, I suppose.' Gavin frowned and tried to sound puzzled, instead of totally disbelieving, which is how he really felt. 'But who gave him a ride to the city? Everybody knew what was going on. The highway here's a dead end. It would have to be somebody from Hickory, and I would've thought everyone knew the kid was missing and that there were search parties out.'

'I don't know Mr—' Powers faltered and looked down at the membership card. 'Mr Packer. Perhaps Doug Riley can visit you and talk to you about it?' Powers' manner was so blank and expressionless it was impossible to judge exactly, but Gavin felt a thrill of unease. Had he detected a tone of menace in Powers' words?

Is he threatening me? Is it a crime to ask questions

now? He smiled and picked up the books. 'I'll see Sergeant Riley soon, one way or another I'm sure. I'll ask him about it then. Well, thank you and goodnight.'

Gavin turned on his heel and left, feeling Powers' eyes boring into his back as he pushed through the entrance. Outside he didn't bother wrestling the books under his arm to ride the bike one-handed. The books were large and glossy-covered, and he was afraid they'd slip and drop. Instead, Gavin kicked the bike off its stand and wheeled it beside him as he walked. When he'd gone a fair distance and felt that he'd be mostly concealed by the darkness, Gavin dared to look back at the library. Powers was still sitting at the desk, his head drooping towards the flat surface again.

It's weird. He's like some battery-operated toy— except the batteries are wearing down. He can't have been like this all the time. It must have only started happening recently. Gavin didn't like the next thought, but he couldn't stop it: *Like the corpses and ghosts—and the UFOs.* He tilted his head back and looked up at the sky. *My God, what am I thinking? Corpses! Is the world going crazy? Am I going crazy?*

He shook the thoughts out of his head and again considered wedging the books under his arm and mounting the bicycle, but now Gavin felt more like walking and thinking things over for himself without Kerry or Michael throwing new ideas at him before he'd had a chance to contemplate the old ones. He didn't feel he needed to get home to his family so urgently now he knew Riley was

270

waiting at Powers' home and the librarian himself was still at work. The walk home would clear his mind and his lungs, and flush his clothing, too. Gavin felt foul from the mess in Powers' home, as if the stench had permeated his clothes, too.

He wryly hoped he wouldn't run into Jake Sanders walking the streets, and with a shock remembered the first night after Jake's death, when Beth had claimed she'd seen him walking past the house.

Why didn't I remember that before? What the hell have I been thinking of? He hurried his pace, then changed his mind and mounted his bike, awkwardly holding the books against his hip.

Gavin got more frightened when he got home. The place seemed empty, although the lights were on. The back door was unlocked and he was momentarily annoyed before his anxiety took over. 'Hello?' he said quietly, his voice echoing through the house. Pushing down his panic he tiptoed through the kitchen and along the hallway. Beth's bedroom door was slightly ajar and Gavin put his head inside. Her bed was still made. It was close to nine o'clock and Beth should have been asleep by now, with school the next day. His fear mounting, Gavin tried the master bedroom. A faint shaft of light fell onto the bed from the doorway as he pushed it open. He was relieved to see Linda and Beth curled up together under the covers. An open book lay beside Linda's head. Gavin guessed Beth had become scared, or maybe suffered a relapse of

271

grief over Jake's death, and Linda had taken her into their bed for a while.

Gavin thought, *I can arrange Jake to come over for a visit, if you think it might help.* He didn't think either Linda or Beth would find that very funny. He wasn't so amused himself.

Normally Gavin would transfer Beth back to her own bed, once she was asleep, but tonight he didn't have the heart. Linda looked deeply asleep too, which wasn't usual, so he didn't want to disturb her either. And finally, Gavin wasn't sure he would sleep himself, thinking of Beth in a separate room. Things were really getting to him, he realised, when he wanted his whole family to sleep in the same room. Tonight that wasn't possible without making a lot of noise moving Beth's bed into the master bedroom—and it would probably cause an argument when Linda found out why he was being so cautious and revealed he hadn't told her the whole truth before. The simple solution was for him to sleep in Beth's bed tonight, and face the argument in the morning.

Gavin felt drained with relief, knowing his family was all right. Finding the house open and the kitchen empty like that had been a nasty shock. The refrigerator offered one cold bottle of home-brewed beer and Gavin gratefully took the top off. Ignoring the cold he went back outside and sat at the garden setting, pouring the beer into a pewter mug he used especially for drinking his home brew. After a minute his nightsight adjusted completely and he could look up at a carpet of stars. They seemed so beautiful and innocent, but now Gavin couldn't help believing the stars must harbour unfriendly things, too. Just like the way the world, with all its beauty, was also home to some of the most terrible places and people.

'What are you doing here?' he asked the sky. 'What do you want?'

Nothing gave him an answer, so Gavin took a deep swig of his beer. A noise from the house made him turn around, thinking Linda had awoken and come looking for him, but it was only one of their cats pushing past the flyscreen door to come into the backyard. This cat was a near-stray, willing to eat any food offered but still very wary of people. Gavin put his hand close to the ground, clicked his fingers and softly called the cat's name. The animal stopped dead on hearing his voice, and stared across the yard at him. Its feline eyes shone a brilliant green while it stayed frozen in mid-step, considering obeying the call. Gavin stayed absolutely still too, not wanting to intimidate the cat with any sudden movements.

He was so engrossed—and now facing the wrong direction—that he didn't see the dazzling falling star streak across the sky. It seemed to come to earth just a short distance from Gavin's home.

14

'DO YOU THINK Gavin was all right?' Kerry asked, settling down on the couch, Monty curled up at her feet.

'Just stunned, like us,' Michael said sitting next to her. 'What an incredible sight.' He couldn't stop a shiver running through him. 'I don't blame Gavin for wanting to get home to his family.'

'I couldn't be alone tonight, either,' Kerry said quietly. 'What's going on, Michael? What's happening in this town?'

'I wish I knew. What started out as a bit of an interesting mystery—like those lights behind your house—has turned into a nightmare. And we can't call for help, by the way.'

'Why not? I was just about to ask—isn't it about

time we told somebody about all this? Haven't we seen enough?'

Michael gave her an apologetic look, then explained what he'd told Gavin about how they were cut off from any form of communication to the outside world. He didn't want to scare her, but he had to go on and explain his suspicions of Doug Riley and how it could be dangerous to try and leave town. Kerry was appalled.

'That's unbelievable! It's like we're prisoners in our own town.'

'That seems to be the idea.'

'Hey—but what about your friend? Is she going to be able to come *in*?'

Michael looked worried. 'I don't know what's happened there. Anne should be here by now. I guess she must have changed her mind and turned around and gone home again. Now she can't get through on the telephone to explain.'

'Are you concerned about her?'

'I guess I am, but I'm also pretty sure she's okay. Even if all our worst fears are true, I figure the worst thing that could have happened to Anne is that Riley somehow stopped her getting into Hickory. A roadblock, or a "road closed" sign. Something like that.' He shrugged. 'At the same time, I'm glad she hasn't got here. We've got enough to worry about, without Anne walking through the door and adding to our troubles.'

Kerry watched him toying with his empty coffee cup. 'Do you miss her?' she asked softly.

He sighed. 'I used to. Up until not so long ago Annie would be on my mind all the time, driving me crazy. But I know we did the right thing splitting up. We used to have some wild arguments over nothing.' He went on to describe the last months of his relationship with Anne Shannon. Kerry listened sympathetically, without interrupting. Michael ended by saying, 'To be honest, lately I've found myself thinking about you, more than anything.' The words came out before he could stop himself. He looked up at Kerry and smiled wryly. 'Sorry. That's the last sort of thing you need to hear right now. I shouldn't have said it. Forget it.'

Kerry was flustered, her face turning slightly red. 'No, it's okay. I—I like you a lot, Michael.' She laughed self-consciously. 'You're right, though. Your timing could be a little better.'

'Don't worry, I'm not going to do anything stupid—' Michael held up his hands and shook his head ruefully. 'I should have kept my big mouth shut. You'll be quite safe on the lounge tonight, okay? I won't come creeping in during the middle of the night.'

Kerry smiled and reached down, patting Monty. 'I've got my trusty guard dog to protect my maidenly virtue.'

There was an awkward silence, then Michael clapped his hands together. 'Right, now that I've finished making an utter fool of myself, what do you want to do tonight? Not that we have a great choice of course, without any television or radio. We can watch another video, if you like. I could suggest we play cards or something, but to be honest my heart wouldn't be in it.'

'I brought a book I've been reading with my stuff from the house. I thought I might curl up and read, if you don't mind.' After they'd left Gavin they'd done a detour of their own to Kerry's house to pick up Monty and some over-night things for Kerry.

'No, it sounds like a great idea. I'll put on some quiet music. I've got a book, too. I've been trying to finish it for months.'

Michael offered Kerry a glass of wine, which she accepted. He had one himself, having run out of beer and not feeling like going down to Mc-Gann's. He put a Van Morrison disc on the player, retrieved his book from the bedroom and sat on the single lounge chair. Kerry had already put her feet up. She briefly looked up from her book to smile at him. It was a slightly sad smile.

'Are you okay?' he asked.

'Yes. It's just that this is nice, sitting here with you and my dog, relaxing reading a book. I wish all this other mess wasn't happening, that's all.'

'Try and put it out of your mind for tonight. There's nothing we can do right now. I'm not sure there's anything we can do anyway—except sit tight and see what happens.'

She nodded, sighing. 'That's why I brought the book. I thought it would be a good way to keep my mind occupied.'

They spent the next few hours comfortably in each other's company. Michael tried to read, but couldn't concentrate. Kerry seemed to be more relaxed and enjoying her book, so to avoid her feeling obliged to make conversation Michael pre-tended to read, staring at the pages while he thought over everything. It was hard to fit all the pieces together and it was tiring to try. Finally Michael felt his eyes drooping once too often, so he yawned and stood up.

'Bedtime for me,' he said, stretching. He looked down at her and became serious. 'Look, I might as well make an even bigger fool of myself. If you want to share my bed instead of sleeping out here, you're more than welcome. I wish I could promise to behave myself, but I'm not sure I could—I thought I'd better warn you.'

'What a romantic,' Kerry said quietly, smiling. Her face turned grave as she considered his offer. 'Okay, I'll be in soon. I'll put some water out for Monty, and his rug, and I'll borrow your bathroom again.'

'Sure,' he said easily, belying his suddenly racing heart. His tiredness had vanished. Michael went into the bedroom, turned on the bedside light and pulled the curtains closed. Then he sat on the bed, uncertain what to do next. He listened to Kerry fussing around in the kitchen and talking to Monty. There was a splashing as she brushed her teeth in the bathroom.

He stood again when she walked into the room. Telling himself there was no point in denying what he wanted to do—or how he felt—Michael put his arms around Kerry's waist and pulled her close. She wrapped her arms around his neck and stared searchingly into his eyes, so he lowered his face and kissed her long and tenderly. When he drew back he said, softly, 'Are you sure about this? I don't want you to do anything unless you really want to.'

278

Kerry hugged him harder, putting her lips next to his ear. She whispered, 'Let's do it now, while we can.'

Michael wasn't sure what she meant. Right then, he didn't want to ask.

She was wearing a windcheater, shirt and jeans. Michael tugged the windcheater over her head, then kissed her again while he unbuttoned the shirt, pulling it back off her shoulders so it fell to the floor. Kerry wasn't wearing anything underneath. Impatiently, he dragged his own shirt and jumper over his head then drew her against him again, feeling her breasts and hardening nipples pressing into his chest. Kissing, they lowered themselves to the bed. They stayed locked together for a while, touching their lips, then Michael moved his mouth down her neck and onto her breasts. Kerry moaned quietly when he teased her nipple with his tongue. He managed to undo the button and zipper on her jeans with one hand, then stopped caressing her so he could pull them off properly. Her panties came with them and Kerry giggled as the bundled clothing caught around her ankles. The jeans turned inside-out as Michael yanked them off her feet. He stared hungrily down at her as she lay completely naked in front of him, then lowered himself on top of her. Kerry pushed him sideways as he came down and wrapped her legs around one of his, rubbing her groin against the fabric of his jeans while she kissed him. Michael held her tight and helped her move hard into him. He could feel her becoming warm and moist.

Soon she said huskily, 'Get undressed, for God's

sake.' He rolled away onto his back and quickly stripped off the rest of his clothes, then came back against her, pushing himself between her legs and sliding one hand down to touch her. Kerry's breathing quickened and Michael could tell she was getting very excited, so he stayed like that, moving his fingers for her. It wasn't long before she suddenly shuddered and moaned, clasping Michael to her with an urgent strength. Then she slowly relaxed, releasing him.

'Wow,' she whispered. 'It's been a while. Hey, I knew this was a good idea,' she added, smiling teasingly at him.

'One of the best I've had,' he smiled back.

'Well, let's keep 'em coming.'

Later, they lay clinched together, drifting off to sleep. Then Michael remembered something.

'Kerry, what did you mean before?' he asked sleepily. 'That we should do this while we can?'

She took a while to reply. 'Well, what's going to happen to us, Michael? I mean, all of us? If we're not supposed to escape from the town. Are we all going to end up like Mrs North—terrified to the point of insanity? Or dead, like Elaine Sanders?' She paused and Michael felt her shiver. 'Maybe we're all just going to disappear, like that boy.'

'They can't make a whole town disappear,' he said soothingly, wishing he felt as confident as he sounded. 'At least we're aware something's going on, so that's in our favour. Don't worry, I don't think any of us are going to disappear.'

15

FOR NO REASON Gavin woke up in the middle of the night. He hadn't forced himself out of a dream, or needed to visit the toilet. Just opened his eyes and was instantly wide awake. And confused. Everything looked different, then the narrowness of the bed reminded Gavin he was in Beth's room. The whole house was deathly quiet. He wondered what had disturbed him.

He slipped out from under the blankets and, wearing only his underwear, padded softly into the hallway and down to the master bedroom. He could hardly see in the darkness, but the black square of the bedroom door told him it was open. He listened for the flushing of the toilet, in case Linda or Beth were there. Gavin was worried he would scare them by suddenly appearing out of the night as they stumbled back to the bed. Looking into his own room he tried to pick out the mounded bedclothes of figures asleep in the double bed, but in the gloom it was hard to see.

In fact, the bed looked empty.

His heart started to beat faster. Gavin pulled the door half-closed then fumbled along the wall of the hallway for the lightswitch. It would throw enough light into the bedroom without waking anyone still asleep. He found the switch and the hall was filled with a glare that blinded him momentarily. Squinting hard he went back to the bedroom door and gently pushed it open, gradually letting in more light until he could see the bed properly. With a shock he saw the covers pulled back. The bed was rumpled and empty.

Moving quickly now he left the bedroom and went to the bathroom door. No light showed beneath it, but that wasn't unusual. Gavin knocked softly and called, 'Linda? Are you in there? Beth?' No-one answered and he knocked harder, uncaring now that he might frighten them. 'Linda? Are you there?' Still there was no reply. Gavin could see there were no other lights on in the house, but he refused to believe the worst— that he was alone in the house—until he was sure. He hurried through to the kitchen, calling Linda's name as he went. He turned on the kitchen light, which illuminated the lounge room, too. Both rooms were empty.

Then he saw that the back door leading out to the yard was wide open. Gavin was sure he'd locked it before he went to bed.

A dread filled him and he rushed through the door, crashing the flywire screen against the wall. The chilly night air hit him, instantly covering his skin with goosebumps and making the hairs on his arms and neck rise. Having turned on all the lights in the house, Gavin's eyes now needed to adjust again to darkness. The night seemed impenetrably black.

'Linda! Beth! Where are you?' There was no answering call. Even the animals didn't stir. Where was Mandy, their labrador? He called the dog's name. Usually she would quickly materialise out of the darkness, wagging her tail and glad of the summons. Gavin waited, but the dog didn't appear. He whispered at the darkness, 'Christ, what's happening?' A strong shiver against the cold ran through him and Gavin realised he had to get dressed. He couldn't go racing off through the night looking for his family without any clothes on—although his first, desperate reactions made him want to run in every direction at once, yelling their names at the top of his voice. Fighting down his panic, he went back inside to Beth's room and quickly dressed. Then he went to his own room, switching the light on this time, to get a heavier jacket. Gavin took a moment to examine everything around him. Nothing looked suspicious or unusual. It simply appeared as if someone had left the bed unmade. Then he noticed a faint, but strange, smell in the air, which he couldn't recognise.

Shrugging the jacket on and finding a pair of gloves in the pocket, he went back to the kitchen and found his torch where it belonged under the sink. Testing the button, the globe flared brightly for a few seconds, then died to nothing. He hadn't replaced the batteries since the search for Ainslie McGregor, when the UFO had killed both his and Michael's torches. Cursing at the delay Gavin opened a drawer and scrabbled through the mess inside, picking out some second-hand batteries he'd kept more out of the habit of not being able to throw anything away, than expecting to get any real use out of them. Reloading the torch with these gave him a weak orange circle of light. It was better than nothing. He'd have to use the torch sparingly.

Heading for the back door again Gavin's eye fell on the wall-mounted telephone. Should he call someone? But who? Doug Riley was now the last person to approach, and that automatically discredited his partner, Constable Griffith, too. Really, Michael Garrett and Kerry Wentworth were the only people Gavin could trust, but it would take too long to call and get them out here. Suddenly it seemed *anything* would take too long—he had to get outside and start searching now.

Standing in the backyard he wondered just what the hell he was going to do. Who was he searching for? Just Linda and Beth? Had they suffered some sort of attack or hallucination, and wandering aimlessly, senselessly, through the night? Or had somebody come and taken them? The last idea left a sick feeling of fear in the pit of his stomach. Gavin again thought of the odd smell in the master bedroom, but couldn't come up with an explanation.

Trying to stay sane and practical—the urge to rush haphazardly off into the night still strong—Gavin started with a careful circuit of the house, using the glow from the lights still on inside to search the perimeter as far as he could. He'd nearly returned to the back door when he found something, and kicked it with his boot. Gavin immediately guessed what it was by the shape and feel of the thing, but he bent down and used a few seconds of his precious torch batteries to examine it more closely. It was a dead chicken, one of the bird's lifeless eyes a bright pin-point reflecting the light. There was no blood or ruffled feathers, as there would be if it had been killed by a predatory animal. Gavin buried his fingers under the fowl's feathers and felt the body. It was still warm beneath the insulation of the feathers. Allowing for the chill of the night, it hadn't been dead long at all.

Casting about he saw two more motionless bundles of feathers, so Gavin got up and went directly to the chicken coop. Using his torch again revealed only two birds remained alive, standing still and shocked-looking among the scattered carcasses of the rest of the brood. He didn't waste any more time there. His eyesight was good enough now to see some distance by the light of the stars and a thin, crescent moon. Gavin could see their milking cow, tethered on a long chain nearby, was still standing. He went over for a closer look and the animal shied away nervously from his approach. Gavin tried again—the cow was normally very comfortable with humans—but it kept as far distant as its chain allowed. At the same time he noticed movement nearby. It was the Packers' three sheep, their green eyes staring at him as they stood hard against the fence, poised to bolt. Obviously they, too, had been badly frightened by something.

Before he had a chance to assess what he'd found—and the fear growing inside him—Gavin heard a dog barking in the distance. He recognised Mandy's familiar bark and made himself stand still and listen. It came from directly behind the house, but a long way away. In that direction lay heavy bush that continued until the next canefields.

Gavin started to run, but immediately his ankle twisted on a tuft of grass and he nearly fell. He swore at the pain, but it wasn't too bad and after gingerly testing his weight on it he limped only a little. The worst problem was being slowed down: if he wanted to go any faster he'd have to use the torch, otherwise he might not be so lucky with the next near-accident. But Gavin didn't want to flatten the torch's batteries any more until he absolutely had to, so he compromised, leaving the flashlight off, but moving at a trot and expecting with each step to fall or trip on some obstacle. Mandy was barking constantly now, a steady yapping which told Gavin something was seriously wrong, but at least acted as a beacon for him.

At his back fence he took a chance on his sore ankle and lightly vaulted the barbed wire. From here on it was bushland. Gavin was reminded of the search for the lost child the other night. He became very conscious that this time he was alone.

Thick trees and bushes grabbed at his clothing

as he pushed his way through. The light was considerably reduced under the canopy of leaves, but Gavin persevered, holding his arms in front of his face as he had in the canefield and bludgeoning his way ahead. Frequently he stopped to listen again for a moment to make sure he was still heading in the right direction. He realised that if Mandy stopped barking he wouldn't have a hope of finding Linda and Beth—if that was what the dog was guiding him towards. He felt blood running down his cheek where a branch had scratched his skin. Now Gavin felt hot inside the jacket, but it was giving him good protection. He kept going, pushing hard and ignoring his breathing, which was coming in short pants. His muscles began to ache, too.

Then he saw a white glow filtering through the bush. It seemed to be coming from something high up and he immediately thought of the UFO they'd encountered in the canefield. Fighting against his urge to hurry, Gavin began to be more cautious. He would do his family no good by bursting into some situation and getting himself into trouble, too. Mandy's barking was loud and clear now. He was getting close.

The small clearing unexpectedly opened up before him. Though the light was brighter, warning he was drawing nearer to *something*, a thick line of bushes hid the open space until Gavin literally fell out of the last bushes. The sight waiting for him on the other side shocked him, leaving him on his hands and knees in the dirt as he stared uncomprehendingly at the scene.

The clearing was bathed in a white, unreal light

from directly overhead. Gavin couldn't see what caused it. On the other side was the dog, still barking furiously, but to no avail. In the centre Linda and Beth stood side by side. Their faces were blank and they held themselves like people in a trance. A grotesque figure was dancing in a tight circle around them, long lanky limbs flailing inexpertly at the air in what appeared to be a parody of graceful ballet. It was a man, dressed in flowing black robes like a priest. As he twisted and turned Gavin glimpsed a white neck-cloth, like a cravat, at his throat. The priest was muttering loudly and continuously, but each time his dancing brought him in front of his captives' faces, he leaned close and spat a question at them.

'*Will you burn?*' he hissed. Linda and Beth didn't move. The priest kept prancing, jigging to a mad melody in his head. He did another circle.

'*Will you dance with me?*' Throwing his head back, the priest howled a cackle of laughter. '*You know, to dance with me is to burn for me. My entire congregation danced in the flames.*'

He performed another circuit of incongruous dancing.

'*You should be joyous in your Choosing. Soothing my illness will bring you closer to your God. I can take you to your God.*' Standing before them the priest froze, cocking his head to one side and staring at the woman and her daughter, but his eyes were suddenly sightless as he looked instead at something within his mind. '*I have even been your God,*' he added, in an almost wistful tone. Then he snapped out of it and went back into the dancing.

288

The white light washed the colour out of everything, as if it could bleach the very life out of the soil of the clearing and the bush surrounding it. Mandy had seen Gavin and settled to a frightened and confused whining. The priest's shadow was a distorted black shape on the ground aping his frenzied movements.

Before the priest could complete another circle Gavin forced himself to act, climbing to his feet and staggering into the clearing. His steps felt leaden, the muscles in his legs straining as though he was wading through deep water.

'Stop! Leave them alone!' he called, his voice hoarse with a sudden feeling of utter exhaustion. 'What are you doing to them? Who the hell are you?'

The priest stopped in mid-step and stared at the intruder. The moment his eyes met Gavin's, any remaining ability Gavin had to move vanished, and he stood slumped and weakened. It needed all of his willpower to keep his head up and watch what would happen. The priest came towards him, not with the awkward dancing movement now, but with a graceful gliding motion, as if he wasn't even touching the ground. He came close, putting his face so close to Gavin's he expected to feel and smell the man's breath. But there was nothing. The priest's skin was white, like a corpse—bringing Gavin a frightening memory of Elaine Sanders sitting in her kitchen with Mrs North. The priest's eyes, however, glowed with a hot, unearthly life.

'I didn't bring you here. I don't want you.'

It took an immense effort for Gavin to choke out

a reply. 'Let my family go. Leave us alone. Who the fuck are you, anyway?'

'*You have disturbed me.*'

'I'm going to kill you, if you don't let them go.' Gavin knew in his heart the threat was empty. He wouldn't have been surprised if the priest laughed again, with the same insane cackling, but he replied matter-of-factly and seemed unmoved by Gavin's anger.

'*This is no business of yours. It is not your choice. It is I who Chooses.*'

'This is my family, you bastard! Let them go!'

'*They will become my family—and you will have no place among us.*'

Gavin felt tears of frustration and rage come into his eyes. 'Why are you doing this? What the hell have we got to do with you? With fucking any of all this?'

The priest drew back and regarded Gavin for a long moment. The dead face was briefly animated by a flicker of confusion and the strange glow in the eyes flared like a struck match. Then the features recomposed themselves into a flat, lifeless visage.

'*My brothers reject me in my illness. I must teach them with loud words, so they* must *listen and they* will *learn.*'

The priest continued to stare at Gavin as he moved away to stand next to Linda and Beth again. With all his strength Gavin tried to follow, begging his limbs to respond, to move. The only parts of his body to stir were the tears in his eyes, suddenly falling down his cheeks. He could only watch in anguish, his vision blurred, as the light filling the clearing closed inwards to concentrate in a single, intense beam over the three figures standing in its centre. The priest stared back at him, his eerie gaze holding Gavin captive.

The priest, Linda and Beth disappeared. An instant later, the beam of light snapped out.

16

THAT NIGHT ARNOLD Connors was minding the cemetery. His confused, maddened mind told him it was the only decent thing to do. In fact he was the sole person in town who *could* do it. He was the custodian of death in Hickory, a man used to grinning cadavers and the disturbing rictus of corpses. He'd witnessed all the mess which was the human form after the life force had departed, and having seen it all, he could ignore it. He could keep his head.

At the same time something else sounded inside him, like a deep instinct he must obey but couldn't recognise, insisting this was a time for staying locked away until it was safe to re-emerge into the world again. Connors didn't understand this. His head was filled with crazy, demanding ideas and soft, insisting voices, all in conflict with the innate urges born from years of habit.

He knew the cemetery was the right place to be. Earlier that night he'd listened to the silence of the town and, like everyone else, heard the quiet shuffling of things moving about the streets outside his home. Things that made even the town's dumbest mongrel dogs stay protectively curled up and whimpering. No-one was supposed to look at these *things*. No-one was allowed to ask what was happening. There was only unquestioning obedience. A necessary lack of reaction.

Connors knew all about reactions. He'd made a game of studying them since he was a boy and his father had introduced him to the undertaking trade. A lifetime of watching people deal with their first glimpse of a dead body had given Connors a whole personal library full of involuntary reactions from the smallest, hissing intake of breath to a complete, screaming emotional breakdown. He had learnt from all of these and taught himself to feel the reactions coming and keep himself under control, to ignore them and still reach out towards a corpse and do his work, as his father expected. That was why Connors was capable now of shutting out the whispering voices in his head—partly, at least—and making his plans to go to the cemetery.

Why must I go to the cemetery?

The question struggled to the surface of his mind through the mire of confusion. The answer was, because Connors knew exactly what was walking the streets of Hickory that night. He hadn't looked out a window—that wasn't allowed. In fact, he'd been quite happy to stay in his house and let the evening slip past, as everyone else was expected to do, too. His wife Charlotte was already in bed, staring mindlessly at a magazine crossword, an unused pencil stub gripped in her hand. Connors had even closed his ears to a soft, slithering noise on the side of his house, as if someone were running their fingers along the wall as they walked past.

Then Connors smelled something. Something that provoked a chain of thoughts louder than the voices he was supposed to be obeying. It was the smells of his trade. An acrid stink of embalming fluids and a cloying stench of flesh turning bad, with an underlying whiff of the perfume Connors used to make his corpses more acceptable.

So Connors knew without looking what was wandering the town during the darkness. It awoke in him a sudden, demented desire to put things right. Being the undertaker in a small community was a large responsibility. The residents of Hickory's cemetery were his charges and they needed looking after properly. They shouldn't be walking the streets.

Connors quietly lost his mind without the slightest warning it was slipping away.

He waited until the slithering noises outside had drifted away, then he went to the small garden shed and took out his long-handled shovel. It was all he would need. Connors knew how to use a shovel so well it was like an extension of his arm. He'd dug many graves himself when he was young, before the council took over those duties in the graveyard and bought a mini-bobcat. Hefting the shovel in the darkness, feeling the smooth wood of the handle against his palms, Connors told himself grave-digging wasn't a trade any more. Not like it was in the old days, when a digger took pride in his ability to carve a hole out of the ground with square corners and deep, straight sides. Tonight, he believed the shovel would again be the tool of his trade.

Connors didn't dress for the biting cold of the night air, but he hardly felt his skin pimple and the hairs on his forearms rise at the chill. He slung the shovel over his shoulder and set off from his yard with a soldierly march. It didn't occur to him to drive. It wouldn't take him long to reach the graveyard this way. As he walked Connors sensed, rather than saw, shapes moving in the darkness around him. Figures shuffling between the buildings and along the verges. He ignored them. It wasn't in his plans to pursue phantoms haphazardly through the streets. Connors was determined to nip this problem in the bud, at the source.

At the grave.

Soon he was striding into the street leading to the cemetery—the same street Ainslie McGregor had ridden down on his bike, hoping for an exciting rendezvous with his friend Kevin. Like Ainslie, Connors noted that only the first few streetlights were working, throwing the far end of the road into darkness. He could just make out the low wall of the cemetery. He didn't mind. The dead didn't scare him in the daytime or at night, and he would be able to see okay. The moon was only just past new, but it was bright in the clear, country air and the stars cast almost enough light on their own anyway.

Connors didn't have a name for the demons he expected to be dealing with, but he did prepare himself to confront something. So he was disappointed when he arrived at the graveyard gates to discover the place looked undisturbed. This wasn't what his madness had wound him up to expect. After a moment's hesitation he decided he couldn't be mistaken. He would wait.

The cemetery wasn't big, but it was old, giving it a size out of proportion to the current population of Hickory. Connors made his way towards the middle of it and picked a flat marble tomb to sit on. He propped the shovel beside him and made himself as comfortable as he could, then concentrated, straining his eyes against the darkness for the first sign of movement. He sharpened his hearing, too—he thought he was more likely to hear something before he saw it.

This was where he began his vigil. The cemetery was his responsibility.

Several hours passed without incident. Then Connors was surprised to find himself aroused from an awkward half-slumber by a familiar sound. He couldn't remember getting sleepy. He jerked upright, feeling a protesting stiffness in his body from the cold. The sound was that of stone moving against stone. He tensed, not moving a muscle, and waited for the noise to come again. He didn't have to wait long, and it came from close by. Picking up the shovel Connors crept in towards it, and as he moved he realised precisely where he should be going. There was only one sealed stonework tomb which might be disturbed without a lot of effort. He headed for it.

It was one of the oldest graves in the cemetery, and one of the first to be constructed as a hollow marble crypt, rather than a dirt-filled grave topped with an ornate lid. The cover of the crypt was cracked in several places, but the quality of the marble was such that the seal still appeared good, so no-one ever disturbed it. Except Connors. Once, when his father had sent him to begin a grave on his own, he had used the opportunity to satisfy his boyish, morbid curiosity and wedged the tip of his shovel into the smallest gap under the lid and experimentally lifted it. The broken section of the lid had risen easily, proving the cracks were completely through the marble. Young Connors had been satisfied with that. Concerned about shifting the stone too much and doing more permanent damage, he did no more.

Now he approached that same grave, slowing as he got closer. The grating noise came again and Connors thought he saw part of the lid shift, but in the darkness he couldn't be sure. Then he saw something unmistakable. Impossible, but recognisable without doubt.

White skeletal fingers curled around the edge of the stone, getting a grip from beneath to push the lid further aside.

With an animal cry Connors stepped forward and swung the shovel like a scythe. The metal of the blade clanged against the marble. The edge of the shovel cleanly lopped through the bones, scattering them to the ground. A howl of pain echoed in Connors' head as he let out his own shout of triumph. Dropping the shovel he quickly heaved the broken section of the lid back into place. It didn't fit exactly, but it was good enough.

'You stay in there, where it's proper,' he grunted, giving the marble a last push to close the gap. He leaned against the grave and allowed himself to feel a flush of victory. His panting breath clouded in the night air as he got his wind back. He'd been right! There were duties to perform here tonight.

More noises came from behind him, close by.

He knew the sound immediately. The rattle of the tiny white stones they often used to dress the tops of graves. Normally he heard this when the barrowloads were tipped onto a new grave. Tonight, Connors knew it was the earth beneath them being disturbed and causing them to move. Snatching up his shovel again he followed the sound, coming to another of the older graves. Here the white stones were rippling and shifting like a shimmering pool of milk in the weak moonlight. As he watched, the surface broke and a pale hand came grasping into the air. This time Connors waited. Another hand appeared, then a larger, distinctive lump began to push its way up at the head of the grave. Holding back until the last moment, Connors swung the shovel again, and saw the blade cut viciously into a ravaged, decomposed face as it came clear of the stones. Again a primal scream of agony filled Connors' mind and he revelled in it, feeling a powerful shiver through his body.

A sixth sense made him whirl around. At his

back, stepping close, was the corpse of a man Connors recognised—more from the rotting clothing the man wore than anything discernible in the ruined features. A farmer he'd buried several years before, who'd been found dead on his tractor at the peak of the planting season. Now it seemed the farmer had more work to do beyond the grave.

Connors slashed out with the shovel once more, but this time the flat back of the blade smacked into the corpse's face and sent the figure reeling to collapse on the ground. There was no cry of pain in Connors' head, but the corpse didn't move again. Carefully he went closer. He realised he was panting again, each breath a laboured heave of his chest. A stench rose up from the motionless human carcass.

'It's back into the ground for you,' Connors said, his voice guttural from his efforts.

The farmer's grave was close, and Connors believed without a doubt that he'd just brought death for a second time to its occupant. Laying his shovel on the body and grabbing the corpse by the ankles, he dragged it through the narrow paths. The top of this grave was decorated with larger, rounded river stones. Connors spent a few frustrating minutes trying to shovel them aside so he could get to the softer earth beneath, but then abandoned his tool and got down on his hands and knees. He picked up the stones one by one, tossing them carelessly away. He barely heard them cracking and ricocheting off the nearby markers and marble tombs. He didn't stop until he was satisfied he could dig with the shovel.

He was more attentive with the soil, piling it properly beside the grave as he worked. Connors didn't know what he'd find when he reached the bottom. An intact coffin? Or one with the lid shattered and the occupant missing? He didn't care. As he dug he decided that if the casket was still sealed he would rebury the corpse on top and simply fill in the hole again. There was no time tonight for niceties.

Connors was too absorbed in his digging to notice the other figures moving around him in the cemetery. He was insanely reliving a proud part of his youth, intent on digging this grave properly, with those square corners and straight, deep sides. Finally, standing waist-deep in the hole, Connors let out a grunt of satisfaction as the shovel struck wood with a hollow sound. It only took a few more minutes to clear the remaining dirt away from the coffin. The lid of the casket, the wood rotting with damp, was split almost its entire length. Connors didn't disturb it further. He climbed out of the grave and looked down at his handiwork.

At the same time a cold pair of hands clamped themselves tightly onto either side of his head.

Connors had time to let out a single cry of shock before the hands jerked with tremendous force. He heard his neck break, a wooden sound loud inside his head. He didn't die instantly. His body went completely limp and he toppled forward, twisting as he fell, to land on his back on the uncovered coffin. There was no feeling in his body, which was numb from the base of his neck down. All he felt was the grit in his hair where the back of his head touched the wood.

Staring up at the square of night sky above him Connors could see the moon perfectly framed by the edges of the grave. He thought it looked beautiful. Then it was obscured briefly as a shovelful of dirt was tossed in. The soil landed on his face. Some got into his mouth, but he couldn't spit it out. More soil dropped down. And more.

The grave slowly filled around him.

17

MICHAEL OPENED HIS eyes, disturbed by a sense that a vehicle had just pulled into his driveway. Beside him Kerry slept on, curled in a ball with her back to him. He watched her shoulders rise and fall with slow, deep breaths, then realised he was able to see her because of the faint, pre-dawn light coming through the window. Michael had taken to leaving the curtains open at night, but only reluctantly. He was torn between a hope of seeing something in the night sky and being fore-warned, or closing the drapes and shutting out the world as best he could—*while* he could—because it was getting too damned scary. He lay and listened, then frowned as he heard a car door slam. Another sound came and it took him a moment to recognise it. It was Monty, softly growling in the lounge room.

Michael quickly slipped out of bed, trying not to wake Kerry, and pulled on his jeans. He didn't wait to put on his shirt and a windcheater, instead grabbing them as he hurried out of the room. His skin tingled with the cold. Even the short-pile carpet of the hallway was chilly against the soles of his feet. In the lounge room Monty wagged his tail in greeting, glad that somebody responsible had appeared. Michael looked through a window and saw a battered utility. It looked vaguely familiar, but he couldn't place it, his sleep-dulled mind refusing to provide the information. Whoever was driving it was out of sight, already on their way to the front door. Turning from the window he hurried through the house, hoping to reach the door and open it before someone knocked or rang the bell and woke Kerry.

He flicked on a light. In the moment he pulled the door aside, the thought came to him that this might not be a person he'd want to invite inside, and he braced himself. But the open door revealed Gavin standing on the step, his hand raised as he was about to knock.

'Gavin, what the—' Michael began, confused. Then he saw the expression on Gavin's face. 'Christ, what's happened? What's wrong?'

Gavin looked haunted, his face unnaturally white in the light from the house. His eyes were red-rimmed. 'They're gone,' he whispered hoarsely. 'He took them. He took them both.'

'Who's gone? Who's been taken?' Michael felt himself go cold with fear. Gavin's reference to somebody taking them *both* could only mean one thing.

'Linda and Beth. They just disappeared into a—a *light*.' Gavin was too shocked to raise his voice above a whisper. Michael reached out and gripped his shoulder, gently leading him into the house and pulling the door closed behind them. He used the moment to gather his thoughts and calm his racing mind.

'Now hang on a second, Gavin. Take it slowly. Are you sure they're missing? They haven't just gone on a trip or something? Perhaps they got scared and they've run away?' Gavin was shaking his head. 'But who? Who are you saying took them?'

'I *saw* it, Mike. I was there, like he enjoyed taking my family away in front of my fucking eyes!'

Michael pressed him down into a chair. 'Who, Gavin? Powers? Or was it Riley?'

'No—nobody like that. It was a priest. A weird-looking priest, dancing around them in a circle and asking them crazy questions. He asked them if they would *burn* for him—' Gavin's voice dropped away and he stared, lost in the memory.

Through his confusion and concern for his friend, Michael realised what Gavin was saying—a priest asking his followers to burn for him. 'My God, Isaiah,' he said, softly. 'I don't believe it. It must have been Isaiah. The Mormon priest who locked his parishioners in their church and set fire to it. You saw the ghost of Isaiah!' The concept was stunning. 'What do you mean, he *took* Linda and Beth? How did he take them?'

'They were standing in this light—a strange light all over the place. Like the one we saw in the cane-field. Then it sort of drew inwards, like a spotlight, and suddenly they all just disappeared.'

Kerry appeared in the entrance to the hallway. She looked still half-asleep and wore Michael's dressing gown pulled tightly around her against the cold. 'What's happened?' she asked dully. 'Gavin, are you okay?'

Michael answered for him. 'Somebody's taken Linda and Beth,' he said gravely.

'Jesus,' she whispered, the news bringing her instantly, fully awake. 'Who?'

'We don't know. It was some—well, some sort of apparition. A ghost, in fact,' Michael ended flatly. Despite all that they had seen so far, it was still hard to say such things aloud. It sounded so impossible. 'The way Gavin describes it, it sounds like it was the ghost of Isaiah, the Mormon priest I told you about.' Michael looked grim.

'I don't understand. How did a ghost take them? Where did he take them?' Kerry was shocked, a trace of hysteria in her voice.

Michael motioned her to stay calm. 'Gavin, you'd better tell us the whole story—from the beginning,' he said softly.

Gavin sat holding his head in his hands, while Michael and Kerry's questions and confusion flowed around him. Now he took a deep, shud-dering breath and began slowly, explaining first how he'd got home last night and found Linda and Beth asleep in his bed. Nobody interrupted him as he took them right through to finally stum-bling back to his house—after getting lost for nearly an hour in the bush on the way. As he spoke Kerry sat next to him and put a comforting hand on his arm.

'What do you think, Michael?' she asked, when Gavin lapsed into a distressed silence.

Michael lowered himself into another chair and frowned, lost in his own hard reasoning for a moment. 'It must have been our UFO again,' he said heavily. 'Now that I'm thinking straighter, Gavin's description of a strange light—especially one that concentrated into some sort of beam just before they disappeared—fits into some of the most classic patterns of UFOs. And remember, we haven't been short on strange lights around here lately, either. So I don't think we're dealing with anything supernatural. Not ghosts, I mean. Unless the proximity of the UFO unintentionally caused Isaiah to appear, like we discussed before. But from what Gavin's said, it sounds like this Isaiah actually went into his house, somehow captured or controlled the two women—ignoring Gavin, for some reason—and took them back to that clearing. It's like somebody, or some*thing*, chose to appear in Isaiah's form, the same way something used Ainslie's shape to lure us into the canefield.'

Gavin spoke, his voice bitter and angry. 'That's something else he said—that Linda and Beth were *chosen*, and that it was him who *chooses* people. This wasn't some alien *being* walking around in human form, like we're saying Powers might be. This was the ghost of a madman—a Mormon priest who burnt and murdered his own followers. You *didn't* see him—dancing and doing that insane chanting—'

Michael cut him off, speaking firmly but sympathetically. 'Gavin, the world's going pretty crazy for us right now, I know. And you feel worse than Kerry and I could possibly imagine. But we *all* have to keep our heads and try to look at things logically. I don't believe the ghost of a homicidal priest from a hundred years ago—no matter how mad he was—would abduct your family into a beam of light from the sky. It doesn't make sense. Remember what you said yourself when we talked about how Ainslie suddenly appeared in front of us in the canefield that night? *You* said it was different. This can't have been the ghost of Isaiah, but somebody or some*thing* using his shape and form, understand? Nothing else fits. I mean, none of us are experts, but it *does* sound more like what I've read about UFO abductions than some kind of ghostly activity. And God knows, the three of us believe in UFOs now.'

'We believe in ghosts, too,' Gavin said stubbornly.

'Gavin, think about this. The possibility that a UFO is involved is our best hope. In a lot of cases of UFO abductions the victims come back. Sometimes they don't have any memory at all of what happened to them. Often they've had to have hypnosis to remember the experience. But they *do* come back. If that's what's happened to Linda and Beth, we can hope there's a chance we can get them back. Otherwise, if we believe that some mad ghost from a hundred years ago has spirited them away—then they're gone forever,' Michael finished brutally. He let that sink in, then added, 'We've got to hope they were abducted by a UFO.

307

Maybe *the* UFO we saw. Then there's a chance we can get them back.'

Gavin finally nodded his head slowly.

As she watched, Kerry worried that Michael may be giving Gavin too much hope. The circumstances looked pretty desperate and hopeless to her. She asked quietly, 'Get them back? How?'

Michael lost some of his self-assurance, his shoulders slumping. 'I don't know,' he sighed. 'I really don't have a clue. But I'm working on it right now.'

'Could we simply confront Powers? Tell him we know everything—even if we don't—and threaten to expose him if he doesn't get Linda and Beth back for us?' Kerry suggested this timidly, frightened by her own idea.

'It's a possibility—' Michael began.

'No,' Gavin stopped him, surprising them with his intensity. 'I think that might be too dangerous. I—I think I may have brought this upon myself.'

Michael and Kerry both stared at him. 'How?' Michael asked.

'I haven't told you yet—but last night I decided I wanted to have a closer look at Powers, so I dropped into the library on the way home and enrolled.'

'Damn it, Gavin! I wish you'd told me. I would have tried to stop you,' Michael said, but he realised it was too late for that and calmed himself. 'So okay, what happened?'

'Nothing, really. I mean, he's certainly not normal any more, that's for sure. And now I've been inside his house and know what to look for, there's a few obvious things. He smells, for a start.

308

He smells bad, and he looks bloody ill. I remember thinking he was like a mechanical clock winding down, or something that runs on batteries, but the batteries are nearly dead. It was weird to see. But there wasn't any real—' Gavin searched for the right word, 'Any real *animosity*, if you know what I mean. I didn't feel threatened or scared. Maybe I should have,' he finished harshly, but his anger was directed at himself.

'Do you believe Linda and Beth were taken because you investigated Powers at the library?' Michael said doubtfully.

'Maybe it was some sort of punishment, or a warning. Maybe he used me as an example.'

'That's crazy. You're just trying to blame yourself for what's happened.'

'It makes sense.'

'No it doesn't. Nothing makes any sense to me any more. Who knows *anything*?'

There was a silence, then Gavin said savagely, 'Riley. Riley knows, I'll bet. In fact, I think I'll go to see him right now and demand he tells me what the fuck's going on—and what the hell he's going to do to get my family back.' He stood and Michael stepped forward and put up his hand.

'Wait, Gavin. That might be as bad as going to see Powers.'

Gavin stared at him defiantly, then his expression collapsed to one of grief and desperation. 'Michael, I've got to do something. I've got to do it *now*. What else *can* I do?'

Michael met his eyes, then spread his arms in a gesture of defeat. 'Okay, okay. You're right, we've got to try something. Short of wandering through

309

the canefields and calling out for the bloody UFO to come back, I can't think of anything else either. But wait for me. I'm coming, too.'

'You don't have to. There's no point in both of us taking a risk.'

'I think you'll have a better chance of staying out of trouble, if you're not alone.' Michael flicked a questioning glance at Kerry, unsure what she wanted to do.

She said, 'If you think you're going to leave me here all alone, think again. I'm coming. Give me time to get dressed.' As she disappeared down the hallway towards the bedroom Gavin looked helplessly at Michael.

Michael returned his look and said, 'She's right. It's probably best we stick together.'

The dawn was a bright orange glow in the sky as they drove into the town. Gavin was behind the wheel, with Michael and Kerry squeezed in beside him in the front seat of his utility. Nothing stirred in the streets. No early-risers, not even a dog or a cat. The houses looked shuttered tight, as if the occupants were expecting a storm.

'Where do we go?' Kerry, sandwiched between the two men, asked in a low voice. 'Do we know where he lives?'

'Beside the police station, I think,' Gavin said. 'Either it's him, or Constable Griffith lives there. Griffith will tell us where to go, if that's the case.'

'Yeah, and immediately get on the telephone and warn Riley we're coming,' Michael said unhappily.

'The phones aren't working at all now. I tried to call you this morning before I left.' Gavin said this simply, but it sounded ominous.

'Jesus!' Kerry cried, jerking forward in her seat to look past Michael. 'What's that? Gavin, stop the car. Go back a bit.'

He quickly braked, then reversed until Kerry held up a hand. She pointed through the window at Bartell's store next to her pharmacy. Behind the closed, double-glass doors of the shop stood a figure staring out into the street. The unmistakable white coat of Mal Bartell was plain to see. Although the notices and advertisements stuck on the glass partially obscured him, it was obviously Bartell himself. Something in the way he held himself, standing absolutely still with his arms by his sides and staring ahead like a sentinel on guard, told them things inside the store were far from normal.

'My God,' Kerry breathed. 'He's *inside* the store. He's been in there all the time. Why?'

'He's barricaded himself in, at a guess,' Gavin said. 'He must have seen something. Maybe he knows something, too, seeing he chose to lock himself away, rather than look for help.'

'He hasn't moved—but he must have seen us.'

'I have a suspicion Mal doesn't feel very well any more. Look at him. You can see the white of his face, it's whiter than his coat. He's in trouble.'

'Should we check on him?'

Gavin answered by pressing his foot down on the accelerator. The utility moved forward. 'No, not now. He's not going anywhere.'

A minute later they pulled up in front of the

police station. Next door was a small weather-board house, the living quarters for the town's resident policemen. Opposite was Hickory's only park, a tiny parcel of lawn with a single bench seat and the narrow, granite spire of the war memorial honouring the district's fallen soldiers. Less than twenty names graced the monument, etched onto a dull brass plaque set into the stone.

'I think there's a light still on in the police station,' Kerry said, pointing.

'We'll try in there first,' Gavin said, pushing his door open. 'Maybe they leave a light on all the time.'

The station was nothing more than a converted house itself. In the rear yard was a pair of concrete cells, each with a wire mesh door, the structure a relic from bygone days. It was a long time since anyone had been held in those cells. Gavin reached the front door of the station first and, seeing it was slightly ajar, didn't bother to knock. He pushed it open and went inside. Kerry and Michael crowded in after him.

There was a wooden reception counter barely large enough to accommodate one person, and behind that a desk. Riley sat at the desk, his feet propped on it. His clothing was dishevelled and he badly needed a shave. He observed their entrance through bleary, red-rimmed eyes. An empty bottle of rum sat on the desk beside his feet. He was very drunk.

18

'AH,' RILEY ANNOUNCED in an overloud voice. 'I wondered how long it would take for someone to come and ask *me*. It took longer than I thought, but at least I was right when I figured it'd be one of you guys. The new faces in town—people from the city who don't know how to mind their own damned business.' He tried to take his feet from the desk and offer a semblance of authority and sobriety, rubbing his hands over his face at the same time, as if he could wipe away its flushed skin and slack expression. He knocked the bottle of rum and it toppled over and smashed onto the polished floor. 'Shit,' Riley mumbled, leaning over for a look.

Gavin's reaction took them all by surprise. He

suddenly vaulted the counter and took three quick steps to the desk and grasped the front of Riley's shirt. He snarled into the policeman's face, 'What are you talking about? What the hell's going on, Riley?'

Gavin's strength had Riley rolling backwards on the wheels of his office chair. At the same time he attempted to push Gavin away and get to his feet, his arms alternately waving to keep his balance and flailing at his attacker. The two men and the chair crashed into the rear wall. Riley, swearing loudly, used the solid wall at his back to hold Gavin at arm's length long enough to stand, then Gavin came swinging in again. Riley wasn't a small man either and they looked like two punch-drunk boxers clinching, yet still trying to land blows.

Michael yelled, 'Gavin! No!' He jumped the counter too, sweeping a pile of brochures to the floor in his haste. Choosing his moment he thrust himself between the two antagonists, forcing them apart briefly. In the fraction of time Gavin used to search for another way to get at the policeman, Michael slammed his shoulder hard into his friend's chest, sending him sprawling to the floor. Then Michael spun around and saw, as he expected, a gleam of satisfaction and impending victory in Riley's eyes, but Michael shoved the policeman back, hard against the wall. He heard the crack of Riley's skull hitting the wood panelling and saw his eyes glaze for a moment.

'No, Riley!' Michael shouted into his face. 'Leave him! You stay right fucking there!' He heard Kerry yelling and glanced over his shoulder.

She was on the floor next to Gavin, putting her weight against his shoulders and telling him to calm down. Gavin could easily have thrown her off, but a flicker of reason came into his face and he stayed where he lay.

Riley sneered and moved. Fearing the worst Michael made to intercept him, but the policeman was only reaching for a small refrigerator nearby. He took out another bottle of rum and a coke and poured a hefty slug of liquor into a drink-stained glass on his desk. He topped it up with the coke. The others watched him silently. Gavin slowly got to his feet.

'It's too late,' Riley said, breathing heavily and dismissing them with a wave. 'By this time tomorrow it'll all be over. You might as well go back home and stay there, like everybody else. Close your doors and have a day off. And tomorrow you can start to forget it.'

Gavin spoke quietly, but with menace. 'Where are my wife and daughter, you bastard?'

This stopped Riley, the drink halfway to his lips. He raised an eyebrow at Gavin. 'They're missing?' He stared into his glass and shrugged. 'He's had a busy night.'

Gavin looked like he was going to attack Riley again, but Michael positioned himself between them. 'Who, Riley?' he asked. 'What are you talking about?'

'John Powers, of course. You know that as well as I do.'

'It wasn't Powers I saw,' Gavin said flatly. 'This was a priest. Some sort of fucking insane priest, who took Linda and Beth right out of our home and into the bush. I woke in time to follow them, but there was nothing I could do. The three of them disappeared.'

'It's still Powers,' Riley said, revelling in his superior knowledge, almost smirking at them. He retrieved the chair from the wall and pushed it back to the desk, where he resumed his previous position with his feet propped on the table, the rum in his hand. He looked at them, assuming an exaggerated air of being in charge, and waited for the obvious questions.

'I don't understand,' Michael said carefully. 'I think it was the ghost of a man called Isaiah, a Mormon priest who lived here about a hundred years ago. At least, that's who it looked like.'

'Ah, *ghosts*,' Riley murmured, looking into his drink again. 'I only wish they *were* ghosts, instead of the damned walking dead. Powers has created quite a problem there,' he said mildly. 'He told me they were supposed to go away once they'd finished their business—the ghosts, I mean. But it appears they're here to stay, and they sure as hell aren't ghosts. Unfortunately, Powers doesn't seem to care.'

'This isn't making any sense,' Kerry said, turning to Michael. 'He's too drunk.'

'Drunk?' Riley smiled crookedly at her. He tipped his glass in salute. 'I'll admit, I'm trying, but I can't seem to get there. Have *you* seen any ghosts, Miss Wentworth? Any zombies—isn't that what Hollywood calls them? Has anything gone *bump* in the night?'

Kerry didn't like being the object of his attention and struggled to answer. Michael saved her by saying, 'We can all see this town's turning into a walking graveyard. I get the impression you can tell us why.'

'Why?' Riley laughed, a drunken and slightly desperate sound. 'Why?' He stopped and stared into space a moment, then he whispered to himself, 'They're looking for their lives. The fucking dead are walking the town, looking for their *lives*, for Christ's sake.' He lapsed into a ruminative silence, gazing down into his drink. Then he gathered himself together and spoke more deliberately. 'I'll tell you, the *original* idea was okay. I'll tell you that for free. That's why we all went along with it. But why Powers is doing what he's doing now—I don't know. He used to tell me everything. Now he just scares the shit out of me.'

'Is he the—the *ghosts* we've seen?' Michael asked. He felt as though he was asking a nervous child, or a madman who might break and refuse to answer at all if Michael said the wrong thing.

'Shit, no—well, maybe sometimes. Mostly they're real—that's my damn problem, like I told you.' Riley drank his rum in one swallow and leaned forward, grasping the fresh bottle by the neck and pouring another. Again, he topped it up with coke, spilling some in his drunken carelessness. The others watched silently, waiting for him to go on. Satisfied with his drink, Riley looked pensively out the window at the lightening sky. 'You know, Powers comes from a civilisation that's thousands of years ahead of us. Literally *thousands*.' He didn't see the tense look exchanged between the three people listening. 'I used to go

317

over to his house and talk to him, but it was like a caveman talking to Einstein. Really, I didn't understand a damned thing. That was before Powers started to go crazy. I *do* know his people do things, and *know* things, which are beyond our comprehension. So, for him to whistle up somebody from the dead—to bring someone's ghost back into our world and to use it, *possess* it—was like us clicking our fingers. Simple. We're talking about Jake Sanders, right?' Riley looked at them slyly, the alcohol accentuating his drooping eyelid. 'Ah—but *why* he did it, that's another thing altogether. Powers told me he could make Hickory just the damn scariest place around. People'd want to leave—and sure as hell no-one would want to come and stay. He could make it a real ghost town, and that'd suit him fine.'

Riley scratched thoughtfully at his nose. 'But that's when I figured he wasn't feeling so well, because he brought back Jake Sanders, and pointed him like a gun at his mother, more for spite than anything. A creature like Powers is supposed to be beyond that sort of feeling—he'd been telling me that for months. Reckoned the next evolutionary step for mankind would be for us to shed our emotions. Says they just get in the way and cause trouble.' Riley paused and took another drink, then his face clouded with disappointment. When he continued, his voice was rambling, the drink taking its toll. 'But Jake's corpse woke up too and didn't go away, and it's going to get worse. Powers called back other spirits. He still didn't notice—or maybe he didn't care—that he was breathing life back into their bloody corpses, too. Now they're all waking up, slowly but surely. I wouldn't be surprised if by the end of the week the entire fucking cemetery is lined up at McGann's front bar demanding a drink. Powers has started something and he doesn't know how to stop it—and like I said, he doesn't care, either. The other night I saw Jake Sanders' mother, large as life but looking deader'n Christ on the cross, waiting outside Mal Bartell's store as if she expected him to open the doors any minute, even though it was two o'clock in the morning. It was after I asked him about that, that Powers told me it was part of his plan, but I didn't believe it. He was losing his grip for sure. I knew he was taking people for a reason too, when he wanted young Ainslie McGregor. He would've had Doctor Stanford's kid as well, but I talked him out of it. I managed to appeal to some weird sense of loyalty, because the doctor's one of us—one of the group who agreed to this crazy set-up in the first place. Maybe Powers got a kick out of doing me a favour,' he added absently. 'Anyway, he just used Kevin Stanford instead. That boy's been at home ever since, sick as a dog and wondering what the hell happened to about twelve hours of his life. He doesn't even know the McGregor kid is gone. He can't remember. I'd say he's better off.'

Riley fell silent. He seemed almost unaware now that the others were in the room, listening to him. The air in the office was thick with his stale, rum-soaked breath.

Michael asked, 'What about Isaiah? The priest?'

'I've never heard of him. But if you say he took your wife and kid, then it was Powers, not some

319

ghost. The thing inside Powers probably has a whole shelf full of crazies he can appear as. John Powers himself is dying and isn't much use any more. This Isaiah is just another shape—another identity. But inside it's still the same *thing*, and if it's got your family, you might as well forget them.' He said this blithely, uncaring how Gavin might feel.

'Why, God damn you?' Gavin snapped, starting to lose his control again. 'Why has he taken them—and where?'

Riley gave them another superior look and tapped the side of his head with his finger, indicating this was something he'd worked out for himself. 'Because he's sick, that's why. I don't mean Powers the man, the poor diabetic son-of-a-bitch sticking needles into himself every day. I'm saying the creature *inside* Powers is sick and he's looking for a cure. That's why he's going crazy and doing weird things now, instead of being the super-intelligent fucking spaceman from the stars he's supposed to be. This whole planet's just one big laboratory for them. It doesn't matter a fuck to him if he plucks a few rabbits for experiments and gets himself fixed up. He tried to get Jake first, and got mad when Jake cheated by dropping his motorbike and killing himself. Then he snatched the McGregor kid, and I know he got some woman travelling the highway into town the other night. So last night it's your wife and daughter's turn, and I heard Jeff Butler's car was found wrecked on the side of the road with no sign of him, too. So I reckon Powers is looking for a cure—and he needs a few *rabbits*.'

'My God,' Michael whispered. All of them were shocked, but Michael and Gavin more so. Gavin's imagination was running wild, tortured by images of his family being subjected to all sorts of ghoulish experiments. Michael was fixed on Riley's words, *I know he got some woman travelling into town the other night.* It had to be Anne Shannon. Anne had been 'taken', as Riley put it, just like Linda and Beth Packer. And worse, it must have happened at least twenty-four, if not forty-eight, hours beforehand. If there wasn't much hope for the Packers, there was none for Anne Shannon.

Only Kerry had the presence of mind left to ask questions which might be of some help. 'What *is* Powers?' she asked, trying to keep a tremor out of her voice. 'Is he a man, or is he—he something else?'

'He *was* a man,' Riley said, noticeably slurring his words now. 'God knows what happened to the poor bastard who used to be John Powers. I figure he's possessed in some way, I guess. Or maybe he's already dead and that thing inside him wears his corpse like a coat.'

'Possessed—like he did with Isaiah, the Mormon priest,' Michael muttered. 'He used that man's body long enough to dispose of all the people living around here, right? And that's what he wants to do again.'

'No,' Riley shook his head adamantly, making himself dizzy and nearly losing his balance on the chair. 'He knew he couldn't get rid of the whole damn town. That's where we came in. First, he wanted us to prepare an area for him, down by the river. The town council had to justify the

321

work, so they built those stupid bloody barbecues. It didn't make sense, because we all figured there was no point in getting somewhere secluded ready, then inviting half the town to go picnicking down there. But Powers did something—I don't know what. Made the place feel bad, so nobody likes to hang around there too long. Even animals and birds stay away from the place—I heard you guys talking about that when we were searching for Ainslie McGregor. Then, of course, once we'd done one thing for Powers, we had no excuse not to do anything else.' Riley was becoming bitter. '"Containment" is what he called it. Censoring the mail and closing down the telephone lines when the time got close. We were supposed to make sure no mention of anything strange happening around Hickory got out. And we got people like Doc Stanford to keep his ear to the ground, listening for anyone getting a little nervous or upset. Powers set up some electronic jamming device to stop any ham radios—that's what's gone wrong with the television and radio reception. Somebody might have got worried too early if they'd figured it was something stopping transmissions *out* of the town, not something preventing us *receiving* anything. And for the last two days Gordon Griffith has been keeping a one-man roadblock just out of town. Now *there's* a man devoted to his duty,' Riley finished dryly.

Michael glanced helplessly at Gavin and Kerry. 'But why? What's the point of all this? What in God's name is going to happen?'

A slow, triumphant smile spread across Riley's face. 'You know what? I haven't got a fucking clue. You'll just have to find out for yourself—and you don't have long to wait, because it happens tonight.'

Michael ignored the flash of panic the words caused and asked carefully, 'And what was in all this for you?'

Riley's smug expression changed to one of helpless confusion. 'Shit, I don't know any more. He promised us anything and everything. It was all possible, nothing was impossible. But he never put a name to it. We never gave him a price and he didn't give us any offers. All the time we just believed we would be rewarded somehow.' Riley shook his head, as if this was the first time he'd realised this flaw in their planning. 'Pretty wild, huh?'

'Where's Powers now?' Gavin asked, his voice thick with suppressed anger.

'At his house, I guess. I wouldn't go near him. He's crazier than a loon. And it's too late to do anything now.'

'Like hell,' Gavin said. 'It's never too late.' He abruptly spun on his heel and walked out of the police station.

Michael looked at Riley and wondered if it was a good idea to leave the policeman alone. In his heart, he realised that Riley was probably right— it was already too late to do anything. He stepped closer to the desk, picked up the bottle of rum and filled the glass still cradled in Riley's hand to the brim.

'You just keep drinking, you useless bastard. You're no good for anything else.'

He put an arm around Kerry's shoulders and

guided her around the counter as they hurried after Gavin. Behind them Riley smiled and raised his glass to their backs, but his eyes were filled with despair.

'Where are we going?' Michael asked, although he already knew. He opened the passenger door of the utility and stood aside to let Kerry get in first.

'To see Powers, of course,' Gavin said grimly.

'Then maybe you shouldn't come along, Kerry,' Michael said. 'We can drop you off at the pharmacy. You can lock yourself in there.'

She stood in the doorway of the car and thought about it. 'No, I don't want us to get separated. I'd go crazy wondering what was happening. But I might stay outside or something—I don't know. Let's see what happens when we get there.' Kerry looked at him and gently reached up to touch his face. 'Are you okay? I heard what Riley said— about Powers picking up a woman on the highway into town. Do you think it was Anne?'

'Who else?' he replied bleakly.

Gavin watched them across the roof of the utility, shocked to realise he wasn't the only one who might have lost somebody close. 'Shit, I missed that, Michael. I'm so caught up in worrying about Linda and Beth.'

'Of course you are. So you should be. Anyway, if it was Anne, he's had her for a couple of days,' Michael said. He didn't need to say more. There was an uncomfortable silence, until Kerry suddenly frowned at something in the distance.

'Guys, look at this,' she pointed down the street.

A wisp of dark smoke, thickening rapidly, was rising into the morning air. 'That's got to be close to my pharmacy.'

'We'd better take a look,' Gavin said, quickly getting into the driver's seat.

They drove the short distance back to the chemist and parked on the opposite side of the street. The smoke was coming from somewhere near the rear of Mal Bartell's store. The shop-keeper was no longer standing behind his doors, which were still closed. The three of them got out of the car and crossed the road. Kerry cupped one hand to her face and leaned close to the window, rapping sharply on the glass with her free hand.

'Mal? Are you still in there? It's Kerry.' There was no answer, so she tried again, and got the same result.

'How can I check around the back?' Gavin asked.

'Just go between the two buildings. There's a low fence at the rear, but you can almost step over it.'

'You guys wait here, in case he answers you. I'll have a look and be back in a minute.' Gavin slipped rapidly down the narrow alleyway. Kerry called out once more for Bartell to answer, but there was no response. Michael walked backwards out onto the road so he could see the spire of smoke. It was now a boiling black cloud.

'This is getting bad,' he called to Kerry.

Gavin reappeared. 'The back doors are locked, but the fire is definitely inside the shop. The smoke's pouring out of an old skylight on the back of the roof.'

'What do we do?' Michael asked. 'Call the fire brigade? Has the town *got* a fire brigade?'

'A voluntary one. God knows if they'll even show up, the way things are right now.'

Gavin was right. Even though it was still early morning, the amount of smoke coming from the roof should have attracted passers-by or alarmed somebody by now. But there were no passers-by. Hickory had closed itself up tight. And nobody was raising an alarm. No-one wanted to get involved any more. Looking up and down the deserted main street, it seemed to Michael that the whole town was turning its back on the fire, ignoring it. It was somebody else's problem.

Gavin was examining the front door. 'This isn't barred or anything, is it?' he asked Kerry.

She remembered when Bartell had shown her the locks on the day of the Sanders' funeral. 'No, just a couple of regular locks and a shot-bolt top and bottom.'

'Okay.' Gavin sprinted over the street to his utility and pulled a heavy shovel from the back tray. Telling Michael and Kerry to stand aside, he used the handle of the shovel like the butt of a rifle, punching it against the glass panelling in one of the doors. The first attempt only made the door rattle, so Gavin didn't hold back with his next try. This time the glass shattered, falling in jagged shards to the ground. Gavin moved back hurriedly in case he got hurt. It made a lot of noise and Michael glanced around, certain they must have attracted some attention now. He thought he saw a curtain twitch in a house on the other side of the road—but that was all. Gavin was leaning carefully half-in the broken frame, fumbling on the other side of the door for the locks. He found them all, unlocking the door, then stepped back and used his boot to push open both doors. More broken glass tinkled to the floor as they swung aside.

'Mind you don't cut yourself,' he told the others as he went inside. Immediately he began calling out to Mal Bartell.

The store was dark and gloomy. None of the neon lights were switched on and most of the windows were covered by signwriting and pieces of paper stuck haphazardly everywhere—Bartell's window acted as an unofficial noticeboard for the town. Gavin figured the lightswitches would be behind the main counter, so he headed that way. The air stank with an acrid, burning smell. Plastics, Gavin decided, and realised the smoke inside was quickly getting heavier. It rasped at the back of his throat and tickled his nose. In a hopeless gesture he cupped his hand over his face in an attempt to filter the air a little before he breathed it. Glancing over his shoulder he saw Kerry and Michael copy him, covering their faces. There was a dull, crackling sound all around them. Gavin looked up at the roof and saw the fibre panelling of the false ceiling shifting and rising. The fire was spreading through the ceiling space faster than in the shop below.

'Mal? Are you still in here?' he yelled. He was about to call again when a barely audible voice came from the far end of the store.

'He wants us all to burn for him.'

Gavin looked back at Michael and Kerry and

saw the alarmed looks on their faces. They'd heard it, too. He shouted, 'Mal? Where are you?'

In a corner of the store, hidden by a high shelf, something collapsed with a clatter of noise. A burst of orange lit the room, filling it with flickering light as a tower of flame began to eat its way through a wall. From where they stood they could see the flames lick hungrily at the ceiling.

'Mal, are you okay?' Gavin called, moving quickly around the shelving.

Behind him, Kerry shouted, 'Mal, it's Kerry!'

The voice came again, louder, as if the speaker were in pain. 'We *must* burn for him. He tells me we *must* burn for him.'

Then they saw him. Mal Bartell was backed into the furthest corner of the store, the flames just centimetres from his clothing. They could see his white coat turning black as it was scorched by the flames. His face was deathly pale and smudged with filth. In his hands he held a large, clear-plastic bottle of liquid. Gavin stopped dead at the sight of him, the other two close behind him.

'Come away from the flames, Mal,' Gavin said gently. Bartell shifted uneasily on his feet, his eyes flicking from side to side.

'Mal,' Kerry said pleadingly. 'Come on, please. You're going to get hurt.' She reached forward and made to step around Gavin to lead Bartell away, but Michael gripped her shoulder, stopping her.

'See what he's holding?' he whispered into her ear. 'Don't go near him.'

It was a two-litre bottle of household kerosene. Kerry told herself she should have recognised it by the light-blue colouring. The flames behind Bartell were roaring now, the storeroom on the other side of the wall where the fire must have started looked like the maw of a furnace. Small explosions began to pop and fizz, as pressurised aerosol cans and lighter fluid reached flash point. Bartell's hair was smouldering. The heat was almost unbearable where Gavin and the others stood. It must have been blistering for Bartell.

'Mal, don't do this,' Michael yelled. 'You don't have to listen to him.'

'You can't *hear* him. He tells us to burn because there is no choice.' The words were choked out, wrung past the need to cry out in pain. Without warning he suddenly tugged at the plastic cap of the kerosene bottle. His face twisted into anguished frustration as the child-proof lock momentarily foiled his efforts.

Gavin whirled around and savagely shoved Michael and Kerry back behind the high shelving. 'Get *back*! Get down behind the shelf!' They tripped and stumbled in their haste to obey, Gavin falling on top of them.

Bartell managed to wrench the cap off and inverted the bottle high in front of him, pouring the contents onto his chest. The blue liquid splashed onto his coat, but only for a moment before the heat and flames ignited the stream of kerosene and, in the same instant, the entire con-tents of the bottle. It exploded with a loud whoosh and Bartell screamed, a shocking, piercing sound.

Crawling on his hands and knees Michael pushed past Gavin and Kerry, risking a glance around the partition. Bartell was a terrible sight.

Similarly, he was on all fours, but the upper half of his body was fiercely on fire. As if he felt Michael's gaze he slowly lifted his head and looked at him, but it must have been impossible for Bartell to see anything, his eyes squeezed closed against the flames sticking to the skin of his face.

Then he started to get to his feet.

Michael didn't wait to see more. 'Move!' he yelled at the others. 'Get out of here! There's nothing we can do!'

Kerry was sobbing, pushing herself upright and away down the aisle with Gavin following. They reached the front door and ran through. Behind them Michael hesitated a moment, stopping to stare back down the length of the shop. The blaze of fire was rapidly consuming the rear of the building. A solid block of writhing flame moved amongst it.

Bartell staggered free of the main inferno, a human torch beyond any help. He launched himself down the aisle towards Michael and crashed into a row of shelving, scattering the goods everywhere. Michael feared for a moment that Bartell was pursuing him, wanting to wrap his flaming arms around his body and incinerate him, too. He threw himself out the door, yelling at everyone to keep clear. At the same moment he registered where Bartell had landed among the smallgoods—in the section where the rest of the inflammables were displayed. More kerosene, and the methylated spirits and cleaning fluids. Bartell must have believed he wasn't burning enough.

Gavin and Kerry stood just beyond the porch,

waiting anxiously for Michael. He spread his arms and shepherded them across the road to the utility. A muffled explosion came from within the shop, then another which blew out one of the windows, showering glass onto the footpath and road. The fire seemed content with this, and settled into a steady, furious blaze working its way along the length of the building.

Dazed, Michael looked around him. Amazingly, neither the explosions nor the fire had brought people running. The street was still almost deserted. Further down the road a few small groups of people gathered near the kerb to peer down towards the fire. Some of them turned away and disappeared indoors when they saw Michael staring towards them. A fire-bell rang faintly in the distance. Finally, a solitary car turned into the street and drove towards them, pulling to a halt behind Gavin's utility.

A middle-aged man got out, his thinning hair dishevelled as if he'd hurried out of his bed. Something about his casual clothing—which didn't suit him—made him unfamiliar. The expression on his face was very grave. His hands hanging loosely at his sides, he stared at the burning building. Kerry was the first to recognise him.

'Doctor Stanford,' she called above the crackling of the flames. 'You're too late.'

He turned towards her, sweeping a glance over the two men as well. 'Is there anyone still inside?' he asked woodenly.

'Mal Bartell is in there. There's nothing you can do.'

Stanford looked back at the fire and stayed silent

331

for a long time. Then he said, 'Sergeant Riley is concerned about you three. You haven't been in town long enough and it—well, shall we say it makes a difference. My best advice to you is to go home now and stay there. By tomorrow everything will be resolved. There'll be nothing to worry about.'

'Go home! We just spoke to Riley,' Michael said, his voice harsh with disgust. 'You're just as bad as he is! What the hell have you people allowed to happen here?' He stepped closer, pushing his face into the doctor's. Michael flung an arm towards the flames. 'Mal Bartell just fucking incinerated himself in his own store and *look* at this place! Nobody cares! Nobody's come running to help! I'll bet that fire-bell is automatic and no-one fucking answers it!'

Stanford returned Michael's glare without flinching. 'Just go home,' he said flatly. Michael stood his ground, wanting more.

'Let's go, Michael,' Gavin called. 'It's no use. We know who we have to see.'

Michael swore and broke away. Without another look at the doctor they all got into the utility. Their clothing stank of the fire and the sweat of their fear. The smell filled the confined space of the cab. As Gavin started the engine Kerry said, 'Christ, what about my pharmacy? The fire will probably spread that far.'

'Is it insured?' Gavin asked, putting the car into gear and pulling away from the curb.

'Of course, but—' Kerry shrugged helplessly.

'Then believe it or not, this could be your lucky day if the fire burns down the chemist as well.'

Gavin parked in front of Powers' house and turned the engine off. In the silence the three of them surveyed the run-down house dubiously.

'What do we do?' Kerry asked quietly. 'Just knock on the door and say "Little pig, little pig, let me in"?'

'Something like that,' Gavin said, opening his door.

Kerry leaned close to Michael. 'Shouldn't we have a weapon of some kind? A gun?'

'Too late now. Who knows if it would make any difference? We still don't really know what—or who—we're dealing with.'

The house looked different in the cold light of day. The yard was overgrown and the fence was on a lean, sections of the wire mesh falling away from the supporting structure. The front gate was open. Gavin led the way, striding so fast he was almost jogging up to the small wooden porch. He hammered on the door, making it rattle in its frame.

'Powers! Open up! I don't care *what* the fuck you are, I want to talk to you.'

Michael had thought Gavin had himself well under control, but he could tell from the strain in Gavin's voice now that he'd been wrong.

'Don't blow it now, Gavin,' he said urgently. Before Gavin had a chance to reply the front door shook, then creaked open.

To their surprise, Jeff Butler the mechanic, not Powers, opened the door. Butler was a disturbing sight. His clothing was torn and smeared with blood. Most of his face was blackened with bruising and his hair was plastered to his scalp by a mixture of dried blood and sweat. His eyes literally danced, skittering and staring in all directions at once. The pupils seemed to burn like hot coals. Butler was alive, but completely insane. Worst of all, he casually held an old, double-barrelled shotgun across his chest.

'What do you want?' His voice was a rasping cough, as if his throat was sore or injured. Gavin was taken aback for a moment, then recovered his anger.

'Where's Powers?'

'He's not seeing anyone. That's why I'm here.' Butler's eyes focused on Kerry and stayed there. 'Hello, Kerry,' he leered. 'I'm glad *you're* here.' One of his hands left the shotgun and dropped to his crotch, absently rubbing at it.

Kerry shuddered and turned away. 'Jesus Christ,' she muttered. 'Why did it have to be *him*?'

'Get Powers,' Michael snapped, angry too, now. 'We're not interested in talking to you.'

'I told you. He's not seeing anyone. Fuck off— but you can leave *her*, if you like.'

Gavin took a quick step forward and grasped the upper barrel of the shotgun with one hand. Butler snarled an animal sound and tried to wrestle it back, but Gavin was far too strong. Standing on the same level he towered over the younger man. He used the shotgun to haul Butler close.

'If you were thinking about using this, you should have been pointing it in the right direction, you fool. Now, where's Powers? Before I break your skinny neck.'

Butler hissed and looked about to relinquish his

grip on the gun in favour of striking at Gavin, but a soft, broken voice from inside the house froze them.

'Let them in, boy.'

Butler backed down reluctantly, trying to take the shotgun with him, but Gavin kept his hold. Then, with an unexpected jerk he snatched it out of Butler's grip. Butler hurriedly retreated into the house. Gavin paused on the threshold, broke open the barrels of the gun and pulled out the shells, pocketing them. He tossed the weapon through the doorway and snapped, 'Leave it!' when Butler apparently made a move to retrieve it.

'Great,' Kerry groaned. 'Why the hell did he do that?'

The foul stench of the house flowed out of the open doorway. It increased tenfold when they stepped into the gloomy interior. Gavin, Michael and Kerry stood in a tight group just inside the entrance and waited for their eyesight to adjust. The broken voice spoke again, directing their attention towards the single lounge chair which, on their last visit, they'd decided was the only one ever used.

'What do you want? Why are you here?'

Powers sat hunched in the chair. He was bent forward, like a man about to vomit between his knees, but his face was raised to glare at the intruders with an ugly expression. Although his physical frame was naturally thin, he appeared still more wasted in his clothes, the jacket falling away from his shoulders and the legs of his trousers deflated around the skinny limbs.

Gavin made to move forward, but stopped in

mid-stride. The anger showed plainly on his face and his hands shook while he flexed his fists open and closed, as if he already had them around Powers' neck. 'It was you, wasn't it?' Gavin hissed. 'Last night. You came to my house and took my family. You looked different, but now I know it was you. Where the hell are they, you bastard? What have you done with my wife and daughter?'

Powers' face showed only a flicker of interest before discarding the emotion. 'I take no-one that does not have a use,' he rasped, dismissing Gavin with the smallest tilt of his head. 'They are necessary for my survival, and I am allowed to use them. It is nothing of your concern.'

'*Nothing of my concern?*' Gavin was momentarily astounded, then his anger flooded back. 'They are my *family*, you fucking freak. You took them, so I figure you can bring them back! If you don't, I'll break every bone in your damn—'

Gavin stopped abruptly. Powers was laughing softly.

Anticipating that Gavin might launch himself at Powers, Butler stepped forward protectively. Incredibly, the young mechanic had hardly moved before he was swept off his feet by some invisible force and thrown backwards against the wall. He screamed, a high, childish sound, and cried out in pain as his back slammed against the wooden panelling. Gavin was grunting with effort, his face twisted with frustration, as he, too, fought against some unseen power. He couldn't get closer to Powers.

'Fools,' Powers spat, though it appeared the

effort exhausted him. 'I can still protect myself.'

Michael grabbed a handful of Gavin's jacket and pulled him away, supporting him as Powers' energy released its hold, leaving Gavin weak and unsteady on his feet.

'Who are you?' Michael whispered hoarsely. 'What are you doing here?'

'Leave. All of you. *Now*,' Powers said, ignoring the question. He sounded threatening, but sickly and tired. Michael briefly wondered how long Powers would last if they pressed him, but the risk seemed too great. He had to remind himself they had no idea what they were dealing with.

'What's going to happen tonight?' he tried, instead. 'We know *something*'s going to happen tonight.'

Powers took a long time to answer. 'It ends. My brothers come.' He suddenly bowed his head and a thin stream of bile escaped his lips, dripping onto the floor.

Kerry tugged on Michael's sleeve. 'We have to get out of here,' she said quietly. 'I think he's dying. God knows what could happen if he does.'

'What? Why? That doesn't make sense.'

Gavin went to move forward again, muttering, 'If he's dying, he's going to tell me everything first.'

Kerry leaned over quickly, holding him back. 'No, Gavin! Leave him! We'll just leave, like he wants.' When Gavin seemed about to ignore her Kerry tightened her grip. 'Christ, Gavin! *Listen* to me! We must leave.'

Gavin surprised her by stopping suddenly, then

as she slackened her hold he lunged in a different direction. In an instant he had Jeff Butler pinned to the wall, one hand tightening around the mechanic's neck. 'But *you're* not dying,' Gavin snapped. 'So you tell me what's happening tonight. And where's Powers put my family, damn you?' In the background Powers laughed again, even weaker this time.

'I couldn't give a fuck about your family,' Butler grated back, choking the words out. 'He says he's changing—preparing himself. I don't know why he's sick, but he could kill you all now if he wanted. Later he'll be worse, but then I'll still be here.' Butler managed a sly look on his slowly reddening face. 'Why don't you try again later? *I'll* kill you then. I'll kill you both—and I'll have her.' His eyes slid to Kerry. Gavin let go, then immediately drove his fist into Butler's stomach. The mechanic gasped in pain and dropped to his knees.

'You don't look in any condition to kill anyone,' Gavin said, turning away.

'Please, we have to go,' Kerry repeated, but Gavin was already heading for the door. She followed, and Michael, after one last look at Powers, went after them.

Once outside, they didn't speak until they'd left the yard. All of them were unconsciously taking deep breaths, clearing the stench of Powers' house from their lungs and nostrils. Gavin opened his car door, but stared at Kerry before he got in. He looked lost and defeated.

'What are you doing, Kerry? I doubt we'll have him in such a position again. I don't think he could've hurt me. He was getting weaker by the second.'

'Exactly,' Kerry said, nodding. 'That's why we had to leave. Look, let's go to my house for a change and I'll explain. I want to check on the place. Believe me, there's nothing we can do for now, anyway.'

'But I can't sit around and do nothing! Who knows what's happening to Linda and Beth? I've *got* to keep looking for them. He must have them hidden somewhere. I might find them!'

'You won't find them,' she said firmly. 'I'm sure of that.'

Gavin seemed about to argue, then Michael said, 'I think she's right, Gavin. They're nowhere you can get to them. For the moment we should get off the streets and rethink what the hell we're going to do. Kerry's place is as good as any.'

Gavin looked distressed, but he eventually nodded and got in the car.

On the way back through town they passed Mal Bartell's store. It was only a framework of roaring flames. The roof of Kerry's pharmacy was well alight too, but she shook her head in response to Gavin's questioning glance and they drove past.

Kerry made them all coffee and put on some toast. But none of them felt like relaxing or drinking coffee, nor were they really hungry. Gavin sat at the kitchen table and stared down at his clasped hands, a despairing expression on his face. Kerry pulled a chair in close to him, while Michael guarded the toaster.

'Did you hear what Powers said?' she asked Gavin quietly.

'When?'

'When Michael asked him what was happening tonight.'

Gavin thought for a moment, then shrugged his shoulders. 'Not really. I guess I was too wrapped up in thinking about strangling him.' He said this lightly, as if he were joking, but Kerry wasn't so sure.

'He said "It ends", and something about his "brothers" coming, remember?'

Gavin shrugged again, uncaring. 'Okay, so what does it mean?'

'Come on, Gavin! Don't give up hope yet. It's got to mean other people, like Powers or whatever's inside him, are coming here to Hickory— tonight. So, why do you think they're coming?'

Gavin started to make an effort, but Michael beat him to it. 'To pick up Powers, obviously,' he said. Juggling hot toast gingerly between his fingers, he came to the table.

'Right,' Kerry said. 'Which is why I stopped you beating the guy to death. I suddenly realised they might not come if they have some way of knowing Powers is dead.'

'But that means he'll have help!' Gavin said, spreading his arms with frustration. 'We had enough trouble with Powers on his own. At least we had him outnumbered—and he wasn't too healthy, either. If more of them come, we won't have a chance.' He dropped his head and blew out a long, tired sigh. 'I just don't understand.'

'Powers is sick—or something like that,' Kerry

went on stubbornly, trying to get through Gavin's despair. 'He's been sick and acting strangely for some time. Riley told us that, too. We probably don't have a hope in hell of getting him to give back Linda and Beth the way he is now. But what if he's not supposed to be like this? What if he's capable of being reasonable, or even compassionate?' Kerry looked at Gavin hard, making sure he was listening. 'Gavin, what if the people coming to get him are reasonable and compassionate?'

Michael chewed listlessly on a piece of toast. He stopped and stared at her. 'Are you suggesting we try and meet them? Ask *them* if Linda and Beth are alive?'

'Why not? If you've met one alien, you've met 'em all,' Kerry said with a twisted smile.

Michael ran his hand through his hair as he thought about this. 'Christ, I suppose there's nothing to stop us trying. But where? Do we just sit on the roof and wait to see where the next flying saucer lands—?' He fell silent as he realised he already knew where it would land. Kerry said it for him.

'We know where it'll happen. Riley told us that, too.'

'The damn barbecue areas,' Gavin said.

19

THE HARDEST THING for Michael, Kerry and
Gavin was to stay put and just wait. So much
seemed to have happened—and was going to
happen—that seemed to demand they do more
than simply sit idle. Gavin prowled restlessly
around the house like a hungry bear, constantly
coming up with suggestions of things they might
do, or places they could look for Linda and Beth.
Michael patiently told him each time there was no
point. Powers must have them somewhere they
couldn't be reached, he was sure of that. No-one
dared remind Gavin it might also be too late to
help his family anyway. Hoping Anne Shannon
might be still alive was stretching the bounds of
credibility too far. For Linda and Beth, everyone

desperately agreed, there was a slim chance.

Often they talked about what was going to occur that night or, at least, speculated about what might take place.

'They're coming to pick him up. Powers, I mean,' Kerry said again, shrugging.

'They've gone to a lot of trouble, just to drop by and give him a ride. You would think UFOs weren't too worried about quick visits, judging by the number of sightings and close encounter reports you hear about,' Michael replied, watching Gavin's constant pacing out of the corner of his eye. 'And why all the preparation—whatever *that* is? Why not just swoop down and pick him up?'

'Maybe he's got something. Something he's been working on.'

'True, he's been here a hundred years or so,' Michael said, nodding. 'It's logical to assume he's here for a reason and possibly working on something. But what?'

'We *know* what he's been working on,' Gavin interrupted, giving them a haunted look.

'Sorry,' Michael said quietly, then added, 'Hey look, don't take what Riley said so literally. The man was very drunk.'

'*Rabbits,*' Gavin whispered, and turned away to resume his pacing.

Time crawled around to lunch. They picked desultorily at some yellowing cheese and pickles Kerry found at the back of her refrigerator. Then Gavin made an announcement.

He stood defiantly in front of Michael and Kerry. 'I've got to get out of this house. I can't just sit here and wait for something to happen.'

'We haven't got much choice, Gavin,' Michael said, but he could see it was going to be a losing argument this time.

'I think we should go for a drive into town. Have a look around. There must be someone else who's still sane, for Christ's sake. We might be able to gather some help together.' At Michael's doubtful look Gavin went on, 'We can keep the car doors locked and the windows up, and have a quick drive through, that's all. We probably won't see a thing. Everybody'll be locked away inside like frightened mice. But I can't stand being cooped up here any longer. I've got to get out for a while.'

'Okay,' Michael sighed, spreading his hands in defeat. 'But at the first sign of trouble we turn tail and run, all right? If I'm going to stick my neck on the block, I want to save it for tonight, when we might achieve something by it.'

'All right,' Gavin nodded, slumping his shoulders with relief.

They took the utility again. Kerry spent a few minutes locking the house up as best she could. Monty was still at Michael's place. They pulled out of the driveway, Michael driving. Gavin wanted to keep his attention free to search their surroundings. The first thing they did was slow down as they passed Kerry's nearest neighbour and scrutinise the house closely. It was shut up tight, but all three of them were becoming used to looking for the right signs—the tell-tale twitch of a curtain as somebody peeked out at the passing vehicle.

'How do they know?' Kerry asked, puzzled. 'How the hell do they *know* that tonight's the night

344

you lock your doors and stay inside? Who told them?'

'Remember what Doctor Stanford said, when we came out of the fire?' Michael narrowed his eyes, thinking. 'He said Sergeant Riley was concerned about us. We hadn't been in town long enough—*and it made a difference.* Now, what the hell does that mean?'

'Some sort of mental conditioning? Maybe some drug they've been putting into the town water supply?'

Michael managed a smile. 'And you're a pharmacist? A drug that makes people lock their doors and windows on a particular night?'

'Well, you know what I mean,' she said, pulling a face.

'Yeah, okay. But the water supply couldn't be it. There's too many farms and properties that have their own rainwater tanks.'

'Then it might be something everybody *does* have. Like milk? Or the meat in the butchers?'

'It sounds crazy,' Gavin muttered. 'But whatever it is—if it's *anything*—then it must be slow-acting if we're not affected. It must be something that takes years to establish a hold.'

They fell silent. No-one could come up with a satisfactory answer. Driving on, Michael kept the pace slow so they could carefully look about them. Finally they swung into the main street. It was deserted, and so far they hadn't seen another moving car.

'Damn, it looks like I'll have to find that insurance policy,' Kerry murmured with a calmness that belied the disappointment in her heart.

Michael brought the car to a halt. Mal Bartell's store was a large square of charred debris. Next to it the pharmacy half-stood like a ruined castle, the outer wall furthest from the main fire still standing, but blackened. The interior of the shop was a twisted mess of melted metals and broken glass. A tenuous framework of aluminium was all that was left of the roof. Everything inside the gutted shell was burnt beyond recognition. At least the outer wall had stopped the fire spreading further.

'It burnt out, from the looks of it,' Gavin said. 'The fire brigade didn't show up. There's no water anywhere.'

As they looked, something stirred within the ashes.

Before their shocked eyes a figure hauled itself painfully upright, pushing the debris away. It was a human being, but only barely recognisable. Two fire-ravaged arms, ending in stumps above the wrist, were held away from a stooped trunk. The knees were bent, as if the legs were only just supporting the weight. The figure's head was a hairless, misshapen lump of charred flesh, stained teeth gaping where the lips had been burnt away. Slowly, one of its ruined limbs waved in a gruesome attempt at beckoning.

Kerry couldn't help a stifled scream of horror. Michael and Gavin each uttered oaths, stunned by the sight.

'It must be Mal Bartell,' Michael said hoarsely. 'My God, he can't be *alive*.'

'He's not alive,' Gavin said flatly. 'He's like Jake Sanders, and Elaine.'

346

'Drive on, Michael, for God's sake!' Kerry fought off a shudder.

The tyres squealed as Michael let the clutch out too quickly, although there was no real need to hurry. Mal Bartell's corpse was in no shape to give chase.

The school was shut down. In fact, everything was closed. Even the front doors of McGann's hotel were drawn together, an unfamiliar sight. Hickory was like a ghost town, or a place evacuated in the face of some impending natural disaster. The soft growl of the utility's motor was the only sound in the streets, beating back off the blank, shuttered facades of the buildings. Michael felt safe enough to wind down the driver's side window and let some fresh air into the cab. Gavin did the same, in order to see better. Michael glanced in his rear-view mirror and braked the car again.

'Look back at the hotel,' he said, staring into the mirror. With difficulty, Gavin and Kerry twisted themselves around in the confined space to stare out the back window. Somebody was now standing under the verandah of the hotel and watching their vehicle.

'He wasn't there when we passed, was he?' Michael asked.

'I don't think so,' Kerry said. 'I looked at the pub pretty hard, thinking it would be the last place on earth to be empty. Who is it, can you see?'

'It's Jake,' Michael said. He glanced at Gavin for confirmation, and received a grim nod in return. Michael wondered aloud, 'Why do they hate us? I'm sure they do. Is it because we're alive,

347

and they aren't? We've still got our lives, while they're out looking for theirs, like Riley said?'

'I don't know anything any more,' Gavin said quietly. 'I don't care about the damned whys and the wherefores, either. I just want my family back.'

Kerry suddenly screamed again, the sound exceptionally loud in the confines of the cab. She had been the first to bring her attention back to the windscreen. Michael snapped his eyes away from the mirror while Gavin turned around. A figure stood directly in front of the car, holding something in its hands.

It was Arnold Connors. He looked almost normal, except for the soil caked into his clothing and skin. Even his face was black, like a coal miner's. The whites of his eyes stood out as they rolled madly in every direction. Worse than this was the unnatural position of his head, lolling uncontrollably like a rag doll's on its broken neck. Connors held the shovel across his chest as if it were a weapon. With an anguished cry he quickly changed his grip and swung the shovel at the windscreen. The blade bounced off the glass with a tremendous noise, leaving behind an opaque, broken starring.

Everyone inside automatically ducked. Then Kerry yelled frantically, 'Get going! Oh God, drive around him!'

Michael didn't need a second urging, but he didn't bother turning the steering wheel. Flooring the accelerator he dumped the clutch and the utility lurched forward, hitting Connors as he poised himself for another strike with the shovel. The impetus scooped Connors onto the bonnet, pressing his face against the windscreen. His crazed eyes glared at them and he screamed inhumanly as he clawed at the windscreen with one hand, leaving behind dark smears as the shattered glass shaved off the tips of his fingers. Michael threw the car across to the other side of the road. With one last, despairing cry Connors slid off the bonnet and disappeared from view. Michael heard the sickening thud of Connors' body hitting the bitumen, and a metallic clang as Connors finally lost his grip on his precious shovel. Through his open window he caught a glimpse of flailing limbs on the road beside the vehicle.

The utility sped down the road, Michael uncaring where they went as long as they put distance between themselves and the horror behind.

'Turn left up here,' Gavin said quickly. Michael obeyed without question. After a few more directions from Gavin he realised they were travelling in a wide circle around the centre of town and back towards Kerry's house.

Turning into Kerry's street, Michael didn't want to scare Kerry any more than she already was, but the question had to asked. 'Do you think we'll be safe here? No-one will come looking for us?'

'Maybe we should just head out to my house,' Gavin said.

'But Powers has already been out there!' Kerry jerked out of a deep, disturbing daydream.

'I don't think Powers is capable of going anywhere now. That's why he's got Jeff Butler, remember? At least at my house there's a fair distance between us and those damn things crawling around town before they can swing another shovel at us.'

They stopped long enough for Kerry to grab some warmer clothes for the coming evening, and a few other bits and pieces she might need. She felt a sense of finality, closing her bedroom door, but when she got back outside she didn't mention it. Then they did a trip out to Michael's house, where he did the same and they put Monty into the back of the utility. Unaware of the circumstances the dog happily wagged his tail, excited by all the activity. At the last minute Michael decided to follow them in his van, so Kerry slid across the seat and drove the utility.

When they arrived at the Packers' small property, Gavin sat in the passenger seat and looked at his house. Kerry could see the past two days were really beginning to take their toll on him. Deep lines of fatigue creased his eyes and he sat slumped, beyond making the effort to sit up straight. Before he had a chance to get out of the car she touched his arm.

'Come on, Gavin. Don't give up hope yet. We all think there's still a chance for Beth and Linda.'

He nodded at the scene in front of them. 'Even the house looks like they're gone,' he said sadly.

Kerry knew what he meant. The home looked forlorn and abandoned, as if all the life, hope and spirit that had gone into building it and the property around it had been somehow taken away. 'There's got to be a chance,' she repeated, but knew she didn't sound very convincing.

Monty was making a fuss of Mandy, Gavin's labrador. Once the two dogs had settled Gavin tied Mandy up to stop her wandering, and that seemed incentive enough for Monty to stick around, too. With the two dogs in the yard Gavin was satisfied they had a warning system should anyone, or anything, choose to pay them a visit. Everyone went inside and now it was Gavin's turn to play host while they again faced the problem of filling the hours until evening. They drank several cups of coffee, then Gavin decided to try keeping busy. There were the dead chickens to bury, for a start.

This took a while, then they checked the rest of the livestock. The sheep were still jittery, but improving. Gavin's cow was calmer too, but she hadn't produced any milk. Kerry offered to make them a meal from the ample supplies in Gavin's kitchen. No-one felt particularly hungry. As the evening finally approached the tension was beginning to build in all of them. But it was essential to keep themselves fit, and none of them had eaten properly all day, so Kerry practically forced the two men to accept her offer. While they were seated around the kitchen table, drinking coffee after the meal, Gavin made an offer of his own.

'I was thinking about tonight,' he announced, looking at Kerry and Michael over the rim of his cup.

'Who isn't?' Michael said lightly.

'No, I mean—there's no point you two coming along. In fact, I don't know why you guys don't get the hell out of town right now. There's nothing to stop you. Why don't you go before it's too dark? I'll go down to the river by myself. It might be better that way.'

Michael had no intention of leaving town, but for the sake of it he asked, 'What about faithful Constable Griffith? He's still out there with his roadblock, don't forget.'

'Now that you know all the facts—well, most of them anyway, I'm sure you could talk your way past him. Tell him Riley's sending you somewhere.'

'And get a bullet in the back as we drive away.'

Kerry was shocked. 'You don't think he'd go that far, do you?'

'Who knows? I'd rather not find out.' Michael looked at Gavin. 'Besides, I have more than a passing interest in tonight's proceedings, too.'

Gavin seemed about to leave it at that, then he said quietly, 'Do you think there's still hope for Anne?'

Michael shrugged. 'It can't be hope*less*.'

'But he's had her probably a day—maybe two— more than he's had the girls. That's not good.'

'No, not really.'

'And if we're all honest with each other, there's not much hope for Linda and Beth either, is there?' Gavin's voice turned hard. There was a silence.

'Look, let's find out together, hey?' Michael said, draining his cup to hide the grim expression on his face.

20

THEY TIMED THEIR drive to the riverside barbecue areas so that they passed through Hickory in the early evening, with enough light left to let them keep an eye on the side-streets and deeper shadows. Because of the damage to the windscreen of the utility they took Michael's van. Taking a risk, Michael retraced their earlier escape path. Arnold Connors' body wasn't lying in the street. The shovel was missing, too.

'You can't keep a good man down,' Michael murmured. No-one found it funny.

As they drove off the main road and under the trees by the river, the last of the sunshine disappeared. The van's headlights gave the landscape a tunnel-like effect as the bushland closed in on either side of the track. Michael took them past the first of the barbecue areas without hesitation.

'Are you going to the last one?' Gavin asked.

'No, further. To Kerry's crop circle—where all the trouble started last time.'

'Makes sense.'

'Won't the car scare them away?' Kerry asked nervously.

'I'm sort of hoping it'll bring them out of the woodwork, really,' Michael said.

'Oh, right.' She nodded and in the reflection of the headlights Michael saw she looked unhappy.

'Perhaps you shouldn't have come.'

'I wouldn't have missed this for the world.'

Gavin startled them both by letting out a short bark of laughter.

Coming over the slight rise and down the other side the headlights illuminated the crushed circle of grass perfectly. New growth was already marring the neatness of it. Michael used the space to reverse the van so it pointed back in the direction they'd come, quipping that they might need a quick getaway. When he turned off the motor and headlights the night seemed to draw in uncomfortably close.

'Jesus, it's dark,' Kerry said unnecessarily.

'No, it's not actually,' Gavin said, pointing through the windscreen at the narrow section of sky they could see above the top of the sugarcane. It was a deep orange. 'The sun's not quite down yet.'

'You're a damn comfort, aren't you?' she said, smiling to rob her words of any offence. 'Where're your torches?'

'Torches have a habit of dying whenever we meet our friends. Mine's well and truly dead,' Michael said. 'And the local stores are temporarily out of stock,' he added wryly. 'What about yours, Gavin?'

'I lost mine in the bush the other morning. I don't even remember dropping it,' Gavin said flatly, killing the moment of good humour.

'Well,' Kerry said, after a short, awkward silence. 'Are we going to wait in the car, or outside? I'm getting kind of warm here, squashed between you two.'

'Fresh air, I think,' Michael decided, opening his door and getting out. As an afterthought he lifted the tailgate of the van, giving them something to sit on. Kerry pressed in close beside him. Gavin walked in small circles, kicking at the grass.

Kerry said, 'Now, for something different, we'll just sit around and see what happens.'

Waiting on the edge of the canefield in pitch dark was hard on their nerves—especially when they thought about what they hoped to meet. At first the tension was fierce. They tried to keep up trite conversations, all the while looking about them for a sign of anything happening. But the time dragged on and nothing occurred. Michael found himself making a conscious effort not to look at his watch, which just made the passage of time even slower. He had expected too much to happen too early. Eventually Kerry relaxed enough to lie back in the van, leaving her legs dangling outside. She answered questions in dull monosyllables, and soon didn't answer at all. Michael thought about trying to make her more comfortable, but decided against disturbing her.

'God knows, I couldn't possibly sleep,' Gavin said, nodding at Kerry.

'It's all this waiting around and the tension.' Michael gave Kerry a fond look. 'She's more exhausted than she knows.'

Gavin began to talk about what had brought him to Hickory. He told Michael of his and Linda's dream of a simpler lifestyle in a cleaner environment, of having more control over how they lived. As he spoke his eyes continually flicked around the bush and canefields close by. When he ran out of things to say, it was Michael's turn. Because he'd already basically explained what had brought him to the town, he heard himself telling Gavin about his relationship with Anne Shannon. It seemed a strange thing to discuss, given the circumstances, but any subject would have done. It was something to fill the hours.

'Damn, I wish we'd brought a flask of rum or something,' Michael grumbled after a while, hunching his shoulders further against the cold.

'We could go for a walk,' Gavin suggested half-heartedly.

'I figure we're in the right place. It wouldn't be wise to go wandering, anyway.'

'It's getting so damned hard to just wait here.'

'There's nothing else to do, is there?'

'This is the longest night of my life,' Gavin said irritably. 'We should be *doing* something, for God's sake. I'd like to go back to Powers' place and grab his skinny fucking—'

Michael cut him off, holding up his hand. 'Gav, be quiet a second. Listen!'

356

Gavin immediately fell silent and cocked his head. Kerry surprised Michael by quietly sitting upright, too. He wondered how long she'd been listening to their conversation.

'It's something on the river,' Michael decided. 'A boat?'

'Let's take a look.'

The three of them moved as quickly as they could, picking their way in the dim moonlight towards the water's edge. As they came closer it wasn't hard to see what had caused the noise. The river was quite wide at this point and there were no overhanging branches to shade its surface.

'Oh God, who is it?' Kerry whispered.

'It must be the kid, Ainslie McGregor,' Michael answered.

It was. Standing on the bank, silhouetted against the silvery surface of the water, stood a small figure. He'd risen out of the shallows, disturbing the water. Although they could see him, it was difficult to pick out any real details. Ainslie's feet were bare, that was obvious from the pale skin standing out against the darker mud. The steadfast gaze which he fixed on the three people watching him was unnerving and frightening. Then his voice came clearly across to them, a tortured sound, yet still high and clear—and with a chilling ring to it that had nothing to do with the words he spoke.

'Tonight you will be joining us. We are becoming stronger, while you are all failing in spirit. It is easier for you to succumb.'

His arms held loosely at his sides, Ainslie began to walk towards them.

Michael and Kerry began to back off, horrified, but Gavin stood his ground and shouted, 'Where's my wife, damn you? And my daughter, Beth? I'm not afraid of you!'

The child's corpse didn't even register Gavin's question, and simply continued moving forward, heading up the slight embankment to where they stood. Michael leaned forward and urgently grabbed the sleeve of Gavin's jacket.

'Gavin, there's no point! This is something different, I'm sure of it. It's got nothing to do with Powers. Remember what Riley said? He said it was something Powers had *started*, but he'd somehow lost control. I don't think we should let him get too close.' When Gavin refused to acknowledge him, and remained staring defiantly at the approaching figure, Michael literally shook him. 'Gavin! This is not who we came to see! And if you confront him, it might ruin any chance you've got of getting your girls back.'

Kerry was trying to edge further away from the approaching corpse, but she was reluctant to lose contact with Michael. 'Please Gavin, for God's sake,' she said. 'Let's keep our distance.'

With an angry snort Gavin spun around and together they all walked quickly away from the water. Behind them they heard a childish peal of laughter. 'So what the hell are we going to do?' he snapped. 'Lock ourselves in the car? We didn't think of *this*.'

'Why not the car?' Michael replied, sounding very shaken. 'At least we can drive away, if need be. We did this afternoon, right?'

'Maybe we should drive away now?' Kerry said,

distraught. 'Gavin's right. We didn't expect this.'

'You two can go!' Gavin grated, throwing an angry look over his shoulder at the river. Ainslie McGregor's corpse stepped onto the flat ground beyond the riverbank. 'I'm not going anywhere. I'm going to see this through, no matter what happens.'

'Then we'll handle one thing at a time,' Michael said, reaching the van. As they passed the tailgate he slammed it closed. Then, as he grasped the handle of the driver's door a stench hit him. It should have warned him, but Michael was in too much of a hurry and his reactions were slow. He'd already opened the door before he realised someone was sitting in the driver's seat.

Arnold Connors jerked his shoulders, his head flopping over on its broken neck to stare at Michael.

Michael let out a strangled cry and fell backwards, only just managing to keep his feet. 'Christ! Stay away from the van,' he yelled, seeing Kerry's silhouette fill the opposite window. She cried out too and disappeared from view. More childish laughter came from somewhere nearby. Michael recovered and dodged around the front of the vehicle. Out of the corner of his eye he saw Connors begin to emerge from the van. Kerry and Gavin were standing together at a safe distance, unsure what to do. Kerry kept glancing nervously towards the water and the slight, menacing figure approaching.

'Let's get to the track,' Michael told them tightly. 'We don't want to get boxed in by the river.'

They went and stood between the wheelruts, waiting to see what would happen next. Kerry was trembling and she moved close to Michael. He wasn't happy having the canefield at his back.

Trying to stay cool, Michael said, 'Gavin, I say we run like hell down the track if something more fucking encouraging doesn't happen soon.' Connors had emerged from behind the van and stopped, swaying drunkenly on his feet, waiting for Ainslie to reach him. Connors now held something in his hands. Michael didn't have to guess what it was.

Ainslie called out, 'You shouldn't run. There's no point. We don't need to run to catch you—and I know how to play catch better than any of you. Even though I'm only a *child*.' The spirit let out another squeal of laughter at this, then added in a much more solemn tone, 'Jake's come to play, too.'

Michael felt dread building inside him and he stared to his right, away from Hickory. A dark figure stumbled out from the sugarcane to stand a short distance down the track. Michael looked desperately at Gavin and Kerry. 'This is getting out of control,' he hissed.

'I'm staying,' Gavin said harshly. 'There's nowhere else for me to go—nothing else I can do. *You* said it. Something's going to happen tonight and *this* isn't it. Powers isn't even here.'

'Guys, I don't think we have a choice, anyway,' Kerry told them quietly, nodding in the opposite direction.

Back towards Hickory the slight rise in the track was silhouetted by a bright, approaching light.

Michael swore and said, 'They're trying to herd us into the canefield.'

'Maybe that's where we should go,' Gavin replied, looking behind them. The black square in the wall of cane, the track he and Michael had followed the laughter down before, seemed to beckon them.

'That's where they trapped us last time! Are you crazy?'

'No—but I can't see anywhere else for—' Gavin stopped, his attention drawn away, then he suddenly yelled triumphantly, 'Jesus, look!'

Another light was beginning to glow, building in intensity, above the cane. Before Michael could decide for himself, Gavin ran into the dark maw of the track and disappeared. Michael hesitated a moment, unsure what to do, but one look at the three corpses now closing in, and the light growing from the Hickory end of the track, convinced him they had no choice but to follow. Grabbing Kerry's hand he said, 'Come on!' and pulled her stumbling after him.

Inside the canefield only a narrow corridor of light penetrated the high tops of the plants on either side. Already they could see Gavin was near the T-junction at the end of the track and about to disappear one way or the other.

'Gavin, wait!' Michael called. 'We should at least stay together.'

Gavin hesitated, then turned to face them. 'Then hurry up,' he said impatiently, his voice even more distant as the surrounding plantation soaked up the sound.

Kerry was moving awkwardly, constantly

twisting around to check behind them. 'They're coming,' she said fearfully. Michael stole a moment to glance behind them, too. Three figures were silhouetted against the open end of the track, the light increasing in brightness behind them. Michael thought he heard a motor and suddenly feared they'd done the wrong thing—run from approaching help. Then he remembered no-one in Hickory was going to help them, and their three dead pursuers didn't seem too concerned about whatever was approaching along the riverbank.

'We seem to be able to outpace them,' he said, more for Kerry's benefit. In fact, he didn't doubt Ainslie McGregor's claim: *We don't need to run to catch you.* 'As long as we keep ahead of them, we should be all right.' As they caught up to Gavin they heard another peal of childish laughter.

'Which way?' Michael asked.

'The same as before. The light seems to be coming from that direction, anyway.'

They moved off together, almost tripping over each other in their efforts to stay close. Gavin paid more attention to the sky, looking at the now-familiar, unearthly white light visible through the plants. It seemed to be growing in intensity. Gavin continued around the next right-angle bend unhesitatingly. Kerry saw something in the shadows out of the corner of her eye and jerked away from it, startled. Michael moved quickly to her.

'It's okay,' he said calmly, keeping her moving. 'It's just a pump of some kind for irrigation. They've got it in a cage.'

'I know. I'm just scared stiff and I wasn't expecting—'

Shocking them all, the pump suddenly burst into life with the staccato roar of a two-stroke motor without an exhaust muffler. The three of them jumped backwards, yelling with surprise. Within seconds a thick jet of water spurted from an open pipe, but the wire caging diffused the burst, causing it to spray in all directions at once. They staggered further away, covering their heads with their arms to avoid getting wet. At a safe distance they stopped and turned, staring at the spuming water.

Shaken, but recovering, Michael shouted above the noise, 'Gavin! We *must* be right! UFOs have been known to do all sorts of crazy things to machinery.' He jerked a finger at the glowing sky above them. 'I'll bet *this* is causing the pump to start all on its own!'

Before Gavin could answer more evil laughter came from behind them. Michael spun around and saw the three dreadful figures standing at the apex of the bend. He thought desperately, *Are they still walking corpses now? Or have they become their own damn ghosts?* Michael couldn't tell—but all three figures were glowing now, matching the unreal white light filling the sky.

'Christ, get *moving*!' Michael yelled, shoving Gavin and Kerry in the back, hard.

The other two didn't bother to turn to see what was wrong. Again shielding their heads they dashed forward through the shower of water. The pump's motor was hammering at a rate far beyond what it was designed for and wouldn't last long, but for now it was throwing out a tremendous amount of water. Just running through the geysers created by the wire caging was enough to give a soaking, turning their clothing heavy and shockingly cold. Despite the dangers, once through the water Kerry wanted to curl up into a shivering ball and give in to the freezing chill, it was so numbing. Michael saw her knees start to buckle and he hooked a hand under her arm and dragged her along. They kept moving to the end of the track, coming to the second T-junction. There they paused and Kerry groaned, hugging herself. Michael's teeth were beginning to chatter, and his whole body shook.

'We're going to the same place, aren't we?' he asked Gavin, a tremor in his voice. They were far enough away from the irrigation pump not to need to shout.

'It looks like it,' Gavin said, pointing towards the side-track where they had encountered Jake, Ainslie and the brilliant light before. This time the light wasn't pouring out of the track itself, but seemed to be concentrated in a blinding mass suspended in the air. 'We should have guessed. I just hope we're going to meet the right people, or whatever they are—not just a congregation of Jake's dead friends!'

Michael suddenly drew Kerry close. 'Damn it, Kerry! If there was any way I could keep you away from this, I would,' he said desperately. 'But I can't leave you alone anywhere now. I should have left you at Gavin's and told you to lock yourself inside. You would have been safe. How stupid are we? We should've have known everybody and every*thing* would be here!'

Kerry turned her pale face up to his, the dark

rings under her eyes made worse by the white light. 'Shut up, Michael,' she said, and even managed a sad smile. 'There's no way I would have let you leave me behind.' Surprising him, her expression turned to a frown. 'Hey, how stupid *are* we? A *congregation*? I'll bet where we're heading is the exact site of Isaiah's old church. This canefield probably swallowed it up years ago.'

Michael was confused by her clear, logical thinking, when everything else was becoming so frightening. Gavin was less impressed, and interrupted tersely, 'Let's get this over and done with. I don't want to waste another second. It might make the difference between life and death for my girls.' He started walking down the track towards the light. Michael and Kerry held each other a moment longer, then followed him, hand-in-hand.

As they walked the laughter started again, alternating from the low, wicked chuckles to squeals of boyish delight. It came from the canefield all around them. Michael guessed that the growing supernatural light was somehow making the three corpses behind them stronger, giving them powers they didn't have before. In some way, they had split their corrupt spirits from their dead bodies, which still shuffled in pursuit of the living. Gavin kept his face forward, refusing to acknowledge what he now knew was deliberate taunting. Michael did the same, with less success. Kerry was the worst, jumping badly at each new sound and staring into the dark shadows, hoping to catch a warning glimpse of whatever caused it. Behind them the irrigation pump clattered to a ruined halt. Now the laughter leapt at them from the near-silence. Only a soft humming filled the air. As they got closer to the side-track and the glaring incandescence hovering above it, the terror of what awaited them consumed all their senses—the numbing wetness of their clothing, even the horror of the dreadful spirits dogging their every step. They came to the side-track and stood squinting, peering between spread fingers, trying to see anything within the incredibly bright light.

Michael's impression was of a large, intricate piece of machinery hidden within the brilliant radiance. Metal and glass-like surfaces reflected shimmering rays of light. There were what appeared to be pipes, or other objects attached in a maze of mechanics and hydraulics.

Kerry and Gavin couldn't see any more than Michael. The light coming from above was too brilliant, burning black spots on their retinas. Wonderingly, Gavin began to walk slowly forward. After a moment's hesitation Michael and Kerry moved with him. The closer they got to the thing hidden within the glare, the harder it was to see anything. Dimly, Michael registered the sound of more laughter behind them. He knew the corpses would be standing at the opening of the side-track now, reunited with their spirits and cutting off any retreat. Moving as close as they dared, Michael, Kerry and Gavin stood bathed in the hot, flaring light. As they watched, two more pin-points of white came alive, then the night was filled with a deafening roar.

Suddenly shadowing the brilliance hanging in the air behind it, a cane-harvesting machine, its augers and blades churning hungrily, lurched towards them out of the light.

The unexpectedness of it—to be struggling with the concept of meeting somebody, or something, totally alien and unknown, only to be suddenly confronted by a very real, earthly threat to their lives, had the three paralysed in the harvester's path. Even as the bellowing machine increased speed, towering over them, the vicious cutting tools throwing clods of dark earth aside, nobody could move. An eternity seemed to pass before Michael finally began to dodge away towards the cane, pulling Kerry with him.

'*No!*' Gavin screamed over the shattering noise of the motor. 'It can move through the cane faster than you can. Back up!'

They stumbled backwards, shielding their eyes against the glare of the harvester's spotlights and the blinding glow of the thing still hanging in the air behind it. A squeal of childish laughter cut through the roaring. Michael glanced behind him. The corpses were waiting. Gavin was yelling again.

'It can't turn! Not *well*, anyway. We have to try and dodge around the back of it, but wait for the last moment! It's got to be at the very *last* moment.'

Michael nodded to indicate he understood, but he was terrified at the thought of trying to slip past the twirling blades. They all stood their ground, about to make the attempt, then Gavin changed his mind and pulled them all back another few metres, giving them extra, precious seconds.

'Split up,' Gavin shouted. 'You take Kerry to

the left, and I'll go right. If I make it, I'll try to get up onto the cab and get control of things. Otherwise, try and get behind the bastard and stay there, okay?' That was all the time he had to explain. It left a lot of things unsaid—like, how the harvester would probably choose to chase one group and that could mean a violent and bloody death. Whoever survived still wouldn't have many options available.

'Wait for it,' Gavin said, his teeth set in a grimace of effort. 'It's got to be at the very last second—'

The corpses behind them let out howls of ghoulish delight, a terrible sound that would unnerve any living human, but the harvester's deafening noise was nearly drowning them out. Gavin lifted his hand, ready to signal the exact instant they should move. The machine was only metres away, the rolling steel blades flashing in the reflected spotlights.

Then it abruptly stopped.

The motor cut out completely and the lights died, flaring briefly before shrinking to impotent, orange-glowing filaments. The harvester coasted forward less than a metre, its tremendous weight dragging it to a halt, and the machine seemed to sag like a huge, tired animal to the ground. The corpses at the head of the track immediately changed their howls to screams of rage.

'Now!' Gavin yelled, recovering first. 'Get around the back of it!' The three of them scrambled forward, not worrying about splitting up. Michael's skin crawled as he pressed close to the inert blades of the harvester, expecting them to burst back to life as quickly as they had stopped, chewing him to pieces. Then they were beyond the harvester and back into the light behind it. Gavin looked up at the cab of the machine as they passed. It was empty. At the same time the quality of the blinding glare around them changed, becoming softer. The screaming from the end of the track cut out suddenly, bringing back the silence of the night, broken only by the quiet humming. It let Gavin hear Michael's soft swearing.

'My God, they're *here*,' Michael whispered. Gavin snapped his attention away from the harvester and back to the track in front of them.

The brilliant light had become a pulsating glow from the cane beyond the end of the track. Standing silhouetted against this, just short of the first plants, was a slight figure. Only a metre tall and built like a child, it stared towards the three people with two eyes that had burning points deep within them. The figure's head was unnaturally large. Stunning them further, it seemed to speak.

'You are safe, for the moment.'

It was impossible to tell where the voice came from, although there was something like a telepathic suggestion that it should be recognised as coming from the alien. It spoke again.

'Where is he?'

Michael was the first to recover, realising who the alien meant, but when he tried to talk his voice came out as a nervous croak. He cleared his throat.

'Powers? He's not here. He's supposed to be, we know, but he's not.'

From the still, listening attitude of the alien it was clear it was digesting this information, formulating a response. *'This is wrong. We should be alone. You should not be here.'*

Gavin found his voice and moved forward suddenly. 'He's got my family! He took them! Can you help me?' He stopped, as if running into a barrier, and a look of confusion spread over his face as he fought against some invisible restraint. Kerry and Michael watched in amazement.

'I have your family now,' the alien said, making a small gesture towards the light behind it. *'We gathered Kann's workplace as we approached. He may call for it, but it will not respond.'*

'You have them? Then set them free, damn you!'

The alien was unmoved by Gavin's passion. He seemed almost to dismiss him, as if having answered his questions sufficiently. Michael sensed it was important to maintain a contact, even if it wasn't resolving the things they really wanted to know.

'What are you going to do here?' he asked, trying to sound challenging.

'We are already doing it.'

Michael looked around quickly. Nothing seemed to have changed. 'What do you mean?' A dizzy spell hit him for a moment and he had to reach out for support. He felt Kerry grip his arm and she asked anxiously if he was all right. Her voice sounded distant and hollow. Then he heard the alien again.

'You will know.'

'I don't give a fuck what you're doing!' Gavin

370

cried angrily, but with an edge of desperation, knowing he was powerless. 'I just want my family back! Why won't you give them to me?'

A new sound grew above the humming. It took a moment for the three humans to realise this wasn't another unworldly trespass, but a more earthly noise. It was the sound of a car's motor as a vehicle worked its way through the canefield towards them. They all turned to look and soon there was the flash of headlights across the mouth of the side-track, only just visible past the bulk of the harvester. Gavin began to swear, distraught at the interruption. The motor cut and in the stillness they heard doors closing and grunts as somebody made a painful, laboured effort to move. Michael looked towards the alien, expecting it to be frightened away by this new intrusion, but instead it emanated an attitude of expectancy and determination. Turning back to the harvester Michael saw a cumbersome, frightening shape struggling past the machine. Then he realised it wasn't just one person, but two, one supporting the other.

'Guess who?' Michael muttered.

Moving out of the shadow of the harvester was Powers, helped by Jeff Butler. Powers looked dreadful. He was obviously weak and his skin was a terrible colour in the white light. Muscles twitched uncontrollably on his face and he was loose-limbed, like a drunk. Despite this, on seeing the tableau in front of him he shook Butler off with an angry snarl and stood alone, swaying, barely staying upright. Butler collapsed to the ground with an anguished cry and lay still.

'I'm here!' Powers called hoarsely, looking past the three people to the alien. 'I've done my work. Now it's time for me to return to myself—to live again.' He began to stagger forward with short, pain-filled steps, but the alien's reply brought him to a halt.

'You are corrupted. You should have told us. You cannot even leave your alien host now. We believed it was happening and I was sent to confirm it. Now I see our fears were correct. You cannot return until your next time. You know that.'

'No! *No!*' Powers moved forward again, stumbling out of control. Michael pulled Kerry aside as he brushed past, leaving in his wake a stench of filth and illness. Powers fell to the ground just short of the alien figure and lay clawing at the thick soil of the wheel-tracks, trying to pull himself to his feet. 'Take me! I have done my work. I *deserve* to return.'

'You are dying. It is not permitted for you to return now. You may corrupt the rest of us. Take comfort that you have done your work well.'

With that the alien turned and moved towards the canefield and the light within it.

'Wait! Wait, for God's sake! My family!' Gavin yelled, his voice breaking.

The alien seemed to hesitate on the edge of the cane, then it paused and half-turned towards the watching humans. *'You must leave here now. Who you know as Powers, we call our brother Kann. Kann is Changing—in your terms he is dying. He is corrupt and will turn to what makes him strongest to survive. He will not allow himself to move on peacefully—and what makes him strongest is what you fear the most.*

You will be right to fear him. You should leave now.'

The figure disappeared among the tall stalks before anyone realised what it was doing. Gavin suddenly understood he was no longer restrained and sprang forward, running towards the cane, ignoring the sprawling shape of Powers as he passed.

Michael ran a few steps after him then stopped, reaching back to grab Kerry's hand. 'We've still got to stick together,' he said, starting after Gavin again and dragging Kerry with him. They took a wider circle around Powers than Gavin had taken. Michael noticed Powers was lying still now. He found time to hope Powers was dead, and surprised himself with the thought. When they reached the cane Gavin had already vanished into the thick growth of plants, but the light coming from the other side was so bright it was possible to see his bulky silhouette. Michael hit out at the stalks, making a path for himself and Kerry. After only a few metres they came to a clearing—and an incredible sight.

A glowing, round craft hovered just above the surface of the crushed cane plants. An area as large again formed a perimeter of broken, flattened stalks. A door in the side of the saucer was closing. Even though the craft was little more than that—an almost featureless, saucer-shaped vessel—it evoked in Michael an incredible sense of wonder at what he was witnessing. He threw his hands up in front of his face, feeling a burning sensation against his skin, and squinted through his fingers. Looking quickly to his side, he saw Kerry doing the same. Beyond her, Gavin stared

373

in hopeless desperation at the saucer. He wasn't bothering to protect his skin and Michael could see tears falling down his cheeks.

The saucer began to rise, the humming noise growing. Gavin let out a meaningless yell of anguish at the departing craft. Then, as it climbed to over ten metres above their heads, a beam of light stabbed down from beneath it. It lasted only a few seconds, but in the instant before the beam snapped out again Michael saw something materialise on the ground beneath the saucer.

Three shapes, lying side by side.

'Gavin! Look!' Michael went to run forward, but several things happened at once. He tripped on the jumbled surface of the crushed cane stalks and began to fall. At the same time the saucer vanished into the air and the sudden lack of light was as effective as if Michael had closed his eyes. Then the light was immediately replaced by a new, similar glow and a growling hum twice that of the saucer. Michael looked up from his prone position and saw another craft, incredibly huge in comparison to the one that just disappeared, climbing from the canefield only a short distance away. This enormous saucer rose majestically into the air and hovered above the field, dwarfing everything and filling the sky. Then it, too, vanished into the night sky with such speed it blurred in Michael's eyesight.

Michael was speechless and lay where he fell, literally too stunned by what he had seen to move. Blackness swamped him again, his pupils contracted and temporarily useless. Vaguely he began to recognise noises around him—movement close by, which he guessed would be Kerry, and a soft sobbing. Gavin was crying.

'Gavin! Didn't you see them?' There was no answer and Michael realised Gavin didn't know what he was talking about. 'Not the saucers—the girls! I *think* it was the girls. They left three people behind as they took off. Didn't you see them? They're in the centre of the clearing.'

The sobbing stopped and there was a long pause, then Michael heard Gavin mutter, 'Oh God, oh God—' before he called, more strongly, 'Where, Mike? Where, for God's sake? I can't see a fucking thing.'

'I can't see anything either,' Kerry cried out nervously.

'Just wait a moment. Your eyes will adjust. Be careful, for Christ's sake. These fallen cane stalks are bloody dangerous.' As he spoke Michael began to see more. He turned his face upwards, deliberately keeping his sight away from the thin, crescent moon, and picked out the brightest stars starting to break up the otherwise uniform blackness of the sky. He turned his attention back to the clearing of broken plants. The shattered stalks, lying like a collapsed spider's web, shone silver in the moonlight. Where the juice had been squashed from the stems they glistened wetly. In the centre of the circle three dark shapes stood out against the cane.

Michael stayed on all fours, picking his way carefully towards them. He heard swearing and looked across to see Gavin trying to walk across the stalks, but the other man kept tripping and falling and was actually making slower progress.

Heavy breathing behind him told Michael Kerry was following his example. He was the first to reach the three bodies. By that time he could see quite clearly.

All of them wore an anonymous garment and only Beth was instantly recognisable from her child's size. Michael had to put his face close to those of the women to determine their identity.

The first was Anne Shannon, and she was obviously dead.

The skin of her face was parchment-like and her mouth hung slackly open. Worse, her eyes stared up at him, unmistakably lifeless. Stamping down his grief Michael moved to Linda and only had time to register that her eyes were closed, but she appeared in better condition—and possibly alive—before Gavin pushed him aside. Gavin glanced at Anne's face and dismissed her as a stranger, then he looked down at his wife and went still.

'Linda,' he whispered, and gently touched his fingers against her cheek. Torn between who to attend to first he looked achingly at his daughter's prone shape.

Linda's eyes snapped open and stared uncomprehendingly up at Gavin. Then a look of deep-seated terror filled them. She sat upright with a jerk, opened her mouth wide and began screaming, a loud, wrenching animal sound so shocking that Michael pulled back a moment and Kerry let out a small squeal of fear before bringing herself under control. Gavin desperately wrapped Linda to his chest in a bear-hug, pressing her face into his clothing and stifling her screams. He rocked her like a child and murmured comforting words. In his arms Linda kept screaming, her body visibly racking with the effort.

Suddenly she stopped and went absolutely still. A dreadful expression of fear and confusion came on Gavin's face and he stared helplessly over the top of Linda's hair at Michael. In the silence Beth began to move and cry softly. Kerry reached out for her tentatively, desperate to offer comfort, but unsure whether the first touch should come from the girl's father rather than a complete stranger. And she was terrified the same thing might happen to Beth. Kerry didn't want a little girl dying in her arms, too.

'Lay her back down,' Michael told Gavin quietly. 'Quickly. She must be going into a severe shock.'

After a long silence Gavin whispered, 'No, she's dead now. I know. I can feel it.' He gripped his wife tighter, holding her face against his body. Michael exchanged a look with Kerry.

'Please, Gavin,' Kerry said, gently. 'Lay her down again. You can't be sure.'

Gavin transferred his stare to Kerry and she almost shrank back at the madness in it. Then he slowly released his hold on Linda so her head fell away from his chest. It lolled backwards. Linda's eyes were still open, but now had the same terrible, vacant gaze that Anne Shannon possessed. A trickle of blood ran from the corner of her mouth. Wordlessly Gavin let them look at her for a few seconds, then pulled her back close to him.

Michael covered his face with his hands and took some deep breaths, trying to calm himself.

Kerry felt her vision swimming, a light-headedness in her mind suggesting that to simply let go, to give in, would be the best cure—the easiest way to rest. But through the blurring of her eyes she saw Beth moving more, and heard the young girl's cries becoming louder. An overwhelming urge to comfort Beth filled Kerry and she fought off the faintness. Shutting out thoughts of what had happened to Linda, she quickly leaned forward to pick Beth up and hold her.

'Michael, help me,' Kerry said, finding Beth's weight awkward. Michael moved closer and lifted Beth onto Kerry's lap. Beth subsided to a steady sobbing, pausing occasionally to draw in long, wet breaths through her tears and running nose. Kerry stroked the back of her head and whispered into the girl's ear. Michael reached over and lay his hand on Kerry's leg, just so he was touching her. He didn't dare touch Gavin.

They all stayed like that a long time, until finally Kerry said softly, 'What shall we do, Michael?'

Michael had been sadly turning their options over in his mind. He kept his voice low. 'Leave the two women here and come and get them in the morning. We could bring the van in and take them tonight, but I think once we're out of the canefield again, none of us will want to come back in. Not at night, anyway. Gavin might try and carry Linda—'

Kerry cut him off. 'But how do you know they'll be here in the morning?'

Michael was puzzled for a moment, then he glanced meaningfully at the sky. 'But they've gone. I expect it's all over.'

'We can't be sure. Riley said it was out of control, and nothing to do with why Powers was really here.' Michael was quiet, unsure of the answer.

The answer came from somewhere else.

A sing-song, broken chant came clearly through the night air. It was in a strange, lilting tongue and Michael barely recognised any of the words. Then he went cold inside as he plainly heard one of the words mixed into the otherwise-unintelligible lyrics.

'*Burning*—'

Michael twisted around and saw a tall, awkward figure walking—no, *dancing*, he realised—around the edge of the clearing. The figure's steps were unaffected by the mess of broken cane plants underfoot. Impossibly, it seemed to him, Michael's fear increased. He looked to Gavin and saw him watching the prancing shape, then recognised the gleam of hatred and revenge in Gavin's eyes.

'Isaiah,' Gavin snarled quietly. With exaggerated care he let Linda's body slip to the carpet of crushed greenery, and tried getting to his feet.

'No, Gavin,' Michael said urgently, quickly reaching out to grasp a handful of clothing. 'Remember what the alien said? This must be Powers in his strongest form. What did he call him—Kann? There's nothing you can do. We just have to get away.'

'I can kill him,' Gavin replied, looking with a murderous glare down at Michael, telling him with his eyes to let go.

'He's already *dead*, Gavin! And the alien inside

379

him is dying, too. There's no point. We've got to get away before he kills *us*.' As Michael said this, he realised it was a very real possibility. He knew it was part of the departing alien's warning.

Gavin clearly wasn't listening. Kerry called to him.

'Gavin, Beth is still alive. You have to get her away, at least. Everything else can wait.'

Now Gavin stared at Kerry and the young girl on her lap, as if noticing Beth for the first time. For a long moment he seemed undecided, then something in his expression of anger broke, and was replaced by a deep sadness. Gavin reached down and lifted Beth into his arms in one strong, smooth movement.

'Okay,' he said gently. 'For the moment, you win. Let's just get the hell out of here.' Then he added, in a flat, emotionless voice, 'We'll come back in the morning.'

Michael didn't comment on that, or repeat Kerry's fears that there may not be any bodies to collect. He kept his attention on the jerking figure of the priest. Isaiah had nearly completed an entire circuit of the clearing and was coming back to the point they wanted to escape through, back to the side-track. 'Let him go past where we want to go,' Michael whispered, unsure if Isaiah could actually hear them. 'That will give us plenty of time to get there and make our way through the cane.' Nobody argued, so they watched in silence. The priest's chanting hadn't stopped or changed, and the word 'burn' came clearly several times. The mad figure finished one circuit and began another.

This time something dreadful began to happen.

As he moved past the wall of cane, at frequent intervals the stalks and the undergrowth around them burst into flame. The priest was setting fire to the canefield, lighting more and more as he moved around the edge of the clearing.

'My God, he's burning the *cane*,' Michael cried, appalled. 'We'll be trapped if we don't move fast!' The cane fire was already starting to spread faster. The priest kept dancing and chanting, though his words were almost drowned by the noise of the flames. The fire ate hungrily at the plants, but it was the undergrowth which burnt most ferociously. This was the weeds and long grass which had grown when the sugarcane was only young. When the plants reached a mature height and density, denying the undergrowth sunlight, the weeds soon died, leaving behind a dry, flammable debris.

There was no breeze to push the fire in any one direction, so it was slowly expanding away from each ignition point. Michael saw licks of flame coming up from beneath the crushed sugarcane too, and he knew they couldn't wait any longer. Making sure the others were following, he started to make his way over the broken plants, crouched over and using his hands as much as his feet to keep moving. Michael felt one of his feet slip between the stalks and threaten to become trapped at the ankle. It needed control not to panic and try hauling it free—it would be an easy way to break bones. Kerry was close behind him. Gavin had the worst of it, cradling Beth with one arm against his shoulder. The nine year old was no small burden, unbalancing him and leaving him with one hand less to use.

Isaiah was two-thirds the way around the perimeter when Michael reached the edge. He found the place they'd entered, the cane plants there already pushed aside and creating an easier passage. Michael stood back and let Kerry and Gavin move ahead of him. He wanted to make sure the ghoulish priest didn't follow—although Michael was beginning to suspect he didn't know they were there. The heat was becoming intense and the whole area was lit up in a lurid orange light from the leaping flames. The noise from the fire was a loud, harsh crackling. Michael put a reassuring hand on Gavin's back as he went past and he was surprised when the other man stopped and looked at him, a despairing expression on his face.

'There'll be nothing left in the morning,' Gavin shouted above the flames.

Michael realised he meant the bodies of the two women. 'We can't take them now,' he yelled back. 'There's no time! We'll get caught in the flames.' Then he added, against his better judgement, 'Perhaps it's best, Gavin.' Michael wasn't sure Gavin understood what he meant, because he merely nodded wearily and moved on. Michael had time for one last look and had an urge to devote this moment to the dead women. He stared into the centre of the clearing, a whispered farewell on his lips.

One of the bodies was gone.

Michael groaned with the shock—and the certainty of what he'd see next. He resisted the impulse to simply turn and leave, instead leaning out of the sugarcane to see Isaiah now quite close, coming towards him as he completed the circuit.

Anne Shannon now danced behind the spirit, aping the priest's prancing movements.

Michael stood and stared a long time, until he was shaken out of it by the smell of his own hair beginning to singe. The two were nearly on top of him, the priest's face a rictus of insane delight. Michael suddenly thought about dodging into the cane, waiting for Isaiah to go past, and reaching out and pulling Anne away—then he remembered she was dead. She *had* to be dead—there had been no doubt about it. He felt someone grab at his clothing and turned to see Kerry, crouched down against the heat, tugging at him.

'Michael, for God's sake! Come on!'

He obeyed, mostly because he didn't want Kerry to see Anne Shannon's dancing corpse—and all that it might forebode for the future.

Breaking out of the cane into the side-track Michael saw Gavin waiting for them. Behind them flames were climbing well above the tops of the plants, casting a flickering glow over everything. Powers' body hadn't moved, stretched across the wheelruts. Jeff Butler also still lay where he'd fallen. No-one gave the two bodies a second glance, pushing past the harvester to the track beyond. Michael's heart was in his mouth, expecting to see the three corpses again blocking their escape, but the entrance to the track was empty save for Jeff Butler's utility. Michael saw Gavin falter a moment, and he knew Gavin was thinking they could have taken Anne and Linda's bodies away had they moved more quickly and realised the utility would be here. Michael forestalled any discussion by pushing ahead of the others.

He said, urgently, 'You drive, Gavin. Put Beth between you and Kerry. I'll ride in the back.' Without waiting for an answer he vaulted into the back tray. He sat impatiently while Gavin and Kerry arranged themselves and Beth in the cab, then Michael breathed a sigh of relief when the motor burst into life. He'd been assuming Butler hadn't had the presence of mind to take the key from the ignition.

It was a close thing. The tracks towards the river brought them back into the fire. Gavin gunned the motor hard, racing between the tall stalks while one side of the canefield began to burn fiercely. In the back Michael covered his head with his arms and felt burning ash falling down on his hands and the back of his neck. Then Gavin turned another corner and they were heading for the river, away from the flames. Michael sat up and looked behind them. A wall of flames stretched out wide, consuming everything in its path. He briefly wondered if they would jump the firebreaks—then decided he didn't care.

They transferred over to the van. No-one had any idea what might happen the next day, but there was no point inviting trouble by being seen driving around in Jeff Butler's vehicle. Once they'd settled in the van Michael turned to look expectantly over his shoulder at Gavin, who clutched Beth protectively to him in the back. But it was Kerry who told Michael what to do.

'It might be best if we put Beth back into her home environment. Familiar surroundings will give her one less thing to cope with. All her toys and favourite things will help.'

Michael nodded wearily and started the van. He took them straight through town without pausing. From the back of the van Gavin couldn't see anything—but he wasn't looking, anyway. Michael and Kerry exchanged looks when they sighted ominous figures several times, lurking in the shadows of the main street. At the Packers' home the two dogs were pleased to greet them, wagging their tails enthusiastically as the van's headlights swept over them. Michael quietly took that as a good sign. The dogs didn't seem concerned or overexcited, as they might be if they had had to deal with any intruders while everyone was away.

Once inside, Gavin disappeared with Beth into her room and didn't come out. Michael helped himself to one of Gavin's home-brew beers and Kerry decided to share it with him. She winced at the unfamiliar taste with her first sip, and sat at the kitchen table opposite Michael.

'Are we safe?' she asked, keeping her voice low.

'I don't know—probably not,' he added reluctantly. 'Still, I doubt the dogs will let anyone unwelcome get too near, even if they warn us with yelps of fear.' He tried to make this sound funny, but it didn't work.

'What do you think we should do?'

'Get out of town.'

'Now?'

'No way. I'm not sure I'll ever travel at night again in my life. Especially around these parts I'd like to see what I'm driving towards, and that means during daylight. We need the rest, anyway. Tomorrow, I vote we take the best vehicle and head for the hills.' Michael saw Kerry's next question coming and said, 'Don't ask me what we're going to do when we get there. Your guess is as good as mine.'

'Who's going to believe us?'

'I might be able to convince someone, as long as I take it carefully and approach the right people. Also, if I'm quick enough, there might be some sort of evidence left around here.'

Kerry frowned. 'Something left? What about those things in the street we saw as we drove here? Isn't that evidence enough?'

'I don't think they'll be around very long. With Powers dead and the UFO gone, I figure there's not enough—well, enough *whatever*—for them to stick around. Know what I mean?'

Kerry nodded, but didn't look convinced.

They began to discuss what they would do once they were safely away from Hickory. Michael hinted he'd like Kerry to stay with him, at least for a while, and she didn't object. They managed to talk for some time without really coming to any firm decisions. Then Gavin appeared in the doorway. He looked awful, but calm.

'I'm going to sleep in Beth's room,' he whispered, throwing a look back towards the bedroom, worried Beth might wake up while he wasn't there. 'You two can sleep in the main bedroom. There's clean sheets in the chest at the foot of the bed, if you like.'

'Thanks, Gavin. We were just thinking about

getting some rest.' Michael paused, considering whether to make some comment about what they should do in the morning, but he let it go. 'Goodnight,' he said, all too aware how trite and inappropriate it sounded.

'Yes, have a good night,' Gavin echoed automatically, his voice dead and emotionless, and turned on his heel.

'We should do it—get some rest, I mean,' Michael said to Kerry. He stood up and offered his hand across the table.

'God knows if I'll sleep,' Kerry said, taking his hand. Then she belied her own words by yawning deeply.

Michael had a dream.

He was moving through an immense space, so vast it was unimaginable. Distances that his human mind should be able to comprehend became meaningless, endless figures. Others were travelling with him, but they were both far ahead and way behind him. It was like being part of an ocean convoy, except the intervals between the individual ships were again incredible distances. Communications from the first ship to the last were impossible. The signals became too dissipated as they moved through space. Each vessel could only contact the next in line—but only just, if they were in the right place at the right time.

It was necessary to encode the signals. Undesirable elements could discover the convoy's plans and attempt to take advantage of that knowledge. But the enormous variety of intelligence existing within the space the convoy travelled through, a very unique type of code was required to remain unbroken. Simple, yet still unique.

Like being in the right place at the right time.

Michael awoke, trembling with excitement at the knowledge that had come to him in his sleep. Other pieces of the puzzle fell into place as he shook the sleep off. A memory came to him, something the alien had said: *You will know.* He realised this wasn't something he'd worked out for himself, but knowledge given to him by the alien. An explanation. That was the cause of the dizzy spell immediately after the alien had spoken the words.

Michael couldn't wait until morning to tell Kerry, he was so excited and wide-awake. He shook her until she stirred, then Kerry's eyes flew open with a startled expression. Michael quickly soothed her, whispering there was nothing to worry about.

'Kerry, I know why the aliens came here!' he said, barely managing to keep his voice down.

'What—?' Kerry blinked in the darkness and asked sleepily, 'Now? Haven't you been sleeping, thinking about it?'

'No, it came to me in a dream! I think the alien gave it to me somehow. That was the dizzy spell.'

Kerry sighed and sat up in bed, pulling the bed-clothes up to her chin. 'I can see you have to tell me now,' she said, only half-serious.

'I might forget it if I go back to sleep.'

'I doubt it, the way you're jumping around, but tell me anyway.'

'Well, they came to receive a signal.'

Kerry was silent a moment. 'A signal?' she said, dryly. 'Is that it? Is that all they were doing here?'

'Yes, but you see it had a special code. They had to be *here* to receive it.' Michael paused impatiently, searching for the right words. 'Look, the earth's atmosphere distorts everything before it reaches the surface, right? UV rays, radio waves— all across the spectrum—radio waves of *any* description are all distorted by the atmosphere. So, if you were to receive a radio signal from outer space, and you were in a precise position on Earth, that signal would be distorted as it travelled through the atmosphere, and that distortion would make it unique—*absolutely* unique, understand?' Kerry stared at him, but didn't say anything. He went on, 'So, conversely it must be possible to use that distortion factor and encode your signals with it. Meaning, if you weren't in the right place at the right time, the signal would be unintelligible to you.'

Still only half-awake, Kerry struggled with it. 'But how do you know where to be?'

'*That's* the system! These people are leap-frogging across space. What they would have received tonight, encoded with the Earth's atmosphere and this exact location, is the where and when of the next place to be—and the encoding for that place, too, obviously.'

'Obviously,' Kerry repeated dully. 'So—what was Powers doing here?'

'He was a sort of guardian. He was supposed to

389

ensure that the area didn't become too populated or dangerous for the rendezvous to take place. That was the "work" he said he'd been doing. And that was why he killed the original settlers who survived the influenza virus and burned them in the church. He probably figured a few more deaths wouldn't make a great difference and it meant he could keep the area clear. Where his calculations went wrong was that we resettled the district anyway. This time, he should have warned off the UFO and sent it to an alternative position, but remember Powers' "work" was finished and he didn't want to be left behind. And he was sick, which was why his judgement was affected—and also why they didn't take him with them.'

' "Corrupted" is what the alien called him,' Kerry said slowly, remembering.

'That's right. And look what he's been doing to this town! It's possible there's guardians like Powers all over the world, doing the same job, and what happens if they become corrupted? This could explain half the supernatural phenomena that's occurred since time began—'

Michael stopped suddenly. He listened hard, and didn't like what he heard.

'What's that?' Kerry whispered, afraid, guessing what the sound was.

'It sounds like gunfire,' Michael said grimly. 'But it's a long way away. Damn, listen to that! You wouldn't think there were that many guns in Hickory. It sounds like World War Three's broken out.' This was an exaggeration, but it was true the amount of gunfire seemed excessive for a small town, even under the strangest circumstances.

390

Michael got out of bed and went to the window, flipping the drapes aside. There was nothing to see. He decided, 'Stay here. I'm going to check on Gavin. He might be worrying about keeping Beth safe.'

Michael quickly pulled on his jeans and padded softly through the house to the kitchen. He didn't turn on any lights and saw Gavin's dim shape standing near a window, obviously listening to the gunfire.

'What do you think?' Michael asked quietly.

'It's something new for us to be concerned about,' Gavin replied, his voice flat with exhaustion. 'But not tonight, I think—not tonight.'

'You should go back to bed. Isn't Beth scared?'

'She's been so scared for so long, I fear she's beyond feeling anything any more. But you're right. I don't want her to wake up alone.'

'I'll stay up for a while, just in case. The dogs will let us know, anyway, if anything comes closer.'

'Yes,' Gavin whispered shortly. He brushed past Michael and went back to Beth's bedroom. Michael frowned after him, wondering if Gavin even knew that he was walking about the house—if he wasn't so shocked and fatigued that he didn't realise what he was doing. Hearing the door to Beth's room click closed, Michael returned to the main bedroom. Kerry was sitting up in the bed waiting anxiously for him.

Michael said easily, 'You know, that's too far away to be Hickory. I reckon that's coming from somewhere else.'

'But where? There's nothing else around.'

'Tell me something I don't know,' he said, trying to smile and keep her calm.

'Shit, will this ever end? Christ, Michael! What are we going to do *now*?'

Michael thought for a long time, then climbed back into bed and pulled her close to him. 'Nothing different. It's far away and I'm not going to go looking for trouble. If trouble wants to come here, then we'll worry about it. I'm sure the dogs will hear anything coming long before we do. My money's still on us waiting until daybreak. It would be too dangerous for us to try anything in the dark. We've got to hang in here until the sun comes up, then I say we make a break for the highway and get out of town.'

'But we have to go through town to get to the highway.'

'Yes,' he admitted. 'That's a bit of a worry—but it's tomorrow's worry.' He sighed and shook his head tiredly. 'You should try and get some more sleep. I'll keep my ears open for a while.

'Sleep! You've got to be kidding.'

But Kerry soon did fall asleep. The gunfire died away within a few minutes and she couldn't stay awake long, even though she felt guilty about not keeping Michael company. Michael didn't do much better. He fought off waves of exhaustion as long as he could, listening for any unusual sounds or the dogs being disturbed, before finally falling into an uncomfortable sleep, still sitting upright with his arm around Kerry. By then, dawn was only a few hours away.

21

MICHAEL WALKED OUT into the kitchen in the early morning and found Gavin standing at the window again, staring out at the new day. Coming up behind him, Michael could see Beth sitting at the table outside. She was absolutely still, looking across the property towards the bushland at the back fence.

'She knows her mother's gone—dead,' Gavin said quietly, without turning around.

'Does she remember how?'

'Not really. I think she became aware of it when she woke up in the middle of the clearing last night. She heard me tell you Linda was dead. Anything before that, she doesn't seem to remember—or she doesn't want to remember. I haven't pressed her about it.'

'What about you?'

'Me?' Gavin turned around. He looked like he hadn't slept for days.

'Are you all right?'

'I'm okay,' he said shortly, then tilted his head towards the window. 'It helps, having to worry about someone else. Otherwise I don't know what I'd be doing. Going crazy, I guess.' Gavin was keeping himself under tight control. Michael wasn't certain whether to go easy on him or tackle their problems now, while Gavin seemed able to cope. He spoke very carefully.

'You realise there's no point in us going back to the canefields, don't you? The fire would have taken care of everything. At least, there's nothing there now that you or I would want to deal with.'

'No, I know that. I've been telling myself that for the last hour, actually,' Gavin said tiredly. 'So, what do you think we should do?'

'Leave town. Let's see if we can get somebody from outside to believe what's been happening here and maybe return with a few reinforcements.' The words reminded him, 'Do you remember hearing that gunfire last night?'

'Yes, but I just really didn't care—like my head subconsciously accepted it was miles away and not worth worrying about. I had other things on my mind, too.'

Michael nodded sympathetically. 'Kerry and I have been talking things over. We thought it might be a good idea to take two vehicles. It will give us a backup.'

'Sounds okay. Beth will want to take Mandy, so

394

I suppose we can put both dogs in the back of your van.'

'They'll come in handy if we need to camp out somewhere. The dogs certainly made me rest easier last night, knowing they were out there.' Michael watched Gavin closely, making sure the other man really was keeping himself together. He seemed utterly calm—still shocked, but calm. Michael had heard of instances where it was the calm ones who suddenly exploded into berserk violence. Gavin was staring out the window at Beth again. Michael said, 'There's no point in all of us going into town to get Kerry's car—and it's got to be hers. It's full of fuel and will be more comfortable. Your ute's got a broken windscreen anyway. You should stay here with Beth and pack anything we'll need. Kerry and I will do a quick dash into Hickory, grab her car and get out again. It won't take us long. Okay?'

'Fine. I'll explain to Beth what we're doing. I'll get her to help me feed up the animals and put out plenty of water. You be careful. Don't stop for anyone. In fact, don't even drive slowly.'

'Don't worry,' Michael said grimly. 'Not even the Pope could flag me down in Hickory today.'

Ten minutes later Michael and Kerry were in the van heading for town. Kerry quickly made a list of things she felt they might need in the most dire circumstances, such as being forced off the highway and having to hide in the bush for a few days. She'd managed to discuss it with Gavin, and he told her what he had already stocked in the house, leaving Kerry with a revised list of items to find in her own home.

'Are you going to need fuel in this thing?' Kerry asked, as the van approached the edge of Hickory.

'No, I should easily have enough to get us to the next town.' Michael reassured himself with a quick glance at the gauge.

'Let's hope the next town's in friendly territory,' Kerry murmured.

They swung into the main street and Michael saw immediately that something was blocking the road ahead. 'Fuck it!' he snarled, bitterly disappointed that things weren't going to go smoothly. Something about the scene ahead of him changed his anger to puzzlement, and he began to slow the van. Kerry glanced at him anxiously.

'What the—?' Michael began, then fell silent, unsure what he was seeing.

'What on earth is that?' Kerry asked for him, fear creeping into her voice.

Four figures stood in the middle of the street. They wore bulky, shapeless garments, and each had a loose-fitting cloth helmet with a tinted visor and breathing apparatus on the front. And they held weapons. It was only the brown and green camouflage patterns, and the heavily armoured vehicle half-hidden in the shadows on the side of the road, that revealed to Michael who they were.

'My God, it's the army!' he said wonderingly. 'And they're dressed in full biological-warfare gear, from the looks of it.'

'Then they must have found what's going on!' Kerry said, her fear changing instantly to elation. Michael pressed his foot back down on the accelerator.

They were still a hundred metres from the

soldiers, who were nervously moving about and hefting their weapons, and regarding the approaching vehicle warily. Out of nowhere another figure appeared next to them, startling the soldiers so much they backed off and raised their automatic weapons. Michael cursed loudly and stomped on the brake pedal, bringing the van to a squealing halt.

'That's Isaiah—or Kann. Or whoever the fuck he is now,' Michael said, his voice full of dread. 'What's he going to do?'

He flung his door open and jumped out onto the road. The soldiers were anxiously shouting instructions to each other, their voices muffled by the protective gear. Michael yelled, 'Stay away from him! Don't go near him!' At his call one of the soldiers levelled his automatic rifle. Michael felt the pit of his stomach go cold at the sight of the tiny black hole in the barrel aimed straight at him. He waited to hear the rattling bark as it fired, and in a reflex action threw his hands up in the air. 'No, not *me*, for Christ's sake! Stay away from *him*!' He felt someone standing next to him and he glanced sideways. Michael was appalled to see Kerry had got out of the van and come around to his side of the vehicle.

It might have been the appearance of the woman which stopped the soldier pulling the trigger and spraying the street with bullets. Then he had other things to worry about.

The soldiers had entered Hickory barely minutes before Michael and Kerry arrived. The four-man patrol had no idea what to expect, but then that was their job—to find out what the hell was going on in the small town. In the last twenty-four hours all of them, including the experienced sergeant leading the patrol, had been given and followed orders the likes of which they had never believed they would encounter in their careers as professional soldiers. Now, only the sergeant had been vaguely briefed on what they might find in Hickory. He was still struggling to believe it.

To him and his men, the place appeared to be a ghost town—though none of them knew just how close to the truth that was. It wasn't unusually early in the day, yet nobody walked the streets, or appeared within the confines of their fenced gardens. There were no vehicles moving anywhere. As they'd travelled towards the town, one of the soldiers noted that for a rural community surrounded by literally thousands of square kilometres of sugarcane, there wasn't a single working tractor or farm vehicle to be seen. Then, as they entered Hickory itself, the men rightly expected the unusual sight and sound of the armoured personnel carrier to excite some reaction from the locals. But nothing happened.

It made them nervous.

Predictably, the burnt remains of Mal Bartell's store and the pharmacy next to it brought the APC to a halt. The sergeant scanned the scene through one of the observation slits. These were hard enough to see through at the best of times, the limited field of vision providing scant information. Being suited-up in full bio-warfare equipment made it twice as hard, and the sergeant found himself wishing he hadn't opted for the tinted visors.

'We'll dismount,' he told the others. 'Bring your weapons.'

They left the motor running. The back doors swung open and the men climbed out, moving away from the vehicle and spreading out slightly, scanning as much of the area as they could at the same time. The sergeant left them and walked over to the ashes. He stepped into the debris, kicking at the mess and turning over some of the larger pieces with his boot.

'I can't see any bodies,' he said loudly. He moved closer to the pharmacy and peered in among the ruins there, but he wasn't game to venture beneath the fragile remains of the ceiling. One of the soldiers, a corporal named Cooper, called out urgently.

'Vehicle coming, boss.'

The sergeant quickly returned to the others and took his place in the defensive formation. In the distance an ordinary van had turned into the main street and was heading towards them. The soldiers heard the engine note fall as the van slowed, and they tensed, expecting the van to turn away suddenly, then the motor picked up again.

'We gave him a fright,' someone murmured.

'Not fucking surprising,' Cooper said dryly. 'I scare myself, dressed up in this shit.'

'Quiet,' the sergeant ordered. 'This bastard might try and run us down, for all we know.'

Then Isaiah appeared, suddenly materialising before their eyes.

'Jesus fucking *Christ*!' one of the men shouted

hoarsely, backing away. 'Where the hell did he come from?'

As a group they drew back towards the APC. The sergeant was yelling, telling them to stay steady. One soldier cocked his weapon and the others automatically followed suit. Isaiah stepped towards them. His priest's garb did nothing to alleviate their fear. He was a dreadful sight. Even though he was a spirit—a true ghost—as a human being he now looked very old. His hair was only sparse, unsightly tufts. The skin of his skull was mottled with disease, as was his face, which was now so withered Isaiah's eyes bulged crazily from their sockets and his yellowed teeth gaped unnaturally. His cheeks had shrunk and tightened, pulling his lips back in a permanent, ghastly smile. He stretched one hand towards the soldiers. It was withered too, an inhuman claw with flesh like parchment.

'You are ill,' he hissed, taking them all in with a searching gaze.

In a nervous reaction one of the soldiers replied, his voice shaky and high-pitched, 'Like fuck! You're the one needing the doctor, mate. Jesus, what the hell do we do, boss?'

Behind Isaiah the men saw the van brake hard to a halt, the tyres locking up. A man jumped out of the driver's side and started yelling at them, telling them to keep away from the ghoulish figure still slowly advancing towards them. The sergeant levelled his automatic rifle and in a panic considered opening up, taking out the weirdo and the guy from the van, too. Then someone else ran around from the other side of the van. The

400

sergeant saw it was a woman—a very attractive woman. He couldn't bring himself to pull the trigger.

'*You are all ill,*' Isaiah spoke again, his words silken and frightening.

It was Corporal Cooper who allowed the flicker of doubt in his mind—he certainly didn't feel *well* at this particular moment. His guts churned with fear at the horrific figure confronting them. He'd been scared since his unit had begun moving into position around the town the previous evening. Their section leaders had told them to expect God-knows-what and to wear full protective equipment. That had to mean something bad was going down.

Inside the helmet Cooper could hear his blood pounding in his ears. Then he saw the old man's eyes fix directly on his. *Where the fuck did he come from?* Cooper lost his orientation, the shouts of his companions sounding distant, unconnected to what he was trying to do himself. In fact, he couldn't remember *what* he was doing any more. Cooper tried to look around, to re-establish his identity, his purpose, but he couldn't tear his eyes away from the old priest's burning gaze. Without realising it, he stopped backing away towards the APC. He didn't hear the shouts of the others to keep moving.

The pounding in his ears filled his whole head now. It felt as if someone was pumping up his skull with fluid. His vision began to swim and a sudden, agonising headache made him cry out. No-one noticed the difference between Cooper's scream of pain and the others' yells of excitement

401

and fear. The last conscious thought Cooper had was of a large bubble of liquid bursting somewhere behind his eyes, releasing the awful pain in a warm flood.

The flood was actually copious amounts of blood that poured from his nose. As Cooper died, the haemorrhage bringing death almost instantly, he expelled his final breath in an explosive burst which sprayed blood all over the inside of his visor. He crumpled to the ground, falling on his back.

'Cooper's down! Cooper's down!' someone shouted unnecessarily. The sergeant steeled himself to jump forward and drag the fallen man back with them.

In the instant he leapt, Isaiah vanished.

His training kept the sergeant moving, even though his mind was stunned, reeling with the effort to understand what was happening. He dropped to his knees next to Cooper and stared down at the soldier's face. At first the sergeant was confused by the black liquid coating the inside of Cooper's visor, then he realised it was blood—the tinting made it appear black. A lot of blood.

'Christ—' he muttered, then snapped over his shoulder, 'Help me get him back in the APC! Move it!' He looked up to see the man and the woman running forward to help. The sergeant jumped aside to let the others pick up Cooper. He faced the two people.

'Stay the fuck back!' he screamed, sounding so crazy both the man and the woman staggered in their attempt to stop suddenly enough. The man held his hand up and started to speak, but the sergeant cut him off. 'You heard me! Stay back!' The man kept coming, still trying to reason with him. The sergeant raised his weapon, pointing it over their heads, and pulled the trigger. The automatic rifle crackled out rounds, sending a shower of brass cartridges around his feet. The two people dropped to the road, the man trying to cover the woman with his body. The sergeant stopped firing and stared down at them.

'I told you to stay *back*!' He was panting and struggled for words. 'You people are *contaminated*,' he snarled finally.

He risked a quick glance over his shoulder and saw the other soldiers looking anxiously out at him from the open back of the APC. The soles of Cooper's boots were visible on the flooring between them. In one swift movement the sergeant turned and jumped into the back of the APC. The moment he was inside the back doors slammed closed. Seconds later the vehicle's motor roared and it moved jerkily off, heading back the way it had come, towards the highway out of Hickory.

Michael and Kerry lay gasping in the fumes of the APC. Kerry groaned with fear and frustration— and pain. She had hit the bitumen hard, and had Michael drop on top of her. He rolled away, then stood and helped her to her feet. He brushed the grit off her clothing and gave her a reassuring hug.

'What *happened*?' she asked, holding him tight.

'I'm not sure. I can only guess Isaiah must have hurt one of them somehow—I don't know. But he

403

didn't even touch them, I could see that. They immediately thought it was some disease or something, the poor bastards. That's why he said we were contaminated.'

They started walking towards the van, Kerry limping. 'But I don't understand,' she said. 'What do you mean, a disease? Why would they think that?'

'Well, maybe not a disease, but that's what they were expecting—some sort of contamination. They were dressed for it. Those biological suits are gas-proof, chemical-proof and even bloody germ-proof. They're not standard issue, that's for sure.'

'So that means they know the UFOs have been here. It's the only explanation. Have the bastards been sitting around watching us all the time? When they could have helped?' Kerry was getting angry.

'Right now, I think anything's possible. If they didn't know already about the alien rendezvous here—which I think is unlikely—it seems they had some sort of contingency plan ready. I guess that's not beyond the realms of possibility. There've been reports and rumours of crashed aliens in the United States since the late fifties. Someone must have taken the idea seriously by now,' he finished wearily.

Michael went around to the passenger side of the van with Kerry and helped her in. As he walked back to the driver's side he saw something moving in the shadows of a large tree some distance away. The movements were painful and laboured, like someone in trouble, and lately that meant it would be someone Michael and Kerry didn't want to meet. He didn't panic, but climbed into the van, started the motor and drove off. Kerry realised he wasn't going to turn off to her house or do a U-turn back to the Packers'.

'Where are we going?' she asked nervously.

'Following the APC.'

'What? Are you crazy? What if that lunatic shoots at us next time?'

'That's why I'm not in any hurry. I doubt that they're on their own. I'm hoping the next soldiers we meet will be different and maybe not so quick to pull the trigger.'

'Christ, Michael! They might be quicker, too!'

He tried to give her a crazy grin. It nearly worked. 'So, duck!'

She stared back at him.

They reached the turn-off where the road became the highway out of town. They had only been travelling along it for a few minutes before Kerry frowned and asked, 'Have we got a flat tyre? It sounds like it.'

Michael weaved the car a little and said, 'No, it doesn't feel like it.' The noise quickly got louder and they both recognised it at the same time.

Michael only had time for a muttered, 'Oh-oh,' before the sound became a shattering noise and a Blackhawk helicopter swooped low over them. The camouflage colouring stood out starkly against the clear blue sky as the aircraft twisted sideways in the air in front of the van, the dark square of the side-gunner's door facing down at them. The helicopter looked like a huge, preying insect about to pounce on the van.

Kerry shouted over the clattering of the rotors. 'What the hell are they going to do? Bomb us, for God's sake?' She was only kidding, but her face was grim when she saw Michael wasn't about to dismiss the idea.

A piercing, metallic voice snapped down at them. 'Turn around. Do not go any further. Return to the town.'

'Well, at least they didn't *start* with shooting,' Michael said. He kept driving. Kerry looked at him in amazement.

'Aren't you going to turn around?'

'Let's see if we can get a little further.' Michael sounded calm, then his control broke a little and he lightly beat his fist on the steering wheel. 'Fuck it, I just want to try and *talk* to someone!'

'Slow your vehicle immediately and turn around. You cannot proceed further.' The Blackhawk was keeping pace with them in an impressive display of flying which maintained the aircraft's sideways profile. The road ahead was straight for some distance before it disappeared in a sweeping bend to the right. Michael said stubbornly, 'Let's try and see what's around this corner.'

'This is your last warning. Turn your vehicle around and return to the town. You are in a quarantined area and cannot leave.'

'Quarantined?' Kerry said, stunned. 'They're not going to try and trap us in the town, are they? Do they know what's walking the damn streets back there?'

'I'm afraid that's exactly what they want to do,' Michael said, instinctively hunching his shoulders as the helicopter dropped its speed a little, allowing the van to come closer. His stomach went cold when he saw the muzzle of a machine-gun suddenly appear from the aircraft's side door. The van was coming into the bend and Michael drove ready to slam on the brakes at the first sign of anything on the road.

It was almost anti-climactic. A jury-rigged barrier of empty oil drums combined with normal hatch-patterned, reflective road signs stretched across the bitumen. A large white sign with red lettering announced the roadblock's purpose.

STOP
TURN AROUND AND GO BACK
YOU ARE ABOUT TO LEAVE A QUARANTINED
AREA WITHOUT AUTHORITY

Michael brought the van to a halt just short of the sign. The Blackhawk hovered about twenty metres above the ground on the other side of the barrier. The crew stared down at the van, faceless in their helmets and dark goggles. Michael could see movement in the distance and what were obviously more army vehicles gathered on the road.

'That sign makes me suspicious,' he yelled to Kerry, the noise from the helicopter deafening. 'They didn't chalk that up in a hurry. They knew they were going to be cordoning off a specific area.'

'But "quarantined" doesn't necessarily mean UFOs,' Kerry shouted back.

Michael agreed with a nod. 'I wonder what they'd do if I tried to go around the sign?'

'For God's sake, Michael! There's no point! They're—'

'I don't think they'll shoot at us. They would have done it by now. Get out of the car and I'll do it on my own, if you like—maybe it's best, anyway.' At Kerry's disbelieving look he shrugged an apology. 'Okay, okay, I'm sorry. I didn't mean that. Look, I think now's the best time to try anything. Probably nobody knows what the fuck's going on. While everything's so confusing, they shouldn't be too quick to start pulling triggers.'

Kerry shook her head in exasperation, but said, 'All right, try it—but I'm not getting out of the car. That will only signal what you're going to do. And if they get upset, let's not push our luck any more after this!'

'That's a deal,' Michael said, putting the van into gear. He slowly swung the vehicle to the left, aiming well off the road to drive around the roadblock.

As soon as it was apparent that Michael was moving past the roadblock instead of turning around, the helicopter's heavy machine-gun started firing out rounds with a loud, staccato hammering. The gunner aimed at the road just beyond the roadblock, the large fifty-millimetre rounds exploding the soft bitumen in a rapid series of black geysers. Small stones and dirt splattered hard against the side of the van and Kerry screamed. Michael let out a yell of fright and stomped hard on the brake, stopping so suddenly the engine stalled. The machine-gun stopped, but the Blackhawk stayed where it was, hovering menacingly close.

Michael said shakily, 'Okay, I think we'll call that pushing our luck far enough.' He restarted the engine and put the van into reverse. Michael could have done a U-turn, but he didn't want any forward movement to be misinterpreted. He flinched as the van began to roll forward for an instant, hoping the gunner in the helicopter didn't have a nervous trigger-finger. Slowly they backed away from the roadblock until Michael was convinced it would be safe to swing the van around.

They both let out sighs of relief as the van headed back towards Hickory. Behind them the noise of the helicopter faded. It seemed the Blackhawk wasn't interested in following them.

'Hey, next time you want to kill yourself, let me know first,' Kerry said, reaction putting a tremor into her voice.

'I'm sorry, but we had to try something. We can't just go back to Hickory and sit there waiting for something to happen. Not if Isaiah and his friends are going to drop in every five minutes.' Michael went quiet, thinking hard for a moment. 'We have to figure out a way of getting a message through to those people.'

'Won't they try and contact us?'

'You'd think so, but I don't know how long it will be now before they try.' An idea came to him and he turned on the van's radio. Twisting the knobs in every direction only brought him harsh static. 'Damn, nothing's changed there. Whatever Powers used to interfere with the airwaves is still working. I'll bet the phones are still out, too. We won't see another patrol—after what just happened to one of their men, they won't be in a hurry to do that again.' He thought some more. 'Maybe Gavin has some ideas. He was in the army reserve for a while and he might know what their standard procedure will be. Otherwise we might have to try this method again.'

'Try again? How? What's wrong with you—do you like getting shot at or something?'

'I was thinking about a different approach,' Michael said calmly. 'Maybe it's time our Mr Riley started making amends for his past actions. The boys in the helicopter might not be so fast to fire at a police car.'

Sergeant Riley had been fighting his own demons—some real, others imaginary. Since his visit from Michael, Gavin and Kerry, the policeman hadn't moved out of the police station's office except to go to the toilet, where he'd swayed so drunkenly his stream of yellowed urine splashed almost everything but the white ceramic bowl.

Riley had been drinking a lot. He was on his fourth bottle and had given up bothering with any mixers. He had a case of rum in a cupboard—a whole case. It was strictly against the rules, but Riley had stopped worrying about breaking the rules a long time before.

It was difficult to spend the allotted petty cash funds in a one-horse town, but he felt he had to, otherwise they'd be reduced. So Riley had long since begun falsifying small receipts and tucking the cash away. It was his 'Christmas fund', he'd wink, whenever he leaned over the counter at Macquarie's garage and added an extra ten dollars to his fuel receipt. No-one was about to argue. Too many of the town's more respected citizens availed themselves of a friendly rum or two and a good chat at the station. Riley knew people liked the feeling of importance it gave them to call the police sergeant by his first name, to sit on the other side of the counter and share a drink. It made them feel special, and maybe just a little above the law. These people felt safe from being included on Riley's annual quota of traffic offences.

Of course, there were some people who weren't ever allowed the privilege of a rum-drinking, off-the-record friendliness with Riley. The sergeant had to keep a balance in the town, have his 'good guys' and the 'bad guys', otherwise the good ones didn't feel so special any more. Even in a town as small as Hickory—or perhaps because it *was* so small—there were politics to be juggled, standards to be kept. Riley had to consider people like Jeff Butler, who, in Riley's opinion, was a smart little bastard who thought he was ten feet tall, bullet-proof, and couldn't stick to a speed limit if you paid him. Now there was one who would never taste his rum.

Jake Sanders had been another one. There were several reasons Riley hadn't hung Jake by his dope-growing neck a long time ago. First, Riley had too much respect for the man's mother. Apart from that, there was the paperwork and extra attention hanging a drug conviction on Jake would bring. Riley knew it wouldn't be a simple case of a bag of green leaf under Jake's pillow. The guy was actively growing plants and regularly selling them in the city. A bust out at Jake's place would be a big-time headache Riley really didn't need.

411

Still, it had irked the policeman the way Jake swaggered around the town in his torn jeans and black leather waistcoat like it was a uniform of his own, affording him an authority of his own, too. In fact, there were a few folks in Hickory who would show Jake more respect than they showed Riley's uniform of the law. That really annoyed Riley. There was no way Jake Sanders would ever drink his rum, either.

Riley didn't know it yet, but Jake was coming for a drink anyway.

The policeman had fallen into a drunken stupor, asleep at his desk, still upright, his head dropped onto his chest. He was snoring wetly, his mouth open. Riley's clothing was a mess—he looked like a man who had been very drunk for several days. His skin was a sickly colour, his hair was an unkempt tangle of damp spikes.

The gunfire woke him up. The few hours he'd slept at least took some of the edge off the alcohol he'd consumed in the last six hours. The sound of automatic rifle-fire was unusual enough to penetrate Riley's deliberate, drunken daze and he opened his eyes slowly, wincing at the electric light filling the police station. For a moment he didn't know what was happening. His immediate concern was the terrible sour taste in his mouth, the sick churning in his stomach, and the headache snapping at his temples. Lifting his head, Riley groaned, and heard the joints in his neck creak and pop.

He cut the groan off suddenly, hearing the rattle of gunfire again in the distance.

'Oh, shit,' he mumbled, pushing himself to his

412

feet. The room spun around him and he needed to lean forward quickly, putting his weight on the desk and closing his eyes until the dizzy spell went away. Eventually it did, but the rebellious boiling in his stomach got worse and Riley knew he had to vomit. He staggered away from the desk, knocking the chair aside as he went, and made his way blindly across to the tiny bathroom on the other side of the building. The stench of stale, splashed urine in there was enough to make Riley drop to his knees and hug the toilet, heedless of the sticky mess he knelt in, and retch uncontrollably for nearly five minutes. Only a thin bile came up. He hadn't eaten anything except for a few biscuits since he'd started drinking. It felt as if he was vomiting up his stomach, until he finally leaned away from the bowl, putting his face against the wall and shutting his eyes. The cool surface of the paint on his flushed skin gave him a moment of relief and he could have fallen asleep again right there, but the smell of urine and vomit slowly got the better of him. The need for fresh air forced him to his feet. Riley yanked on the toilet's old-style chain impatiently several times before it obliged with a rush of water.

Now he stumbled to the front door, hearing more gunfire as he went. On his way he looked towards the windows. The outside world they framed was totally black, and Riley had to concentrate, focusing his sickened eyesight on the clock mounted high on the wall. It was four o'clock in the morning. For a moment he considered it a funny time for anyone to be awake and firing a gun, but this was followed by his first really lucid thought for some time—nothing was unusual in Hickory any more.

As he walked down the few small steps into the police station's front yard, the cold night air struck him like a slap in the face, sobering him a little more, but also making his head spin again. Once more he had to close his eyes and work hard to stay upright, the blood pounding in his ears as he pressed his fingers against his temples. The moment slowly faded.

The black, chilly night offered Riley two pieces of information. First was the slightly louder sound of the gunfire, and the second was an orange glow in the sky to his right. The gunfire was a real puzzle. With an exhausted grunt and a nod which made his headache stab harder, he confirmed to himself that it was automatic rifle-fire. Short bursts, not prolonged volleys, but the rate and consistency of firing had to be from an automatic weapon. To Riley's knowledge nobody in Hickory had a gun like that, but it wasn't impossible. Some of the farmers were real gun-nuts—or worse, used to be—and many had God-knows-what rusting away in arsenals stashed under their beds. As the firearms laws had become more strict, it was easier to push these weapons further under the bed than to come clean and admit you'd smuggled a souvenir home from the Vietnam War, or something like that. The only comforting thought for Riley was that the gunfire sounded too far away and definitely wasn't coming from the town itself—which further supported his suspicion that some farmer on one of the outer properties was letting loose with an old, but dangerous, relic.

The glow in the sky was easier to recognise. Riley had seen it many times before. One of the canefields was burning—maybe more than one. The trouble there was, the crushing season hadn't started yet. Nobody was supposed to be burning anything yet. He decided to deal with gunfire first.

There was a certain amount of drunken bravado in this, but at the same time Riley was well aware that all sorts of things had been wandering the streets of Hickory lately. None of these, however, struck him as the sort that would bother with high-performance weaponry. So Riley figured that confronting a madman with a gun might at least guarantee he'd be dealing with a human being.

Riley's own handgun was in the top drawer of his desk. He could have taken a shotgun, or even the department-issue sharp-shooter rifle which was locked in a cupboard, but the thirty-eight revolver was a standard part of his everyday uniform. To go investigating gunfire and be armed to the teeth himself was inviting a long-range sniping shot before he even got close. Riley started to congratulate himself on his smooth, professional thinking, then he got a nasty reminder of the condition he was in. The revolver was in the upper drawer of the desk, but the ammunition he kept in the bottom drawer as a safety precaution. Now, as he flipped the chamber open and tried to load the shells, the gun kept moving from side to side. The bullets were slippery and awkward between his shaking fingers. He dropped several rounds which clattered condemningly onto the linoleum floor. Riley realised he was still very drunk.

Rather than slow himself down, keeping calm and acting as his newly discovered responsibility should dictate, Riley slammed the revolver back on the desk, uncaring that half the chambers were still unloaded. He grabbed at the half-empty bottle of rum next to it and took a deep swig. His throat and stomach, both still raw from the vomiting, rebelled, and he nearly brought the liquor straight back up. Riley fought hard and kept the rum down. His face screwed up against the pain.

A voice called to him from the darkness beyond the front door.

'Hey man, looks like I'm just in time to have a drink.'

Riley spun around at the croaked words, his stomach turning into a cold pit of fear. Someone had walked up the steps to the open door. There was a brief moment as the figure crossed the short verandah into the light, but Riley realised who it was without even looking.

It was the sound of worn motorcycle boots dragging their heels across the timber flooring.

Jake Sanders stepped into the police station. With him came the stench of decaying flesh and thick, dried blood. Jake's face and hands were still chalk-white, but the flayed, open areas of skin where the bitumen had cruelly ripped at him gave glimpses of the grey, dead meat beneath. The clothes were the same—Jake hadn't been dead long enough for the cloth of his jeans or his leather jacket to begin rotting. He stopped at the counter and glared with empty eyes at Riley. Then, with a dreadful purpose, like an automaton that knew where to go without having to acknowledge the obstacles in front of it, Jake began to make his way around the front desk.

'I'm coming for my rum now, Sergeant Riley.'

In his horror Riley froze where he stood, staring at the corpse walking towards him. He snapped out of it with a jerk and let out a small groan of fear.

'Stay the fuck away from me, you freak,' he snarled, snatching up the revolver. Jake ignored him and kept moving slowly towards Riley's desk. The policeman didn't wait any longer. He lifted the gun and aimed, the barrel trembling wildly.

The first shot missed, the sound of it slamming hard at Riley's eardrums in the confined space. It took him a moment to dazedly register the splintered hole in the wall beyond Jake. The next pull of the trigger fell on an empty chamber and Riley let out a howl of dismay. The third was loaded and the bullet tore away a chunk of flesh from Jake's upper arm, splattering blood and mess on the wall behind him. Jake was knocked sideways slightly, then continued his advance, oblivious to the gaping wound. Riley's next shot fell again on an empty chamber.

His reason collapsed and he let the revolver fall from his hand as he backed away from the corpse. He felt his shoulder-blades touch the rear wall. Jake's eyes didn't leave Riley's, but he paused at the desk and reached out blindly for the rum bottle, grasping it by the neck. Jake raised it to his lips and tipped his head back, his Adam's apple bobbing obscenely as he drank. Riley was horrified to see wetness seeping from the wounds in Jake's face, trickling down to soak his neck. The corpse's mouth and cheeks were too damaged to hold the liquor.

Jake removed the bottle from his lips without re-inverting it. Rum splashed noisily to the floor until he banged it back on the desk.

'We should talk, you and I.'

His face white, Riley whispered, 'What in God's name could we talk about?'

'My crimes—the crimes you had me committing. Without trial or justice.'

Riley's terror deepened. He was loose-limbed and realised with a shock that he was on the verge of wetting himself. 'I never booked you for anything,' he said hoarsely. 'I never even accused you of any damned thing.'

'You hated me. You hated what I was, because I was stronger than you.'

'I didn't *hate* you, damn you. I just thought you were—different, that's all,' Riley pleaded. The soft threat in the corpse's voice was terrifying.

'I am stronger now. We are all becoming stronger. The dead are living again. You should join us.'

'No!' Riley cried. Unbidden, a vision of himself as Jake was now filled his mind—he saw his eyes glazed with death and his skin decaying and flaking away in grey pieces. Jake picked up the bottle again and offered it to the policeman.

'Drink with me now. You will become stronger.'

Riley screamed. Jake was offering him death. He had to get out of the police station—get away from this living corpse. The rear door beckoned, just metres away. Riley lunged for it and instantly

418

found himself outside, Jake's laughter echoing behind him. The night was completely black. His nightsight ruined, Riley ran headlong away from the building. He'd only gone a few metres when he understood he'd been tricked—crouched, stinking corpses with their grasping hands would be waiting for him in the darkness. He looked around desperately, expecting to see something loom out of the night towards him, something reaching with rotting, skeletal hands. He was a fool! He should have stayed in the light! A bulkier blackness on his right caught his attention. It was the old gaol cells, unused now for years.

Frantic with fear, it occurred to Riley he could back into one of the tiny cells and close the iron gates behind him. Nothing could get him then! Only the spiders and the cockroaches, and they were nothing compared to the horrors Riley believed were waiting for him within every shadow. Quickly he crossed to the simple stone block that contained the two cells, little better than dog kennels, with stout metal-barred doors. Riley slipped inside one cell and pulled the gate closed behind him. It moved with a harsh, protesting squeal of rusting iron. He needed to slam it several times before the lock engaged. Riley believed that somewhere on his key ring was the key that would let him out—but he didn't care. Feeling safer, he fell back onto the cold concrete and hugged his knees to his chest like a frightened child. It didn't take long before a silhouette blocked out the night sky visible between the bars. Jake's soft, mocking laughter slapped off the walls of the cell. Riley closed his eyes and prayed with all his might for the horrors to go away.

Instead, something touched him in the darkness.

Riley screeched and cowered away. A small black object scuttled around him, squeaking. A rustling began in the opposite corner—something was moving among the dead leaves and rubbish gathered there. Riley stared into the darkness, but couldn't see anything. He managed to keep silent, but another scream wasn't far from his lips. It was nearly forced from him when the cell gate was rattled with tremendous strength, as if the hinges were being torn from the stone. Jake laughed again.

'There is nowhere you can hide from us. Join us, and be stronger.'

Riley tried to close his mind to Jake's hissing, mocking voice. Out of the darkness fingers brushed against Riley's face, like a macabre lover's touch.

He had locked himself in with the spirits of long-dead prisoners. Their ghosts were still alive in the walls.

The cells hadn't been used for a long time, but in the past they'd been occupied a lot, especially just after they were built. The pioneers of Hickory had struggled with the local natives, and the European settlers' answer was to throw the ignorant savages into these cells. Sometimes, after being cruelly beaten as examples, men had died in them, the lessons taken too far. White men had died in them, too: one committed suicide by slashing his wrists with a concealed knife and slowly bleeding to death. He had been gaoled for

thrashing his wife senseless, then become filled
with remorse as the narrow, rough walls and the
barred gate closed in on him.

These were the anguished spirits that, given
substance by the same corrupted force that made
the dead of Hickory's cemetery walk the streets,
began grasping for Riley as he sat hunched against
the cold stone at the back of the cell. Fingers
brushed his skin, or plucked at his clothing. Whispering voices, telling of pain and misery, filled his
mind. At one point Riley felt an intense coldness
against his ear, as if some tortured spirit had put
its lips there to ensure its story of horror would be
heard properly. Crying softly with terror, Riley
alternatively drew himself into a small ball, shutting everything out, then suddenly windmill his
arms or slap at the air around him, as if he was
trying to drive away insects buzzing about his
head. All the time Jake's wicked laughter came
through the bars at the head of the cell. Riley
waited for the plucking fingers to start literally
tearing at his skin, ripping off pieces. Vaguely he
registered that his rump was soaked, that he was
sitting in dampness. At the same time a smell hit
him: the stench of blood. Riley knew it was the
suicide's blood, welling out of the walls and floor
and pooling around him. Involuntarily, his mind
began to shut down, turning off each of his senses
as they were assaulted afresh by every new terror.
Soon he no longer heard the cries of agony inside
his head, and he opened his mouth wide, concentrating on breathing through it, rather than suffering the taint of blood in his nostrils. Eventually he
wasn't even flinching from the spectral touches

421

and jabs that taunted his body. Riley was turning into an unfeeling mound of human flesh, cut off from everything around him, becoming like the very stone of his prison.

But Jake didn't stop laughing.

Although Michael felt they didn't have a minute to waste, he knew they had to get Kerry's car. Gavin would be becoming anxious if he and Kerry were late returning—more so after hearing the automatic gunfire, which seemed closer, now. But it couldn't be helped. Michael drove as fast he could to Kerry's, then kept watch outside while she went in and quickly crammed some essentials from the kitchen into a cardboard box. When she had loaded this into the boot of her car she waved Michael on, but he waited until she was behind the wheel and moving before he drove off, keeping a close eye on the rear-view mirror. They arrived back at the Packers' property without incident. Gavin and Beth watched the two vehicles pull up.

'What the hell's happening?' Gavin called to them, before Michael had even shut down the motor. 'I saw a gunship buzzing the town—a Blackhawk, I think.'

'There were soldiers in the middle of town.'

'Soldiers? What sort of soldiers?'

'Ours, of course—though you wouldn't think so.' Michael got out of the van, stopped, and gathered his thoughts, then leaned back against the van and quickly told the whole story. Kerry joined him, occasionally filling in details he missed. Gavin listened without interrupting, his face becoming grimmer with every passing minute. Beth regarded the two of them with wide, staring eyes, and huddled herself protectively against her father's legs. He absently put a hand on her shoulder.

'So, what do you think, Gavin?' Michael finished. 'Do you know what they're doing?'

'I can't think of anything that isn't already bloody obvious to all of us. They've sealed off the town and they're treating it as some sort of biological disaster of a totally unknown type. Isaiah made sure of that, when he killed that soldier—and how the hell did he do *that*, I wonder?'

Tentatively, Kerry said, 'Well, I think I know what he *is*—what he's become. I've been thinking a lot about Isaiah—terrified of what he might turn into,' she admitted softly. 'The alien said Isaiah would turn to what made him strongest in an attempt to survive. So it must have been while he *was* Isaiah, that the alien inside the priest was most powerful. Remember he told you, Gavin, that Linda and Beth were "chosen"? It's like an insane religious doctrine. And the "burning". Normally it's associated with cleansing, but I think it's a twisted re-enactment of how he killed those poor people in his church, incinerating them all to death. So now Isaiah is the spirit of that insane priest *and* the alien that was Powers. God knows what he's capable of.' She hesitated, uncertain. 'And there's something else, I think.' She paused.

Michael quietly prompted her. 'Go on, Kerry. We're listening.'

'Did you notice how old he looked? Older, I think, than he did last night in the canefield.'

423

'I thought so, too,' Michael said slowly. 'But I wasn't sure—or that it really mattered.'

'He's dying, like the alien said he would. And the form he's taken is dying with him.'

'Then he could already be dead,' Gavin said, reluctantly joining in the discussion. 'He looked ancient as it was.'

'I think that might depend on how long Isaiah lived,' Kerry explained, turning to him. 'Remember the records showed Isaiah disappeared into a "shining door and he vanished into the air"? No-one saw him actually die. It's possible this alien—' She stopped, searching for a name.

'Kann,' Michael reminded her gently.

'Okay—Kann. Well, it's possible Kann kept Isaiah alive far beyond a normal, earthly life-span.' Kerry struggled for the right words, gesturing in frustration. 'It's like Kann has Isaiah's life stored up to use, like a human battery, but every time he uses the image like he did last night—and this morning—some of that resource is spent and Isaiah's image appears closer to Isaiah's real age and physical condition. *That's* why he looked older this morning. And if Kann is trying to prevent his own death, fighting against it like the alien said, and trying to survive, every time he appears as Isaiah, he's using up that time, too.'

Gavin was sceptical. 'So all we have to hope for is that Isaiah will keep popping up every now and again, because eventually he's going to run out of some supernatural gas? And that will be the end of him?'

Kerry held her hands up and looked sorry she'd

424

said anything. 'I wish I could explain it better. It's just an idea. Maybe we should just forget it.'

'No,' Michael said quickly. 'At least one of us has got an idea. It sort of sounds like good news.'

'The bad news is, whenever he *does* appear, we'd better be damn careful,' Kerry said. 'He's not going to waste any of the time he has left. And he's determined to survive.'

This made them silent for a moment. Michael said, 'Okay, if that's what we're dealing with, then *what* is he doing? Does he still insanely think he's got "work" to do, even though the other aliens left him behind? Is he keeping the area clear for more UFOs?' Michael saw that Gavin didn't understand, and remembered that he hadn't had a chance to explain his dream to him. He decided to leave that until later, adding instead, 'Or has Isaiah just turned really malicious? Did he kill the soldier for fun, or out of spite?'

Gavin replied bleakly, 'I'm scared he knew *exactly* what he was doing. Those men were an advance party of scouts reconnoitring the town. The survivors have gone back with a story that even being *close* to one of the inhabitants is enough to cause death—there's no physical contact needed. And those guys were in the best protective suits money can buy, so all their scientific people will be saying they're dealing with something extremely dangerous and completely beyond their experience. The authorities will close this town up tight. Nobody will be allowed out, and the army won't be coming in for another look in a hurry, either. Isaiah has got us trapped by our own people and he's got the run of the town. He knew what he was doing—I'd say he's got something planned.'

'Jesus, Gavin,' Michael said quietly. 'You're both crediting Isaiah with a lot more intelligence than I am. As bad as it sounds, I still think of him as some sort of possessed spirit—a real damn *ghost* with a nasty streak. Surely he can't be capable of such logical thinking!'

'Maybe not,' Gavin shrugged. 'But that's what he's achieved, whether he wanted to or not. And Isaiah *may* be a ghost, but somehow Kann is still alive, and I guess that means he's trapped in Isaiah's spirit. That doesn't make him incapable of *thinking*—logically or otherwise.'

'But there must be a way out of this town,' Kerry said desperately. 'Those soldiers are still *people*! We must be able to communicate with them somehow—tell them not to shoot and let us talk it over.'

'That's why I want to try again,' Michael told Gavin. 'This time I want to take Riley with me. I'm hoping a police car with flashing lights, and Riley in full uniform, might get us close enough to talk to somebody.'

'Do you think Riley will do it?'

Michael laughed for a moment, but it was a humourless sound. 'He has to now. He's in just as much trouble as we are.'

They began to move towards the house. Michael wanted to spend some precious minutes having a quick bite to eat and a drink, and they still had to discuss who was going to go back into Hickory to face Riley. Gavin tried to argue that perhaps they should wait and see what the army's next move would be. As they walked Beth turned her face up to her father's.

'Will the soldiers attack us back, Dad?' she asked in a small voice.

'No, darling,' he replied with a smile, reaching down to give her a reassuring hug. 'I don't think they'll ever want to do that.'

'But they think we attacked them, don't they?'

'No, they're just being very careful,' Gavin said easily, but he shot a look at Michael.

When they were all inside the kitchen, Beth wandered towards her bedroom to check for the hundredth time there was nothing she'd rather take, instead of the limited choice Gavin had let her pack.

Once she was out of earshot, Michael frowned and murmured, 'Talk about "out of the mouths of babes"! She couldn't be right, could she? The army doesn't believe this is some sort of alien *attack*?'

'I guess we should consider it a possibility,' Gavin said soberly.

'Does it really make much difference?' Kerry asked, but she wasn't expecting Gavin's chilling reply.

'It could make a big difference to how they choose to finally resolve the problem—if they decide a final resolution is what they need.'

It didn't take long for Michael to convince them that another attempt had to be made to contact the soldiers, this time with Riley and the police car. And again, it had to be Michael and Kerry who tried it. Much as Gavin hated being left behind, he didn't want anyone else looking after Beth, and they didn't want the young girl anywhere near the danger if it could be helped. In the end, they decided that if Michael and Kerry were successful, the first thing they would do is convince the soldiers to run another patrol into the town to collect Gavin and Beth.

This time as Michael and Kerry drove through the main street towards the police station, a new sight greeted them at McGann's hotel. Someone had hanged themselves on the upper floor, outside the rooms on the corner of the upstairs verandah. As Michael's van approached the building, the dangling body with its lolling head, and the taut rope connecting it to the roof above were plainly silhouetted against the clear sky. Michael and Kerry both saw it at the same time. The black shape of the hanging body was sickening and frightening.

'Dear God,' Michael said, twisting his head to look up at the verandah as they passed. 'Can you see who it is?'

'Not really,' Kerry replied, her voice thick. 'Maybe if we stopped, but I don't want to do that. It's a girl, I think.'

'One of the barmaids, maybe,' he said sadly.

'Is this what we're all expected to do, Michael? Kill ourselves? Is that what Powers, or Isaiah, or Kann, whatever his damn name is, is hoping we'll all do?'

'Perhaps. At least so far, you and I haven't been behaving the way the rest of the town has, obeying some type of mental programming or hypnotic

428

suggestion.' He reached over and squeezed her hand. 'Don't worry, I'm not about to hang myself just yet.'

'Sometimes it doesn't seem like a bad idea,' Kerry muttered, alarming Michael. Both were too busy watching either side of the road for anything dangerous to say anything more until they pulled up outside the police station. Sitting in the van at the kerbside, they studied the place for a while.

'The front door's still open,' Kerry said.

'The way he was drinking, he's probably flat out on the floor in a coma.'

'That'll be damned handy for us.'

Michael let out a snort of laughter. 'It won't do him any good. I feel Mr Riley can be held responsible for a lot of things. Now's his big chance to make amends. Not even a bloody coma is going to let him get out of it. I'll wake him up somehow.'

Kerry gave Michael a sideways glance. She knew him well enough now to almost take for granted the extra strength and power he possessed in his arms and shoulders. She had a fleeting memory of the first time she had noticed his heavier build when he had walked from her pharmacy. She realised Michael Garrett would not be a good man to have working against you.

'Let's have a look,' he said, opening his door.

Michael went over to the Ford police car parked in the driveway. He put a hand on the bonnet— it was cold. The car hadn't been anywhere for a while, he guessed. They walked together cautiously up to the front door and paused just short of the verandah. There was no sound from inside at their approach, and Michael turned to Kerry and raised his eyebrows before gesturing they should go on. The lights were still on inside the station, despite the bright sunlight outside.

'Oh-oh,' Michael said in a low, tense voice. 'Somebody's been here—or they're still here. Can you smell it?' The putrid smell of rotting meat, unmistakable for what it represented in Hickory now, lingered in the air. Michael wound himself up, ready for anything.

'Michael, look,' Kerry said, pointing behind him. Michael had walked straight through the door to the front counter. Now he turned to see the inside of the doorframe, where Riley's bullet had smashed into the woodwork, the beams so old they might have been iron. The damage wasn't obvious from the outside, though it was plainly caused by gunfire from this side. Apart from the splintered timber, there was the mess of blood and traces of flesh which had been Jake Sanders' shoulder. The blood hadn't dried yet, and showed a browning stickiness against the paintwork.

'The army came here?' Kerry whispered.

'No, I don't think so.' Michael was looking around the police station again. He saw some of the thirty-eight rounds Riley had dropped in his drunkenness. 'There,' Michael pointed. 'I'd say Riley did this himself. He had a visitor he didn't like. He shot at them as they came through the door.'

'Is this the gunfire we heard last night?'

'Hell, no. The place would be shot to pieces if what I heard last night happened here. I'd say Riley took a few shots himself—maybe a couple more, if some went straight out the door.' Michael

430

moved around the counter into the main part of the office, searching carefully as he went. Now he could see the thirty-eight revolver lying on the floor, but he didn't touch it.

'So what the hell happened?' Kerry said, following him.

'Let's see if we can work it out. Finding Riley might help.'

It took only a minute to determine that Riley wasn't in the building. Michael found the empty rum bottles scattered about the place and counted them aloud, letting Kerry know how intoxicated Riley must have been. 'Maybe he drank himself to death,' he added lightly, but the expression on his face conceded it wasn't so far-fetched. Without much hope he tried the handle on the small steel safe in one corner. It was locked. Kerry, checking the bathroom, back-stepped rapidly away from the sour odours of vomit and stale urine.

'We'll have to try the residence next door,' Michael told her.

'Let's hope he's not still trigger-happy.'

'Good point.' Michael hadn't thought of that. There had to be more than one gun in the place.

The house next door was unlocked too, but the doors were closed. Michael tried the handle and felt it turn, then changed his mind and rapped hard on the front flyscreen, rattling the aluminium in its frame. There was no response.

'Passed out on the bed?' Kerry asked.

'There's only one way to find out.'

They moved inside. It was only a small house and typical in its design. It didn't take long to confirm it was empty. The only thing Michael was able to determine was that Riley lived there, not his partner Griffith. Until then, he hadn't been so sure.

'We can take a look outside, and that's about all, damn it,' Michael said, disappointed. 'Otherwise we'll have to start searching the town for him, and I don't fancy doing that, to be honest.'

Kerry knew he was talking about the hanging corpse at McGann's hotel. The town could be filling with such horrors. She forced herself to think aggressively, rather than give in to the urge to return to Gavin's property and simply hide until everything went away. She knew that wouldn't be an answer. 'We should check out the back here,' she said carefully. 'And out the back of the police station. Then maybe we should search the station again and find his car keys. Maybe there's a spare set hanging on a wall somewhere.' Reluctantly, she added, 'It might be worth a try for us to drive the police car out to the soldiers, even without Riley, as long as we can make the lights flash and everything.' She stopped and held a finger up, another idea coming to her. She turned and disappeared through a doorway, returning a minute later with one of Riley's police shirts in her hand. 'You could wear this,' she said. 'Make sure your arm's hanging out the window so they can see the badges. It might make all the difference.'

'You're thinking way ahead of me,' Michael said. 'You're right, we'll check out the back first, then I'll turn the police station upside-down for those keys. There must be a spare set somewhere.' Silently, he hoped Riley wasn't conscientious enough to have locked them in the safe.

Riley's house backed onto a canefield. It was a

long yard, the cane nearly fifty metres away, because the police station adjacent needed room for the cells built behind it. There was nothing to see in the house's yard—not even a garden shed. Michael found himself warily eyeing the sugarcane and wondering if it was worth a closer inspection. Kerry called out.

'Look at that, Mike,' she said, nodding towards the police station.

He saw immediately. The morning was still early enough for the sunlight to have a decided slant, and it cut a bright square into the gloom of the two concrete cells at the rear of the police station. Someone was in one of the cells. A blue-trousered leg lay against the bars in the sunlight.

'Shit,' Michael said softly, feeling another piece of his planning coming apart. 'That's all we need.' He started towards the low fence.

'Michael! Are you sure we should go so close?'

'I must have a closer look,' he replied, sounding very unhappy about it. 'He's probably still got the keys on him. If I can get them, it could save us a lot of time and trouble.' Kerry swore at the logic of it, then followed. They approached the cells cautiously. Michael kept glancing nervously around, aware that whoever—or whatever—had visited Riley and prompted the gunfire could still be nearby. Kerry kept close behind him.

Riley sat sideways across the cell, his back against one wall and one leg leaning on the metal bars. His eyes stared sightlessly at the opposite wall. The crotch of his pants was damp and there were other wet stains down the front of his shirt. A stink of vomit hit them from the cell.

433

'Christ, I don't know how much of this I can take,' Kerry whispered. 'What killed him? Has he shot himself?'

'I can't tell,' Michael said, kneeling close to the cell door. 'I don't think I want to know. Believe it or not, there's some good news here.' He pointed down at the policeman. Gleaming silver in the sunlight, hanging from a spring-loaded clip on his belt, was a bunch of keys. Michael could easily reach them through the bars, so he gingerly put his hand between the metal struts.

In the instant Michael unclipped the keys and drew his hand back, Riley screamed and leapt to his feet, scuttling back into the shadows of the cell. Michael was so startled he yelled out and fell backwards onto Kerry, who also let out a cry of horror in her surprise.

Riley's hoarse voice echoed out at them from the cell. 'Stay *away* from me, you dead fuckers!'

Kerry was already back on her feet and tugging at Michael, urging him to run from the cell. Michael resisted her, and sat and looked into the dark interior.

'Wait,' he told her. 'Wait a moment.' In despair she stopped, then heard the sound coming from the cell.

It was a soft sobbing.

'Riley?' Michael called in amazement. 'Are you okay? Are you *alive*?'

Riley was distraught, his voice soft and breaking. 'Keep *back*, damn you. You can't get me in here. You might as well fuck off.'

'Riley, it's Michael Garrett. And Kerry Wentworth. We're not what you think we are—

we're alive, for God's sake. We're okay.'

This prompted a harsh bark of laughter. Michael slowly got to his feet and moved nearer to the cell gate.

'Be careful, Mike! He might still be armed, remember.'

He moved quickly to one side. 'Jesus, thanks. I'm not thinking.' He called into the cell, 'Riley, talk to me. What happened? Are you okay?'

'Go *away*, fuck you.'

'Riley, we need your help.' Michael gave Kerry a quick glance that told her he didn't think threatening Riley or getting angry would achieve anything. His appeal brought another burst of desperate laughter, which subsided to a derisive snorting interspersed with annoyed muttering. While Michael was considering his next words Kerry stepped closer.

'Michael, he's locked himself in there. He can't do us any harm, can he? If we want, we can leave him in there and still do it ourselves. We've got the keys and one of his shirts.'

Michael thought about it, then grimly shook his head. 'The guys running the army cordon must at least have a list of the authorities in Hickory. They'd only have to ask me some trick question to prove I was Riley—his official police number would be enough—and they'd know I wasn't the real thing. And we've already seen what they can do when they get a bit nervous.'

'Christ Almighty.' Kerry rubbed her face wearily. 'But this guy's about as stable as a rocking horse. How the hell can he help?'

'Even if we just take him along, it can give us a

few more options. Maybe a few more answers we wouldn't otherwise have.' Michael looked at Kerry, willing her to agree. He wasn't really any happier about the choices they had, but he was prepared to take a risk. She looked helplessly back at him. He turned back to the cell.

'Riley? Listen carefully. The army's here. They've surrounded the town and quarantined us off. They won't even talk to us.' Michael deliberately avoided mentioning the army's readiness to open fire at anyone approaching the cordon. 'We need someone with some authority—like you—to get them to listen to us—' Michael stopped, surprised. Riley had moved quickly out of the deeper shadows at the back of the cell to stand at the cell door, gripping the gates with both hands.

'It was the army?' he whispered. 'Last night, I heard the army? All that gunfire?'

'They must have arrived during the night,' Michael nodded, cautious at the sudden change in the policeman. Tears filled Riley's eyes and he let out a quiet moan of despair.

'They're here to kill us all,' he said, still whispering. 'If Jake Sanders and the rest of the fucking walking corpses don't kill us in our beds, the army will come in and finish off the job.' His body slumping, Riley turned and began to walk back towards the rear of the cell.

'No, wait!' Michael called desperately. 'They don't do that sort of thing in this part of the world—you know that! This is the nineties, for Christ's sake! They just won't talk to me, because I'm a civilian, but I know they'll talk to *you*.

436

You're the sergeant of police in Hickory, right? Why the hell would they want to shoot you?'

'What choice have they got?' came the beaten, sickened reply.

'They've got no choices right now! That's why we have to go out and try talking to them—*give* them a choice!' Michael saw Kerry had gone pale at Riley's conviction that the army would come into Hickory and kill everyone. He wished he could logically point out that it couldn't happen, but there wasn't any such argument. Gavin had already hinted it might be possible.

Riley hadn't answered Michael's last plea, so he decided to change tactics. 'Look Riley, think about this. Are you listening? If we try and talk to the soldiers outside of town, I believe the very *worst* they'll do is lock us up somewhere safe and isolated, and ask us damn questions and do tests for months, right? But at least we'll be out of Hickory! Don't you want that?'

There was a long silence from inside the cell. Kerry put her lips against Michael's ear. 'Do you really think they'd do that? Keep us for months, I mean?'

He slipped his hand into hers and said quietly, 'Right now, I wouldn't care if they locked us away for years—as long as you and I were together,' he added with a soft smile. Kerry tried to smile back, but the distressed look in her eyes told Michael that their personal relationship was the furthest thing from her mind.

Riley shuffled back to the bars. Like a tired child that knows it's beaten, but is still wanting to escape its cot, he tugged experimentally at the metal. It shifted slightly, but didn't open.

'All right, you have the key there,' he said desperately.

His voice was so low Michael needed a moment to realise what the policeman had said.

Riley was compliant about everything Michael wanted to do. The sergeant became like a cooperative drunkard, silently obeying each command. Michael took them around the side of the police station, instead of walking through it, in case Riley saw something which could trigger off violent memories of the night before. Michael was certain something terrible had happened—it was obvious from the policeman's mental state and the stains on his clothing, but he wasn't about to ask.

Michael made Riley sit in the passenger seat of the police car, then he went around to the driver's seat himself. Before he got into the car he took the police shirt from Kerry, quickly stripped off his own sweater and T-shirt, and shrugged into it. When he was dressed again he said to Kerry, 'I'm sorry, but there's only one way I can think of doing this.' Ignoring her alarmed look he went on, 'Will you go back inside the station and get his gun? It's on the floor near his desk, and there's a few rounds of ammunition lying around, too. I want to stay here and keep an eye on him.' After a moment of hesitation Kerry walked quickly into the building and reappeared less than a minute later carrying the gun. She gave it, and three shells, to Michael. There was one still left in the chamber. He shook it out into the palm of his hand.

Michael dry-fired the weapon, showing Kerry how simple it was and familiarising himself with the handgun at the same time. 'See?' he said. 'It's very easy. You only have to pull the trigger. If this was loaded, it would be firing now.' Kerry nodded and watched him put the four rounds into the chamber. She was taken aback when he held the gun out to her.

'Why me?' she said. 'You'd be better—in fact, I'm not so sure this is a good idea, Michael. If they know we're armed they might not be—'

Michael cut her off. 'I want you to sit in the back seat with this. If Riley goes crazy, or looks like endangering you and me in any way, then I want you to shoot him.' Kerry was going white, so Michael spoke more forcefully. 'I'd do it myself, Kerry, but I think the army people will expect a male policeman to be driving the car. Even if you put on this shirt, we couldn't disguise that you're a woman.'

She took the gun reluctantly, saying, 'I really don't think I could shoot him, no matter what he's doing.'

'Well, it'll make me feel better at least, knowing I've got some help in the back seat if he goes nuts. But don't worry. I doubt if he'll do anything to harm us—and for God's sake don't pull the trigger if he looks like throwing himself out of the car. Just let it happen.'

Kerry slid into the rear seat of the sedan and sat in the middle, not bothering with any safety belts. She held the gun awkwardly between her knees, pointing the barrel carefully towards the floor. Behind the wheel Michael fumbled with the large bunch of keys until he found the right one. The car started first time, the motor a powerful growl. He let it warm up for a while, then dropped the automatic gear selector into reverse and backed out of the driveway. 'Well, here goes nothing,' he said tightly, choosing the drive gear. The car moved smoothly forward. From the moment he had sat in the passenger seat, Riley hadn't altered his steadfast stare out the windscreen. The stench from his clothing quickly filled the car and Michael wound down his window. Kerry did the same, the wind rushing through and whipping at her hair.

The township was still eerily deserted. With a dreadful feeling, Michael began to seriously consider the possibility that some sort of mass suicide might have occurred behind the closed doors of the homes. It was nearer to midday now, and there had been gunfire in the main street and an army helicopter overflying the town, yet still the residents of Hickory were staying inside. The corpse hanging from the upstairs balcony of the hotel now possessed a more foreboding significance. Riley didn't even look up at the body as the police car cruised past.

When they turned onto the main highway again Michael slowed right down and cocked his head out the window. 'I can hear the helicopter, but it must be a long way away,' he said to Kerry. It appeared pointless to speak to Riley, who remained zombie-like.

'It's over there,' she said, pointing through her

window. Michael searched for a moment and finally saw it—a distant speck moving quickly just above the horizon.

'It must be doing a quick sweep of the outer farms. The boys at the end of the road will see us coming soon, and no doubt whistle up the chopper before we can get too close.'

Riley spoke, startling them. His voice was totally devoid of emotion, a flat and inflectionless monotone. 'They can't,' he said, without turning his face away from the windscreen. 'They have no radio communications. Powers had some sort of jamming device hidden around here. It'll still be working.'

'God damn, that's right! Well, I wouldn't have thought it, to be honest,' Michael said enthusiastically. 'I would've said the armed forces' more sophisticated stuff would operate okay, despite Powers' jamming. But shit, that'll be giving them a big headache,' he added absently. It was almost like a small victory for their side. 'I'm almost sorry we're in this white car now. The helicopter's got the best chance of spotting us. At least we've got the right vehicle to move fast. Maybe we can get to the first line of the cordon before the chopper knows what's going on.'

He put his foot down hard on the accelerator and the police car surged forward. They quickly reached the roadblock with the quarantine sign and Michael slowed, steering the car around it without hesitation. There was a shaking rattle as the tyres passed over the new holes in the bitumen caused by the helicopter's gunfire that morning. Now it was a straight run towards the distant figures, the

441

images flickering slightly as a heat-haze came off the road. Again Michael pushed the pedal to the floor and the engine began to roar, the car immediately gaining speed. Michael wasn't sure—the haziness made things deceptive—but he thought the shapes at the end of the road began to scurry about with more urgency. He figured they would have heard the car approaching by now, the motor's noise carrying clearly in the country air.

The edges of the road were usually littered with the carcasses of animals struck down by speeding trucks, but beyond the first roadblock there was a profusion of dead kangaroos, bandicoots and even a young bull. On all of them the slick of blood was still wet and bright red.

'Michael, these animals have been *shot*,' Kerry said, appalled. 'All of them.'

'Of course,' he said, grimly. 'That would be the gunfire we heard last night—the army clearing out the area.' He looked in the rear-view mirror and saw her confusion. 'Animals can't read "keep out" signs, so there's only one way to stop them moving beyond the perimeter.'

Kerry's face was sad and tears glittered in her eyes. Annoyed, she brushed them away and didn't mention the slain animals again. Michael turned his attention back to the road. He let out a groan as a vivid flare arced into the sky from somewhere ahead. However, it seemed the flare wasn't needed.

'The helicopter's coming,' Kerry called. Michael didn't bother to look. He could hear the sound of the aircraft's rotors now above the noise of his own vehicle. He grimly concentrated on driving. The police car was doing one hundred and sixty kilometres an hour and still accelerating. Michael didn't dare take his attention away from the road. He didn't want to go crashing into the barriers at the end—just to get there before the helicopter. Suddenly he cursed himself for not thinking straight. Glancing down at the car's dashboard showed him two switches which were obviously not part of the car's standard equipment. One was marked 'lights' and the other 'siren'.

'It's going to get noisy!' he yelled and slapped both switches down. The whooping of the siren filled the cabin. Michael stole a glance at Riley. Amazingly, the policeman was unperturbed and sat in the same manner, unaffected by all the noise and fuss, still gazing out the windscreen in front of him. Through Riley's window Michael saw the surroundings flying past them at a frightening speed.

The speedometer was touching on one hundred and ninety when the steering wheel began to shake unnervingly. Michael wanted to stay at that speed, but the vibration scared him too much. He backed off a little. There wasn't far to go. Now he needed to judge their arrival very carefully. If he stopped the police car too late, they might think he was going to smash his way through the roadblock, and bring a storm of gunfire down upon them. Stopping too early would leave them trying to shout explanations over an impossible distance. Normally, it wouldn't be a difficult thing to do, but Michael wasn't used to hurtling along at such a speed.

As he started to brake Michael realised he might

have indeed left it too late and he stamped hard down on the pedal. The wheels didn't lock, but the rear of the car rose high in the air and the three people inside were thrown forward. The Blackhawk helicopter thundered over the top of them at the same moment, so low it seemed the undercarriage of the aircraft might scrape the roof of the car. As it continued its sweep in front of them Michael saw the deadly snout of the machine-gun poking from the side door. The police car jerked to a halt, the wheels locking at the last moment, and the car rocked on its suspension. The clattering of rotors faded as the machine moved further away, Michael flicked off the siren and lights, then killed the motor.

The sudden quiet was disconcerting, as if the world beyond the car's windows was holding its breath in anticipation of what would happen next. The scene in front of them heightened the atmosphere of tense expectation. Michael found himself wondering belatedly if this had been a good move. The army were obviously very serious about maintaining the roadblock.

It was less than a hundred metres away.

The armoured personnel carriers had been brought on a low-loader semi-trailer. Painted dark green, the powerful prime mover with its tray still attached was parked at the most acute angle they could achieve across the road, completely blocking it. Beyond the truck and half-hidden to Michael's sight by the groups of axles and wheels was an assortment of Landrovers, canvas-covered trucks and the APCs. Everything was dappled with camouflage colouring, as were the uniforms of the soldiers now deploying themselves urgently in every direction. In the distance Michael picked out the drooping rotors of one or maybe two more Blackhawks. The airborne chopper was flying in a wide circle around the area. The closest soldiers were taking cover behind the wheels of the low-loader. An APC was manoeuvring clumsily, lurching backwards and forwards and trying to move into a position to provide more protection.

All the soldiers were armed.

'God damn,' Michael muttered, awed by the sight. 'Who do they think we are—the Russians? There's half an army here!' On a sudden thought he twisted around to Kerry. 'For Christ's sake, keep that revolver well out of sight.' She didn't need any further urging. Michael sat and looked out at the scene, suddenly uncertain what he'd hoped to achieve. Finally, he took a deep breath and said, 'Well, here goes—'

He slowly opened his door. Michael could almost feel the tension grow among the watching soldiers. Stepping out of the car he hesitated, tempted to stay behind the dubious protection of the open door, but he immediately reasoned they might interpret that as trying to conceal a weapon, so Michael took a step backwards and closed it. He felt naked and exposed. Too late, he realised his jeans and sneakers were now belying the policeman's shirt he wore. He flinched as an authoritative voice snapped out from behind the truck, anonymous among the camouflage fatigues.

The voice said, 'Turn around and return to the town—*now*.'

Recovering, Michael shouted back, 'We need to

talk to someone! There is something terribly wrong. You're making a mistake. We need help.'

The soldier—an officer, Michael guessed correctly—wasn't going to hear reason very easily. His response wasn't a surprise.

'You are not allowed beyond the boundaries of the town. Do *not* attempt to come any closer, or you will be shot.' The officer gestured and a group of soldiers quickly scuttled from behind one set of wheels to behind the prime mover. They ran crouched over, their weapons held ready.

Even though Michael had known what to expect, the officer's words turned him cold. He somehow knew the soldiers wouldn't hesitate to shoot if he made the wrong move.

'For God's sake!' he called, hearing a tremor in his voice. 'We're not even armed! All this is completely unnecessary.'

The officer immediately replied, 'You are considered a risk to the health and security of the nation. Until we can ensure that risk is negated, you must stay within the quarantined area.'

The Blackhawk flew close overhead, drowning out any possible exchanges for a minute. Michael instinctively ducked, remembering the machine-gunning that morning. His mind was working furiously. *A risk to the health and security of the nation! We are in fucking serious trouble.*

'You don't understand!' he almost screamed, getting in first over the noise of the Blackhawk. 'There are things happening that we must explain. You have to listen to us. You will be in no danger, I promise you.'

The voice was unrelenting. 'You must not

approach the barriers. Turn around and return to the town. Negotiations are not an option.' The denial was in more than the officer's words. His tone was harsh and unyielding—and Michael heard a touch of fear, too. He figured all of them would be well aware of the patrolling soldier's death. They would all be scared, faced by an invisible and fatal enemy.

'For God's sake, who is the senior officer in charge? Can I talk to him? There must be a way we can talk.' But the reply was exactly what Michael didn't want to hear.

'I *am* the senior officer, and I'm telling you for the last time—get back in your vehicle and return to the town. Stay in your homes until you are told otherwise.'

Or until you guys napalm the fucking street, Michael told himself, and was shocked by the thought. It was no longer beyond the bounds of possibility. He was getting nowhere fast.

The sound of another car door opening dragged his attention away. Turning around, Michael worried that it might be Kerry with the revolver still in her hand. But it was Riley. The policeman emerged from the car with all the calm and poise of someone who fully expects to be respected. He held himself straight, his arms stiff by his sides. Michael wondered if the soldiers could see the ashen face and the trembling fists Riley was clamping against his thighs. Like Michael, Riley closed the door, but he took several steps forward, stopping just beyond the police car's front fenders. From behind the barriers came the rattle of weapons being cocked.

447

Michael snapped, 'For God's sake, Riley! Stay back!'

Riley didn't acknowledge him, but faced the wall of trucks and armed men without any apparent fear. He called out.

'I am Sergeant Owen Riley, sergeant of police at Hickory. It's within my authority to order your men to put down their weapons and allow us safe passage through. I want to speak to the commanding officer in person.'

The moment of silence in the soldiers' ranks showed their confusion. Only Michael and Kerry, aware of the circumstances, recognised the strength and recklessness in Riley as evidence of his unstable mind. Michael thought, *He's lost his mind. He's gone insane, and we didn't even notice he was so far gone. Why the hell didn't I see it?* He considered moving around to the front of the car and grabbing hold of Riley, but he figured any movement could spark off a tragedy. Michael tried to push away the thought that he was also being a coward, but it persisted.

'Stay *back*,' came the response, its spontaneity another indication the soldiers were flustered by Riley's bravado. It was followed by a more formal order.

'Get back in the car and return to the town.'

Michael swore under his breath as Riley took another step forward, shouting now, 'This is my town—these are my people. You have no right to do this! Order your men to let us through—'

The officer cut him off, almost frantically. 'Do *not* come any closer! There will be *no* negotiations. Return to the town and stay in your homes.'

Michael called, 'Riley! For Christ's sake come back! We have to do this bloody carefully.'

Riley turned around and looked at Michael. He spread his arms in a gesture of helplessness and said softly, 'I'm not going back to that town. Not after last night. He'll only come back for me again.'

Michael was too surprised to reply. Riley swung his pleading stance back towards the soldiers, the momentum of it causing him to take a small step forward.

'You have to listen—'

There was a shocking rattle of gunfire as one of the soldiers pulled the trigger of his weapon. Michael would never know if the rifleman was ordered to do so, or if he took matters into his own hands. The bullets punched into Riley's chest, pushing him backwards as if he'd been shoved by a giant hand. The front of his shirt disintegrated in a spraying mess of blood and cloth. He fell against the car and stayed propped up for long seconds by muscle spasms locking his legs, before he silently collapsed to the ground.

The officer was yelling at everyone to cease firing, although only one man had started shooting. In the back of the car, Kerry screamed and ducked down behind the front seat. Michael was paralysed with fear, fully expecting to feel bullets slamming into his body, too. It took him a long moment to realise the firing had stopped and he was safe—for the moment. He discovered he was holding his hands well above his head.

The only sounds now were urgent hisses of talk floating out from behind the truck, and an alarmed squawking of birds leaving the nearby treetops. Michael didn't dare move. Finally the officer's voice came clearly, but with a trace of despair and panic.

'Leave him where he is. Take the car and return to the town. Stay in your homes until we tell you.' There was a pause and the officer's desperation filled the silence. 'Stay *in* the damn town, damn you. We are *not* fucking around here!'

Michael had to make a conscious effort to lower his arms, their muscles frozen. Without taking his eyes off the barrier and the crouched-over shapes moving behind them with their weapons, he groped blindly behind him for the door handle of the police car. He didn't even flinch again when the Blackhawk passed close overhead with a shattering roar. Michael knew now, with a stunning certainty, there would be no escape down the highway out of Hickory.

22

KERRY HAD ALREADY gone over all her ideas with Michael during the drive back from the cordon. Now she offered to play with Beth inside the house, while Michael and Gavin discussed what they could do. Keeping their voices low, they talked outside, sitting on the garden furniture.

'What will the army do, Gavin? Any ideas?'

Gavin sighed. The lines on his face—not there only two days before—showed the toll his grieving and the pressure to keep going were taking on him. 'I was only a reservist private, Mike. Not a brigadier-general. My guess is probably as good as yours, really.'

'Didn't they ever tell you about biological

warfare—how they would combat it? I figure that's how they'll be treating this.'

'No, but what they've done so far makes sense, even if it is extreme. Killing off the animals to stop the spread of any disease is excessive, for example. They could have merely maintained their perimeter and perhaps shot anything that threatened to slip through the net. And there's the birdlife. There's no way they can keep that contained, so wiping out everything else doesn't make much sense, really.'

As if to give Gavin's words credence, a large crow noisily flapped over the house and settled on a fence-post. It glared at the two men angrily, its eyes glittering in the sunlight. Michael watched it for a moment. 'You know, I understand what Isaiah did this morning—whether he did it intentionally doesn't matter. He scared the living daylights out of the army and now they're not going to come near the place until they can figure a safe way of doing it. I can also understand why the army is killing off everything they can—to stop the spread of anything.' Michael paused, frowning. 'But they did all that shooting last night, right? Before the scene with Isaiah.'

Gavin was nodding. 'It means they are deadly serious. We were in enough trouble without having Isaiah prodding them along, too.'

'So, when do they start killing off the rest of us, for Christ's sake?'

'Come on, Mike. Let's not panic. The whole situation is unprecedented. We have to base our thinking on the fact that they can't possibly have faced anything like this before, and they are just as much in the dark about what to do next as we are. I guess they'll be watching the surviving soldiers of that patrol very closely—and I figure that's our only hope. If those men are okay and they stay that way, then perhaps the people in charge will eventually try some limited contact again.' Suddenly exasperated he added, 'Look, I don't know. Who knows?'

'No, that sounds right,' Michael said carefully. 'But how long will they wait? How long will they watch those soldiers—a sort of incubation period, I guess—until they decide they're going to be okay?'

'Think of it this way,' Gavin said. 'We don't know—and *they* don't know, either. Chances are they'll pick a figure out of the air and stick to it. If you were in their shoes, how long would you say?'

Michael knew what Gavin was trying to do, so he answered quickly without thinking. 'Twenty-four hours.'

'That's what I'd say, too. They'll be thinking they haven't got too much time to waste.'

'Damn, I don't like that idea. It means we'll at least have to get through another night in town, before we *might* have a chance to talk our way out of here.'

'That's right,' Gavin said soberly. 'We've been pretty lucky, so far.'

'What if the helicopters take a break tonight? They can't have unlimited fuel supplies, so they must ease off at least. What's to stop us walking out of here then? Through the canefields, I mean? They can't have a ring of soldiers completely around the town, surely.'

'I haven't been out to the roadblock, so you tell me how many soldiers they've brought out.'

'I couldn't even guess,' he said. 'But a hell of a lot. It's a big camp.'

'It doesn't need many to maintain the roadblock,' Gavin said. 'The rest will be out patrolling a line, a set distance from the town. That's what that second Blackhawk would've been doing—dropping off patrols at regular intervals. Those guys will be as nervous as hell and probably keeping very close together. I wouldn't be surprised if somebody ends up shooting another soldier by accident tonight, they'll be that keyed up. With enough men and aggressive patrolling, it shouldn't be too hard to keep the area sealed up tight. A trained person might slip through, but not three people, a kid and two dogs,' Gavin finished, smiling sadly.

Defeated, Michael looked around the surrounding property. 'How long will it be before Jake gets out here to pay us a visit? Riley was terrified at the idea of Jake coming back. That's why he pushed *his* luck too far.'

Gavin didn't answer, but sat staring out across the yard. Both men stayed deep in thought for a while. Finally Michael said, 'Maybe we should be thinking about holing up somewhere safer.'

'Where? What are you thinking of?'

Michael gave him an odd look, then began to explain. 'Nothing's the same any more—for us, anyway. Maybe we should be looking at less rational solutions—something a little off the wall. I mean, God knows the whole damn world's turned upside-down at the moment.' He paused and saw Gavin getting impatient. 'I'm just wondering if we might be safer in the church, in town.'

Gavin took a while to reply. 'Maybe we should pick up a few videos and watch them, too. Some Dracula movies might give us a few hints, and I think Linda planted some garlic around here—' he stopped and tiredly waved an apology. 'I'm sorry. I know what you mean, but I'm not sure the Hollywood filmmakers ever really bothered to get their facts right. It's possible the church is some sort of sanctuary against these damn things, but it's a hell of a risk. The church is almost smack in the middle of town. I'd hate to be outnumbered by walking fucking corpses. The cemetery is only a short stroll down the road from the church, remember. We could start quite a party.'

Michael was nodding reluctantly. 'I know. I wish we knew more about what we're dealing with. But I've been thinking and you know— you're right. Jake and the others seem to be walking *corpses*, like a living dead. You can run over them, like we did in the car—or you can even shoot them, judging by the wall at the police station, although I guess it didn't do much good. Isaiah's different, though. He seems to be able to pop up like a damn jack-in-the-box almost any time. He's twice as scary to me. That's why I'm grasping at straws and thinking the church could be a safe place to be.'

'I suppose we mustn't discount it as a possibility. How can we find out?'

'All we have to do is go there now, during daylight when we can keep our eyes peeled for any danger. Basically, if old Father Johnson is still alive and kicking, it must be okay.'

'Father Johnson is half-senile at the best of times,' Gavin said doubtfully.

'I don't care if he's completely insane, as long as he's alive and unharmed. Otherwise, we can only barricade ourselves in out here, but we know closed doors aren't going to be much of a deterrent for Isaiah.'

Gavin bowed his head and thought about it. Then he stood up, wiping the palms of his hands on his jeans. 'Well, it's a better plan than mine—but that's only because I haven't got one.'

It was difficult to explain the circumstances to Beth without scaring her senseless with the truth. Gavin told her a version of the dangers they faced, watering down the facts as much as he could. Beth accepted it all with a surprising calm. Kerry whispered to Michael that it actually made sense—as a child, Beth had been imagining and fearing these sorts of things all her life. It wasn't particularly astonishing to be told that bogeymen lived after all. It was only the adults who, having been convinced for many years that such things did not exist, were having trouble adjusting their thinking.

'And there's something else,' Kerry told him. 'I just tried asking her gently if she could remember anything of *before* we found her in the canefields— I mean, if she recalled any of her time with the aliens. Guess what? Beth didn't have a clue what I was talking about. It's like her memory of that time has been completely erased. In fact, it's more than that. I was worried it might scare her, just asking her to think about it, but Beth's a total blank. Not only can't she remember, but she sort of switches off and becomes very vague,' Kerry finished with a helpless shrug. 'I don't know—it's strange.'

'It might be her own natural defence mechanism, like a mental block,' Michael said, puzzled.

'Maybe, but I have a hunch it's something the aliens have done. It's so complete.'

'Well, perhaps they know best. Otherwise Beth might be raving mad or hysterical with those memories. God knows what she went through.'

'Yes,' Kerry nodded thoughtfully. 'I suppose it's best that she is this way, for the moment, anyway.'

Michael decided the police car might make any soldiers too nervous after the trouble at the road-block. In comparison, loading everyone into the van and Kerry's car gave Michael an absurd feeling they were all going off on a family outing. Michael would drive his van with Gavin in the passenger seat. Kerry would follow. Spread between the two vehicles were several bags of food and warm clothing, bottles of drink and extra blankets, and finally the two dogs in the back of the van. The dogs were a subject for debate, because Gavin was concerned it might be kinder to leave them behind on the property, to let them run and take their chances. But Michael was more practical—and more attuned to the emotions of both Beth and Kerry. The dogs, he said, still served as the best pairs of eyes and ears they could get, and if the army swept through the town with their indiscriminate policy of killing all the animal life the dogs wouldn't stand a chance roaming alone. Gavin reluctantly agreed, and Michael saw a look of relief on Beth's face. It was worth it, just for that.

After starting the van's motor Michael took a moment to stare at the Packers' property. He had a feeling he would never see it again, and wondered if Gavin was having the same thoughts. Then he let in the clutch and drove out the driveway.

There was another body in the town. Another hanging. This time on the large poinciana tree in the schoolyard. The shade underneath had seen generations of Hickory children sit on the low benches, eating their lunch. Now somebody had used the bench seats to reach the branches above, tie a thick rope around a bough, fasten a noose around their own neck and simply step forward into space. As they passed, Michael could see the corpse's feet just touching the dirt below. Whoever it was had obviously been sufficiently determined to die to resist the urge to stand on tiptoe and support their own weight—or maybe they had simply got too tired to keep the effort up. Prudently, Michael had seated Beth in the back of the van where it was difficult for her to see outside, and the dogs kept her occupied. Otherwise, it would have been a miracle if she hadn't glanced towards her own schoolyard.

The body still dangled from the upstairs verandah of McGann's hotel.

It was close to midday. The sun was bright and the resulting shadows deep. Still no-one openly walked the streets. Michael was completely at a loss about what was happening. Among the entire population of Hickory, small though it was, he expected *somebody* to get curious—surely they couldn't all be 'conditioned' in some way? Driving through the streets he looked past the footpaths into the shadowy areas beyond. It was hard to tell if he was actually seeing something, or if his over-wrought senses were playing tricks, but Michael felt he spied movement. Furtive figures drifting within the shade. He was tempted to try to drive closer and see exactly who and what they were, but quickly decided this was no time to be side-tracked. Besides, he would have to leave the car to get a good look, and Michael didn't like that idea.

They reached the church without incident. Typically, the building was made of weatherboard, the overlapping planking starting to separate in places through age and a lack of regular maintenance. The paint was peeling, leaving large scabs of dark, exposed wood. The church had been designed and built in the classic way—a long, narrow build-ing with a pointed roof and a small spire mounted over the front alcove. The double front doors had a short verandah attached with stairs leading off each side. It was an area for the Father to greet or bid farewell to his flock. A rough wooden chair was squeezed into one corner of the porch. Like the police station, there was a residence for the incumbent priest next door.

The two vehicles pulled up in front of the church together, raising a small pall of dust. Michael leaned out his window and called to Kerry.

'Stay in your car a second. We'll check it out.'
Seeing her nod, he turned to Gavin. 'Tell Beth
to stay in the van, too. You and I'd better have
a look first.' He listened to Gavin extract a
severe promise from Beth not to open her door,
then Michael got out of the van. Gavin followed
him.

The front door of the church opened at a touch.
Michael eased his way through and called out a
cautious hello. There was no answer. Behind him,
Gavin did the same, but again no-one replied. The
inside of the church was like a picture-postcard
scene—the epitome of a serene place of worship.
It was dim, though the gloom was brilliantly cut
by shafts of sunlight coming through the leadlight
windows, the colours in the glass lending themselves to the light. Heavy, full-length drapes
framed each window, their material dropping to
the floor. Dust motes hung in the air, swirling
slightly now with the opening of the door. The
only jarring note was the two rows of ceiling fans
stretching the length of the church.

The two men walked slowly towards the altar,
their footsteps echoing emptily. The floors and
pews were polished, lacquered timber. Only the
walls boasted a coating of light green paint, the
pale colour highlighting carved figurines of Christ
on the Cross and a selection of framed, fading
prints depicting famous religious scenes.

'Hello?' Michael called again. 'Father Johnson,
are you in here?'

Gavin looked around the altar and the several
small niches behind it, each containing some arte-
fact of Father Johnson's trade. 'It looks all set up

for the next service—which is probably how it normally would be.'

Michael found a narrow door, and opening it discovered a tiny cloakroom. Two vestments were hanging on hooks. 'I'd say you're right. It seems there's nobody here. The good Father must be in his home. I suppose the only thing we can do is knock on his front door and ask.'

'It *sounds* simple,' Gavin muttered.

They retraced their steps back down the aisle, moving faster now. Just as they reached the front door a voice called out to them, stopping them cold.

'Can I help you?'

Startled, Michael and Gavin spun around quickly. Standing next to the altar now was Father Johnson. In the wall beside him a connecting door was clicking shut, cutting off a square of sunlight. Michael had noticed the door before, but judged that it was never used—for no reason other than it *looked* like a door that was never opened. Father Johnson was a surprising sight, dressed in the full-length white raiment of his office, a gold cross emblazoned on the front of his flowing robe.

'Father Johnson?' Michael said, looking carefully. 'Remember me? I'm Michael Garrett. I came to see you about a year or so ago, and I've sinced moved into Hickory a few months back.'

'I remember you, Mr Garrett. And this is Mr Packer, I believe.' The priest's voice was soft-spoken, but not gentle. It had a hard edge to it.

'Gavin—Gavin Packer,' Gavin responded automatically. Like Michael, he was unnerved by the priest's sudden appearance, even though the swinging door explained it.

'Why have you come to my church? You haven't attended a service before now.'

Michael took a few steps back down the aisle and tried to get a better look at the priest. 'Father, are you—aware of what's happening in Hickory right now?'

Father Johnson turned his head slightly, so he was looking sideways at Michael. When he answered, he whispered in a rush, the sibilant sounds reverberating around the walls.

'There is *evil* in the streets!'

Michael kept his voice non-committal. 'Have you seen it?'

'Of course. My eyes have been opened to this for many years.'

'But *what* have you seen?' Gavin interrupted. 'Have you been close to it?'

'It will not ever come close to me.'

'Then, has it been inside the church? Have you ever found anyone—anyone evil—in here lately?'

Father Johnson paused and looked at them carefully. 'This is a sacred and powerful place.'

Michael went back to Gavin and said, very quietly, 'Great. This guy's as nutty as a fucking fruitcake. Talking in riddles doesn't help—but I don't want to get too blunt with him in case he thinks *we're* evil and he chucks us out into the street.' Michael gestured at the church around them. 'If I understand him properly, then we might have made a good move here. It *is* sacred ground, after all. Maybe Isaiah and his friends can't come too near the place. I'd rather put up

462

with him than them,' he jerked a thumb towards Father Johnson.

'Okay, see what he says,' Gavin said reluctantly. Michael turned to the priest.

'Father, we want to shelter in your church. We think it must be safer. There's ourselves, Gavin's daughter Beth and Kerry Wentworth, the pharmacist—you'd know her, I expect.'

There was another pause, longer this time, then Father Johnson said, 'Bring them inside. With such a congregation I feel a service is warranted. We will pray together for the Darkness to be lifted from our town. But first I will refresh myself, while you call your people into the church's protection.' The priest moved slowly to the connecting door, opened it and disappeared into the sunshine. The door closed by itself behind him.

'Damn,' Michael swore, softly. 'We might have found the best place to hide out, but he's crazier than I thought. I don't want to appear ungrateful, but the last thing I want to do is say prayers all day and night.'

'I'm more concerned we didn't get a closer look at him. Does he always talk like that? Are you sure he's okay?'

'I remember him as being pretty old-world in his speech, and he's undoubtedly lost a few more marbles in his head—so he's not exactly *okay*. But he sounds like himself, if you know what I mean.'

'Then we'll have to humour him, I suppose. If he gets too much—' Gavin stopped. A car horn was beeping urgently. The two of them rushed outside. Kerry stood beside her car, her hand through an open window to press the horn button.

463

'We've got company coming,' she said anxiously, and pointed down the road. In the distance a man was coming towards them. Normally, he would have been unrecognisable that far away, especially with his slumped posture, the bowed head hiding his face and anonymous, dragging footsteps. But the long shovel over one shoulder left Michael with no doubts about who it was.

'Well, Gavin?'' he said tightly. 'What do you think? We haven't got much time. We either drive away again or we try the church.'

Gavin looked torn. 'We have to try the church,' he decided heavily. 'Otherwise we might be running away all day, until we run out of places to go—and probably end up back here anyway. At least now it's daylight and we might be able to see it's not going to work before it's too late. Grab Beth for me, will you? I want to get something out of your van.'

Kerry pulled open the van's side door and beckoned Beth out. Filling the younger girl's arms with blankets and a bag, she hustled her towards the church's front door. Before she followed, she leaned back into the van herself and snatched up some things. Michael was busy with the dogs, unceremoniously hauling them out by their collars and half-carrying them to the door, shoving them through without caring what Father Johnson might think about animals in his church. Michael felt they needed all the help they could get, and he still believed the dogs would come in handy. He didn't want to leave them outside, where they might get hurt or be scared away.

Gavin was under the back tailgate of the van,

rummaging around among the tools. He emerged with the two-metre-long ratchet pole for the bumper jack. It was a heavy piece of metal with serrations down one edge for the jack mechanism to lock onto. Gavin hefted it experimentally in his hand and looked vaguely unsatisfied.

Down the street Connors was in plain view now, still slowly approaching. A cloud of flies buzzed around his head.

'Get inside now and stay there,' Michael told Kerry as she emerged from the church for another load. 'Have you still got the gun?' She nodded, patting the bulging pocket of her jacket.

Michael was the last to go inside. He took a final look at Connors, but the corpse didn't raise its face. Slamming the door behind him Michael immediately called for Gavin to help. Between them they placed one of the heavy pews against the doors, barring it. Then, as an extra precaution, they balanced a second on top of the first to add more weight. All the time Michael expected to hear Father Johnson's shouts of outrage suddenly coming from the other end of the church. He wondered what he should do about the connecting door to the Father's home. He wanted to block it right then, but knew he should call Father Johnson into the church with them.

But what if, for some misguided reason, the old priest didn't want to come? Michael didn't have time to argue.

The leadlight windows were the only ones providing daylight for the church. There was no clear glass through which Michael could try and get a look at Connors' progress. Consequently, he felt blind and regretted barricading the door so quickly. He would have preferred to watch Connors as long as he could and then try to decide what he was going to do.

'Gavin, yell out for Father Johnson to get the hell in here, will you? Everybody else go up the other end of the church.'

Nobody argued. Kerry hurried Beth up the aisle. The two dogs, their claws slipping noisily on the polished wooden floor, scampered around with the excitement. Michael stayed near the door and listened, straining his ears for the first sound that Connors had arrived on the other side. At first the noise of the others making their way up the aisle prevented him hearing anything, then they settled down and anxiously watched him. Gavin had quickly opened the side door and called out for Father Johnson, but received no answer. Closing it again, he stood braced and ready, watching the door for its first, smallest movement, the jackpole in his hands in case someone other than the priest tried to come in.

Heavy footsteps landed on the porch. Michael held his breath, half-expecting to have Connors' shovel suddenly smashing into the door panelling. The footsteps shuffled for a while and there was a faint metallic ringing as the blade of the shovel struck something. Then Michael heard a creaking sound. It took him a moment to understand what was happening—Connors had seated himself in the chair.

He was going to wait.

A noise from behind made Michael spin around. Gavin tensed himself as the side door began to

466

open. Father Johnson stepped through, closed the door calmly, and walked towards the altar without sparing a glance for Gavin. The priest went to a small cupboard and took out a handful of candles, then busied himself placing them in holders on and around the altar. After watching him in amazement for a long moment, Gavin suddenly put the jackpole down and threw his weight against the nearest pew. Before anyone could help him, he man-handled it across the side door. Even the noise of this didn't distract Father Johnson from his tasks at the altar, where he continued to prepare himself and the church for a service. Incredibly, he was ignoring everything happening around him, as if he were alone in the church.

From the front door Michael called, speaking very clearly. 'Father Johnson, Arnold Connors, the funeral director, is outside. Connors has been *dead* nearly two days, if not longer. Can you explain that, Father?' Frightened by Connors' arrival, Michael let the pressure get to him for a moment. 'Can you do anything *about* that, Father?' he asked harshly.

Father Johnson was lighting the candles, striking matches one after the other, touching the flame to three or four candles before he needed to strike a new match. There were over twenty candles in all. Finally, when they were all lit, the priest faced the rows of empty church pews and spoke loudly, as if his entire congregation filled the seats.

'We must pray to God for guidance.'

Without waiting for a response he began to pray in a stentorian voice, the words echoing around the inside of the church. Mandy, the labrador, got

467

upset and began to bark, setting Monty off, too. Beth hurried to quieten them both down. Gavin moved down to Michael.

'Jesus, it's just what we need,' he said, grimacing. 'He's really out of his mind. He looks sick, too. His face is as white as a sheet. Look at him.'

Father Johnson was a daunting sight. He gripped the edges of his altar with fierce strength while he glared out at his invisible audience, exhorting them to heed his prayers and find deliverance in his message. He offered the empty pews absolution, eternal life in the Hereafter and peace of mind for their mortal journey on God's earth. Within a minute he was almost ranting with zealous abandon. The candles around the altar flickered and trembled as he shook their mountings. The firelight danced on his white skin and glittered in his eyes. The interior of the church seemed to grow darker.

The blade of Connors' shovel crashed with a tremendous ringing against the front door.

Beth screamed and Kerry immediately wrapped her arms tightly around the girl, comforting her. Both dogs leapt away from Beth and rushed snarling back down the aisle, skidding to an untidy halt at the front door. Hackles raised, they barked furiously at the wooden panelling.

'It looks like we could have made a bad choice,' Gavin called to Michael, shakily.

'Maybe not. Let's wait and see what he's going to do.'

The shovel clanged against the outside of the church again. This time it wasn't directly on the door, but on the wall next to it. Half-hopeful, Michael looked at Gavin.

'See? He's moving around the building. Is he trying to get in, or is he just mad that he *can't* come in?'

Father Johnson raised his voice slightly to combat the noise of the shovel and the barking dogs. Apart from this, he didn't acknowledge any of what was happening. The shovel struck again, on the corner of the building this time. One of the framed prints dropped from its hook to the floor. The edge-on impact made the glass explode out of the frame with a bang. The dogs began to move, following the sounds around the building, Michael lunged down and grabbed them both by their collars so they wouldn't run through the broken glass. Gavin quickly came to his aid, taking Mandy.

'Can Connors come inside? That's what we need to know,' Michael shouted over the dogs, who were still barking madly. 'He can bash on the outside all week for all I care—if he can't come inside.'

The shovel slammed into the side wall.

Gavin looked desperately up at Father Johnson. 'He must know! He can't have been blind to everything that's been happening. These bastards have been wandering the streets for two days now—more, probably. This church is right in the middle of town and only a minute's walk from the cemetery where all these fucking spooks must be coming from. If any of them were going to step inside here, they would've done it by now—and *he* would know about it.'

Michael nodded quickly, then indicated for Gavin to hold Monty, too. 'I'll try and get some sense out of him.'

He sprinted up the aisle to the altar, ignoring the splintering crash of the shovel as it struck the outside wall again. Michael was surprised by the amount of heat coming from the candles. He stood for a moment, just to one side, but in plain view of the priest. Father Johnson didn't appear to even notice him, but kept up his strident sermon to the empty pews. Michael didn't wait any longer.

'Father, you must listen to me! Please, forget the service for a minute. I need to know if these people—these *living dead*—can come inside the church. Have you seen them? Have they threatened you, before now?'

The priest ignored him, except to inject a trace of worry into his shouted sermon, as if he were running out of time.

The shovel smashed again.

'*Father Johnson!* For Christ's sake, forget the sermon and talk to me!'

Michael was yelling, trying to get through to the priest. Scared too much by everything, Beth burst into wild crying in Kerry's arms. Kerry held her tighter and rocked her a little, whispering soothing words into Beth's hair. Michael could only spare them a sympathetic glance, before turning his attention back to Father Johnson. Michael suddenly figured he might have a chance of getting an answer out of the priest if only he could get him away from the altar—the priest's source of power and authority.

With one determined sweep of his forearm, Michael brushed aside the candles mounted on his side of the altar. They scattered to the floor, spilling wax. Most of them stayed alight. Father Johnson didn't respond. His eyes, riveted to a point somewhere near the back of the church, weren't even attracted to the fluttering, falling flames. Michael realised that to pull the priest aside, he would have to release the man's death-like grip on the altar.

'Father, I'm sorry, but you've got to stop this,' Michael said grimly. He slipped his hand over the priest's nearest wrist, intending to squeeze the tendons painfully so Father Johnson's fingers would involuntarily open. At Michael's touch, the priest suddenly fell silent and turned his face towards him. In that same moment, Michael understood something dreadful.

Father Johnson's skin was as cold as ice, and slick with moisture. Horrified, Michael stared up into the priest's face. As he looked, a small cockroach came out of Father Johnson's slackly-open mouth, ran across his cheek and disappeared into his hairline.

Arnold Connors' shovel punched a hole through one of the leadlight windows with an explosion of glass. The rest of the window crumbled prettily to the floor, a deadly cascade of coloured shards.

Michael stumbled backwards away from the priest. Twisting around and getting his balance, he rushed to pull Kerry and Beth away, too. 'Get away from him! Quick! Move up the centre of the church. No! Don't worry about those,' he added urgently, as Beth made an attempt to grab some of her things from the pile around them. Glancing over his shoulder Michael saw Father Johnson's corpse slowly bending over, starting to pick up the fallen candles. With a sudden change of mind, Michael began throwing the blankets and extra clothing down the aisle towards Kerry, who scooped it up. Once again, the priest seemed oblivious to their presence. As he moved around the altar, picking up the candles and relighting those that had been extinguished, he began his shouted sermon again, yelling the holy words angrily at the walls and pews around him. Michael, carrying the last of their supplies away from the altar, dropped them at Kerry's feet and nimbly dodged around her. He ran to Gavin, who still stood near the door, holding the dogs.

'The priest is *dead*,' he said, shocked. 'I mean, he's *already* fucking dead! We locked ourselves in here with a damn corpse.'

The circumstances were bad enough, but Gavin's face turned a shade even paler. He stared at the priest and let his breath out in a slow whistle when it appeared Father Johnson wasn't immediately threatening them. 'Christ, what a mess! How could we be so blind? I *knew* we should have taken a closer look. There was something about him—oh shit, Michael! That must mean Connors can come *in*, too. As soon as he finds a way.'

The next leadlight window burst inwards with a tremendous noise, the shovel poking through the shattered framework for a moment until the dead hands pulled it back. The broken glass flew far enough to shower over Kerry and Beth.

'We have to get out of here,' Michael said. He

looked towards the last broken window. The same thoughts were going through Gavin's mind. Connors seemed to be making his way around the building. Soon, he would be going around the back, and he wasn't moving fast. If they were quick, everyone could get out the front doors and run for it. 'One person go for the van,' Michael said. 'Get it started and away from the church. Everyone else can just run for it and get in the van when they're a safe distance away and there's enough time—'

Michael stopped. Something in Father Johnson's preaching had caught his attention. The two men looked towards the priest and saw him moving away from the altar. He was clutching several lit candles.

'Only his burning can cleanse the Evil which has come into my church. The Darkness can be cast out, and we can do his work in the flames.'

The dead priest touched one of the burning candles to the long drape framing the nearest window.

The material was old and very brittle. And dry. The fire took hold with startling speed, racing up the curtain and setting it completely aflame within seconds. The painted wall beside it immediately began to blister and pop with the heat. Uncaring of the fire licking at his clothing as he passed, Father Johnson moved on to the drape on the other side of the window and set that alight, too. He started towards the next window. Behind him, Connors' shovel smashed through the last remaining window on the opposite side.

'We have been Chosen to do his work. The

flame can burn the Darkness from our souls. We should embrace the flame.'

Watching, Michael was both appalled and fascinated at how fast the flames were growing, catching on the wooden walls and the timber window frame. Then he snapped out of it and yelled at Gavin, 'This place will burn to the ground in minutes! We haven't got any more time to waste. We *must* get out now.'

Gavin nodded his answer. He was still holding the dogs, who had reverted to worried whimpering at the leaping flames. 'Take these two for a moment,' he told Michael. Free of the dogs, Gavin went to the first broken window and cautiously poked his head out. Looking to his left, he was just in time to see Connors shuffling slowly around the back of the building. He went back to Michael and surprised him by bodily picking up the labrador, Mandy. His boots crunching on the broken glass Gavin returned to the window and, being careful not to cut himself on the shards still lodged in the frame, he half-lowered, half-threw the dog outside. Then Gavin did the same with Monty.

'The dogs will follow us, as soon as we get outside,' Gavin said loudly, gesturing as he went past for Michael to help him clear away the pews blockading the front door. Straining at the weight, they threw them aside, then Michael hesitated, before he swung open the doors. He saw Gavin picking up the steel jackpole again. This helped Michael come to a decision. It was his van anyway—he knew best how to start it in a hurry.

'I'll go for the van,' he explained. 'The rest of

474

you forget the food and blankets—just get out of the church and run like hell down the road and stay in the *middle* of it. Don't stray off onto the verges or go near any houses. We don't know who's in them any more. I'm sure Connors can't move fast, so you should be safe. I'll get away just as quick as I can—even quicker, if the van starts all right, so don't worry about me. I'll pick you up just a few metres down the road and we'll be well away from here, okay? Now, everyone ready?'

The roaring flames in the church were very loud now, almost drowning out Father Johnson's preaching. He was moving between the pews, heading for the drapes on the opposite side of the church.

'Let me go first,' Gavin said, showing them the jackpole. 'You three run out behind me. As soon as you're clear, I'll follow.'

There wasn't any time to argue. Michael cried, 'Here we go!' and threw open the doors. The flames inside the church growled their approval at the sudden rush of air. Gavin stepped out and blocked the steps on the side of the alcove where they expected Connors to appear, forcing Kerry, Beth and Michael to run down the opposite stairs. As he ran to the van, fumbling in his pocket for the keys, Michael wondered if he hadn't been too careful. Connors hadn't appeared yet. It looked as though there would have been time to load everyone into the van. Kerry and Beth were already a fair distance down the street. Then Michael saw that Gavin hadn't moved. He was waiting for Michael to get the van safely started, rather than leave his friend in danger. Michael was about to shout out over the roof of the van, before he got inside, for Gavin to run too. At that moment Connors came around the corner of the church. He hadn't bothered smashing the windows on that side, but kept moving as if he knew there was better prey at the front of the church.

Without warning, the corpse swung its shovel at Gavin. Gavin used his jackpole as a staff, holding it with two hands and blocking the blow. The stench of Connors' decomposing body washed over Gavin and he was stricken almost enough to retch uncontrollably. Connors was slow, dragging the shovel back to start another swing, and Gavin had time to change his grip on the jackpole and hit out hard. The steel caught Connors flush on the temple, crushing the skull and making his head, with its broken neck, flop over comically to the other shoulder. A dark fluid splashed across the spoiled skin on his cheek.

But it had no effect on Connors' efforts to kill Gavin. He slashed with the shovel again, missing as Gavin stepped quickly backwards.

In the van Michael was doing the only thing he could—get the motor started so Gavin could make his own escape. He twisted the key and stomped on the accelerator. The engine turned over sluggishly and Michael knew, in his haste, he was flooding the carburettor. Reluctantly, he lifted his foot. A moment later the motor caught, ran unsteadily, then cleared itself with a clattering roar and a cloud of blue smoke from the exhaust pipe. Michael rammed the gear lever into reverse and backed away from the church. He saw the building already had flames climbing out of the roof outside. Then, swinging the van onto the road Michael braked and yelled at Gavin.

'Come on! Let's get going, you bloody idiot.'

For a dreadful moment it looked like Michael called out at exactly the wrong moment. Gavin turned to look at him as Connors was laboriously swinging the shovel once more. He turned back in the last instant and saw the blow coming, deflecting it away with the jackpole, then he twisted away from Connors and began sprinting down the road. Michael drove after him, slowing down as he drew level. Surprising Michael, Gavin slid open the side door and tumbled inside. He lay there, gasping for breath. On the road ahead of them Kerry was carrying Beth and still running—though not so fast now, as over her shoulder she could see the van coming up behind her. The two dogs ran excitedly around her.

Michael was right. Connors was incapable of following them at any speed and no-one else appeared to give them more trouble. He had time to stop completely and let Kerry and Beth climb into the back of the van with Gavin. The dogs didn't need any invitation, leaping easily over the prone humans in the way.

'Now where?' Gavin yelled towards the cabin. 'Any more bright bloody ideas?'

'Kerry's house,' Michael called back without turning. 'I think we can make it safely. All we have to do is get through the town.'

But driving through the streets soon showed them the centre of Hickory had changed. Whereas before the place had looked deserted, now more people were walking the footpaths than would ever be seen on a busy day. Except none of them should have been able to walk.

By all appearances, everyone on the streets of Hickory today was dead.

Mrs North stood in front of the burnt-out ruins of Mal Bartell's store, patiently waiting where the front door used to be, as if she were expecting the store to open at any moment. She ignored a stirring among the ashes nearby, where a half-limbed, blackened figure thrashed among the debris. Similarly, Jake Sanders and another man Michael couldn't recognise were standing at the doors to McGann's hotel. As the van went past Jake's dead eyes locked onto Michael's, and Michael had trouble breaking away from the terrible gaze. It had a strange, inviting quality and Michael could almost have stopped the car and got out. He forced himself to lean forward and look upwards at the upper balcony instead. The corpse hanging there was now kicking its legs and squirming, alive again, but trapped by the noose into endlessly reliving its own death.

'Did you see Jake?' Gavin said, from the back.

'Yes.'

I think he wants us to join him for a drink, Michael was going to add, but stopped himself. Now they were passing the school.

The hanging body there also moved, scraping at the soft soil beneath its feet, digging it away and making its situation worse. Two young boys seated on nearby swings calmly watched the corpse's efforts. One of them was Ainslie McGregor, Michael could see. The other he didn't know, but he could guess. It looked like Ainslie

478

had his best friend, Kevin Stanford, as a playmate again. Michael sadly wondered how a young boy like Kevin would kill himself, then he remembered the boy's father was a doctor with a surgery attached to his house. There would be drugs of some sort. Kevin had probably ingested everything he could find. An overdose of something would kill him eventually, or perhaps he inadvertently swallowed a deadly cocktail.

Some of the houses sprinkled along the main street among the shops and businesses now had their owners wandering dazedly within their gardens. They all had the blank-faced look of people emerging from a deep, dream-filled sleep. With a flicker of hope Michael suddenly doubted all of them were actually dead—but then he reminded himself he'd made that mistake about Father Johnson, too.

It was possible the entire town was populated by walking corpses—people who had met or made their deaths, only to discover there was to be no resting in peace.

Michael was so absorbed in watching the scenes to either side of the street he nearly didn't see the line of men walking down the centre of the road towards him. At the last moment Michael swore and swung the van violently away, bringing cries of fear and dismay from the three in the back as people and dogs went everywhere. One front wheel rode up onto the kerb before Michael could bring the van to a halt. He stared out the driver's side window.

There were nearly a dozen men marching down the road in single file. They all wore their best clothes—or what had been once their best—and Michael saw many of them had tarnished medals pinned to their chests. On most of them the cloth of their jackets had rotted so much the medals hung crookedly, or had fallen off completely, leaving gaps like broken teeth. The shuffling corpses were doing their best to keep a straight line and hold their decaying bodies erect. A sense of awe filled Michael as he realised what he was witnessing.

These were the town's returned soldiers. They were marching again, down the main street of Hickory. Michael remembered something Riley had said: *The dead were trying to find their lives.* These corpses were trying to find their moment of glory.

The moment was broken when Gavin snapped, 'Move it, Michael. Someone's getting too close.'

In the rear-view mirror Michael saw another ragged corpse—someone who'd been in the grave a long time—shuffling towards the back of the van. It was a terrible sight, most of the flesh hanging away from the skull in rotting strips. There were no eyes, just empty sockets, and no lips either, giving the head a ghastly, grinning appearance. There was no telling how long the corpse had been moving about the streets, or why it did so. But the van stopped in front of it obviously gave the cadaver a purpose. It dragged itself along with an effort and began clutching at the vehicle with one wasted, skeletal arm.

'Jesus Christ,' Michael muttered, sickened. The motor was still running. He quickly found first gear and drove off the footpath. He silently prayed

480

he hadn't done any serious damage, hitting the kerb. The first few metres told him the steering was okay—they'd been lucky.

They made Kerry's house without any further mishaps. All over town, or at least the parts of it they saw, was the same. Some of the things moving through the streets were obviously living dead, like Jake Sanders and Mrs North. Others were so sick-looking and uncomprehending of their surroundings it was impossible to tell what sort of condition they were in. Michael didn't care any more. He was only concerned about the people in the van.

He told everyone to go upstairs into Kerry's kitchen, including the dogs. As they went, moving quickly and looking nervously about the yard, Michael called to Kerry, 'Have you got any tools—garden tools?'

She was confused for a moment, then replied, 'There's a pile of rusty things under the house. I'm not even sure what's there—they were there when I got the house. I think there's a shovel.'

Michael waved his thanks and said to Gavin, 'Help me, will you?'

Puzzled, Gavin joined Michael to search among the old tools and farming implements stacked in one corner under the house. Michael was pleased when he found a rusting axe and a long crowbar. He gave the axe to Gavin.

'Now what do we do? Cut down a tree?' Gavin asked, perplexed.

'Close,' Michael said. 'Go up the rear stairs and cut them out instead, as you go. I'll see if I can wrench some of the front ones out while you do it, but the axe will probably do the best job.'

Gavin looked up at the house on its high stumps. 'I get you,' he said, slowly. 'But what about Isaiah? It won't stop him.'

'I don't know if there's anything we can do about him, but we *can* do something about those fucking living corpses. If we're up there, and they're down here, with no stairs in between, I think we'll be pretty safe.'

It was hard work, especially with the old and inadequate tools. The axe did prove the better of the two, smashing rather than cutting the wooden steps out of the supporting rails. This was good enough, Michael figured. Most of the corpses they'd seen in town were having enough trouble simply walking. There was no way they could climb the steep and splintered railings. The house was raised a little over two metres off the ground. It wasn't that far to drop down when they wanted to leave, and a determined, fit and healthy person wouldn't have much trouble climbing back up, if need be. But it wasn't fit and healthy people Michael was worried about.

When they'd finished Michael and Gavin looked out at their handiwork. In the distance a tower of black smoke climbed into the blue sky—the church was burning to the ground.

'This gives us some breathing space,' Michael said, nodding down at the ruined stairs. 'We should get through tonight—maybe longer, like this. If anyone's going to drop in for a visit, they'll have trouble getting to the front door,' he added dryly. 'Apart from this, we can only take one day at a time and hope the army comes to its senses.'

'Do you think we might get some visitors? Who?'

'Those corpses in town—even the old and rotting ones—seemed somehow attracted to us, did you see it? I don't know why—but I think it's like I said before. They *hate* us for living. I'm worried some of them are making their way out here right now, as if we three are the Pied Pipers of Hickory for the dead.' Michael suddenly let out a snort of laughter, then lowered his voice. 'The whole damn cemetery might come for a visit. It seems being dead just isn't good enough any more.'

23

THE SOLDIERS BEHIND the barriers were professionals—men and women who had joined the army for a career. But of the entire company blockading the highway out of Hickory, only a few of them had ever fired a shot in anger. Some of them had seen active service in trouble spots around the world, fulfilling United Nations peacekeeping roles and undertaking hazardous duties, sometimes getting involved in 'firefights'—brief, confusing exchanges of weapons fire usually over before anyone was aware they had begun.

Nobody had seen anything like this.

No-one had seen somebody gunned down in cold blood, the way Sergeant Riley had been. It affected some of them deeply, despite their training. Some men, like Private First Class Milton Casey, were in a mild form of shock after seeing what a Steyr automatic rifle could do to a human being. Every time he relived those seconds in his mind, seeing again the bullets ripping into the policeman's chest, Casey felt a cold sweat cover his face and a funny, shivering feeling creep through his body. He knew he should talk to someone about it. It seemed there were 'counsellors' for everybody and everything these days and this unit was no exception. Several counsellors were included in the task force to deal with just such a problem as Casey's. But Private First Class Milton Casey was only twenty years old, had served two years in the army already, and was expected by his peers—even more than by his officers—to tough these things out. It's what made a good soldier. He knew a real rifleman couldn't go running for a comforting pat on the head every time things got a little hot.

Each time it resurfaced into his consciousness, he tried to block his mind to the image of Riley being punched to the ground by the bullets. And Casey ignored the flush of perspiration popping out of his skin like beads of ice, and the slightly dizzy, disorientating feeling that came with the sudden shivers. Casey wasn't surprised when he started hallucinating too, after a moment of shock. He told himself his imagination was working overtime.

He was supposed to be watching the highway towards town in case someone else came up with the idea of rushing the blockade in a high-speed vehicle while the Blackhawks were too far away.

485

But his eyes kept locking onto the fallen, bloodied body of Sergeant Riley still lying on the road where he'd dropped. Even though in reality the distance prevented it, Casey seemed to be able to see every detail of the body, his imagination filling in the parts his eyes couldn't pick out. Riley lay on his back, his torn chest glistening red in the sunlight, his arms and legs flung wide. Casey could see one of the hands, covered in blood, touching the black bitumen. His imagination told him that after so long in the sun, the fingers of that hand would be gummed together now by the blood.

Casey saw the hand suddenly flex, the fingers separating and breaking the bond of the congealed gore, then lying still again. That was all.

The private froze, his mouth half-open in amazement and fear. Had he seen it? Had he *really* seen it? He quickly looked around at the other soldiers manning the barriers, but it seemed he was the only one taking his duty seriously and still watching down the road. The other guys were calling to each other, swapping cigarettes and stories. The officers weren't complaining. The man responsible for pulling the trigger on the policeman was a celebrity at the moment and getting all the attention. Casey was close enough to see the man was trying to stay cool, but his face was pale. Casey wished some of the others had been doing their jobs and watching the highway. Maybe they would have seen the corpse move, too. Now he didn't know what to do. Casey knew he wasn't one hundred per cent fit at the moment. He wasn't thinking straight, and seeing that policeman shot down was playing hell with his head. Trying to keep calm, he reasoned it wasn't so surprising after all that his eyes would begin playing tricks on him, too. And besides—what was he thinking of?

The guy was dead—there was nothing surer than that. Dead people don't move.

Leaving the body in the middle of the road had been a major decision—but was only a stop-gap measure. The officers commanding the army task force were still in a huddled conference. No-one really knew what to do. Shooting the policeman hadn't been ordered, but then again the soldiers were told not to let anyone—and that meant *anyone*—cross the barricade, and the man had appeared to be about to do just that. It may have been a little premature, gunning him down like that when a warning shot might have sufficed, but the officers realised that seeing the biological warfare suits being used in earnest was putting the fear of God—or worse—into the men. Under the circumstances, nobody was going to act in half-measures. In effect, the soldier had been obeying orders with an initiative no-one else might have found the courage to use.

But the problem hadn't been solved. In fact, it compounded itself. The policeman couldn't walk away, which would have been the most desirable conclusion to the confrontation. Now the army had a corpse lying within a hundred metres of their perimeter. With the evidence they had at their disposal at the moment, supplied by the patrol that had been into town earlier that morning, the corpse had the potential to contaminate anyone who went near it with a deadly virus—'virus' being the only word available to describe what had killed Corporal Cooper. Bringing the policeman's body through the barricade to examine it, or even just for the sake of decency, contradicted the logic behind killing him in the first place. Leaving him out there on the road was okay for the moment, if a little callous— until the wind changed and blew their way, or it rained and running water brought the virus into their midst anyway.

Obviously, something had to be done.

Corporal Cooper's body wasn't a much better proposition. They had him in the huge medical trailer at the rear of the blockade. Cooper's corpse had come amongst them before anyone knew the dangers. The best they'd been able to do was keep him sealed in his bio-warfare suit and hope that whatever got in there to kill him wouldn't get out again. It was slightly illogical, but so far it seemed to be working. The other soldiers were isolated, too, in a small camp of their own until somebody figured out what to do with them.

Medical Corpsman Overman was the only man allowed to work inside the medical trailer now. It wasn't his choice, but he'd been the one to help the returning patrol frantically unload Cooper's body—there'd been a thread of hope the man wasn't dead—into the mobile hospital. Overman could have been in a much worse position, but the sergeant of that patrol at the last moment clamped his hand over Overman's as the medic reached for Cooper's uniform.

488

'Don't unseal the suit,' the sergeant said, his face white. 'Not yet. Can you tell if he's dead—beyond help—without undoing the suit?'

Dealing with the first real casualty of his career and feeling slightly panicked, Overman was flustered. 'I can try listening for a heartbeat,' he said finally.

'Then do that. Nothing more.'

Overman realised the sergeant was very frightened. He used a stethoscope and pressed it hard against the material of the uniform. Normally it wouldn't have been considered conclusive, but Overman shook his head and said, 'I can't hear a thing. I think he's dead.'

'Then that's good enough,' the sergeant said hoarsely. Outside the trailer a Landrover full of officers pulled up with a squeal of tyres. The sergeant hurried towards the doorway to stop them coming inside, saying again to the medic as he left, 'Whatever you do, don't unseal his suit. Do you understand me?' He didn't wait for a reply.

Medical Corpsman Overman was ordered to keep himself confined to the medical trailer—with Cooper's corpse for company. Someone was despatched to drive far enough down the highway to re-establish radio contact and arrange a second trailer to be hauled out to replace his. Overman worried what his fate might be, once it arrived. For the moment he'd kept himself busy re-sterilising everything and passing it outside in sealed bags in case it had to be used. It was mundane work and Overman did it listlessly, suspecting everything he touched would be destroyed anyway, as soon as replacements arrived. He only continued with it to keep his mind occupied.

It wasn't long after that he heard gunfire coming from the barricades and somebody shouted to him that a man had been killed. Once the initial excitement died down Overman applied himself to his work more vigorously, thinking he might be doing something useful after all. The replacement hospital would be days away, but people were being hurt now.

Overman could guess what must have happened in the nearby town. The task force was ordered to contain any living thing within the cordon they'd thrown around Hickory, and someone must have tried to escape. He was shocked to realise that that person must have been shot dead. He knew the orders were expected to be taken seriously, but it took an incident like this to hammer the point home. He figured the government must have a secret biological-warfare unit out here somewhere—it was isolated enough—or a chemical plant, and something dreadful had gone wrong, contaminating the local population. This whole scene had to be a very bad mess for them to shoot on sight. Overman silently put a wager on germ-warfare being involved. The chemical weapons wouldn't have the potential to spread indiscriminately across the country. *The poor bastards,* he thought. *Anyone still alive is probably dead already. They just don't know it yet.* Overman tried not to let his mind stray to wondering how seriously the Command would be treating *him*, and his possible exposure to a deadly virus. Was he already dead, too?

Even though the thought that he was wasting

his time was still strong in his mind, Overman kept re-sterilising bandages, gauze pads and packets of cotton wool. Most of these were in air-tight seals of their own, but he had proof lying on a bunk behind him, covered by a sheet, that air-tight packaging wasn't much protection against whatever the soldiers had been exposed to in the town. Overman began to consider how illogical everything was—the idea of confining him to the mobile hospital in case he'd been infected by Cooper's corpse. The hospital itself wasn't sealed completely, so if they were trying to guard against something in the air inside the trailer, they were kidding themselves. No doubt Overman himself would be contaminated, but so could everyone else for kilometres around, depending on the nature of the virus. The perimeter around the town was a joke against an airborne disease. In fact, bringing Cooper's body through the barricade meant nothing. Germs didn't recognise roadblocks and armed soldiers. Every member of the task force could already be on borrowed time.

The thought turned Overman cold. He shook it away. To try and regain his sense of humour he turned to the sheet-covered corpse at the other end of the trailer.

'You are causing me a lot of stress,' he told it. 'And to think I was only trying to help you, you ungrateful bastard—' the words died on his lips. Overman frowned at the shape underneath the white cloth and tried to decide why he suddenly found it unsettling. The answer came to him quickly—but he didn't appreciate it.

If he didn't know better, Overman could have sworn the body had moved slightly.

Private First Class Casey couldn't take his eyes off Riley's corpse now. There was something about it. In the same way that a thing—a human, or an animal—can be unmistakably dead by a certain something, or *lack* of something, in its appearance, Sergeant Riley's corpse exuded a sense of life. The more Casey stared at the bloodied remains, the more he became convinced that soon it would move again. The thought gave Casey a sick feeling in his stomach, adding to the effects of seeing Riley gunned down.

But he couldn't tell anyone. No-one would believe him. The other soldiers on the barricade had become even more relaxed now, some leaving their positions and gathering together to talk. Still, the officers and sergeants weren't complaining, as long as the troops didn't stray from the barricade. The highway on the other side of the side-on semi-trailer was straight for some distance. There would be plenty of warning. And nobody else was worried by the dead body. It was dead.

Casey's position was mostly in the shade of the truck. It was a mild time of year, but he imagined lying in the sun for any lengthy period would get too warm after a while. It would be hot out there on the bitumen. Casey could see a flicker of movement over the corpse and realised it would be flies, feeding on the blood. As he watched a thick cloud of insects suddenly rose momentarily from the corpse, then settled again. Casey's apprehension

492

tightened. What had disturbed them? Movement? He glanced quickly around, but nobody else was watching. He swore under his breath, a long sequence of continuous expletives, but it didn't ease the squirming in his gut. He was back to staring at the body again, and heard himself willing the corpse not to move.

But it did. One of the legs was slowly drawn up, like a man taking a high step, pulling the knee closer to his chest.

'Oh Jesus,' Casey muttered in a low, quavering voice. Then he called out, before he could stop himself, 'Sergeant! Over here!'

The sergeant had joined one of the groups of chatting soldiers. The panic in Casey's voice made everyone fall silent and the sergeant moved quickly to him. The other soldiers immediately went back to their positions. Squatting down next to Casey, the sergeant peered anxiously up the road. A Blackhawk was circling nearby, drowning out any possibility of hearing any approaching vehicles, and the highway in front of the roadblock was clear. He looked at Casey, puzzled.

'What is it?'

'The body, Sarge. Watch the body.'

'Watch the—? What the hell are you talking about?'

'Just watch it, for Christ's sake!'

Casey's pleading tone had the sergeant take him seriously for a few seconds and he waited. Nothing happened. 'What am I supposed to be seeing?' he asked, getting annoyed.

'It's moving.'

'Moving? The fucker's dead, Casey. In fact, I

haven't seen anyone more dead than that bastard. Are you blind? Did you see how many rounds he took, before—?'

'I tell you, he's fucking moving!' Casey cut him off. 'I've seen it.'

'Christ,' the sergeant sighed, and turned to call down the line of the barricade. 'Has anybody else seen the corpse moving? Casey here says the guy's starting to feel better.' Only a few of the soldiers bothered to answer with a negative. There were several stifled laughs.

'No-one else has been watching,' Casey said, gritting his teeth.

The sergeant took this as a criticism of his own behaviour. He snapped back, 'Everything's under control here, Casey. I don't need you to tell me what to do, or how to fucking do it. You stick to your job and I'll keep to mine, okay—'

The sergeant's words slowed then faded into silence. As he'd spoken, he'd kept his eyes on Riley's body.

This time the corpse rolled slightly and slowly flipped one hand over to join the other, like a sleeping man trying to roll onto his side.

'*Jesus Christ Almighty,*' the sergeant whispered, staring. 'What the fuck is going on here?' He suddenly jumped up and moved down the line, alternatively ordering everyone back to their positions and anxiously yelling for Lieutenant Borne, his commanding officer. Borne appeared from nowhere and the sergeant led him back to Casey's position, explaining as they went what was happening.

'This is crazy,' Borne said, dropping down

494

beside Casey. 'How long has he been moving? Do you think he's still alive?' he asked Casey.

Communication between the ranks was normally quite informal, but Casey was one of those soldiers who still held his officers slightly in awe. He wasn't used to speaking to them so directly. 'About ten minutes, I think,' he answered uncertainly.

'Ten minutes! Why didn't you say something earlier?'

'I—I didn't think anyone would believe me. The sarge here thought I was—' But the sergeant cut off Casey's reply with a look.

Before anyone could say more Riley's corpse rolled again once, twice, then with an obvious effort turned completely over until it flopped facedown on the bitumen.

There was an audible whisper of shock and amazement from the line of watching soldiers. Borne was at a loss what to do. He heard a commotion start somewhere behind him, in the rear of the task force's camp, but he told himself to ignore it. It would have to be somebody else's problem—all of a sudden he was too busy here. A thought came to him and Borne ordered one of the nearest men to go searching for one of the senior officers. As the man hurried away, Borne silently chastised himself for not thinking fast enough.

'What are we going to do, sir?' The sergeant asked. 'Do you think he's still alive?'

'What are you talking about, of course he's still alive!' Borne snapped back, but then something made him add exasperatedly, 'But how the hell *can* he be? Who is this guy—fucking Rambo?'

'Lieutenant,' Casey said urgently. 'He's getting up.'

'Christ, this is impossible.'

They fell silent, watching in fascination and fear as Riley's corpse struggled to stand. The arms strained, trembling, to push the torso off the ground. Fresh rivulets of blood appeared out of the shirt-sleeves, flowing down from his chest and running over his elbows and forearms. Slowly Riley drew his legs up underneath him too, until he squatted on all fours. He stayed that way for a long time while the soldiers anxiously looked on. Then, like a punch-drunk fighter who doesn't know when to quit, Riley got to his feet. He stood, swaying visibly, his back to the barricades. After nearly a minute, during which Borne sensed the corpse was slowly gaining strength, Riley stumbled around in a small circle to face the soldiers. Borne heard somebody nearby quickly say a short prayer.

Riley's chest was a shattered, bloody mess. Blood now soaked his trousers and arms. He stood still, the blood dripping off the ends of his fingers, his hands held close to his sides. Borne could see dirt caked into one of the corpse's eyes, but the other was clear and glared at them with a hate made all the more terrifying by the total lack of any other emotion, or glow of real life. Riley took a tottering step forward, then another.

A new voice spoke behind Borne. He turned to see the task force second-in-command, Major Collins, his face white, watching Riley's painful progress towards the barricade.

'Take him down, again,' he said flatly.

Casey was crouched down behind one of the trailer's wheels. He twisted around, staring at the newcomer.

'You heard me, soldier! Open fire and take him out. Don't let him get any closer.'

The sergeant glared down at Casey, but his anger was more an effective method of hiding his own horror and confusion. 'For fuck's sake, Casey! What are you waiting for—written confirmation?'

Without answering Casey slowly thumbed the safety catch off his Steyr and put the weapon to his shoulder. Beyond the sights on the barrel Riley's figure blurred, then cleared again. Casey ignored his training and drew in a deep breath to steady himself, then pulled the trigger.

The rifle was on automatic, spitting out a stream of bullets. Casey remembered enough of his training to realise Riley was still too far away for very accurate firing with the Steyr, so he kept his finger pressed and hosed his aim slightly, seeing the rounds suddenly strike Riley and send him staggering backwards. The corpse fell and Casey tried to follow him down, the bullets chewing pieces out of the bitumen. Riley jerked and trembled, the rounds striking home. Casey stopped firing when the sergeant clamped a hand on his shoulder. The silence following was more shattering than the shooting.

'God damn, he must be a tough one,' the sergeant said grimly. 'But I'll bet he won't get up from that.'

Riley did.

Even more slowly, each movement a trembling effort—no-one could guess if the corpse felt the agony of its injuries—Riley dragged himself upright to confront the barriers again. The latest wounds showed in his upper arms and legs. One round had passed cleanly through the cheeks of his face leaving flapping pieces of skin and giving the watchers glimpses of blood-reddened teeth. Twisting his body to haul his useless legs forward one at a time, Riley began a stumbling walk towards the soldiers.

'My God,' Collins said hoarsely, then in a stronger voice ordered, 'Do it again, man! Shoot him down.'

Casey didn't need to hear it twice. His own fear was building and pulling the trigger of his weapon was an outlet akin to screaming, a personal release. The Steyr snarled again, the shiny brass cartridge cases cascading onto the ground around him. Other soldiers took his firing as a cue and opened up, too. Caught in a hail of fire Riley went down more quickly. Again, his body was subjected to extra rounds after he fell, his figure twitching on the bitumen like a man in a restless sleep. Several people had to call repeatedly for a cease-fire before all the Steyrs were silent.

The policeman got up again.

This time as Riley began to pick himself up from the road, the soldiers could see one hand had been blown cleanly off at the wrist, leaving a bloody stump. More rounds had hit him in the face, making such a gored mess its features were unrecognisable. The corpse staggered, barely capable of supporting its own weight on legs broken by the bullets. It only lasted a moment before Riley pitched forward face-down onto the road. The soldiers collectively held their breath, praying it was finished, but the corpse reached forward with its good hand and hauled itself a few centimetres closer to the barricade, leaving a smear of blood and flesh on the bitumen.

Major Collins turned to Casey's sergeant and said harshly, 'Go find the armoury sergeant and tell him I want a rocket-propelled grenade unit with four rounds, and a half-dozen hand grenades here *now*. No arguments, no red tape or fucking acquisition forms, just get them here.'

The sergeant ran off. Watching him leave, Borne saw some of the riflemen closest to the barriers the corpse was moving towards begin to edge backwards. Riley had already dragged himself several metres forward, but he still had a way to go.

'Keep your positions, damn you!' Borne yelled. The soldiers flinched, but did as they were told. Collins was briefing another soldier, telling him to relay what was happening to the task force's commander.

The corpse completed half the distance to the barricade before the sergeant returned with another man helping him carry the weapons. He looked towards Riley and realised it was getting too close for comfort when it came to grenades, but he didn't complain.

'All hell's breaking loose out the back, too,' he announced breathlessly.

'All right,' said Collins sharply. 'But they'll have to look after themselves. We've got too many of our own problems here.' He looked at the grenade launcher speculatively a moment. 'Get your best shooter onto that and three others with a hand grenade each. I want you to literally blow that bastard to pieces, understand? You'd better be quick too, or you'll be blasting us in the process.'

The sergeant stared at him, then nodded and hurried away. As he left another soldier ran up to Collins and began talking to him urgently. The major listened intently, nodding and glancing towards the rear, as if he might see what the soldier was explaining.

The sergeant picked the men he knew were the best and explained what was expected. They carefully orchestrated how they would do it. First, three men would prime the hand grenades and wait as long as they could, then lob them towards the corpse. The man firing the rocket grenade would try and judge his shot so the projectile would arrive at its target at the same time. The combination of the four simultaneous explosions should be enough to achieve the result they wanted.

They had to duck under the trailer and stand on the other side of it. Although the truck was only a token barrier the men felt exposed and vulnerable. It was strange to have that mass of metal and machinery at their backs—and frightening to have nothing between them and the crawling corpse. The sergeant went with them and called out the sequence of orders. Drill-like, he ordered the priming of the hand grenades and counted down aloud to the moment they must be thrown. As the grenades arced through the air the gunner steadied his aim and fired. The rocket-propelled grenade left the launcher with a whooshing noise and visibly streaked across the short space towards Riley. It hit the corpse squarely, hurling it backwards. Watching from behind the barriers, Borne realised with a sick feeling the projectile had literally buried itself inside the policeman's body. An instant later the three thrown grenades landed close by, bouncing spectacularly on the hard bitumen. The five soldiers were in the act of dropping to the ground when all four grenades detonated in a ripple of explosions.

The noise of the blasts was sharp and very loud. Shrapnel and pieces of bitumen lashed against the barricades. The sergeant felt the sting of concussion and flying grit, but knew he wasn't seriously hurt. His ears ringing, he slowly raised his head and looked.

A pall of smoke was drifting away down the road towards the town. The sergeant found time to register this meant the wind was on their side, for the time being, when it came to anything nasty in the air. Then he saw the shallow, irregular crater blown out of the bitumen. Pieces of something were strewn wide, nothing bigger in size than a human hand. It was only possible to recognise some of these bits as having belonged to the policeman by the shreds of blue cloth that still clung to them. By a mixture of good luck and good training Major Collins' wishes had been carried out almost to perfection.

The men closest to Collins expected to see him satisfied. He'd dodged for cover behind one of the trailer's wheel assemblies and now re-emerged to inspect the results. But instead of being grimly content about a job well done, he turned to Borne and said, 'Well, that's one of them out of the way. Bring the weapons and follow me. I believe we may need them again.'

He turned on his heel and walked away, leaving Borne staring in amazement after him.

Overman went back to his sterilising equipment and started working again, telling himself he needed to keep himself busy. He also convinced himself he wasn't purposely putting himself at the opposite end of the medical trailer to Cooper's body. For five minutes he operated the steriliser. Anything he touched or moved made a noise which seemed unnaturally loud in the confines of the mobile hospital. Overman was on edge, more than before. When the sound of automatic gunfire came through the sealed windows Overman jumped so nervously he dropped the handful of field dressings he was about to sterilise. They scattered over the floor.

Treading on them in his haste, he rushed to the window. He had to press his face to the glass to look towards the barricades where he knew the firing must be coming from. Overman couldn't see anything. For a moment he believed he glimpsed a wisp of blue smoke drifting through the air, but the window was smeared and it might have been his imagination. A noise from the other end of the trailer made him spin around.

Cooper was sitting up, the sheet falling away from his body.

'Oh dear, oh *shit*!' Overman mumbled, feeling himself go numb.

Cooper began to shiver, then the trembling turned to real convulsions. He jerked so violently on the narrow bunk it seemed certain he would soon fall over the edge. Overman reacted quickly, obeying his training and his instincts—which proved to be wrong. Cooper's cloth head-cover with its visor and breathing apparatus were attached to the lower parts of the suit by two press-seal lines. Overman was convinced Cooper was trying unsuccessfully to breathe, so he ran forward and gripped the bottom flap of the helmet and pulled hard, ripping it away over the back of Cooper's head and exposing the soldier's face.

Cooper's eyes fixed on Overman. They were blood-red instead of white, around the cornea, and the cornea itself was opaque and lifeless. The skin of Cooper's face was white like dirty paper. The blood in his body had already settled to the lowest parts of his body. Cooper had been dead long enough for that.

Overman realised he was still dead.

With a scream he backed away, then with a tremendous effort clamped down on his hysteria. Vaguely he heard people shouting outside and realised the army hadn't been so trusting. There were soldiers detailed to keep an eye on him and now they were panicked by his scream.

What would happen if I rushed out the door? They would probably gun me down, like they must have done to some other poor fuck down at the barricade.

503

Overman backed all the way to the other end of the trailer. He felt a sink there press against the small of his back. One of the trailer's doors was to his left, but opening it might bring a burst of rifle-fire. He was certain the soldiers guarding the hospital were told not to give a damn about the trailer itself, as long as they kept anyone contaminated inside it.

Alive or, if necessary, dead.

Contaminated! Christ, they'll kill me without asking a thing. The bastard pulling the trigger will probably get a fucking medal for saving the world.

At the other end of the trailer Cooper let himself fall sideways to the floor, then used the bunk beside him to lever himself back to his feet. He stood unsteadily, groping at the air around him for support. Suddenly he tried to rush forward, but he was facing the side of the trailer and there was nowhere to go. Cooper cannoned into the shelving, dislodging a shower of implements to clatter noisily to the floor. He tried again, turning slightly, but the wrong way. After two more attempts he ran head-first into the end of the trailer. The savage impacts seemed to have no effect on him.

Overman watched in horror, knowing it was only a matter of time before the blind, but living, corpse found a clear path down the centre of the trailer. The entire hospital was rocking as Cooper slammed into the walls. From outside the trailer Overman heard another long burst of automatic fire and in his panic he desperately figured there might be too much happening elsewhere for anyone to care about what was going on here.

He had no time to think about the outside world any more. Finally, the dead soldier had turned until he faced the aisle. When Cooper rushed forward this time he travelled half the length of the trailer before veering off-course slightly and tripping on a chair, bringing him crashing to the floor. He lay there a moment, groping at nothing. Overman realised Cooper was reaching for him. Somehow the dead man could sense the living, and he wanted to get at Overman.

The medic began a mutter of panicked oaths. 'God damn, God damn, God *damn*! I'm going to fucking *die* in here.'

Cooper struggled to his feet and went still. Overman held his breath, knowing the corpse was trying to locate him. Then Cooper spoke, a broken whisper.

'Am I dead?'

Overman couldn't stop himself from answering, grasping at the chance of safety. 'I can help you,' he said quickly. 'If you stay calm and take it easy.'

Cooper instantly turned at the sound of his voice and lunged forward, his hands grasping. With a cry of terror Overman flicked the latch of the door next to him and fell out of the trailer, tumbling down the short steps to land sprawling on the ground. The sunshine blinded him and people were yelling at him urgently, but he immediately jumped to his feet and in the glare recognised the shape of the open door. Overman threw himself against it, slamming it closed again. Then he collapsed, suddenly sobbing, back onto the dirt. With his back against the steps of the trailer he could feel it moving as Cooper's corpse raged inside, searching for him. Overman prayed he wouldn't be able to operate the door lock.

'Overman, don't move!'

Overman looked up, his eyes adjusting to the sunlight, and blurred by the tears. A ring of soldiers stood around him. Some held their weapons in a way Overman didn't like. All of them regarded him warily, like he was some sort of escaped animal. Recognising the voice, he realised it was none other than the task force commander himself, Lieutenant Colonel Exeter, who was calling the orders.

'You were told not to leave the hospital. What's happening in there?'

Overman looked around the soldiers. They appeared to him as judge, jury and possibly executioners as well. Finally he picked out Exeter standing to one side. A nervous-looking adjutant was beside him. Overman whispered, 'For God's sake, it's Cooper, sir. He—he woke up, I think. He's going crazy in there.'

Exeter's voice was cold—but oddly not very surprised. 'You told us Cooper was dead.'

'I swear he was—sir. There was no heartbeat.' Overman shook his head slowly and stared down at the ground, suddenly lost in the memory as his mind slipped into a mild form of shock. 'Christ, he still *looks* dead. His face, and his eyes—'

'His face?' Exeter snapped. 'What about his face?'

'It—it was white, like a sheet. Like there was no blood left in the guy—' Overman's words trailed away as he realised what he was saying. Panic started to grip him again. Some of the watching soldiers took a few steps further back and changed the grip on their weapons.

'You unsealed his suit?' Exeter asked grimly.

'I didn't mean to—' Overman fell silent and covered his face with his hands. He started to cry again. Dimly he heard Exeter conferring with someone else and the Lieutenant Colonel saying quietly, 'If that's what Collins wants to do, tell him it's his call. He's the man on the spot and I trust his judgement. In fact, tell him when it's over to bring that fire-power here. We may need it, too.' Overman still had the medical trailer against his back. It rocked violently and there was the sound of smashing glass. Cooper's corpse was tearing the place apart. Overman looked up at Exeter.

'What am I going to do, sir?' he pleaded. His stomach tightened with fear. Overman wouldn't have been surprised to see Exeter pull out his revolver and shoot him like a rabid dog.

'There's only one thing you can do, Overman. There's only one place you can go, now.' Exeter's voice was flat and hard. He looked away, scanning the soldiers nearby until he found a corporal. 'Corporal, use four men to escort Overman to the barricades and release him on the other side. Make sure he keeps walking towards the township.' Without giving the corporal a chance to question him, Exeter turned back to his adjutant. 'John, spread the word right now that Medical Corpsman Overman is to be held inside the quarantined area. We don't want him talking his way back through the perimeter after nightfall, or taking food from friends.'

Another resounding crash came from inside the trailer. This time one of the outside walls actually bowed out slightly. Exeter looked at the trailer, weighing up his next move. He said, wearily, 'Get the engineers to tow this down the highway, attach as many charges as it needs, and blow it and the damn thing inside it sky-high. If Major Collins is correct, we don't want any of it left in one piece.'

The adjutant didn't ask if the Lieutenant Colonel meant the trailer, or Cooper's corpse inside it.

Overman stayed where he was for some minutes. He sat on the ground, his arms hugging his legs and his head dropped down on his knees. He only flinched slightly when a loud, multiple explosion came from the direction of the barricades. Cooper still rampaged inside the trailer behind him. Then Overman felt something hit him and he looked up to see a thick rope on the ground next to him. Holding the other end was the corporal assigned to escorting him away.

'Tie it around your waist, Overman,' he called harshly.

'What? Why—'

'Just *do* it, Overman.'

Overman did as he was told, then too late realised what the rope was for. If he tried to escape or went mad, they could shoot him dead and still be able to drag him outside the task force area.

Humiliated, feeling like a criminal and totally at a loss as to what else he could do, Overman stood and began walking towards the barricades. The corporal followed, holding the rope with one hand and his rifle with the other. The four escorting soldiers kept a wide berth, but walked in the same direction. As Overman moved through the camp people saw him coming and kept their distance. When he came to the barricades the corporal motioned for him to keep going, Overman ducked under the semi-trailer and walked down the road as far as the rope allowed him. It brought him to a halt next to a shallow crater surrounded by thrown dirt and pieces of stuff wrapped in blue cloth.

'This is it,' the corporal called, his voice still hard. 'Untie the rope and keep going—and don't think about coming back. Nobody wants what you've got, Overman.'

Overman didn't reply, but slowly unknotted the rope and let it fall to the ground. He turned his back to the barricades and began walking down the highway. There was a creeping feeling between his shoulder-blades. He half-expected to feel bullets slamming into him before he got out of range.

Overman walked all the way to the first roadblock at the bend in the road. The glimpse of something in the distance gave him a goal to strive for. But when he reached it and realised what it was— nothing, really—a deep despair overtook him and he suddenly sat on the ground and began sobbing once more. After several minutes he found the strength to stumble off the bitumen and lie down

509

in some shade, his back against a tree. A Black-hawk swooped over low, but he didn't care. Overman was almost beyond caring about anything. A severe exhaustion flooded through him without warning and Overman closed his eyes. He fell asleep. Later, his eyes flickered open momentarily when a massive explosion occurred far behind the army's barricades. The engineers were destroying the mobile hospital along with Cooper's still-raging corpse inside. But shock and fatigue still had a strong grip on Overman and he slipped back into sleep again.

When he awoke properly, with a start, it was late afternoon. He needed some time to remember where he was and why, and Overman immediately had to fight off a return of the despair that had crippled him before. He began to reason with himself, sometimes speaking aloud. What could he do? It didn't take him long to realise Lieutenant Colonel Exeter was right—there was only one place he could go.

'There's got to be somebody in that fucking town who can help me,' he said to the dirt between his boots. 'The whole damn town can't be sick.'

Overman began walking again, not hurrying so he would save his energy. Occasionally the Black-hawk flew close. The first time, Overman looked up and saw the anonymous, goggled faces staring down at him from the side-gunner's door, dispassionately watching him the way a child observes an insect crawling across the ground. After that, Overman didn't look up again. An hour later he was beginning to feel tired again and his feet hurt.

As a medical corpsman the army hadn't been too concerned with his fitness, unlike the regular foot-soldiers. But seeing buildings signalling the edge of Hickory in the distance against a lowering sun gave him a second wind and Overman kept going. Another thirty minutes later he realised the first structure was a roadhouse, and that made him feel better, figuring that the local petrol station in a small community was a good place to start when it came to finding out what was happening in the town, and it would still be open after-hours. Now he hurried his pace.

Someone was standing beside the road at the edge of the station's concrete apron. It was dusk by now, the shadows deep, the only light coming from a slash of orange still hanging on the western horizon. Overman could see it was a big man, shabbily dressed and carrying what looked like a shovel over his shoulder. Motionless, he was watching Overman approach. The soldier felt wary, but knew he was running out of choices.

'Hello there!' he called, trying to keep the anxious tremor from his voice. 'I need some help.'

The man didn't answer him. Silhouetted against the dying sunlight, his face was only a dark blob to Overman. He moved closer.

'Look, I'm sorry. I know things are a little crazy right now, but none of it's my fault, really.' Overman spread his arms in a mute plea for understanding. 'I mean, I don't know what the fuck's going on either, but now they've made me come here and I haven't got a clue what I'm going to do—' He stopped and glared up at the sky. The

511

Blackhawk was doing another close sweep and the roar of the rotors was drowning out Overman's voice. 'For fuck's sake!' he snarled, looking up again. 'Why can't they leave me alone. I'm *here*, aren't I?' He took another step towards the other man and drew in a deep breath, preparing to shout over the noise of the helicopter.

He looked back in time to see the shovel scything through the air at his head.

The blade caught Overman cleanly at the base of his neck, severing his spinal cord and nearly decapitating him completely. With a strange, tired sigh Overman dropped to his knees and stayed that way for a moment.

Long enough, in fact, for Connors to swing his shovel again and finish the job.

When the engineers detonated their charges around the medical trailer, Lieutenant Colonel Exeter and Major Collins were meeting in the commander's private caravan. The reverberations slapped against the sides of the van. Exeter was scanning a well-thumbed report, looking one more time for clues which might give him some answers, and comparing the details with what had happened in the last hour. The report concerned a young couple who had been killed in a motor vehicle accident near Hickory. After being held in the town's small morgue for a short time they'd been transferred to the city.

It had been while they were in the funeral parlour's preparation room that the two corpses had come back to life and attacked the staff. In the

512

end, they'd had to be literally cut to pieces before they were stopped.

There was only one obvious course of action the authorities could take—seal up Hickory until nothing could escape, alive or dead. From then on it would be guesswork for everyone.

The commander looked up at the sound of the explosion. 'That's the end of that,' Exeter said quietly. 'We just demolished a million-dollar unit to get rid of one man.'

'It wasn't just one man,' Collins reminded him.

'God knows what he was, in the end. The same applies to your policeman. What's worrying me more, Robert, is the methods we have to employ to get rid of them. What if the whole town's like them? The entire population? If the media finds out how we're handling this, we'll all be shot at dawn.' Exeter pressed his lips together in an expression of frustration, then he absently patted his pockets for his cigarettes. 'Christ, we haven't been here twenty-four hours yet and I'm already looking seriously at our final option—levelling the town and burying everyone in it. Can you believe that?'

Collins shook his head slowly. 'I used to think this cordon was a violent overreaction. That we should have been approaching the whole business quietly and more scientifically, not with these draconian contain-or-kill orders. But after seeing what I saw this morning, I've changed my mind. That policeman was God-damned terrifying.' Collins paused, then tried to be more conciliatory. 'But there *must* be something else we can try first!'

'Is there?' Exeter raised his eyebrows. 'Well,

Robert. You'd better think of it fast. Without immediate radio communications at my fingertips it's my decision, and the only fact I have in front of me now is we don't have much time. We're kidding ourselves if we think we can contain this thing much longer. We would be failing in our duty if we don't move soon. Even if that means destroying the town completely and making sure there's no survivors.'

'Survivors?' Collins made a noise, half-laughing and partly a cry of disbelief. 'From what we've seen today, we can't even have any damned *bodies*.'

24

AT KERRY'S HOUSE everyone was getting decidedly more nervous. Nothing had happened. The expected visits from any of the number of corpses now inhabiting Hickory didn't eventuate. No-one could guess why. There was one moment during the afternoon when Michael thought somebody was under the house, but it was impossible to tell for sure without hanging out the door and being dangerously exposed at the same time. The dogs were unsettled too, walking to and fro about the house and growling softly.

'Did you hear something, Gavin?' Michael asked, watching Monty do another circuit of the lounge room. 'These dogs aren't happy.'

'No, but maybe they can hear something we can't.'

Beth and Kerry sat on a rug in the centre of the room. Kerry was showing her a large picture atlas and making a game out of it. Michael asked them to be quiet for a moment and they all sat and listened intently. There was nothing, but both the dogs were still on edge.

'It must be something in the distance,' Gavin concluded reluctantly. 'Maybe it's that damn helicopter upsetting them. He's zooming all over town again for some reason.'

'Do you think he could be looking for us because we were the ones who went out to the roadblock?' Kerry asked.

'I doubt it. They must be blind if they can't see the police car out at Gavin's place. No, I agree with Gavin. These dogs must be hearing something beyond our range, but we'd best be on our guard,' Michael said.

'Be on our guard?' Gavin laughed, but there wasn't much humour in the sound. 'I've been on my damn guard since I woke up this morning. I'm sick to death of waiting for something bad to happen.'

That was when they heard more automatic rifle-fire crackling in the distance. The three adults looked at each other, but said nothing. Even when a ripple of small detonations sounded, it seemed pointless to attempt to guess what was going on. Only Gavin made a short comment, cocking his head and thinking a moment.

'Grenades, I would say,' he said quietly. Michael looked at him and shrugged helplessly.

Sometime later a large explosion slapped against the house, rattling the windows in their frames. Everyone jumped nervously and Gavin got up and ran quickly to the front door for a look. Monty began to bark, but Kerry quietened him down.

'So what the hell was *that*?' Michael asked, joining Gavin at the doorway. They had to lean outwards slightly to see in the right direction. On the horizon a tower of smoke was climbing into the sky.

'I don't know,' Gavin said slowly. 'It was big, whatever it was. An accident, maybe?'

'Has one of the helicopters crashed?' Kerry called from the lounge.

'No such luck,' Michael told her. He pointed at a Blackhawk moving along another part of the skyline. 'He doesn't seem too concerned about the explosion. If it was an accident, you'd think he'd turn around and buzz over there real quick to see what was wrong.'

Gavin shook his head and turned away from the door. 'I hate this. I hate not knowing what the fuck is going on,' he said harshly. 'And why are they leaving us alone? Not the army—those *things* walking the streets, I mean. I expected Arnold Connors with his bloody shovel to be trying to smash this house off its stumps by now.'

'I don't understand it either,' Michael said, following him. 'But at the moment I'm grateful for any breaks we get. We can do without Arnold Connors, if you ask me.'

'I know, I know,' Gavin waved a hand tiredly. 'It's getting to me, that's all.'

By late afternoon all of them were getting

hungry. Kerry despaired, because everything had started happening at the wrong time, as far as food stocks in her house were concerned. She had nothing that would constitute a meal for three adults and a young girl. The tinned food she'd kept stored for emergencies was still lying in the middle of the church aisle along with the spare blankets and clothing—or had been burnt to ashes, if the church had been destroyed completely by the fire. She still had plenty of dog food, so she fed the two animals. Looking down at the meaty chunks oozing from the tins Kerry wondered if that might be a final resort for them— eating dog food. The idea made her feel ill. Finally, Kerry baked a cake. It seemed an incongruous thing to do, given the circumstances. Cakes were supposed to be for happy occasions. It wasn't a nutritious meal, but it had bulk and did the job of quietening growling stomachs. As they ate, Gavin and Michael discussed attempting a raid the next day on nearby homes for some better supplies. They agreed that if they met anybody alive and well, they would invite them to join their group—safety in numbers being the principle. Otherwise, it was going to be survival of the fittest.

During the last light of the day something happened to make Michael fear they might not have much time left. Gavin had taken a calculated risk and dropped to the ground, then had the dogs lowered down to him so they could have a run before it got too dark. Now man and beasts were safely back inside, Michael stood in the doorway, casually looking out. He watched one of the

518

Blackhawks hovering somewhere near the edge of town. In the dusk it was a dark, moving shape against the slightly lighter sky, except for its navigation lights, which were blinking brightly red and green. Suddenly a machine-gun opened fire from the aircraft's side door. A brilliant stream of red tracers reached down to the ground. From where Michael watched it looked beautiful, like a flickering laser beam. Only the faint chattering of the gun under the noise of the machine's rotors gave away the deadly nature of it.

The Blackhawk danced away from where it hovered, the machine-gun stabbing at the earth intermittently.

'Oh-oh,' Michael muttered, then called, 'Gavin! Come and look at this.' Gavin was already on his way, having heard the gunfire. 'Something's happened. They're upset. Look, that Blackhawk's blasting away at anything it can see now.'

'This doesn't look good,' Gavin said grimly. Only minutes earlier Michael had turned on most of the lights in the house. Now Gavin did a quick round of the rooms and switched them all off again, explaining as he went, 'We'd better not draw any attention to ourselves. We could well be the only house in Hickory using electric light tonight. We'll stick out like a sore thumb and that Blackhawk might consider us a target. If it comes any closer, we'd better stay away from the doors and windows, too. He's probably got night-sight equipment.

'Are we going to have to sit here in the dark?' Beth asked, her voice trembling.

Gavin went over and put a comforting hand on

her head. 'Only while the helicopter's in the air,' he said gently. 'Don't worry, we've got Mandy and Monty with us, and they can see ten times better in the dark than we can.'

They all ended up sitting on the floor together in the lounge room with both the front door and the back kitchen door left open. This way they could see plenty of the sky on two sides of the house. For the next hour they frequently saw the Blackhawk's navigation lights moving through the night against the backdrop of stars and heard the thudding of its rotors. The machine-gunning came less frequently, but still the brilliant red tracers occasionally leapt downwards. A second helicopter appeared, but it didn't do any firing. In the darkness it was hard to see exactly what it was doing. Finally the sound of both helicopters' engines faded and didn't return.

'Show's over for the night?' Michael said.

'Maybe,' Gavin replied quietly. Beth was falling asleep on his lap. 'I couldn't guess at anything any more. I didn't have much of a clue in the first place.'

'Who did?' Michael replied, unable to keep a trace of bitterness out of his voice.

Kerry couldn't sleep. Gavin and Beth lay huddled together on the floor, both had their eyes closed. Michael tried to stay awake, feeling it was his duty to keep alert for any signs of danger, but he slowly slipped from sitting up, to lying on his side and with his head propped on one elbow, to finally rolling onto his back. He kept whispering to

Kerry, but his words became fewer and eventually he didn't say anything for a long time. Kerry carefully leaned close and listened to his deep, regular breathing. In the darkness she smiled. Kerry didn't mind. They all should be getting as much sleep as they could while they had the chance. It only really needed one pair of eyes and ears to stay awake and she was too nervous and jittery to sleep, so it might as well be her.

She could have gone to her bedroom and tried sleeping there—even taking Michael with her— but Kerry had deliberately stayed away from her room from the moment they returned to the house. Having Beth with them, it seemed unfair to Kerry that she should have somewhere private she could retreat to while the younger girl didn't. And besides, it seemed more important than ever now that they should all stay together, so Kerry had sat with them on her lounge room floor and didn't go near her bedroom. Michael must have tacitly agreed, because he never suggested they should go to bed there, either.

She jumped slightly when Monty suddenly got up from where he was curled on a rug. The dogs were still very uneasy and no amount of soothing or even threatening had managed to settle them down. Monty padded silently through the house and stood silhouetted against the night sky at the back door. Very softly, he growled.

'Come on, Mont,' Kerry whispered, quietly getting up. 'You'll wake everyone. I wish you'd do this when there was a good reason, instead of being so damned touchy all the time.' She went quickly to the dog and ran a calming hand down his back, feeling the hackles raised along his spine. Still, he wasn't too upset and Kerry looked out the back door not expecting to see anything worth worrying about, except perhaps a bandicoot or another stray dog wandering out of the canefields.

Instead, she saw something that made her blood freeze and her hand stop in mid-stroke down the dog's back.

An all-too-familiar light was shining among the trees down by the river.

Kerry spun around and hurried back to Michael. She dropped to her knees beside him on the floor and shook his shoulder.

'Michael!' she hissed urgently. 'Wake up. They're back.'

Michael instantly opened his eyes, but stared uncomprehendingly at her in the darkness. 'What—' he began, then his mind began to clear and he sat up painfully, his muscles aching from sleeping on the floor. 'Who's back? Connors?' Suddenly he looked frightened. 'Christ, not Isaiah?'

'No, none of them. The UFOs!' Kerry tugged at him to get up and look for himself. Michael didn't need any urging. Behind them Gavin stirred and woke, slowly realising something was happening. Michael had to push past Monty, who still stood in the doorway, growling. As an afterthought Kerry reached down and grabbed the dog's collar in case he tried to jump down to the ground.

'God damn, what are they doing back?' Michael murmured to himself as he stared out at the shimmering brightness. He tilted his head, listening. 'I can't hear any helicopters, but I'll bet they'll come running.'

Gavin came up behind them, squeezing into the doorway for a look. 'They probably can't see it. There's no clouds to reflect the light and that roadblock is a fair way out of town.' He looked at the light for a long time. 'Yes, what *are* they doing here?' He sounded pleased, like a man who is given an unexpected second chance to reclaim an old debt. Kerry looked at him, a worried expression on her face.

'How do we know it's the same ones?' she asked.

'We don't, but it's a pretty safe assumption. We're better off trying to work out what they're doing back here,' Michael said.

'What did the alien say in the canefields last night?' Kerry said, screwing her face up as she concentrated. 'Everything was so fantastic! You'd think every detail would be etched into our memories, but it's like a sensory overload, too. I can't remember his exact words.'

Slowly, as he recalled everything, Michael said, 'He told Powers he had to be left behind because he was corrupted. He had to wait until his "next time"—but I remember thinking afterwards that it didn't make sense. Powers should have diverted the rendezvous to an alternative location, but he didn't, because it was his last duty as a guardian— or whatever he called himself—and he was supposed to be picked up and taken home. So, when was there going to be a "next time"?' He paused, looking at the light again. 'Have they changed their minds, realising that Powers hasn't got another opportunity to escape?'

'It hardly seems likely a superior intelligence like them would be capable of such a simple misunderstanding,' Kerry said doubtfully.

'That's right. So the misunderstanding must be ours. We've missed something.'

Gavin said carefully, 'Then how about this for a theory? He said Powers must wait until his next time, right? *His* next time. Powers was dying, we know that. Riley told us and I guess he was supposed to know. But does it mean Powers would go through some sort of reincarnation? Back to some sort of spirit form, then he could start again and he *could* go home? That could be what he meant by his "next time".'

'It makes sense,' Michael nodded slowly. 'It makes even more sense really, than the idea of the aliens leaving Powers behind in any shape or form. That doesn't sound like the logical behaviour of a so-called superior intelligence, either.'

There was a silence as they all thought this over. Kerry said bitterly, 'So after all this, you're saying he gets to escape after all.'

'Assuming we're right, and he gets to the cane-field and back to the UFO, it's possible.'

'But what will this spirit form be? Will he still be Isaiah, or Powers? Or will he be this Kann and something completely different? Back to an alien, like the others?'

'What difference does it make?' Michael suddenly sighed and turned away from the doorway. 'Anyway, I doubt it'll have any effect on our particular problems. The army probably won't even see the UFO leaving, or at least they won't have a chance to do anything about it.'

'That's right,' Kerry said, getting angry. 'After turning the place upside down, killing innocent people—including Linda, damn him—he gets to sail over the army's roadblock and disappear into the wild blue yonder without a care or regret. You call that a superior intelligence?'

But Michael wasn't going to join her in her anger. Her words had made him stop and stare at her. An idea began to form in his head. 'Jesus, Kerry. What if we could talk them into giving us a ride? Over the army—'

'Michael, now you've got to be kidding,' she cut him off. 'Or are you going crazy?'

'Why not?' He spread his arms, then lowered his voice so Beth couldn't hear him in the lounge room. 'Basically, we asked them to give us the girls back and they did, didn't they? They're obviously capable of some sort of compassion. Perhaps they'll do this, too.'

'But why should they? We're nothing to them, Michael. Little more than laboratory rats, most likely. We'd just be taking more unnecessary risks trying.'

Gavin spoke, his voice soft but intent. 'But if we had Powers, we might be able to force them to do it.'

Michael was stunned and he looked at Gavin a moment before replying. 'Now *that* might be an unnecessary risk—but it might also have a better chance of succeeding.'

'That's even crazier!' Kerry cried, then she remembered to keep her voice low. 'How the hell do you expect to keep an *alien* captive, for God's sake! They *must* be infinitely smarter and more capable than us.'

'But remember there was a time when Powers

needed Jeff Butler to protect him, when he was going through a change and wasn't able to look after himself. What if this is one of those times, too?'

'And how are you going to tell the difference before he decides to throw you around the room the way he did Jeff Butler?'

'Look, there's really only one way we can do it,' Gavin interrupted quietly. 'We have to find him, see what sort of form or condition he's in, and *then* work out if we can do anything about it.'

'Great!' Kerry said, throwing her hands up in the air. 'We've just spent the last two days trying to avoid the bastard, and now you're suggesting we go *looking* for him.'

There was a silence, then Michael said, 'I guess his house is the obvious place to look first.' Kerry's expression said she couldn't believe Michael was even contemplating the idea.

'No,' Gavin said, shaking his head. 'I'm thinking of something Powers said when I went to enrol in the library. He said something about books being the source of power. I thought he was talking about knowledge, but now I'm not so sure. I reckon the library is the first place to look.'

'Okay. That's as good as any. It's before his house too, so we can go on from there if need be. We'd better get moving soon, though.'

'Now,' Gavin nodded. 'That UFO isn't going to hang around any longer than it has to. It might be too late already.'

Michael turned to Kerry, his voice pleading, but firm. 'Kerry, we've got to try this. We don't have any choice. That helicopter began shooting at anything it saw. We might have just been lucky it was close to dusk. Tomorrow, with a full day of daylight available, God knows what they'll try and do. If we've got the slightest chance of getting out of here tonight, we must try it.'

'Michael's right,' Gavin added. 'And if this doesn't work, we might have to keep going and take our chances in the canefields with the army patrols—try and get out of the area completely. I agree, there's no saying what the army will do in the new day. At least if we check out this Powers thing and there's no hope there, it'll be into the early hours of the morning by then and we might catch the soldiers at their least alert.'

Kerry looked from one to the other and saw the determined expressions on their faces. Then she thought about enduring another whole day and possibly a night too, in the house with no food, all the while waiting for the helicopters to come and start machine-gunning the streets. And there was always Arnold Connors, who might come and pay them a visit with his shovel.

'I'll have to scrounge together some more warm clothing for me and Beth,' she said finally. 'I left the best we had in the church, apart from this jacket. Are you two guys going to need anything extra?' They shook their heads, then Michael stepped forward and gave her a quick hug.

'It'll be okay, you just wait and see. We'll get out of here yet.'

Kerry nodded and broke away, still feeling she was being steamrolled into an idea that didn't have as much merit as she would have liked. At the same time, she recognised they had very few options available.

She walked down the hallway to her bedroom door and opened it, letting herself through. Inside the room her hand hovered over the lightswitch, and she stopped herself just in time. Even though the helicopters weren't around, she figured somebody might be keeping watch, and an electric light could be all they needed to see before they sent the Blackhawks into the air again. Kerry had a trunk at the end of her bed and she headed for this, bending down to see the latches in the gloom.

That was when she realised something was wrong. A bad smell was coming from a corner of the room, and she had an instinctive feeling somebody was in the bedroom with her.

Before she could turn around or cry out something struck her head very hard. Kerry fell forward onto the bed. Someone shoved her at the same time to ensure she collapsed onto the mattress. The pain in her head was crippling, blinding her and it was as if she'd been thrown into deep, dark water. She could hardly move and felt suffocated. As someone leaned over her, enveloping her in a fetid stench, Kerry tried to fight back, but her arms and legs wouldn't respond. With all her will she wanted to strike out, but the most movement she could manage was a trembling of the muscles in her arms as they lay uselessly on the bed. A cry of terror was locked in her throat, her vocal chords paralysed, too. The darkness swam around her, broken by bright pin-points of light in her vision. The figure bending over her was unrecognisable, but the foulness filling her nostrils told Kerry what it was.

Her sobs, still trapped inside, turned to

anguished, silent screaming as she felt the flaps of her jacket pushed aside and callused fingers rip at the clothing at her waist until they got to the bare skin beneath. They pushed her shirt up and tore her bra down without breaking the clasp, exposing her breasts. The hands kneaded them both at the same time, the fingers rolling and pinching her nipples painfully hard. Kerry's shirt kept falling back down, covering her, and after impatiently flicking it back up and out of the way several times the hands tired of this and moved back down to her waist. Kerry felt the button and zipper of her jeans wrenched open, then they were tugged roughly off over her hips and down to her knees. Her panties were dragged down next, the elastic snapping. Kerry was terribly aware of the cold air against her nakedness. One hand tried to push her thighs apart, but the jeans at her knees stopped this. The other hand forced itself between her legs, the pubic hair catching in broken nails, then fingers probed at the soft flesh there, searching for the opening.

Something seemed to click within the pain inside Kerry's mind and she began to regain full consciousness again, the strength flowing back into her muscles. One part of her tried to stay submerged in the stupor, knowing the truth awaiting her when she became fully aware. The scream finally broke out, a strangled, sobbing sound. Kerry lashed out weakly with one fist, but didn't strike anything.

Suddenly the room and her bed were filled with other presences. Hot, furry bodies landed heavily on the mattress. Sharp claws scratched her flesh

529

as they flung themselves at her attacker with a shocking noise of snarling and yelping. Kerry tried to curl herself into a ball and got tangled with one of the animals, the jeans around her knees making things worse. She realised there was a clear space to one side and with an effort rolled over, falling to the floor beside her bed, just in time. Her attacker was knocked down to take her place on the mattress, the frantic dogs ripping at his flesh.

Michael was at the back door again, staring out at the light down by the river. Absently, he held Monty's collar again so the dog wouldn't leap out of the doorway. Kerry's scream turned his heart to ice. The dog broke from his grip and ran growling to Kerry's bedroom, the labrador Mandy close behind. Michael burst through the bedroom door after them, flicking on the light by slapping at the wallswitch hard. The glare made him blink for a moment.

What he saw filled Michael with such emotions he stopped breathing and stared. He experienced an intense hate. Kerry's half-naked body crouched on the floor told him what had happened and Michael instantly wanted to kill whoever was responsible. At the same time he felt an overwhelming compassion for Kerry that brought tears to his eyes. He wanted to scoop her up and hold her, and tell her nothing had really happened and promise her nothing ever would. She looked so vulnerable and hurt, it broke his heart to see it.

Gavin pushed into the room behind him and Michael heard his sharp intake of breath at the scene.

The dogs were savaging someone on the bed. It was difficult to recognise who it was, the dogs were big and concealed most of their opponent, who was thrashing weakly at them. Then Michael noticed the oil-stained overalls—and something on the floor, poking just out from the bed on the opposite side to Kerry. It was the butt of the old double-barrelled shotgun.

Now Michael felt a chilling calm.

Ignoring the dogs doing their vicious work on the bed, he bent down and easily lifted Kerry up, cradling her in his arms. Gavin moved aside to let him get through the door and saw the look in Michael's eyes telling him to wait—and do nothing. After gently putting Kerry down on the lounge room rug beside a stunned Beth, Michael told the young girl quietly, 'I need you to be a big girl now, Beth. Kerry needs you to help her this time. I want you to hold her tight until I come back.' Without waiting for Beth's reply he returned to the bedroom.

The smell in the room was horrific. The dogs were easing off. They were tiring and their victim no longer responding. Michael stepped around the foot of the bed and picked up the shotgun, reversing his grip so he held it by the barrel, like a club. He looked at Gavin.

'Pull the dogs off.'

Gavin didn't argue. Timing his move carefully, he caught both the dogs by their collars and dragged them back. Mandy had her teeth fastened around an arm and pulled a long flap of flesh away with her.

Jeff Butler lay sprawled across the bed. One side of his body was blackened by fire, including his scalp, half of which still had hair, the other was bald, burnt skin. His face, neck and arms were now a gored mess—but none of the wounds were bleeding. There was no heartbeat to pump the blood away. Butler had been dead since Powers shrugged him off his shoulder the night before. His ruined eyes glared at Michael. One hand slowly reached down and rubbed at his groin.

'Give me the girl. She wants me.'

Michael swung the shotgun hard. The side of the butt smashed into Butler's face, but because he lay on a mattress the corpse bounced back to almost upright. This suited Michael. He hit him again, and again, each time slamming the rifle butt into Butler's face. The corpse quickly became unrecognisable, its facial features crushed into its own broken skull. Several teeth were imbedded into the bottom lip. Still Butler waved his arms and legs in an effort to move away.

'For God's sake, Michael,' Gavin said, shocked. He was struggling to keep both the dogs under control. Then he thought the better of asking Michael to take it easy, and said instead, 'Hey, if that thing's loaded you might blow yourself in half.'

This stopped Michael abruptly. He stared down at the weapon in his hands, then quickly spun it around and broke open the chambers. It was loaded. Snapping the barrels closed again he quickly walked to the end of the bed. Without pausing he cocked both hammers, put the gun to his shoulder and lined up on Butler's head. The corpse, completely blinded by the beating, was groping at the sheets for a purchase so it could haul itself upright. Michael pulled the first trigger.

The roar of the weapon was deafening in the confined space. The corpse was punched back into the mattress, its face shredded by the concentrated leadshot. The room filled with blue smoke. Taking his cheek away from the butt, but not lowering the shotgun, Michael watched the corpse intently. He thought he could hear Beth crying in the lounge room.

'Come on, that must be enough, Michael,' Gavin said softly.

Butler's corpse twisted its fingers into the bedding and slowly drew itself upright.

Michael pulled the second trigger. This time Butler's head flew back so violently the neck obviously broke. When it tipped deliberately forward again to fall against the chest, white shards of skull were visible within the mutilated flesh of the face.

'Jesus Christ,' Gavin whispered. He suddenly twisted around and man-handled the protesting dogs through the door, closing it behind them. Then Gavin reached over and led Michael away from the bed.

'Give me the gun, Michael.'

Michael silently passed it over. He was watching the corpse which, incredibly, was again beginning to stir.

Gavin was giving Michael instructions. 'Open the door, hold it for me, and for God's sake don't let the damn dogs in again.'

Michael did that, using his body to block the doorway, while he held the handle on the other side. Gavin used the butt of the shotgun as a hammer, lining it up carefully on the inner door-handle and smashing down hard. After three strikes the metal knob broke off. Bringing the shotgun with him Gavin slipped through the opening, pushing Michael out of the way, and slammed the door closed.

'There. Even if he finds the fucking door, he won't be able to open it.'

Suddenly exhausted, Michael nodded gratefully. He felt emotionally and physically drained.

In the lounge Kerry had dressed herself. She still sat on the floor, holding Beth close. The younger girl was crying. The two dogs were competing for attention. Kerry was keeping one hand free to alternately pat both of them. Michael shoved them out the way and sat down next to Kerry. He wrapped an arm around her and hugged her hard, leaning over to kiss her hair at the same time. Michael felt a large bump on her scalp with his lips and quickly pulled back, using his fingers to part her hair and examine it.

'Are you all right?' he asked gently.

She nodded, winced, then whispered, 'Yes, I'm okay. A bit of a headache, I guess.'

'Are you sure? What—did he do?' Michael instantly regretted asking.

She looked at him, then pressed her lips together determinedly before saying, 'I was too stunned to move at first, but I could feel everything. He—he touched me, that's all. That's all he was able to do, before the dogs came in.' Kerry fell silent and

534

fought off tears. 'My God, Michael. He was in there *all day*, just waiting for me. These creatures aren't just the dead, living again. They're *possessed.*'

'We should have guessed,' Michael said angrily. 'It's my fault for not thinking. It was always too good to be true. Now we know why Connors or somebody else like him didn't come. Somehow they knew Butler was already here, and they left it up to him. You're right—there's more to these things than just a collection of walking zombies.'

'We have to make a move,' Gavin told them. He was standing at the back door. 'The bedroom light might be bringing us more unwanted attention. I don't want to go in there again and turn it off. It's probably too late for that, anyway.' Through the walls they could hear slithering, bumping sounds coming from the bedroom.

Michael held Kerry a moment longer, then nodded slowly.

There was a small table-lamp in the lounge room. Gavin shattered the ceramic base, leaving him with a globe socket on the end of a short cable. Adding an extension lead to this, and being careful not to break the bulb, he lowered the light out the front door to shine under the house. Then, with Michael sitting on his legs to hold him, Gavin jack-knifed his body out the doorway, hanging partially upside-down. He stayed this way for nearly a minute, swinging the light in different directions and having a close look into the shadows.

'It looks clear,' he called. Michael helped him back inside. Gavin was red-faced. 'As far as I can see, there's nobody down there—no more nasty surprises hiding in wait for us.'

'Then let's not give them a chance to catch up,' Michael said.

Gavin went first, dropping out the door to the ground. Michael lowered Beth down to him next, then helped Kerry out. Handling the dogs out the doorway was awkward, and Gavin gave Michael a strange look as they did it. With everyone safely on the ground they ran to the van. Kerry jumped into the back with Beth. The dogs automatically followed. But as Michael went to run around the front of the vehicle to the driver's side Gavin caught his sleeve and drew him close.

'Michael, we can't take the dogs.'

Michael looked at him, as if to say he knew Gavin was probably right, but he said, 'Yes, we can. We'll take them as far as we can, at least.'

'If we have to sneak through the canefields between army patrols, the dogs will give us away.'

'And they might give us advance warning, too. They could be a help, if we muzzle them or something.'

'That won't keep them quiet enough—you know that.'

Michael put his face close to Gavin's and kept his voice low. 'Turning them loose is exactly the same as killing them—the army will see to that. And the girls are aware of it, too. Those dogs probably just saved Kerry's life. If we dump them now, Kerry will be worried sick with guilt and Beth won't stop crying. The dogs are a comfort for all of us, so I want to hang on to them as long as I can. They attacked Butler, don't forget. They could still be a help in town, or at Powers' house. And even if we're forced into the canefields, they might ultimately act as a distraction for us, giving us a chance to slip through.'

Gavin was already nodding. 'Okay, I see your point—but for God's sake, let's make sure we don't get into any really bad trouble just over a couple of dogs.'

'Don't worry, we won't let it come to that.'

Once more they found themselves in Michael's van, travelling through town. He didn't turn the headlights on, in case it attracted too much attention. At the beginning of Kerry's street they moved back into the streetlight areas, so it wasn't too hard to see. People still walked aimlessly everywhere, but in the dark it was impossible to see any details. Some seemed to stop and watch the van drive past.

It was the main street Michael was most worried about. As he turned into it Gavin, in the passenger seat, said, 'There's lights up ahead. See? In the distance.'

Gavin frowned, trying to decide. 'I've got a feeling I know where that is,' he said carefully.

'The library?'

'You guessed it.'

'So, does anyone want to guess what's going to happen now?' Michael muttered.

With the lights blazing up ahead Michael felt it was safe to turn the van's headlights on. The glare picked out figures shuffling along the footpaths. There were no lights in any of the houses or shops. McGann's hotel was completely dark. Michael suddenly stamped his foot down on the accelerator and the van gained speed quickly.

'What are you doing?' Gavin asked, looking worried.

'Not giving them a chance,' Michael said grimly. 'Maybe we can bolt through the main street before anyone realises we're coming.' He glanced over his shoulder and saw the white oval of Kerry's frightened face. 'Hang on back there! We're going to do this in a hurry.'

The van sped along the road, the shops and streetlights on either side seeming to rush past. The road ahead looked clear and Michael was sure they were going to make it okay, when someone stepped out onto the street in front of them and turned to face the headlights.

Michael had the presence of mind not to brake or even swerve to avoid them. He only yelled out, 'Hang on!' again and gripped the steering wheel tight. He recognised the dead face of Mrs North glaring at them with eyes full of hate. Her corpse was crushed against the windscreen for a long moment before slipping downwards, leaving a smear of mess on the glass. There was a sickening bump as the wheels rode over the body. Michael didn't slow down. He didn't even bother looking in the rear-view mirror. The library was just ahead.

They pulled to a skidding halt in the car park opposite the main doors. It looked like every light in the building was on, a blazing beacon in the otherwise darkened town.

'Look,' said Gavin, though it was hardly necessary.

Somebody was sitting at the reception desk.

Gavin thought it was Powers himself, because he was in exactly the same position as when Gavin had seen him in the library before. The head was bowed, hiding the face, and held close to the surface of the desk. The noisy arrival of the van didn't cause the person to look up. Then Gavin realised the head was almost bald.

It was Isaiah.

Michael and Gavin got out of the van at the same time. Michael leaned back in the window. 'Maybe you should stay out here,' he said to Kerry.

'No way,' she answered quickly. 'This is no time to split up, Michael. And you're not leaving us out here with all these damn things walking the streets.' She slid open the door, making sure the dogs didn't get out.

'But it might be twice as dangerous inside.'

'At least we'll be together.' Kerry took Beth's hand and helped her out of the van. She closed the door and looked defiantly at Michael.

'All right,' he said reluctantly. 'At least, will you please stay back?'

'I'm not going to go near him, if I can help it. I'll look after Beth.'

Michael was satisfied with that.

Gavin led the way to the entrance. The doors weren't locked. The four of them cautiously let themselves in. Still the figure at the desk did not stir. There was a foul smell in the air. Michael moved closer to Isaiah. He bent over, trying to get a look at his face.

Isaiah had aged incredibly. The skin over his cheekbones was stretched like dry parchment, as if the smallest touch would split it open. The flesh was stained with cancers. Only the smallest tufts of hair still clung to his scalp. His eyes were open and stared sightlessly down at the desk. A thin line of drool dripped from the corner of his mouth. Isaiah's neck, and the hands lying flat in front of him, revealed that this rendering of the mad priest was little more than a skeleton with the barest minimum of flesh and sinew. If he were a real, living human being Michael doubted Isaiah would be alive.

Michael looked at Kerry. 'You must be right— or bloody close to it. There's no way this guy would be alive if he wasn't kept that way by some sort of artificial means or higher technology.'

'Is he dead now?' Gavin asked, moving forward.

'I don't know. I'm not going to jump to any conclusions, that's for sure.'

Both of them circled warily around the priest seated at the desk.

'Can you touch him?'

Michael looked around for something to use, rather than touch Isaiah with his own hand. Gavin couldn't wait, and reached towards the priest.

Isaiah suddenly lifted his head and glared at Gavin.

'You can join us. It is time. The church and every-one in it must burn.'

Gavin jerked backwards. He flicked a nervous glance at Michael, before saying impulsively, 'Nobody's joining anyone, you bastard. Your friends have come back to take you home, but we're not going to let you go anywhere.'

Isaiah kept his eyes fixed on Gavin, and slowly stood. He looked like a frail, very ill old man—except for the hate and evil twisting his wasted face. A gleam of understanding crossed his features, then disappeared again to be replaced by madness.

'My brothers wait for me to Change. I am still strong—stronger. I will not Change, and you will join us.' Isaiah's voice turned silken and he held a hand out, palm up, as if he held something in it and was offering it to Gavin. *'I already have your wife.'*

Kerry cried a warning, seeing the anger exploding inside Gavin, out of control. A terrible black rage consumed him. She suddenly realised—too late—that this was always going to happen, the first opportunity Gavin had to confront Isaiah. 'No, Gavin! Michael, keep him back!'

Gavin stepped forward. 'You have my wife? You *murdered* my wife!' He lashed out back-handed, striking at Isaiah's face. Gavin's hand passed through the priest's head, and Isaiah brought his full, maddened gaze to stare with mocking, defiant amusement at Gavin. There was a flicker of brilliant light in the room lasting only an instant.

'You want to kill me? I kept this fool priest alive for a hundred years more than he deserved. With more like him, I will live for another thousand.'

Michael moved quickly to Gavin and put a hand on his shoulder. 'For God's sake, Gavin! Stay back! We've only got to wait—the UFO wouldn't be in the canefields without good reason. They must know he's dying. Don't listen to him!'

But Gavin shrugged him off. He looked

bemused, trying to understand how he might inflict some injury on the mocking spectre. Gavin had struck out in anger without thinking, forgetting the priest might prove to be nothing but an ethereal spectre. Gavin needed something—or someone—tangible to vent his grief and fury on. Ignoring Beth's added sobbing cry for him to stop, he moved forward again. This time he tried punching Isaiah in the chest with all his strength. The gaunt figure moved backwards mockingly, the black priest's garment billowing around his limbs like a shroud. Still he glared at Gavin with sneering disdain.

'Do you want to see your wife? I tell you, she is with us. Join us, and you will be with her again.' Isaiah turned his head to look slyly at Beth. She shrank back against Kerry. 'You can bring the girl with you.'

Gavin let out a roar of rage and picked up the single chair behind the desk. He swung it at the priest and let out an anguished sound of frustration as the chair cut harmlessly through the spectre. Gavin was angered beyond reason and he tried again, lifting the chair high. Michael, who was moving closer, had to step hurriedly clear. This time Gavin swung the chair so hard the momentum of his blow made him lose his grip. The chair didn't even hit Isaiah, but crashed into the bookshelves behind him. The priest let out a chuckle of amusement. Gavin was twisting around, looking for another weapon.

When he turned back, his hands still empty, Isaiah had vanished.

He reappeared standing calmly, but stooped and

weakened, between the shelves, the same teasing smile on his face. *'See my strength? My brothers say I will Change. They are wrong. Join us and feel this strength. Bring the girl. Bring all of you.'* As Isaiah said this, more of the brilliant light began to flash and flicker in the room, like flashbulbs going off one after the other. Michael realised the light was coming from Isaiah himself.

The spirit was suddenly concerned too, looking around to see the light being reflected off the walls. Gavin stood still and stared, his anger unabated as he tried to discover a way he could attack the priest.

Michael cried, 'For God's sake, leave him, Gavin. Look at him! He's dying. We'll get our chance.'

Kerry pressed Beth's face against her so she couldn't see.

Two more figures stepped into view, moving into the aisles behind Isaiah. Jake Sanders and Ainslie McGregor. Isaiah turned back to Gavin and, despite losing control, his smile broadened, showing diseased gums around yellowed teeth.

'Now we can all burn together.'

Kerry screamed at the sight of the two corpses, making Beth scream with her. Michael rushed over to the girls protectively, expecting Gavin to do the same.

But Gavin threw himself at Isaiah.

'No!' he yelled, reaching out. Snarling his anger, Gavin wrapped himself around the priest, hugging the skinny figure to his body. There was a shocked moment of indecision as Gavin realised he'd succeeded—he was suddenly able to hold the

grinning spectre. But it was as if he'd lunged at a column of solid rock. His weight and strength didn't move the priest. The blinding light flashed and crackled in the room, searing the air now and building in intensity. Michael went to pull Gavin back, but there was a brilliant flash of flame and intense heat, making him throw a hand up in front of his face.

Isaiah became a core of white-hot fire, flaring like magnesium and enveloping Gavin. Gavin screamed with pain, but didn't let go his hold. The books and shelves around them burst alight with licking tongues of heat climbing quickly up to the ceiling. The floor was instantly scorched black. The two figures clasped together became enveloped in a pillar of fire. There was a tremendous noise, like a giant blowtorch, coming from the flame.

Gavin was still screaming—still alive and trapping Isaiah in his arms, when the two of them toppled over. A wave of blistering heat washed over Michael, Kerry and Beth, and they were forced back further, although Michael had again been trying vainly to edge closer to help Gavin. All of them were crying and calling out. Gavin was already as good as dead. There would be no saving him. The shaft of blinding white flame swelled until it completely obscured Gavin and his captive. The sound of it was joined by the hungry spitting of fire eating at the wooden bookshelves and spreading through the library.

Michael and the girls could do nothing except watch. After nearly a minute the incandescent blaze began to ebb, shrinking in size slowly until it turned into a ball of heat. It finally vanished, leaving behind a conventional flame flickering around the edges of a pit in the floor.

Gavin and Isaiah had disappeared.

Michael called out desperately, 'Gavin! Where are you? Are you here? For God's sake—' But he knew in his heart it was pointless. There was no denying what they'd just seen. He crept forward once more, holding up his arms to shield his face from the heat of the burning ceiling and book-shelves, until he could look down into the hole in the floor. The edges of the broken timber were glowing embers and Michael could see the library's wooden foundations below had hot-spots of smouldering red embers and the earth was black-ened. Coating everything in a thin layer was a fine white ash.

Michael realised this was all that remained of his friend.

Tears filling his eyes, he suddenly remembered the two corpses and Michael looked up at the aisles. Jake and Ainslie had retreated back to the rear of the library, watching Michael with dead eyes through the flames between. Michael spun around and spread his arms in a mute, helpless appeal to Kerry. She was crying hard, watching him and clutching Beth to her. As she stared back at Michael he saw the expression on her face change and her eyes focus on something behind him. The hairs on the nape of his neck prickled and he turned back around, expecting anything.

Suspended above the smoking hole in the floor, at the same height as Michael's chest, was a shim-mering orb of light. It hung there motionlessly.

Instantly, Michael understood what he was looking at was a similar thing to what led him to fall into the river the evening they'd been searching for Ainslie McGregor. He held his breath, fascinated and frightened at the same time. He made a conscious mental effort to push back the grief and shock of Gavin's death so he could deal with this.

'What is it?' Kerry called, her voice trembling.

Michael replied, surprising himself that he knew the answer. 'It's Isaiah,' he said wonderingly. 'It's what Isaiah has become—he's finished his Changing. That wasn't any ordinary fire. That was Isaiah dying. This is his "next time". That white flame must have been a cleansing—'

'But where's *Gavin*?'

'Gavin's dead, Kerry,' Michael said flatly. 'I don't know what in God's name he hoped to do—'

He stopped mid-sentence. Something fantastic was happening in the air. A figure was forming among the smoke climbing from the smouldering floorboards. It shimmered, then solidified.

It was Gavin, standing suspended in mid-air in front of him. Michael was stunned, his senses reeling. He tried to say something, but the words wouldn't come out. Michael didn't even know what he wanted to say. Instead, as he stared at the apparition and struggled to find his voice, he realised Gavin held the glowing orb in the palm of his out-stretched hand. Then Beth spoke, startling them.

'He wants us to go to the canefield,' she said, her voice flat and emotionless.

Michael spun around. 'What?' Keeping one eye

on the ghost he went quickly to the young girl and knelt down next to her. Beth's face was blank. She was listening to some inner voice. 'How do you know?' Michael asked her, trying to stay calm. 'Can you hear him?'

'Of course I can hear him.' Beth spoke like someone keeping an impossible clamp on her inner torment.

Michael glanced up at Kerry. She stared back with a small, helpless shrug of her shoulders.

'So, what's he saying, Beth?' Michael said, gently. 'What is your father saying?'

'He wants us to go to the canefield,' Beth repeated in a monotone.

Michael looked back at the spectral figure. In that instant Gavin vanished, taking the orb with him.

Michael closed his eyes, then shook his head, as if to clear it. It was all becoming too much—he suddenly wasn't sure if he could keep things, including himself, under control.

'Michael!' Kerry shouted, the noise of the flames getting louder. 'Do you believe her? Can she hear him?'

He nodded wearily. 'She can obviously hear somebody, but can we be sure it's Gavin? It might be some sort of trap.'

'If he said we should go to the canefields—he must mean the same place, right?'

'Yes, but it's probably what Isaiah—or Powers, whoever the fuck he was—would tell us, too. I don't know what the hell we should do, to be honest.' Michael stared into Beth's empty eyes, as if the answer would be there. Instead, Kerry spoke.

547

'What else? Go to the damn canefields!'

Michael was amazed at Kerry's calm acceptance. 'Kerry, we don't know what the fuck we're dealing with any more. We just saw Gavin get *incinerated*, for Christ's sake—'

'We just saw Gavin do something for us!' Kerry cut him off vehemently. 'Maybe he did it only for Beth, but I'd like to believe he did it for you and me, too. He took whatever Isaiah was going to throw at us *all*. We can't let him down, after that. He's telling us to go to the canefields. I say we should do it—and do it now. That was *Gavin*, Michael. Not a walking fucking corpse like Jake Sanders, or a freak like Isaiah. It was Gavin Packer, and he was trying to tell us something— to go to the canefields.'

Michael was confused and frightened. 'But why should we listen to him? None of the other walking fucking corpses have been exactly helpful.'

'This isn't the same, Michael. I don't know why and I know he was angry beyond reason, but I believe Gavin just sacrificed himself for us, and that's made him *different* from the others. It's *got* to be that!'

Michael stared at Kerry and saw the strength of the conviction in her eyes. It gave him fresh courage and he shook his mind free of the apathy that Gavin's death and the apparent hopelessness of their situation had allowed to take hold of him. His next thought was the realisation that the fire in the library was getting dangerous for them. They had to get outside.

'Okay, we don't have a lot of choice,' he said flatly.

Kerry looked relieved Michael was coming to his senses again and she picked up Beth, holding the girl to her chest. Michael ran ahead and opened the front doors for them.

Outside, the chill night air was like a slap in the face after the heat of the flames. Michael expected there would be trouble waiting for them in the darkness too, but the way seemed clear. There was no sign of Jake or Ainslie—he guessed they were still trapped in the library—or anybody, living or dead. Kerry got into the passenger seat first, and lifted Beth onto her lap. Michael was already behind the wheel, turning the ignition. The motor caught quickly and he moved off. In the back the two dogs eagerly tried to get some attention and the sudden movement took them off-guard, making them scrabble to keep their balance.

Michael glanced in the rear-view mirror. The flames coming from the library were turning into a spectacular sight in the clear night. He glanced at Kerry and saw now that she was the one losing her self-control. Tears were shining in her eyes again.

'Not now, Kerry,' he said, his voice harsher than he wanted. 'Don't think about it—don't think about him.' He dropped his eyes to Beth for a moment. 'Let's get out of this nightmare, first,' he finished softly.

'I know,' she said quietly. 'I wonder where he is now?' She was looking out at the night through her side window. Beth surprised her by answering instead.

'He's with us,' she said simply. 'Don't you know?'

The drive through Hickory was uneventful. Michael feared the events at the library might have somehow aggravated everything—that the corpses walking the streets would be angered or disturbed by Isaiah's 'Changing'. But the van's headlights showed them little. Only a few people still stood in the streets like zombies. It was impossible to tell with most of them if they were dead or alive. This time there was no Mrs North to step out in front of the speeding vehicle, and that was all Michael cared about.

His nervousness got worse as they left the main road and started down the track leading to the barbecues and the canefield. The darkness seemed more threatening, but he knew it was his imagination. Glancing in his rear-view mirror he saw the glow of the burning library. Michael wondered how long it would be before the soldiers at the cordon noticed it too, and sent a helicopter to investigate.

He didn't stop near the river, but drove straight down the side-track and into the cane. Heading in the right direction now Michael could see a glow in the air—the lights of the UFO reflecting off dust and insects attracted by the glare. When he turned into the track with the final corner ahead, the same side-track was obvious with its bright square of white light shining onto the cane opposite. Michael swung around the bend and had to brake hard—he'd forgotten about the cane harvester filling the track, its tall silhouette blocking some of the glare. The van's headlights showed him the machine was blackened by the fire, some of its parts melted by the heat. At the same time

Michael realised what was different about the sugarcane, too. It was burnt. Now the stalks stood on their own, charred and looking strangely bare without the usual undergrowth filling the gaps between each plant.

Michael turned off the motor and silence flooded in. He looked across the cab at Kerry. Her face was pale and frightened. 'Come on,' he said gently. 'We've come this far. We can't back off now.'

'What are we going to do?'

'See if anybody's home. After that, I wouldn't have a clue.' He tried to sound encouraging, but it didn't really work.

She nodded and opened her door. Beth needed to be carried. She seemed to have somehow completely detached herself from her surroundings now. Every now and then Kerry heard her murmuring softly to herself. She said 'Daddy' more than once and Kerry wondered if Beth really was talking to her father's spirit, or if her young mind had finally given in to the terror and slipped into an abyss of madness. She was like a big rag doll, totally compliant and apparently unaware of anything happening around her. Kerry hoped Beth was only in some form of shock.

Michael came around to Kerry's side of the van and picked Beth up. Silently, he was in a quandary. If their journey back to this canefield was to have any success, then the two dogs had come as far as possible. Michael had to set them free now, but at the same time he didn't want them running around and complicating things. He couldn't bring himself to lock them in the van, either.

Michael had no idea what might happen in the next few minutes.

In the end, his compromise served two purposes. Michael left the passenger-side door open. The dogs could squeeze between the front seats and escape that way, when they eventually realised they could. This meant Michael wasn't blatantly releasing or trapping them, and thereby maybe triggering hysterics in Beth.

Michael led the way with Kerry pressing close behind. The burnt sugarcane was wilted, and as he pushed past the harvester it was hard not to brush against either the machine or the fire-blackened plants. The air was filled with the smell of ash, and fine puffs of it clouded around their footsteps. The white light from the UFO became blinding as they moved out of the cane harvester's shadow. Beyond the limit of the track it was possible to see the round, saucer-shaped disc on the ground behind the fire-stripped cane.

And standing before it at the very end of the track was the same figure as before—a child-like person with an unusually large head. Even with the brilliant light behind it, Michael could see again the burning gleam from deep within the alien's eyes. Even though he was expecting—hoping for—exactly this, the moment still took Michael's breath away.

They came to a halt just past the cane harvester. Michael put Beth on the ground, but kept hold of her hand. Kerry stood close on his other side. She threw a worried glance at Beth, thinking that the sight of the UFO might be the catalyst for bringing back any dreadful memories of her time with the aliens, but Beth was looking towards the white light with an expression on her face of childish wonderment. At least that was something—not the vacant gaze of madness.

Michael didn't call out, but stared defiantly at the alien.

After a long moment of staring back, the alien moved down the track towards them. It stepped lightly and Michael almost thought its feet weren't actually touching the ground, except for the same small wisps of ash rising up from each footfall. When the alien was within a few metres of them it cocked its head to one side, like a curious animal, and regarded them intently with its unsettling fiery gaze.

'Where is our brother?'

A trite cliché slipped unbidden into Michael's mind, *Hard questions first.* He cleared his throat. 'We've come to talk to you.'

'What could we discuss? There is nothing common. We have come only to retrieve our brother after his Changing.'

'We want you to help us.' Michael had a sudden urge to abandon tact and diplomacy, so he added, making his tone hard, 'You owe it to us.'

'This is none of our affair.'

'One of your people started this whole damned thing!'

'And he has Changed. It is finished.'

'Look, Changed—Chosen, whatever it's about, I don't give a damn. Have you got any idea what he's done to this town?' Michael couldn't tell if the alien's reply was a simplistic stubbornness to avoid the issue, or if it was incapable of arguing.

'Where is our brother?'

Michael felt his anger rise. 'Why the hell should we know?'

'It is your fate to bring him to us. That is why we wait without searching.'

'It's our fate? What's *that* supposed to mean? Are you trying to tell me—'

Michael was interrupted by a slight shifting in the air close by. He held his breath, certain of what he was about to see.

Gavin appeared, still holding the shining orb in his outstretched hand.

The spirit's eyes stared at nothing. He stood like a statue, an inner light giving him substance. There was no acknowledgement of the people near him. The alien became still—the only display of emotion of any kind it was to show—then it moved closer to the ghost and studied it closely for a long moment.

'He has our brother.'

'That's right.' Michael couldn't stop himself sounding slightly triumphant. 'He was holding Powers—or Kann, as you think of him—when he Changed.'

'Tell him, he must be released.'

Michael hesitated, unsure of what was happening now or how to go on. He glanced at Kerry and saw she was thinking hard. She surprised him by speaking out, loud and clearly.

'He won't release your brother until you can guarantee safe passage for his daughter away from the town.'

The alien turned its gaze towards Kerry and Michael saw her steel herself, but she steadfastly returned the stare.

Michael said, 'The army has surrounded the town and won't let anyone leave. They're killing everything that tries to move beyond the perimeter. We think tomorrow they'll begin killing everything inside the town, too. That's your damned *brother's* fault as well,' he added harshly.

Now the alien turned towards Michael. *'Tell him, he must be released.'*

'No. You must get us to safety first.'

Michael understood he had no real idea what he was demanding, or what would be involved. Only his instincts were telling him it must be possible. These people were capable of almost anything. And Gavin's spirit was dedicated to the same purpose, Michael knew that instinctively, too. The alien was taking a long time to reply and Michael believed they were on the threshold of a breakthrough—the whole crazy idea just might be about to work. He didn't expect the alien's next move.

It simply turned and began walking away towards the light.

'Hey, wait!' Michael shouted, caught by surprise. 'Where are you going?'

Kerry called out too. 'Please don't go! We need your help, damn you!'

But the alien didn't pause or turn back. It moved in the same light-footed manner to the end of the track and disappeared into the intense glare of the UFO.

'Jesus, Michael,' Kerry cried, after a stunned silence. She was bitterly disappointed, they'd seemed so close. 'Why's he leaving? Was it too much to ask?' Kerry looked at Gavin's spirit,

which hadn't moved. She was suddenly tempted to blame it for the failure.

Michael was on the point of thrusting Beth into Kerry's arms, before sprinting down the track towards the UFO hoping of getting in one last appeal to the alien. In the same moment they heard the dogs start barking—a frantic mixture of fear and defiance.

'Christ, now what's happening?' he groaned fearfully. Instead of running after the alien he hurried back past the cane harvester. A stray piece of cane whipped him across the face, but Michael ignored it. Staring down the track, he could see in the light still coming from the UFO that the dogs had stayed in the van. Their dark shapes were framed in the windows. Then Michael saw what they were barking at.

Beyond the van, at the opening of the track, figures were beginning to gather. He immediately recognised Mrs North, and a smaller shape which he first thought was Ainslie McGregor, then Michael realised it must be Kevin Stanford. Ainslie and Jake couldn't have got here from the library so quickly—but Michael bet they were on their way.

The whole intersection was filling with the walking dead of Hickory. They'd been waiting in the cane, attracted by the UFO, and had hidden themselves from the arriving, living humans. Now, like an angry mob, they were revealing themselves.

Michael felt the blood drain from his face. 'Why do they hate us?' he whispered to himself. But such questions didn't matter any more. They were going to be trapped if they didn't move fast.

556

Michael rushed back to Kerry and seized her arm. 'We're in big trouble,' he said urgently. 'We have to get back in the van—you'll see why,' he added when she looked like protesting. Michael bent down and scooped Beth into his arms, then set off at a run back past the cane harvester. He heard Kerry cry out behind him as she saw what was gathering at the mouth of the track. He yelled over his shoulder, 'Just get in the van. We'll drive right over the bastards if we have to!'

That was exactly what it seemed Michael would have to do. More figures pressed in behind the others. After clambering into the driver's seat Michael tried to see out the back window, but the excited dogs kept getting in the way, their yelping rattling Michael's nerves more. He gave up and started the motor instead, pleading aloud as he turned the key for everything to work. The engine burst into life and Michael immediately slammed the lever into reverse gear, turning the wheel hard. He let the van push far into the cane, front and rear, as he squeezed a reverse-turn in the narrow track. Then the headlights were shining on the throng of corpses, their white faces full of hate glaring back.

'God, Michael, we'll never get through them,' Kerry said, despairing. 'Even if you run straight over them.'

'We've got no choice other than to try,' he told her grimly. 'Hang on—this is going to be rough.' He gunned the motor hard and dumped the clutch.

The van lurched forward only a few metres, then suddenly came to a halt again. Everything stopped without warning—the motor, the headlights, all went completely dead.

Michael stared unbelievingly at the brilliant light in his rear-view, then he hit his fist against the steering wheel. He cried out in anguish, 'No! Not now, you bastards! Not *now*!'

'Michael, what's happening? What's wrong with the car?'

'The UFO's drained the battery—killed off all the fucking electrics!'

'Dear God,' Kerry whispered. The look on her face was one of absolute terror. There was no hope left now. They were trapped. Still, she asked helplessly, 'What can we do?'

Michael stared back her, his mind filled with fear, and regrets, and a deep sorrow that they had failed. He knew they could try running into the cane—and that was what they had to do now. But Michael also doubted they would survive until the morning. The odds were getting too high against them.

He felt this might be the last chance he had to speak to Kerry, even if it was just one last, stolen moment, before they tried their escape—the rest of their time together would be full of terror and running. He wanted to tell her so many things and had no time to say any of them properly. Out of the corner of his eye he saw the crowd of people begin moving down the track towards them. Then his vision began playing tricks on him. For a moment he believed it was the start of a mental breakdown, the first symptoms that his mind could no longer cope.

The cab of the van was filling with a strange blue

light. In the back, the dogs fell instantly silent. Michael was still looking at Kerry and her image wavered. He thought he was going to faint and tried fighting against it. He couldn't leave Kerry and Beth to face everything without him. A dull roar built inside his head and Michael felt the blood pounding at his temples. Despite all his efforts, he knew he was losing consciousness.

The last thing he saw was Kerry's eyes widening with shock as she watched him.

25

MICHAEL OPENED HIS eyes. Something was wrong.

A brilliant glare made him shut them again. He felt hot, a slick of perspiration coating his face. With the bright light beyond his eyelids, he slowly opened them this time, letting his pupils adjust.

Michael found himself staring up at a beautiful, clear blue sky.

He was lying on the ground. The smell of lush grass filled his nostrils. Suddenly his memory reawakened and he panicked, sitting up too fast and making himself dizzy.

'How the hell—' he began, then saw Kerry and Beth curled up on the ground beside him. Kerry's eyes were opening too and Michael saw in them the same confusion and panic he had been through. He quickly reached out to her.

'Kerry, take it easy,' he said gently. 'Brace yourself for a bit of a shock.'

She focused on him, then made the same mistake of sitting up too hastily. 'Whoa,' she said, putting a hand to her forehead and waiting for the faintness to fade. Then she saw the scenery around them. She turned her head slowly, astonished as she took in their surroundings. 'What? Where the *hell* are we?' she asked incredulously.

'That's a good question,' Michael replied, with a calm he didn't really feel.

The countryside around them was hilly, green pastureland neatly divided by wire fences. In the distance some black-and-white cows grazed contentedly. Michael could hear traffic on a road, but he couldn't see it. He judged by the sunlight and the freshness of the day it was still early morning. The three of them were under a wide tree, but the climbing sun had left Michael just outside the shade, which was why he was hot and perspiring. Beth was still sleeping easily.

'We're a long way from Hickory, I can tell you that,' he told Kerry, once they'd had more time to look around them.

'A *long* way,' she agreed, nodding.

Michael stifled a disbelieving laugh. 'You know what this means? I guess the alien came through! God damn, they got us out of there—' He stopped, amazed. It seemed so fantasic. 'Do—do you remember anything?'

Kerry frowned, concentrating. 'No, not a thing. There was a blue light, then nothing. Hell, I

561

thought we were finished!' Kerry added, her own memories flooding back.

'I remember thinking I was having a mental breakdown. They must have zapped us out somehow.'

Michael was suddenly concerned. 'Hey, what about Beth? Is she okay?' He leaned forward to see past Kerry. Beth was lying motionless on the ground beside them, looking as if she was in a deep sleep.

'She looks peaceful enough,' Kerry said, lowering her voice. 'Remember what she was like? Like she was—possessed or something. What's she going to be like when she wakes up?'

'I don't know. I guess we'll just have to look after her. She's got no-one else now.'

'Should we wake her? Let her know she's safe?'

'I'd say she already knows, from the expression on her face.'

'Maybe Gavin told her—before we were taken away. That she was going to be okay.'

'Maybe.'

They lapsed into a thoughtful silence. Already, in the safety and calm surrounding them now, it was difficult to accept the memories of what had happened to them during the last few days. It all seemed so unreal—so impossible.

Kerry asked, 'What do you think's happened to Hickory?'

'I suppose we were taken away last night, so I'd say today will see the finish of Hickory, one way or another. It might be safer if we were never heard to ask,' he added soberly.

'That won't be easy—people will be asking us

all sorts of tricky questions when we try and get back on our feet.'

'Yes, we'll have some explaining to do, but we'll work out a few lies and stick to them. Maybe we can say we were out of town the whole time. I'll bet the army will have a good story to stop us going back.'

Kerry shuddered. 'I don't want to go back—ever.'

'No, I don't think you'll see me going near the place, either,' he said with a wry smile.

Michael had been watching the brow of a nearby hill, thinking he'd seen movement there. He was right. The two dogs suddenly appeared, playfully tail-chasing each other. 'Look! I don't believe it!' Michael said, pointing.

Kerry screwed her face up with amazement and joy. 'Mike, they brought the *dogs* out with us?'

Monty and Mandy saw them and ran at full speed towards them. Michael and Kerry both got to their feet to ward off the happy attack. Kerry was delighted as she bent over and patted them both.

'Do you think they did it on purpose?'

A frown crossed Michael's face, but he hid it before Kerry noticed. 'They must have done it on purpose,' he said confidently. 'I doubt they're capable of accidents like that. Maybe they didn't realise we don't consider dogs quite as important as humans and just naturally included them.'

'Of *course* they're important,' Kerry said, laughing. She was so pleased, she didn't notice the note of concern in Michael's voice.

He decided not to mention what worried him.

In fact, Michael found himself believing it *was* entirely possible the aliens had brought the dogs out of the canefield by accident.

And that had him wondering if anything else might have been brought out of Hickory, too.

G.M. Hague

Ghost Beyond Earth

Spine-chilling suspense.
Relentless action.
Stark terror.

An old man is possessed and tormented by an ev
spirit.

The ghost of a little girl returns to terrorise her isolated
outback home.

A house in an affluent suburb becomes a place o
worship for followers of the black arts.

Crew members begin to die as a cryogenics experi
ment in a space station goes horribly wrong.

Seemingly unconnected occurrences – yet linked by
one figure: ex-priest, Matthew Kindling.

Fighting for his sanity and his life, relentlessly pursued
by darkness, Kindling is inexorably propelled towards
a confrontation with an evil beyond human imagining

Read his story ... if you dare.